George Gilfillan

Specimens - With Memoirs of the Less-Known British Poets

Vol. III

George Gilfillan

Specimens - With Memoirs of the Less-Known British Poets
Vol. III

ISBN/EAN: 9783337093266

Printed in Europe, USA, Canada, Australia, Japan

Cover: Foto ©Andreas Hilbeck / pixelio.de

More available books at **www.hansebooks.com**

SPECIMENS

WITH MEMOIRS OF THE

LESS-KNOWN BRITISH POETS.

With an Introductory Essay,

BY THE

REV. GEORGE GILFILLAN.

IN THREE VOLS.

VOL. III.

EDINBURGH: JAMES NICHOL.
LONDON: JAMES NISBET & CO.   DUBLIN: W. ROBERTSON.
M.DCCC.LX.

CONTENTS.

THIRD PERIOD—FROM DRYDEN TO COWPER.

CONTENTS.

CONTENTS.

SPECIMENS, WITH MEMOIRS,

OF THE LESS-KNOWN BRITISH POETS.

THIRD PERIOD.

FROM DRYDEN TO COWPER.

SIR CHARLES SEDLEY.

SEDLEY was one of those characters who exert a personal fascination over their own age without leaving any works behind them to perpetuate the charm to posterity. He was the son of Sir John Sedley of Aylesford, in Kent, and was born in 1639. When the Restoration took place he repaired to London, and plunged into all the licence of the time, shedding, however, over the putrid pool the sheen of his wit, manners, and genius. Charles was so delighted with him, that he is said to have asked him whether he had not obtained a patent from Nature to be Apollo's viceroy. He cracked jests, issued lampoons, wrote poems and plays, and, despite some great blunders, was universally admired and loved. When his comedy of ' Bellamira ' was acted, the roof fell in, and a few, including the author, were slightly injured. When a parasite told him that the fire of the play had blown up the poet, house and all, Sedley replied, ' No ; the play was so heavy that it broke down the house, and buried the poet in his own rubbish.' Latterly he sobered down, entered parliament, attended closely to public business, and became a determined opponent of the arbitrary measures of James II.

To this he was stimulated by a personal reason. James had seduced Sedley's daughter, and made her Countess of Dorchester. 'For making my daughter a countess,' the father said, 'I have helped to make his daughter' (Mary, Princess of Orange,) 'a queen.' Sedley, thus talking, acting, and writing, lived on till he was sixty-two years of age.   He died in 1701.

He has left nothing that the world can cherish, except such light and graceful songs, sparkling rather with point than with poetry, as we quote below.

TO A VERY YOUNG LADY.

1 Ah, Chloris! that I now could sit
   As unconcerned, as when
Your infant beauty could beget
   No pleasure, nor no pain.

2 When I the dawn used to admire,
   And praised the coming day;
I little thought the growing fire
   Must take my rest away.

3 Your charms in harmless childhood lay,
   Like metals in the mine,
Age from no face took more away,
   Than youth concealed in thine.

4 But as your charms insensibly
   To their perfection pressed,
Fond Love as unperceived did fly,
   And in my bosom rest.

5 My passion with your beauty grew,
   And Cupid at my heart,
Still as his mother favoured you,
   Threw a new flaming dart.

2

6 Each gloried in their wanton part,
   To make a lover, he
Employed the utmost of his art,
   To make a Beauty, she.

7 Though now I slowly bend to love,
   Uncertain of my fate,
If your fair self my chains approve,
   I shall my freedom hate.

8 Lovers, like dying men, may well
   At first disordered be,
Since none alive can truly tell
   What fortune they must see.

SONG.

1 Love still has something of the sea,
   From whence his mother rose;
No time his slaves from doubt can free,
   Nor give their thoughts repose.

2 They are becalmed in clearest days,
   And in rough weather tossed;
They wither under cold delays,
   Or are in tempests lost.

3 One while they seem to touch the port,
   Then straight into the main
Some angry wind, in cruel sport,
   The vessel drives again.

4 At first Disdain and Pride they fear,
   Which if they chance to 'scape,
Rivals and Falsehood soon appear,
   In a more cruel shape.

    5 By such degrees to joy they come,
           And are so long withstood;
       So slowly they receive the sum,
           It hardly does them good.

    6 'Tis cruel to prolong a pain;
           And to defer a joy,
       Believe me, gentle Celemene,
           Offends the winged boy.

    7 An hundred thousand oaths your fears,
           Perhaps, would not remove;
       And if I gazed a thousand years,
           I could not deeper love.

JOHN POMFRET,

THE author of the once popular 'Choice,' was born in 1667. He was the son of the rector of Luton, in Bedfordshire, and, after attending Queen's College, Cambridge, himself entered the Church. He became minister of Malden, which is also situated in Bedfordshire, and there he wrote and, in 1699, published a volume of poems, including some Pindaric essays, in the style of Cowley and 'The Choice.' He might have risen higher in his profession, but Dr Compton, Bishop of London, was prejudiced against him on account of the following lines in the 'Choice:'—

> 'And as I near approached the verge of life,
> Some kind relation (for I'd have no wife)
> Should take upon him all my worldly care,
> Whilst I did for a better state prepare.'

The words in the second line, coupled with a glowing description, in a previous part of the poem, of his ideal of an 'obliging modest fair' one, near whom he wished to live, led to the suspicion that he preferred a mistress to a wife. In vain did he plead that he was actually a married man. His suit for a bet-

4

ter living made no progress, and while dancing attendance on
his patron in London he caught small-pox, and died in 1703, in
the thirty-sixth year of his age.

His Pindaric odes, &c., are feeble spasms, and need not detain us. His 'Reason' shews considerable capacity and common sense.   His 'Choice' opens up a pleasing vista, down
which our quiet ancestors delighted to look, but by which
few now can be attracted.   We quote a portion of what a biographer calls a 'modest' preface, which Pomfret prefixed to his
poems :—'To please every one would be a new thing, and to
write so as to please nobody would be as new; for even Quarles
and Withers have their admirers. It is not the multitude of
applauses, but the good sense of the applauders which estab-
lishes a valuable reputation ; and if a Rymer or a Congreve say
it is well, he will not be at all solicitous how great the majority
be to the contrary.' How strangely are opinions now altered!
Rymer was some time ago characterised by Macaulay as the
worst critic that ever lived, and Quarles and Withers have now
many admirers, while 'The Choice' and its ill-fated author are
nearly forgotten.

THE CHOICE.

If Heaven the grateful liberty would give,
That I might choose my method how to live,
And all those hours propitious fate should lend,
In blissful ease and satisfaction spend,
Near some fair town I 'd have a private seat,
Built uniform, not little, nor too great:
Better, if on a rising ground it stood,
On this side fields, on that a neighbouring wood.
It should within no other things contain,
But what are useful, necessary, plain:
Methinks 'tis nauseous, and I 'd ne'er endure,
The needless pomp of gaudy furniture.
A little garden, grateful to the eye;
And a cool rivulet run murmuring by,

On whose delicious banks, a stately row
Of shady limes or sycamores should grow.
At the end of which a silent study placed,
Should be with all the noblest authors graced:
Horace and Virgil, in whose mighty lines
Immortal wit and solid learning shines;
Sharp Juvenal, and amorous Ovid too,
Who all the turns of love's soft passion knew;
He that with judgment reads his charming lines,
In which strong art with stronger nature joins,
Must grant his fancy does the best excel;
His thoughts so tender, and expressed so well;
With all those moderns, men of steady sense,
Esteemed for learning and for eloquence.
In some of these, as fancy should advise,
I'd always take my morning exercise;
For sure no minutes bring us more content,
Than those in pleasing, useful studies spent.
I'd have a clear and competent estate,
That I might live genteelly, but not great;
As much as I could moderately spend,
A little more sometimes t' oblige a friend.
Nor should the sons of poverty repine
Too much at fortune; they should taste of mine;
And all that objects of true pity were,
Should be relieved with what my wants could spare;
For that our Maker has too largely given,
Should be returned in gratitude to Heaven.

THE EARL OF DORSET.

THIS noble earl was rather a patron of poets than a poet, and
possessed more wit than genius. Charles Sackville was born on

the 24th January 1637. He was descended directly from the famous Thomas, Lord Buckhurst. He was educated under a private tutor, travelled in Italy, and returned in time to witness the Restoration. In the first parliament thereafter, he sat for East Grinstead, in Surrey, and might have distinguished himself, had he not determined, in common with almost all the wits of the time, to run a preliminary career of dissipation. What a proof of the licentiousness of these times is to be found in the fact, that young Lord Buckhurst, Sir Charles Sedley, and Sir Thomas Ogle were fined for exposing themselves, drunk and naked, in indecent postures on the public street! In 1665, the erratic energies of Buckhurst found a more legitimate vent in the Dutch war. He attended the Duke of York in the great sea-fight of the 3d June, in which Opdam, the Dutch admiral, was, with all his crew, blown up. He is said to have composed the song, quoted afterwards, 'To all you ladies now at land,' on the evening before the battle, although Dr Johnson (who observes that seldom any splendid story is wholly true) maintains that its composition cost him a whole week, and that he only retouched it on that remarkable evening. Buckhurst was soon after made a gentleman of the bed-chamber, and despatched on short embassies to France. In 1674, his uncle, James Cranfield, the Earl of Middlesex, died, and left him his estate, and the next year the title, too, was conferred on him. In 1677, he became, by the death of his father, Earl of Dorset, and inherited the family estate. In 1684, his wife, whose name was Bagot, and by whom he had no children, died, and he soon after married a daughter of the Earl of Northampton, who is said to have been celebrated both for understanding and beauty. Dorset was courted by James, but found it impossible to coincide with his violent measures, and when the bishops were tried at Westminster Hall, he, along with some other lords, appeared to countenance them. He concurred with the Revolution settlement, and, after William's accession, was created lord chamberlain of the household, and received the Order of the Garter. His attendance on the king, however, eventually cost him his life, for having been tossed with him in an open boat on the coast of Holland for sixteen hours, in very rough weather, he caught an illness from which he never recovered. On 19th January 1705–6, he died at Bath.

During his life, Dorset was munificent in his kindness to such men of genius as Prior and Dryden, who repaid him in the current coin of the poor Parnassus of their day—gross adulation. He is now remembered mainly for his spirited war-song, and for such pointed lines in his satire on Edward Howard, the notorious author of ' British Princes,' as the following :—

> 'They lie, dear Ned, who say thy brain is barren,
> When deep conceits, like maggots, breed in carrion ;
> Thy stumbling, foundered jade can trot as high
> As any other Pegasus can fly.
> So the dull eel moves nimbler in the mud
> Than all the swift-finned racers of the flood.
> As skilful divers to the bottom fall
> Sooner than those who cannot swim at all,
> So in this way of writing without thinking,
> Thou hast a strange alacrity in sinking.'

This last line has not only become proverbial, but forms the distinct germ of ' The Dunciad.'

SONG.

WRITTEN AT SEA, IN THE FIRST DUTCH WAR, 1665, THE NIGHT BEFORE AN ENGAGEMENT.

> 1 To all you ladies now at land,
>   We men at sea indite;
> But first would have you understand
>   How hard it is to write;
> The Muses now, and Neptune too,
> We must implore to write to you,
>   With a fa, la, la, la, la.
>
> 2 For though the Muses should prove kind,
>   And fill our empty brain;
> Yet if rough Neptune rouse the wind,
>   To wave the azure main,

Our paper, pen, and ink, and we,
Roll up and down our ships at sea.
    With a fa, &c.

3 Then if we write not by each post,
    Think not we are unkind;
Nor yet conclude our ships are lost,
    By Dutchmen, or by wind;
Our tears we'll send a speedier way,
The tide shall bring them twice a-day.
    With a fa, &c.

4 The king, with wonder and surprise,
    Will swear the seas grow bold;
Because the tides will higher rise
    Than e'er they used of old:
But let him know, it is our tears
Bring floods of grief to Whitehall stairs.
    With a fa, &c.

5 Should foggy Opdam chance to know
    Our sad and dismal story,
The Dutch would scorn so weak a foe,
    And quit their fort at Goree:
For what resistance can they find
From men who've left their hearts behind?
    With a fa, &c.

6 Let wind and weather do its worst,
    Be you to us but kind;
Let Dutchmen vapour, Spaniards curse,
    No sorrow we shall find:
'Tis then no matter how things go,
Or who's our friend, or who's our foe.
    With a fa, &c.

7 To pass our tedious hours away,
    We throw a merry main;
Or else at serious ombre play:
    But why should we in vain
Each other's ruin thus pursue?
We were undone when we left you.
      With a fa, &c.

8 But now our fears tempestuous grow,
    And cast our hopes away;
Whilst you, regardless of our woe,
    Sit careless at a play:
Perhaps, permit some happier man
To kiss your hand, or flirt your fan.
      With a fa, &c.

9 When any mournful tune you hear,
    That dies in every note,
As if it sighed with each man's care,
    For being so remote,
Think how often love we've made
To you, when all those tunes were played.
      With a fa, &c.

10 In justice you can not refuse
    To think of our distress,
When we for hopes of honour lose
    Our certain happiness;
All those designs are but to prove
Ourselves more worthy of your love.
      With a fa, &c.

11 And now we've told you all our loves,
    And likewise all our fears,

In hopes this declaration moves
Some pity from your tears;
Let's hear of no inconstancy,
We have too much of that at sea.
With a fa, la, la, la, la.

JOHN PHILIPS.

BAMPTON in Oxfordshire was the birthplace of this poet. He was born on the 30th of December 1676. His father, Dr Stephen Philips, was archdeacon of Salop, as well as minister of Bampton. John, after some preliminary training at home, was sent to Winchester, where he distinguished himself by diligence and good-nature, and enjoyed two great luxuries,—the reading of Milton, and the having his head combed by some one while he sat still and in rapture for hours together. This pleasure he shared with Vossius, and with humbler persons of our acquaintance; the combing of whose hair, they tell us,

'Dissolves them into ecstasies,
And brings all heaven before their eyes.'

In 1694, he entered Christ Church, Cambridge. His intention was to prosecute the study of medicine, and he took great delight in the cognate pursuits of natural history and botany. His chief friend was Edmund Smith, (Rag Smith, as he was generally called,) a kind of minor Savage, well known in these times as the author of 'Phædra and Hippolytus,' and for his cureless dissipation. In 1703, Philips produced 'The Splendid Shilling,' which proved a hit, and seems to have diverted his aspirations from the domains of Æsculapius to those of Apollo. Bolingbroke sought him out, and employed him, after the battle of Blenheim, to sing it in opposition to Addison, the laureate of the Whigs. At the house of the magnificent but unprincipled St John, Philips wrote his 'Blenheim,' which was published in 1705. The year after, his 'Cider,' a poem in two books, appeared, and was received with great applause. Encouraged by this, he projected a poem on the Last Day, which all who are aware of the difficulties of the subject, and the limitations of the author's genius, must rejoice that he never wrote. Consumption and asthma removed him prematurely on the 15th of February 1708, ere he had completed his thirty-third year. He was buried in Hereford Cathedral, and Sir Simon Harcourt, afterwards Lord Chancellor, erected a monument to his memory in Westminster Abbey.

Bulwer somewhere records a story of John Martin in his early days. He was, on one occasion, reduced to his last shilling. He had kept it, out of a heap, from a partiality to its appearance. It was very bright. He was compelled, at last, to part with it. He went out to a baker's shop to purchase a loaf with his favourite shilling. He had got the loaf into his hands, when the baker discovered that the shilling was a bad one, and poor Martin had to resign the loaf, and take back his dear, bright, bad shilling once more. Length of time and cold criticism in like manner have reduced John Philips to his solitary 'Splendid Shilling.' But, though bright, it is far from bad. It is one of the cleverest of parodies, and is perpetrated against one of those colossal works which the smiles of a thousand caricatures were unable to injure. No great or good poem was ever hurt by its parody:—the 'Paradise Lost' was not by 'The Splendid Shilling'—'The Last Man' of Campbell was not by 'The Last Man' of Hood—nor the 'Lines on the Burial of Sir John Moore' by their witty, well-known caricature; and if 'The Vision of Judgment' by Southey was laughed into oblivion by Byron's poem with the same title, it was because Southey's original was neither good nor great. Philip's poem, too, is the first of the kind; and surely we should be thankful to the author of the earliest effort in a style which has created so much innocent amusement. Dr Johnson speaks as if the pleasure arising from such productions implied a malignant 'momentary triumph over that grandeur which had hitherto held its captives in admiration.' We think, on the contrary, that it springs from our deep interest in the original production, making us alive to the strange resemblance the caricature bears to it. It is our love that provokes our laughter, and hence the admirers of the parodied poem are more delighted than its

12

enemies. At all events, it is by 'The Splendid Shilling' alone
—and that principally from its connexion with Milton's great
work—that Philips is memorable. His 'Cider' has soured
with age, and the loud echo of his Blenheim battle-piece has
long since died away.

THE SPLENDID SHILLING.

> ". . . . . Sing, heavenly Muse !
>   Things unattempted yet, in prose or rhyme,"
>   A Shilling, Breeches, and Chimeras dire.

Happy the man who, void of cares and strife,
In silken or in leathern purse retains
A Splendid Shilling: he nor hears with pain
New oysters cried, nor sighs for cheerful ale;
But with his friends, when nightly mists arise,
To Juniper's Magpie or Town-Hall[1] repairs:
Where, mindful of the nymph whose wanton eye
Transfixed his soul and kindled amorous flames,
Chloe, or Phillis, he each circling glass
Wisheth her health, and joy, and equal love.
Meanwhile, he smokes, and laughs at merry tale,
Or pun ambiguous, or conundrum quaint.
But I, whom griping Penury surrounds,
And Hunger, sure attendant upon Want,
With scanty offals, and small acid tiff,
(Wretched repast!) my meagre corpse sustain:
Then solitary walk, or doze at home
In garret vile, and with a warming puff
Regale chilled fingers; or from tube as black
As winter-chimney, or well-polished jet,
Exhale mundungus, ill-perfuming scent!
Not blacker tube, nor of a shorter size,
Smokes Cambro-Briton (versed in pedigree,
Sprung from Cadwallader and Arthur, kings

---

[1] 'Magpie or Town-hall:' two noted alehouses at Oxford in 1700.

Full famous in romantic tale) when he
O'er many a craggy hill and barren cliff,
Upon a cargo of famed Cestrian cheese,
High over-shadowing rides, with a design
To vend his wares, or at the Arvonian mart,
Or Maridunum, or the ancient town
Ycleped Brechinia, or where Vaga's stream
Encircles Ariconium, fruitful soil!
Whence flow nectareous wines, that well may vie
With Massic, Setin, or renowned Falern.
    Thus while my joyless minutes tedious flow,
With looks demure, and silent pace, a Dun,
Horrible monster! hated by gods and men,
To my aërial citadel ascends,
With vocal heel thrice thundering at my gate,
With hideous accent thrice he calls; I know
The voice ill-boding, and the solemn sound.
What should I do? or whither turn?   Amazed,
Confounded, to the dark recess I fly
Of wood-hole; straight my bristling hairs erect
Through sudden fear; a chilly sweat bedews
My shuddering limbs, and, wonderful to tell!
My tongue forgets her faculty of speech;
So horrible he seems!   His faded brow,
Entrenched with many a frown, and conic beard,
And spreading band, admired by modern saints,
Disastrous acts forebode ; in his right hand
Long scrolls of paper solemnly he waves,
With characters and figures dire inscribed,
Grievous to mortal eyes; ye gods, avert
Such plagues from righteous men! Behind him stalks
Another monster, not unlike himself,
Sullen of aspect, by the vulgar called
A Catchpole, whose polluted hands the gods,
14

With force incredible, and magic charms,
Erst have endued; if he his ample palm
Should haply on ill-fated shoulder lay
Of debtor, straight his body, to the touch
Obsequious, as whilom knights were wont,
To some enchanted castle is conveyed,
Where gates impregnable, and coercive chains,
In durance strict detain him, till, in form
Of money, Pallas sets the captive free.
    Beware, ye Debtors! when ye walk, beware,
Be circumspect; oft with insidious ken
The caitiff eyes your steps aloof, and oft
Lies perdue in a nook or gloomy cave,
Prompt to enchant some inadvertent wretch
With his unhallowed touch.   So (poets sing)
Grimalkin, to domestic vermin sworn
An everlasting foe, with watchful eye
Lies nightly brooding o'er a chinky gap,
Protending her fell claws, to thoughtless mice
Sure ruin.   So her disembowelled web
·Arachne, in a hall or kitchen, spreads
Obvious to vagrant flies: she secret stands
Within her woven cell; the humming prey,
Regardless of their fate, rush on the toils
Inextricable, nor will aught avail
Their arts, or arms, or shapes of lovely hue;
The wasp insidious, and the buzzing drone,
And butterfly, proud of expanded wings
Distinct with gold, entangled in her snares,
Useless resistance make: with eager strides,
She towering flies to her expected spoils;
Then, with envenomed jaws, the vital blood
Drinks of reluctant foes, and to her cave
Their bulky carcasses triumphant drags.

15

So pass my days.   But, when nocturnal shades
This world envelop, and the inclement air
Persuades men to repel benumbing frosts
With pleasant wines, and crackling blaze of wood;
Me lonely sitting, nor the glimmering light
Of make-weight candle, nor the joyous talk
Of loving friend, delights; distressed, forlorn,
Amidst the horrors of the tedious night,
Darkling I sigh, and feed with dismal thoughts
My anxious mind; or sometimes mournful verse
Indite, and sing of groves and myrtle shades,
Or desperate lady near a purling stream,
Or lover pendent on a willow-tree.
Meanwhile I labour with eternal drought,
And restless wish, and rave; my parched throat
Finds no relief, nor heavy eyes repose:
But if a slumber haply does invade
My weary limbs, my fancy's still awake,
Thoughtful of drink, and, eager, in a dream,
Tipples imaginary pots of ale,
In vain; awake I find the settled thirst
Still gnawing, and the pleasant phantom curse.
    Thus do I live, from pleasure quite debarred,
Nor taste the fruits that the sun's genial rays
Mature, john-apple, nor the downy peach,
Nor walnut in rough-furrowed coat secure,
Nor medlar, fruit delicious in decay;
Afflictions great! yet greater still remain:
My galligaskins, that have long withstood
The winter's fury, and encroaching frosts,
By time subdued (what will not time subdue!)
An horrid chasm disclosed with orifice
Wide, discontinuous; at which the winds
Eurus and Auster, and the dreadful force

16

Of Borcas, that congeals the Cronian waves,
Tumultuous enter with dire chilling blasts,
Portending agues.   Thus a well-fraught ship,
Long sailed secure, or through the Ægean deep,
Or the Ionian, till cruising near
The Lilybean shore, with hideous crush
On Scylla, or Charybdis (dangerous rocks!)
She strikes rebounding; whence the shattered oak,
So fierce a shock unable to withstand,
Admits the sea; in at the gaping side
The crowding waves gush with impetuous rage,
Resistless, overwhelming; horrors seize
The mariners; Death in their eyes appears,
They stare, they lave, they pump, they swear,
      they pray;
Vain efforts! still the battering waves rush in,
Implacable, till, deluged by the foam,
The ship sinks foundering in the vast abyss.

WE may here mention a name or two of poets from whose verses we can afford no extracts,—such as Walsh, called by Pope 'knowing Walsh,' a man of some critical discernment, if not of much genius; Gould, a domestic of the Earl of Dorset, and afterwards a schoolmaster, from whom Campbell quotes one or two tolerable songs; and Dr Walter Pope, a man of wit and knowledge, who was junior proctor of Oxford, one of the first chosen fellows of the Royal Society, and who succeeded Sir Christopher Wren as professor of astronomy in Gresham College. He is the author of a comico-serious song of some merit, entitled, 'The Old Man's Wish.'

SIR SAMUEL GARTH.

OF Garth little is known, save that he was an eminent physician, a scholar, a man of benevolence, a keen Whig, and yet an admirer of old Dryden, and a patron of young Pope—a friend of Addison, and the author of the ' Dispensary.' The College of Physicians had instituted a dispensary, for the purpose of furnishing the poor with medicines gratis. This measure was opposed by the apothecaries, who had an obvious interest in the sale of drugs; and to ridicule their selfishness Garth wrote his poem, which is mock-heroic, in six cantos, copied in form from the ' Lutrin,' and which, though ingenious and elaborate, seems now tedious, and on the whole uninteresting. It appeared in 1696, and the author died in 1718. We extract some of the opening lines of the first canto of the poem.

THE DISPENSARY.

Speak, goddess! since 'tis thou that best canst tell
How ancient leagues to modern discord fell;
And why physicans were so cautious grown
Of others' lives, and lavish of their own;
How by a journey to the Elysian plain
Peace triumphed, and old Time returned again.
Not far from that most celebrated place,
Where angry Justice shows her awful face;
Where little villains must submit to fate,
That great ones may enjoy the world in state;
There stands a dome, majestic to the sight,
And sumptuous arches bear its oval height;
A golden globe, placed high with artful skill,
Seems, to the distant sight, a gilded pill:
This pile was, by the pious patron's aim,
Raised for a use as noble as its frame;
Nor did the learn'd society decline

18

The propagation of that great design;
In all her mazes, nature's face they viewed,
And, as she disappeared, their search pursued.
Wrapped in the shade of night the goddess lies,
Yet to the learn'd unveils her dark disguise,
But shuns the gross access of vulgar eyes.
   Now she unfolds the faint and dawning strife
Of infant atoms kindling into life;
How ductile matter new meanders takes,
And slender trains of twisting fibres makes;
And how the viscous seeks a closer tone,
By just degrees to harden into bone;
While the more loose flow from the vital urn,
And in full tides of purple streams return;
How lambent flames from life's bright lamps arise,
And dart in emanations through the eyes;
How from each sluice a gentle torrent pours,
To slake a feverish heat with ambient showers;
Whence their mechanic powers the spirits claim;
How great their force, how delicate their frame;
How the same nerves are fashioned to sustain
The greatest pleasure and the greatest pain;
Why bilious juice a golden light puts on,
And floods of chyle in silver currents run;
How the dim speck of entity began
To extend its recent form, and stretch to man;
To how minute an origin we owe
Young Ammon, Cæsar, and the great Nassau;
Why paler looks impetuous rage proclaim,
And why chill virgins redden into flame;
Why envy oft transforms with wan disguise,
And why gay mirth sits smiling in the eyes;
All ice, why Lucrece; or Sempronia, fire;
Why Scarsdale rages to survive desire;

When Milo's vigour at the Olympic 's shown,
Whence tropes to Finch, or impudence to Sloane;
How matter, by the varied shape of pores,
Or idiots frames, or solemn senators.
　　Hence 'tis we wait the wondrous cause to find,
How body acts upon impassive mind;
How fumes of wine the thinking part can fire,
Past hopes revive, and present joys inspire;
Why our complexions oft our soul declare,
And how the passions in the features are;
How touch and harmony arise between
Corporeal figure, and a form unseen;
How quick their faculties the limbs fulfil,
And act at every summons of the will.
With mighty truths, mysterious to descry,
Which in the womb of distant causes lie.
　　But now no grand inquiries are descried,
Mean faction reigns where knowledge should preside,
Feuds are increased, and learning laid aside.
Thus synods oft concern for faith conceal,
And for important nothings show a zeal:
The drooping sciences neglected pine,
And Pæan's beams with fading lustre shine.
No readers here with hectic looks are found,
Nor eyes in rheum, through midnight watching,
　　drowned;
The lonely edifice in sweats complains
That nothing there but sullen silence reigns.
　　This place, so fit for undisturbed repose,
The god of sloth for his asylum chose;
Upon a couch of down in these abodes,
Supine with folded arms he thoughtless nods;
Indulging dreams his godhead lull to ease,
With murmurs of soft rills and whispering trees:
　20

The poppy and each numbing plant dispense
Their drowsy virtue, and dull indolence;
No passions interrupt his easy reign,
No problems puzzle his lethargic brain;
But dark oblivion guards his peaceful bed,
And lazy fogs hang lingering o'er his head.

SIR RICHARD BLACKMORE.

OUR next name is that of one who, like the former, was a
knight, a physician, and (in a manner) a poet. Blackmore was
the son of Robert Blackmore of Corsham, in Wiltshire, who is
styled by Wood *gentleman*, and is believed to have been an
attorney. He took his degree of M.A. at Oxford, in June 1676.
He afterwards travelled, was made Doctor of Physic at Padua,
and, when he returned home, began to practise in London with
great success. In 1695, he tried his hand at poetry, producing
an epic entitled 'King Arthur,' which was followed by a series
on 'King Alfred,' 'Queen Elizabeth,' 'Redemption,' 'The
Creation,' &c. Some of these productions were popular; one,
'The Creation,' has been highly praised by Dr Johnson; but
most of them were heavy. Matthew Henry has preserved portions in his valuable Commentary. Blackmore, a man of excellent character and of extensive medical practice, was yet
the laughingstock of the wits, perhaps as much for his piety as
for his prosiness. Old, rich, and highly respected, he died on
the 8th of October 1729, while some of his poetic persecutors
came to a disgraceful or an early end.

We quote the satire of John Gay, as one of the cleverest and
best conditioned, although one of the coarsest of the attacks
made on poor Sir Richard :—

VERSES TO BE PLACED UNDER THE PICTURE OF SIR R. BLACKMORE,
CONTAINING A COMPLETE CATALOGUE OF HIS WORKS.

See who ne'er was, nor will be half read,
Who first sang Arthur, then sang Alfred;

Praised great Eliza in God's anger,
Till all true Englishmen cried, Hang her ;
Mauled human wit in one thick satire,
Next in three books spoiled human nature ;
Undid Creation at a jerk,
And of Redemption made —— work ;
Then took his Muse at once, and dipt her
Full in the middle of the Scripture ;
What wonders there the man grown old did,
Sternhold himself he out Sternholded ;
Made David seem so mad and freakish,
All thought him just what thought King Achish ;
No mortal read his Solomon
But judged Reboam his own son ;
Moses he served as Moses Pharaoh,
And Deborah as she Sisera ;
Made Jeremy full sore to cry,
And Job himself curse God and die.
    What punishment all this must follow ?
Shall Arthur use him like King Tollo ?
Shall David as Uriah slay him ?
Or dext'rous Deborah Sisera him ?
Or shall Eliza lay a plot
To treat him like her sister Scot ?
No, none of these ; Heaven save his life,
But send him, honest Job, thy wife !'

CREATION.

No more of courts, of triumphs, or of arms,
No more of valour's force, or beauty's charms ;
The themes of vulgar lays, with just disdain,
I leave unsung, the flocks, the amorous swain,
The pleasures of the land, and terrors of the main.
How abject, how inglorious 'tis to lie
Grovelling in dust and darkness, when on high
Empires immense and rolling worlds of light,
To range their heavenly scenes the muse invite ;
I meditate to soar above the skies,
To heights unknown, through ways untried, to rise ;
I would the Eternal from his works assert,
And sing the wonders of creating art.

22

While I this unexampled task essay,
Pass awful gulfs, and beat my painful way,
Celestial Dove! divine assistance bring,
Sustain me on thy strong extended wing,
That I may reach the Almighty's sacred throne,
And make his causeless power, the cause of all things,
    known.
Thou dost the full extent of nature see,
And the wide realms of vast immensity;
Eternal Wisdom thou dost comprehend,
Rise to her heights, and to her depths descend;
The Father's sacred counsels thou canst tell,
Who in his bosom didst for ever dwell;
Thou on the deep's dark face, immortal Dove!
Thou with Almighty energy didst move
On the wild waves, incumbent didst display
Thy genial wings, and hatch primeval day.
Order from thee, from thee distinction came,
And all the beauties of the wondrous frame.
Hence stamped on nature we perfection find,
Fair as the idea in the Eternal Mind.
See, through this vast extended theatre
Of skill divine, what shining marks appear!
Creating power is all around expressed,
The God discovered, and his care confessed.
Nature's high birth her heavenly beauties show;
By every feature we the parent know.
The expanded spheres, amazing to the sight!
Magnificent with stars and globes of light,
The glorious orbs which heaven's bright host compose,
The imprisoned sea, that restless ebbs and flows,
The fluctuating fields of liquid air,
With all the curious meteors hovering there,
And the wide regions of the land, proclaim

The Power Divine, that raised the mighty frame.
What things soe'er are to an end referred,
And in their motions still that end regard,
Always the fitness of the means respect,
These as conducive choose, and those reject,
Must by a judgment foreign and unknown
Be guided to their end, or by their own;
For to design an end, and to pursue
That end by means, and have it still in view,
Demands a conscious, wise, reflecting cause,
Which freely moves, and acts by reason's laws;
That can deliberate, means elect, and find
Their due connexion with the end designed. ·
And since the world's wide frame does not include
A cause with such capacities endued,
Some other cause o'er nature must preside,
Which gave her birth, and does her motions guide;
And here behold the cause, which God we name,
The source of beings, and the mind supreme;
Whose perfect wisdom, and whose prudent care,
With one confederate voice unnumbered worlds
    declare.

ELIJAH FENTON.

THIS author, who was very much respected by his contemporaries, and who translated a portion of the Odyssey in conjunction with Pope, was born May 20, 1683, at Newcastle, in Staffordshire; studied at Cambridge, which, owing to his nonjuring principles, he had to leave without a degree; and passed part of his life as a schoolmaster, and part of it as secretary to Charles, Earl of Orrery. By his tragedy of ' Mariamne ' he secured a moderate competence; and during his latter years, spent his life comfortably as tutor in the house of Lady Trumbull. He died in 1730.

His accomplishments were superior, and his character excellent.
Pope, who was indebted to him for the first, fourth, nineteenth, and
twentieth of the books of the Odyssey, mourns his loss in one
of his most sincere-seeming letters.   Fenton edited Waller and
Milton, wrote a brief life of the latter poet,—with which most of
our readers are acquainted,—and indited some respectable verse.

AN ODE TO THE RIGHT HON. JOHN LORD GOWER.

WRITTEN IN THE SPRING OF 1716.

1 O'er Winter's long inclement sway,
　　At length the lusty Spring prevails;
And swift to meet the smiling May,
　　Is wafted by the western gales.
Around him dance the rosy Hours,
And damasking the ground with flowers,
　　With ambient sweets perfume the morn;
With shadowy verdure flourished high,
A sudden youth the groves enjoy;
　　Where Philomel laments forlorn.

2 By her awaked, the woodland choir
　　To hail the coming god prepares;
And tempts me to resume the lyre,
　　Soft warbling to the vernal airs.
Yet once more, O ye Muses! deign
For me, the meanest of your train,
　　Unblamed to approach your blest retreat:
Where Horace wantons at your spring,
And Pindar sweeps a bolder string;
　　Whose notes the Aonian hills repeat.

3 Or if invoked, where Thames's fruitful tides,
　　Slow through the vale in silver volumes play;
Now your own Phœbus o'er the month presides,
　　Gives love the night, and doubly gilds the day;

25

Thither, indulgent to my prayer,
Ye bright harmonious nymphs, repair,
  To swell the notes I feebly raise:
So with aspiring ardours warmed
May Gower's propitious ear be charmed
  To listen to my lays.

4 Beneath the Pole on hills of snow,
    Like Thracian Mars, the undaunted Swede[1]
  To dint of sword defies the foe;
    In fight unknowing to recede:
  From Volga's banks, the imperious Czar
  Leads forth his furry troops to war;
    Fond of the softer southern sky:
  The Soldan galls the Illyrian coast;
  But soon the miscreant Moony host
    Before the Victor-Cross shall fly.

5 But here, no clarion's shrilling note
    The Muse's green retreat can pierce;
  The grove, from noisy camps remote,
    Is only vocal with my verse:
  Here, winged with innocence and joy,
  Let the soft hours that o'er me fly
    Drop freedom, health, and gay desires:
  While the bright Seine, to exalt the soul,
  With sparkling plenty crowns the bowl,
    And wit and social mirth inspires.

6 Enamoured of the Seine, celestial fair,
    (The blooming pride of Thetis' azure train,)
  Bacchus, to win the nymph who caused his care,
    Lashed his swift tigers to the Celtic plain:

[1] Charles XII.

26

There secret in her sapphire cell,
He with the Nais wont to dwell;
   Leaving the nectared feasts of Jove:
And where her mazy waters flow
He gave the mantling vine to grow,
   A trophy to his love.

7 Shall man from Nature's sanction stray,
   With blind opinion for his guide;
And, rebel to her rightful sway,
   Leave all her beauties unenjoyed?
Fool! Time no change of motion knows;
With equal speed the torrent flows,
   To sweep Fame, Power, and Wealth away:
The past is all by death possessed;
And frugal fate that guards the rest,
   By giving, bids him live To-Day.

8 O Gower! through all the destined space,
   What breath the Powers allot to me
Shall sing the virtues of thy race,
   United and complete in thee.
O flower of ancient English faith!
Pursue the unbeaten Patriot-path,
   In which confirmed thy father shone:
The light his fair example gives,
Already from thy dawn receives
   A lustre equal to its own.

9 Honour's bright dome, on lasting columns reared,
   Nor envy rusts, nor rolling years consume;
Loud Pæans echoing round the roof are heard,
   And clouds of incense all the void perfume.
   There Phocion, Lælius, Capel, Hyde,
   With Falkland seated near his side,

Fixed by the Muse, the temple grace;
Prophetic of thy happier fame,
She, to receive thy radiant name,
Selects a whiter space.

ROBERT CRAWFORD.

ROBERT CRAWFORD, a Scotchman, is our next poet. Of him we know only that he was the brother of Colonel Crawford of Achinames; that he assisted Allan Ramsay in the 'Tea-Table Miscellany;' and was drowned when coming from France in 1733. Besides the popular song, 'The Bush aboon Traquair,' which we quote, Crawford wrote also a lyric, called 'Tweedside,' and some verses, mentioned by Burns, to the old tune of 'Cowdenknowes.'

THE BUSH ABOON TRAQUAIR.

1 Hear me, ye nymphs, and every swain,
    I'll tell how Peggy grieves me;
Though thus I languish and complain,
    Alas! she ne'er believes me.
My vows and sighs, like silent air,
    Unheeded, never move her;
At the bonnie Bush aboon Traquair,
    'Twas there I first did love her.

2 That day she smiled and made me glad,
    No maid seemed ever kinder;
I thought myself the luckiest lad,
    So sweetly there to find her;
I tried to soothe my amorous flame,
    In words that I thought tender;
If more there passed, I'm not to blame—
    I meant not to offend her.

23

3 Yet now she scornful flies the plain,
    The fields we then frequented;
  If e'er we meet she shows disdain,
    She looks as ne'er acquainted.
  The bonnie bush bloomed fair in May,
    Its sweets I'll aye remember;
  But now her frowns make it decay—
    It fades as in December.

4 Ye rural powers, who hear my strains,
    Why thus should Peggy grieve me?
  Oh, make her partner in my pains,
    Then let her smiles relieve me!
  If not, my love will turn despair,
    My passion no more tender;
  I'll leave the Bush aboon Traquair—
    To lonely wilds I'll wander.

THOMAS TICKELL.

TICKELL is now chiefly remembered from his connexion with
Addison. He was born in 1686, at Bridekirk, near Carlisle. In
April 1701, he became a member of Queen's College in Oxford.
In 1708, he was made M.A., and two years after was chosen
Fellow. He held his Fellowship till 1726, when, marrying in
Dublin, he necessarily vacated it. He attracted Addison's
attention first by some elegant lines in praise of Rosamond, and
then by the 'Prospect of Peace,' a poem in which Tickell,
although called by Swift Whiggissimus, for once took the Tory
side. This poem Addison, in spite of its politics, praised highly
in the *Spectator*, which led to a lifelong friendship between
them. Tickell commenced contributing to the *Spectator*, among
other things publishing there a poem entitled the 'Royal Progress.' Some time after, he produced a translation of the first
book of the Iliad, which Addison declared to be superior to

Pope's. This led the latter to imagine that it was Addison's own, although it is now, we believe, certain, from the MS., which still exists, that it was a veritable production of Tickell's. When Addison went to Ireland, as secretary to Lord Sunderland, Tickell accompanied him, and was employed in public business. When Addison became Secretary of State, he made Tickell Under-Secretary; and when he died, he left him the charge of publishing his works, with an earnest recommendation to the care of Craggs. Tickell faithfully performed the task, prefixing to them an elegy on his departed friend, which is now his own chief title to fame. In 1725, he was made secretary to the Lords-Justices of Ireland, a place of great trust and honour, and which he retained till his death. This event happened at Bath, in the year 1740.

His genius was not strong, but elegant and refined, and appears, as we have just stated, to best advantage in his lines on Addison's death, which are warm with genuine love, tremulous with sincere sorrow, and shine with a sober splendour, such as Addison's own exquisite taste would have approved.

TO THE EARL OF WARWICK, ON THE DEATH OF MR ADDISON.

If, dumb too long, the drooping muse hath stayed,
And left her debt to Addison unpaid,
Blame not her silence, Warwick, but bemoan,
And judge, oh judge, my bosom by your own.
What mourner ever felt poetic fires!
Slow comes the verse that real woe inspires:
Grief unaffected suits but ill with art,
Or flowing numbers with a bleeding heart.
    Can I forget the dismal night that gave
My soul's best part for ever to the grave?
How silent did his old companions tread,
By midnight lamps, the mansions of the dead,
Through breathing statues, then unheeded things,
Through rows of warriors, and through walks of kings!
What awe did the slow solemn knell inspire;
    30

The pealing organ, and the pausing choir;
The duties by the lawn-robed prelate paid:
And the last words that dust to dust conveyed!
While speechless o'er thy closing grave we bend,
Accept these tears, thou dear departed friend.
Oh, gone for ever! take this long adieu;
And sleep in peace, next thy loved Montague.
To strew fresh laurels, let the task be mine,
A frequent pilgrim at thy sacred shrine;
Mine with true sighs thy absence to bemoan,
And grave with faithful epitaphs thy stone.
If e'er from me thy loved memorial part,
May shame afflict this alienated heart;
Of thee forgetful if I form a song,
My lyre be broken, and untuned my tongue,
My grief be doubled from thy image free,
And mirth a torment, unchastised by thee!
    Oft let me range the gloomy aisles alone,
Sad luxury! to vulgar minds unknown,
Along the walls where speaking marbles show
What worthies form the hallowed mould below;
Proud names, who once the reins of empire held;
In arms who triumphed, or in arts excelled;
Chiefs, graced with scars, and prodigal of blood;
Stern patriots, who for sacred freedom stood;
Just men, by whom impartial laws were given;
And saints, who taught and led the way to heaven;
Ne'er to these chambers, where the mighty rest,
Since their foundation came a nobler guest;
Nor e'er was to the bowers of bliss conveyed
A fairer spirit or more welcome shade.
    In what new region, to the just assigned,
What new employments please the embodied mind?
A winged Virtue, through the ethereal sky,

From world to world unwearied does he fly?
Or curious trace the long laborious maze
Of Heaven's decrees, where wondering angels gaze?
Does he delight to hear bold seraphs tell
How Michael battled, and the dragon fell;
Or, mixed with milder cherubim, to glow
In hymns of love, not ill essayed below?
Or dost thou warn poor mortals left behind,
A task well suited to thy gentle mind?
Oh! if sometimes thy spotless form descend,
To me thy aid, thou guardian genius, lend!
When rage misguides me, or when fear alarms,
When pain distresses, or when pleasure charms,
In silent whisperings purer thoughts impart,
And turn from ill a frail and feeble heart;
Lead through the paths thy virtue trod before,
Till bliss shall join, nor death can part us more.

That awful form, which, so the heavens decree,
Must still be loved and still deplored by me,
In nightly visions seldom fails to rise,
Or, roused by fancy, meets my waking eyes.
If business calls, or crowded courts invite,
The unblemished statesman seems to strike my sight;
If in the stage I seek to soothe my care,
I meet his soul which breathes in Cato there;
If pensive to the rural shades I rove,
His shape o'ertakes me in the lonely grove;
'Twas there of just and good he reasoned strong,
Cleared some great truth, or raised some serious song:
There patient showed us the wise course to steer,
A candid censor, and a friend severe;
There taught us how to live; and (oh! too high
The price for knowledge,) taught us how to die.

Thou hill, whose brow the antique structures grace,
32

Reared by bold chiefs of Warwick's noble race,
Why, once so loved, whene'er thy bower appears,
O'er my dim eyeballs glance the sudden tears?
How sweet were once thy prospects fresh and fair,
Thy sloping walks, and unpolluted air!
How sweet the glooms beneath thy aged trees,
Thy noontide shadow, and thy evening breeze!
His image thy forsaken bowers restore;
Thy walks and airy prospects charm no more;
No more the summer in thy glooms allayed,
Thy evening breezes, and thy noon-day shade.
　　From other ills, however fortune frowned,
Some refuge in the Muse's art I found;
Reluctant now I touch the trembling string,
Bereft of him who taught me how to sing;
And these sad accents, murmured o'er his urn,
Betray that absence they attempt to mourn.
Oh! must I then (now fresh my bosom bleeds,
And Craggs in death to Addison succeeds,)
The verse, begun to one lost friend, prolong,
And weep a second in the unfinished song!
　　These works divine, which, on his death-bed laid,
To thee, O Craggs! the expiring sage conveyed,
Great, but ill-omened, monument of fame,
Nor he survived to give, nor thou to claim.
Swift after him thy social spirit flies,
And close to his, how soon! thy coffin lies.
Blest pair! whose union future bards shall tell
In future tongues: each other's boast! farewell!
Farewell! whom, joined in fame, in friendship tried,
No chance could sever, nor the grave divide.

———

JAMES HAMMOND.

THIS elegiast was the second son of Anthony Hammond, a brother-in-law of Sir Robert Walpole, and a man of some note in his day. He was born in 1710; educated at Westminster school; became equerry to the Prince of Wales; fell in love with a lady named Dashwood, who rejected him, and drove him to temporary derangement, and then to elegy-writing; entered parliament for Truro, in Cornwall, in 1741; and died the next year. His elegies were published after his death, and, although abounding in pedantic allusions and frigid conceits, became very popular.

ELEGY XIII.

He imagines himself married to Delia, and that, content with each other,
they are retired into the country.

1 Let others boast their heaps of shining gold,
　And view their fields, with waving plenty crowned,
　Whom neighbouring foes in constant terror hold,
　And trumpets break their slumbers, never sound:

2 While calmly poor I trifle life away,
　Enjoy sweet leisure by my cheerful fire,
　No wanton hope my quiet shall betray,
　But, cheaply blessed, I'll scorn each vain desire.

3 With timely care I'll sow my little field,
　And plant my orchard with its master's hand,
　Nor blush to spread the hay, the hook to wield,
　Or range my sheaves along the sunny land.

4 If late at dusk, while carelessly I roam,
　I meet a strolling kid, or bleating lamb,
　Under my arm I'll bring the wanderer home,
　And not a little chide its thoughtless dam.
34

5 What joy to hear the tempest howl in vain,
   And clasp a fearful mistress to my breast!
   Or, lulled to slumber by the beating rain,
   Secure and happy, sink at last to rest!

6 Or, if the sun in flaming Leo ride,
   By shady rivers indolently stray,
   And with my Delia, walking side by side,
   Hear how they murmur as they glide away!

7 What joy to wind along the cool retreat,
   To stop and gaze on Delia as I go!
   To mingle sweet discourse with kisses sweet,
   And teach my lovely scholar all I know!

8 Thus pleased at heart, and not with fancy's dream,
   In silent happiness I rest unknown;
   Content with what I am, not what I seem,
   I live for Delia and myself alone.

      *   *   *   *   *

9 Hers be the care of all my little train,
   While I with tender indolence am blest,
   The favourite subject of her gentle reign,
   By love alone distinguished from the rest.

10 For her I'll yoke my oxen to the plough,
   In gloomy forests tend my lonely flock;
   For her, a goat-herd, climb the mountain's brow,
   And sleep extended on the naked rock:

11 Ah, what avails to press the stately bed,
   And far from her 'midst tasteless grandeur weep,
   By marble fountains lay the pensive head,
   And, while they murmur, strive in vain to sleep!

12 Delia alone can please, and never tire,
   Exceed the paint of thought in true delight;
   With her, enjoyment wakens new desire,
   And equal rapture glows through every night:

13 Beauty and worth in her alike contend,
   To charm the fancy, and to fix the mind;
   In her, my wife, my mistress, and my friend,
   I taste the joys of sense and reason joined.

14 On her I'll gaze, when others' loves are o'er,
   And dying press her with my clay-cold hand—
   Thou weep'st already, as I were no more,
   Nor can that gentle breast the thought withstand.

15 Oh, when I die, my latest moments spare,
   Nor let thy grief with sharper torments kill,
   Wound not thy cheeks, nor hurt that flowing hair,
   Though I am dead, my soul shall love thee still:

16 Oh, quit the room, oh, quit the deathful bed,
   Or thou wilt die, so tender is thy heart;
   Oh, leave me, Delia, ere thou see me dead,
   These weeping friends will do thy mournful part:

17 Let them, extended on the decent bier,
   Convey the corse in melancholy state,
   Through all the village spread the tender tear,
   While pitying maids our wondrous loves relate.

WE may here mention Dr George Sewell, author of a Life of
Sir Walter Raleigh, a few papers in the *Spectator*, and some
rather affecting verses written on consumption, where he says,
in reference to his garden—

'Thy narrow pride, thy fancied green,
(For vanity's in little seen,)
All must be left when death appears,
In spite of wishes, groans, and tears ;
Not one of all thy plants that grow,
But rosemary, will with thee go ;'—

Sir John Vanbrugh, best known as an architect, but who also wrote poetry ;—Edward Ward (more commonly called Ned Ward), a poetical publican, who wrote ten thick volumes, chiefly in Hudibrastic verse, displaying a good deal of coarse cleverness ;—Barton Booth, the famous actor, author of a song which closes thus—

'Love, and his sister fair, the Soul,
    Twin-born, from heaven together came ;
Love will the universe control,
    When dying seasons lose their name.
Divine abodes shall own his power,
When time and death shall be no more ;'—

Oldmixon, one of the heroes of the 'Dunciad,' famous in his day as a party historian ;—Richard West, a youth of high promise, the friend of Gray, and who died in his twenty-sixth year ;—James Eyre Weekes, an Irishman, author of a clever copy of love verses, called 'The Five Traitors ;'—Bramston, an Oxford man, who wrote a poem called 'The Man of Taste ;'—and William Meston, an Aberdonian, author of a set of burlesque poems entitled 'Mother Grim's Tales.'

RICHARD SAVAGE.

THE extreme excellence, fulness, and popularity of Johnson's Life of Savage must excuse our doing more than mentioning the leading dates of his history. He was the son of the Earl of Rivers and the Countess of Macclesfield, and was born in London, 1698. His mother, who had begot him in adultery, after having openly avowed her criminality, in order to obtain a divorce from her husband, placed the boy under the care of a poor woman, who brought him up as her son. His maternal grandmother, Lady Mason, however, took an interest in him, and placed him at a grammar school at St Alban's. He was afterwards apprenticed to a shoemaker. On the death of his nurse, he found some letters which led to the discovery of his real parent. He applied to her, accordingly, to be acknowledged as her son; but she repulsed his every advance, and persecuted him with unrelenting barbarity. He found, however, some influential friends, such as Steele, Fielding, Aaron Hill, Pope, and Lord Tyrconnell. He was, however, his own worst enemy, and contracted habits of the most irregular description. In a tavern brawl he killed one James Sinclair, and was condemned to die; but, notwithstanding his mother's interference to prevent the exercise of the royal clemency, he was pardoned by the queen, who afterwards gave him a pension of £50 a-year. He supported himself in a precarious way by writing poetical pieces. Lord Tyrconnell took him for a while into his house, and allowed him £200 a-year, but he soon quarrelled with him, and left. When the queen died he lost his pension, but his friends made it up by an annuity to the same amount. He went away to reside at Swansea, but on occasion of a visit he made to Bristol he was arrested for a small debt, and in the prison he sickened, and died on the 1st of August 1743. He was only forty-five years of age.

After all, Savage, in Johnson's Life, is just a dung-fly preserved in amber. His ‘Bastard,’ indeed, displays considerable powers, stung by a consciousness of wrong into convulsive action; but his other works are nearly worthless, and his life was that of a proud, passionate, selfish, and infatuated fool, unredeemed by scarcely one trait of genuine excellence in character. We love and admire, even while we deeply blame, such men as Burns; but for Savage our feeling is a curious compost of sympathy with his misfortunes, contempt for his folly, and abhorrence for the ingratitude, licentiousness, and other coarse and savage sins which characterised and prematurely destroyed him.

THE BASTARD.

INSCRIBED, WITH ALL DUE REVERENCE, TO MRS BRETT, ONCE COUNTESS OF
MACCLESFIELD.

In gayer hours, when high my fancy ran,
    The Muse exulting, thus her lay began :

'Blest be the Bastard's birth! through wondrous
    ways,
He shines eccentric like a comet's blaze!
No sickly fruit of faint compliance he!
He! stamped in nature's mint of ecstasy!
He lives to build, not boast a generous race:
No tenth transmitter of a foolish face:
His daring hope no sire's example bounds;
His first-born lights no prejudice confounds.
He, kindling from within, requires no flame;
He glories in a Bastard's glowing name.
  'Born to himself, by no possession led,
In freedom fostered, and by fortune fed;
Nor guides, nor rules his sovereign choice control,
His body independent as his soul;
Loosed to the world's wide range, enjoined no aim,
Prescribed no duty, and assigned no name:
Nature's unbounded son, he stands alone,
His heart unbiased, and his mind his own.
  'O mother, yet no mother! 'tis to you
My thanks for such distinguished claims are due;
You, unenslaved to Nature's narrow laws,
Warm championess for freedom's sacred cause,
From all the dry devoirs of blood and line,
From ties maternal, moral, and divine,
Discharged my grasping soul; pushed me from shore,
And launched me into life without an oar.
  'What had I lost, if, conjugally kind,
By nature hating, yet by vows confined,
Untaught the matrimonial bonds to slight,
And coldly conscious of a husband's right,
You had faint-drawn me with a form alone,
A lawful lump of life by force your own!
Then, while your backward will retrenched desire,

And unconcurring spirits lent no fire,
I had been born your dull, domestic heir,
Load of your life, and motive of your care;
Perhaps been poorly rich, and meanly great,
The slave of pomp, a cipher in the state;
Lordly neglectful of a worth unknown,
And slumbering in a seat by chance my own.
　'Far nobler blessings wait the bastard's lot;
Conceived in rapture, and with fire begot!
Strong as necessity, he starts away,
Climbs against wrongs, and brightens into day.'
Thus unprophetic, lately misinspired,
I sung: gay fluttering hope my fancy fired:
Inly secure, through conscious scorn of ill,
Nor taught by wisdom how to balance will,
Rashly deceived, I saw no pits to shun,
But thought to purpose and to act were one;
Heedless what pointed cares pervert his way,
Whom caution arms not, and whom woes betray;
But now exposed, and shrinking from distress,
I fly to shelter while the tempests press;
My Muse to grief resigns the varying tone,
The raptures languish, and the numbers groan.
　O Memory! thou soul of joy and pain!
Thou actor of our passions o'er again!
Why didst thou aggravate the wretch's woe?
Why add continuous smart to every blow?
Few are my joys; alas! how soon forgot!
On that kind quarter thou invad'st me not;
While sharp and numberless my sorrows fall,
Yet thou repeat'st and multipli'st them all.
　Is chance a guilt? that my disastrous heart,
For mischief never meant, must ever smart?
Can self-defence be sin?—Ah, plead no more!
40

What though no purposed malice stained thee o'er?
Had Heaven befriended thy unhappy side,
Thou hadst not been provoked—or thou hadst died.
　　Far be the guilt of homeshed blood from all
On whom, unsought, embroiling dangers fall!
Still the pale dead revives, and lives to me,
To me! through Pity's eye condemned to see.
Remembrance veils his rage, but swells his fate;
Grieved I forgive, and am grown cool too late.
Young, and unthoughtful then; who knows, one day,
What ripening virtues might have made their way?
He might have lived till folly died in shame,
Till kindling wisdom felt a thirst for fame.
He might perhaps his country's friend have proved;
Both happy, generous, candid, and beloved,
He might have saved some worth, now doomed to
　　　fall;
And I, perchance, in him, have murdered all.
　　O fate of late repentance! always vain:
Thy remedies but lull undying pain.
Where shall my hope find rest?—No mother's care
Shielded my infant innocence with prayer:
No father's guardian hand my youth maintained,
Called forth my virtues, or from vice restrained.
Is it not thine to snatch some powerful arm,
First to advance, then screen from future harm?
Am I returned from death to live in pain?
Or would imperial Pity save in vain?
Distrust it not—What blame can mercy find,
Which gives at once a life, and rears a mind?
　　Mother, miscalled, farewell—of soul severe,
This sad reflection yet may force one tear:
All I was wretched by to you I owed,
Alone from strangers every comfort flowed!

> Lost to the life you gave, your son no more,
> And now adopted, who was doomed before;
> New-born, I may a nobler mother claim,
> But dare not whisper her immortal name;
> Supremely lovely, and serenely great!
> Majestic mother of a kneeling state!
> Queen of a people's heart, who ne'er before
> Agreed—yet now with one consent adore!
> One contest yet remains in this desire,
> Who most shall give applause, where all admire.

THOMAS WARTON THE ELDER.

THE Wartons were a poetical race.   The father of Thomas and
Joseph, names so intimately associated with English poetry, was
himself a poet.   He was of Magdalene College in Oxford, vicar
of Basingstoke and Cobham, and twice chosen poetry professor.
He was born in 1687, and died in 1745.   Besides the little
American ode quoted below, we are tempted to give the following

VERSES WRITTEN AFTER SEEING WINDSOR CASTLE.

> From beauteous Windsor's high and storied halls,
> Where Edward's chiefs start from the glowing walls,
> To my low cot, from ivory beds of state,
> Pleased I return, unenvious of the great.
> So the bee ranges o'er the varied scenes
> Of corn, of heaths, of fallows, and of greens ;
> Pervades the thicket, soars above the hill,
> Or murmurs to the meadow's murmuring rill ;
> Now haunts old hollowed oaks, deserted cells,
> Now seeks the low vale-lily's silver bells;
> Sips the warm fragrance of the greenhouse bowers,
> And tastes the myrtle and the citron flowers ;—
> At length returning to the wonted comb,
> Prefers to all his little straw-built home.

This seems sweet and simple poetry.

AN AMERICAN LOVE ODE.

FROM THE SECOND VOLUME OF MONTAIGNE'S ESSAYS.

Stay, stay, thou lovely, fearful snake,
Nor hide thee in yon darksome brake:
But let me oft thy charms review,
Thy glittering scales, and golden hue;
From these a chaplet shall be wove,
To grace the youth I dearest love.

Then ages hence, when thou no more
Shalt creep along the sunny shore,
Thy copied beauties shall be seen;
Thy red and azure mixed with green,
In mimic folds thou shalt display;—
Stay, lovely, fearful adder, stay.

JONATHAN SWIFT.

IN contemplating the lives and works of the preceding poets in this third volume of ' Specimens,' we have been impressed with a sense, if not of their absolute, yet of their comparative mediocrity. Beside such neglected giants as Henry More, Joseph Beaumont, and Andrew Marvell, the Pomfrets, Sedleys, Blackmores, and Savages sink into insignificance. But when we come to the name of Swift, we feel ourselves again approaching an Alpine region. The air of a stern mountain-summit breathes chill around our temples, and we feel that if we have no amiability to melt, we have altitude at least to measure, and strange profound secrets of nature, like the ravines of lofty hills, to explore. The men of the sixteenth and seventeenth centuries may be compared to Lebanon, or Snowdown, or Benlomond, towering grandly over fertile valleys, on which they smile— Swift to the tremendous Romsdale Horn in Norway, shedding abroad, from a brow of four thousand feet high, what seems a

43

scowl of settled indignation, as if resolved not to rejoice even over the wide-stretching deserts which, and nothing but which, it everlastingly beholds. Mountains all of them, but what a difference between such a mountain as Shakspeare, and such a mountain as Swift!

Instead of going minutely over a path so long since trodden to mire as the life of Swift, let us expend a page or two in seeking to form some estimate of his character and genius. It is refreshing to come upon a new thing in the world, even though it be a strange or even a bad thing; and certainly, in any age and country, such a being as Swift must have appeared an anomaly, not for his transcendent goodness, not for his utter badness, but because the elements of good and evil were mixed in him into a medley so astounding, and in proportions respectively so large, yet unequal, that the analysis of the two seemed to many competent only to the Great Chymist, Death, and that a sense of the disproportion seems to have moved the man himself to inextinguishable laughter,—a laughter which, radiating out of his own singular heart as a centre, swept over the circumference of all beings within his reach, and returned crying, 'Give, give,' as if he were demanding a universal sphere for the exercise of the savage scorn which dwelt within him, and as if he laughed not more 'consumedly' at others than he did at himself.

Ere speaking of Swift as a man, let us say something about his genius. That, like his character, was intensely peculiar. It was a compound of infinite ingenuity, with very little poetical imagination—of gigantic strength, with a propensity to incessant trifling—of passionate purpose, with the clearest and coldest expression, as though a furnace were fuelled with snow. A Brobdignagian by size, he was for ever toying with Lilliputian slings and small craft. One of the most violent of party men, and often fierce as a demoniac in temper, his favourite motto was *Vive la bagatelle*. The creator of entire new worlds, we doubt if his works contain more than two or three lines of genuine poetry. He may be compared to one of the locusts of the Apocalypse, in that he had a tail like unto a scorpion, and a sting in his tail; but his ' face is not as the face of man, his hair is not as the hair of women, and on his head there is no crown like gold.' All

44

Swift's creations are more or less disgusting. Not one of them is beautiful. His Lilliputians are amazingly life-like, but compare them to Shakspeare's fairies, such as Peaseblossom, Cobweb, and Mustardseed; his Brobdignagians are excrescences like enormous warts; and his Yahoos might have been spawned in the nightmare of a drunken butcher. The same coarseness characterises his poems and his ' Tale of a Tub.' He might well, however, in his old age, exclaim, in reference to the latter, ' Good God! what a genius I had when I wrote that book!' It is the wildest, wittiest, wickedest, wealthiest book of its size in the English language. Thoughts and figures swarm in every corner of its pages, till you think of a disturbed nest of angry ants, for all the figures and thoughts are black and bitter. One would imagine the book to have issued from a mind that had been gathering gall as well as sense in an antenatal state of being.

Swift, in all his writings—sermons, political tracts, poems, and fictions—is essentially a satirist. He consisted originally of three principal parts,—sense, an intense feeling of the ludicrous, and selfish passion; and these were sure, in certain circumstances, to ferment into a spirit of satire, ' strong as death, and cruel as the grave.' Born with not very much natural benevolence, with little purely poetic feeling, with furious passions and unbounded ambition, he was entirely dependent for his peace of mind upon success. Had he become, as by his talents he was entitled to be, the prime minister of his day, he would have figured as a greater tyrant in the cabinet than even Chatham. But as he was prevented from being the first statesman, he became the first satirist of his time. From vain efforts to grasp supremacy for himself and his party, he retired growling to his Dublin den; and there, as Haman thought scorn to lay his hand on Mordecai, but extended his murderous purpose to all the people of the Jews,—and as Nero wished that Rome had one neck, that he might destroy it at a blow,—so Swift was stung by his personal disappointment to hurl out scorn at man and suspicion at his Maker. It was not, it must be noticed, the evil which was in man which excited his hatred and contempt; it was man himself. He was not merely, as many are, disgusted with the selfish and malignant elements which are mingled in man's nature and

45

character, and disposed to trace them to any cause save a Divine will, but he believed man to be, as a whole, the work and child of the devil; and he told the imaginary creator and creature to their face, what he thought the truth,—'The devil is an ass.' His was the very madness of Manichæism. That heresy held that the devil was one of two aboriginal creative powers, but Swift seemed to believe at times that he was the only God. From a Yahoo man, it was difficult to avoid the inference of a demon deity. It is very laughable to find writers in *Blackwood* and elsewhere striving to prove Swift a Christian, as if, whatever were his professions, and however sincere he might be often in these, the whole tendency of his writings, his perpetual and unlimited abuse of man's body and soul, his denial of every human virtue, the filth he pours upon every phase of human nature, and the doctrine he insinuates—that man has fallen indeed, but fallen, not from the angel, but from the animal, or, rather, is just a bungled brute,—were not enough to shew that either his notions were grossly erroneous and perverted, or that he himself deserved, like another Nebuchadnezzar, to be driven from men, and to have a beast's heart given unto him. Sometimes he reminds us of an impure angel, who has surprised man naked and asleep, looked at him with microscopic eyes, ignored all his peculiar marks of fallen dignity and incipient godhood, and in heartless rhymes reported accordingly.

Swift belonged to the same school as Pope, although the feminine element which was in the latter modified and mellowed his feelings. Pope was a more successful and a happier man than Swift. He was much smaller, too, in soul as well as in body, and his gall-organ was proportionably less. Pope's feeling to humanity was a tiny malice; Swift's became, at length, a black malignity. Pope always reminds us of an injured and pouting hero of Lilliput, ' doing well to be angry' under the gourd of a pocket-flap, or squealing out his griefs from the centre of an empty snuff-box; Swift is a man, nay, monster of misanthropy. In minute and microscopic vision of human infirmities, Pope excels even Swift; but then you always conceive Swift leaning down a giant, though gnarled, stature to behold them, while Pope is on their level, and has only to look straight before him.

46

Pope's wrath is always measured; Swift's, as in the ' Legion-Club,' is a whirlwind of ' black fire and horror,' in the breath of which no flesh can live, and against which genius and virtue themselves furnish no shield.

After all, Swift might, perhaps, have put in the plea of Byron—

> ' All my faults perchance thou knowest,
> All my madness none can know.'

There was a black spot of madness in his brain, and another black spot in his heart; and the two at last met, and closed up his destiny in night.   Let human nature forgive its most determined and systematic reviler, for the sake of the wretchedness in which he was involved all his life long.   He was born (in 1667) a posthumous child; he was brought up an object of charity; he spent much of his youth in dependence; he had to leave his Irish college without a degree; he was flattered with hopes from King William and the Whigs, which were not fulfilled; he was condemned to spend a great part of his life in Ireland, a country he detested; he was involved—partly, no doubt, through his own blame—in a succession of fruitless and miserable intrigues, alike of love and politics; he was soured by want of success in England, and spoiled by enormous popularity in Ireland; he was tried by a kind of religious doubts, which would not go out to prayer or fasting; he was haunted by the fear of the dreadful calamity which at last befell him; his senses and his soul left him one by one; he became first giddy, then deaf, and then mad ; his madness was of the most terrible sort—it was a ' silent rage ; ' for a year or two he lay dumb; and at last, on the 19th of October 1745,

> ' Swift expired, a driveller and a show,'

leaving his money to found a lunatic asylum, and his works as a many-volumed legacy of curse to mankind.[1]

BAUCIS AND PHILEMON.

In ancient times, as story tells,
The saints would often leave their cells,

---

[1] It has been asserted that there were circumstances in extenuation of Swift's conduct, particularly in reference to the ladies whose names were connected with his, which *cannot be publicly brought forward.*

And stroll about, but hide their quality,
To try good people's hospitality.
    It happened on a winter night,
As authors of the legend write,
Two brother-hermits, saints by trade,
Taking their tour in masquerade,
Disguised in tattered habits went
To a small village down in Kent,
Where, in the strollers' canting strain,
They begged from door to door in vain,
Tried every tone might pity win;
But not a soul would let them in.
Our wandering saints, in woful state,
Treated at this ungodly rate,
Having through all the village passed,
To a small cottage came at last,
Where dwelt a good old honest yeoman,
Called in the neighbourhood Philemon;
Who kindly did these saints invite
In his poor hut to pass the night;
And then the hospitable sire
Bid Goody Baucis mend the fire;
While he from out the chimney took
A flitch of bacon off the hook,
And freely from the fattest side
Cut out large slices to be fried;
Then stepped aside to fetch them drink,
Filled a large jug up to the brink,
And saw it fairly twice go round;
Yet (what is wonderful!) they found
'Twas still replenished to the top,
As if they ne'er had touched a drop.
The good old couple were amazed,
And often on each other gazed;

48

For both were frightened to the heart,
And just began to cry,—'What art!'
Then softly turned aside to view
Whether the lights were burning blue.
The gentle pilgrims, soon aware on 't,
Told them their calling, and their errand:
'Good folks, you need not be afraid,
We are but saints,' the hermits said;
'No hurt shall come to you or yours:
But for that pack of churlish boors,
Not fit to live on Christian ground,
They and their houses shall be drowned;
Whilst you shall see your cottage rise,
And grow a church before your eyes.'
   They scarce had spoke, when fair and soft
The roof began to mount aloft;
Aloft rose every beam and rafter;
The heavy wall climbed slowly after.
   The chimney widened, and grew higher,
Became a steeple with a spire.
   The kettle to the top was hoist,
And there stood fastened to a joist;
But with the upside down, to show
Its inclination for below;
In vain; for a superior force,
Applied at bottom, stops its course:
Doomed ever in suspense to dwell,
'Tis now no kettle, but a bell.
   A wooden jack, which had almost
Lost by disuse the art to roast,
A sudden alteration feels,
Increased by new intestine wheels;
And, what exalts the wonder more,
The number made the motion slower;

The flier, though 't had leaden feet,
Turned round so quick, you scarce could see't;
But, slackened by some secret power,
Now hardly moves an inch an hour.
The jack and chimney, near allied,
Had never left each other's side:
The chimney to a steeple grown,
The jack would not be left alone;
But up against the steeple reared,
Became a clock, and still adhered;
And still its love to household cares,
By a shrill voice at noon declares,
Warning the cook-maid not to burn
That roast meat which it cannot turn.

The groaning-chair began to crawl,
Like a huge snail, along the wall;
There stuck aloft in public view,
And with small change a pulpit grew.

The porringers, that in a row
Hung high, and made a glittering show,
To a less noble substance changed,
Were now but leathern buckets ranged.

The ballads, pasted on the wall,
Of Joan of France, and English Moll,
Fair Rosamond, and Robin Hood,
The little Children in the Wood,
Now seemed to look abundance better,
Improved in picture, size, and letter;
And, high in order placed, describe
The heraldry of every tribe.

A bedstead, of the antique mode,
Compact of timber many a load,
Such as our ancestors did use,
Was metamorphosed into pews;

Which still their ancient nature keep,
By lodging folks disposed to sleep.
  The cottage, by such feats as these,
Grown to a church by just degrees;
The hermits then desired their host
To ask for what he fancied most.
Philemon, having paused a while,
Returned them thanks in homely style;
Then said, 'My house is grown so fine,
Methinks I still would call it mine;
I 'm old, and fain would live at ease;
Make me the parson, if you please.'
  He spoke, and presently he feels
His grazier's coat fall down his heels:
He sees, yet hardly can believe,
About each arm a pudding-sleeve;
His waistcoat to a cassock grew,
And both assumed a sable hue;
But, being old, continued just
As threadbare, and as full of dust.
His talk was now of tithes and dues;
He smoked his pipe, and read the news;
Knew how to preach old sermons next,
Vamped in the preface and the text;
At christenings well could act his part,
And had the service all by heart;
Wished women might have children fast,
And thought whose sow had farrowed last;
Against Dissenters would repine,
And stood up firm for right divine;
Found his head filled with many a system;
But classic authors,—he ne'er missed 'em.
  Thus, having furbished up a parson,
Dame Baucis next they played their farce on;

Instead of home-spun coifs, were seen
Good pinners edged with colberteen;
Her petticoat, transformed apace,
Became black satin flounced with lace.
Plain 'Goody' would no longer down;
'Twas 'Madam' in her grogram gown.
Philemon was in great surprise,
And hardly could believe his eyes,
Amazed to see her look so prim;
And she admired as much at him.

Thus happy in their change of life
Were several years this man and wife:
When on a day, which proved their last,
Discoursing on old stories past,
They went by chance, amidst their talk,
To the churchyard to take a walk;
When Baucis hastily cried out,
'My dear, I see your forehead sprout!'
'Sprout!' quoth the man; 'what's this you tell us?
I hope you don't believe me jealous!
But yet, methinks, I feel it true;
And, really, yours is budding too;
Nay, now I cannot stir my foot—
It feels as if 'twere taking root.'

Description would but tire my Muse;
In short, they both were turned to yews.
Old Goodman Dobson of the green
Remembers he the trees has seen;
He'll talk of them from noon till night,
And goes with folks to show the sight;
On Sundays, after evening-prayer,
He gathers all the parish there,
Points out the place of either yew:
'Here Baucis, there Philemon grew;

52

Till once a parson of our town,
To mend his barn cut Baucis down.
At which 'tis hard to be believed
How much the other tree was grieved,
Grew scrubby, died atop, was stunted;
So the next parson stubbed and burnt it.'

ON POETRY.

All human race would fain be wits,
And millions miss for one that hits.
Young's Universal Passion, pride,
Was never known to spread so wide.
Say, Britain, could you ever boast
Three poets in an age at most?
Our chilling climate hardly bears
A sprig of bays in fifty years;
While every fool his claim alleges,
As if it grew in common hedges.
What reason can there be assigned
For this perverseness in the mind?
Brutes find out where their talents lie:
A bear will not attempt to fly;
A foundered horse will oft debate
Before he tries a five-barred gate;
A dog by instinct turns aside,
Who sees the ditch too deep and wide;—
But man we find the only creature,
Who, led by folly, combats nature;
Who, when she loudly cries, Forbear,
With obstinacy fixes there;
And, where his genius least inclines,
Absurdly bends his whole designs.
  Not empire to the rising sun
By valour, conduct, fortune won;

Not highest wisdom in debates
For framing laws to govern states;
Not skill in sciences profound
So large to grasp the circle round,
Such heavenly influence require,
As how to strike the Muse's lyre.

　Not beggar's brat on bulk begot;
Not bastard of a pedlar Scot;
Not boy brought up to cleaning shoes,
The spawn of Bridewell or the stews;
Not infants dropped, the spurious pledges
Of gipsies littering under hedges,
Are so disqualified by fate
To rise in church, or law, or state,
As he whom Phœbus in his ire
Hath blasted with poetic fire.
What hope of custom in the fair,
While not a soul demands your ware?
Where you have nothing to produce
For private life or public use?
Court, city, country, want you not;
You cannot bribe, betray, or plot.
For poets, law makes no provision;
The wealthy have you in derision;
Of state affairs you cannot smatter,
Are awkward when you try to flatter;
Your portion, taking Britain round,
Was just one annual hundred pound;
Now not so much as in remainder,
Since Cibber brought in an attainder,
For ever fixed by right divine,
(A monarch's right,) on Grub Street line.

　Poor starveling bard, how small thy gains!
How unproportioned to thy pains!

54

And here a simile comes pat in:
Though chickens take a month to fatten,
The guests in less than half an hour
Will more than half a score devour.
So, after toiling twenty days
To earn a stock of pence and praise,
Thy labours, grown the critic's prey,
Are swallowed o'er a dish of tea;
Gone to be never heard of more,
Gone where the chickens went before.
How shall a new attempter learn
Of different spirits to discern,
And how distinguish which is which,
The poet's vein, or scribbling itch?
Then hear an old experienced sinner
Instructing thus a young beginner:
Consult yourself; and if you find
A powerful impulse urge your mind,
Impartial judge within your breast
What subject you can manage best;
Whether your genius most inclines
To satire, praise, or humorous lines,
To elegies in mournful tone,
Or prologues sent from hand unknown;
Then, rising with Aurora's light,
The Muse invoked, sit down to write;
Blot out, correct, insert, refine,
Enlarge, diminish, interline;
Be mindful, when invention fails,
To scratch your head, and bite your nails.

Your poem finished, next your care
Is needful to transcribe it fair.
In modern wit, all printed trash is
Set off with numerous breaks and dashes.
To statesmen would you give a wipe,

You print it in italic type;
When letters are in vulgar shapes,
'Tis ten to one the wit escapes;
But when in capitals expressed,
The dullest reader smokes the jest;
Or else, perhaps, he may invent
A better than the poet meant;
As learned commentators view
In Homer, more than Homer knew.

Your poem in its modish dress,
Correctly fitted for the press,
Convey by penny-post to Lintot;
But let no friend alive look into 't.
If Lintot thinks 'twill quit the cost,
You need not fear your labour lost:
And how agreeably surprised
Are you to see it advertised!
The hawker shows you one in print,
As fresh as farthings from a mint:
The product of your toil and sweating,
A bastard of your own begetting.

Be sure at Will's the following day,
Lie snug, and hear what critics say;
And if you find the general vogue
Pronounces you a stupid rogue,
Damns all your thoughts as low and little,
Sit still, and swallow down your spittle;
Be silent as a politician,
For talking may beget suspicion;
Or praise the judgment of the town,
And help yourself to run it down;
Give up your fond paternal pride,
Nor argue on the weaker side;
For poems read without a name
We justly praise, or justly blame;

And critics have no partial views,
Except they know whom they abuse;
And since you ne'er provoked their spite,
Depend upon 't, their judgment's right.
But if you blab, you are undone:
Consider what a risk you run:
You lose your credit all at once;
The town will mark you for a dunce;
The vilest doggrel Grub Street sends
Will pass for yours with foes and friends;
And you must bear the whole disgrace,
Till some fresh blockhead takes your place.
    Your secret kept, your poem sunk,
And sent in quires to line a trunk,
If still you be disposed to rhyme,
Go try your hand a second time.
Again you fail: yet safe 's the word;
Take courage, and attempt a third.
But just with care employ your thoughts,
Where critics marked your former faults;
The trivial turns, the borrowed wit,
The similes that nothing fit;
The cant which every fool repeats,
Town jests and coffee-house conceits;
Descriptions tedious, flat, and dry,
And introduced the Lord knows why:
Or where we find your fury set
Against the harmless alphabet;
On A's and B's your malice vent,
While readers wonder what you meant:
A public or a private robber,
A statesman, or a South-Sea jobber;
A prelate who no God believes;
A parliament, or den of thieves;
A pick-purse at the bar or bench;

A duchess, or a suburb wench:
Or oft, when epithets you link
In gaping lines to fill a chink;
Like stepping-stones to save a stride,
In streets where kennels are too wide;
Or like a heel-piece, to support
A cripple with one foot too short;
Or like a bridge, that joins a marish
To moorland of a different parish;
So have I seen ill-coupled hounds
Drag different ways in miry grounds;
So geographers in Afric maps
With savage pictures fill their gaps,
And o'er unhabitable downs
Place elephants, for want of towns.

But though you miss your third essay,
You need not throw your pen away.
Lay now aside all thoughts of fame,
To spring more profitable game.
From party-merit seek support—
The vilest verse thrives best at court.
And may you ever have the luck,
To rhyme almost as ill as Duck;
And though you never learnt to scan verse,
Come out with some lampoon on D'Anvers.
A pamphlet in Sir Bob's defence
Will never fail to bring in pence:
Nor be concerned about the sale—
He pays his workmen on the nail.
Display the blessings of the nation,
And praise the whole administration:
Extol the bench of Bishops round;
Who at them rail, bid —— confound:
To Bishop-haters answer thus,
(The only logic used by us,)

'What though they don't believe in ——,
Deny them Protestants,—thou liest.'
　　A prince, the moment he is crowned,
Inherits every virtue round,
As emblems of the sovereign power,
Like other baubles in the Tower;
Is generous, valiant, just, and wise,
And so continues till he dies:
His humble senate this professes
In all their speeches, votes, addresses.
But once you fix him in a tomb,
His virtues fade, his vices bloom,
And each perfection, wrong imputed,
Is fully at his death confuted.
The loads of poems in his praise
Ascending, make one funeral blaze.
As soon as you can hear his knell
This god on earth turns devil in hell;
And lo! his ministers of state,
Transformed to imps, his levee wait,
Where, in the scenes of endless woe,
They ply their former arts below;
And as they sail in Charon's boat,
Contrive to bribe the judge's vote;
To Cerberus they give a sop,
His triple-barking mouth to stop;
Or in the ivory gate of dreams
Project Excise and South-Sea schemes,
Or hire their party pamphleteers
To set Elysium by the ears.
　　Then, poet, if you mean to thrive,
Employ your Muse on kings alive;
With prudence gather up a cluster
Of all the virtues you can muster,
Which, formed into a garland sweet,

Lay humbly at your monarch's feet,
Who, as the odours reach his throne,
Will smile and think them all his own;
For law and gospel both determine
All virtues lodge in royal ermine,
(I mean the oracles of both,
Who shall depose it upon oath.)
Your garland in the following reign,
Change but the names, will do again.

But, if you think this trade too base,
(Which seldom is the dunce's case,)
Put on the critic's brow, and sit
At Will's the puny judge of wit.
A nod, a shrug, a scornful smile,
With caution used, may serve a while.
Proceed on further in your part,
Before you learn the terms of art;
For you can never be too far gone
In all our modern critics' jargon;
Then talk with more authentic face
Of unities, in time, and place;
Get scraps of Horace from your friends,
And have them at your fingers' ends;
Learn Aristotle's rules by rote,
And at all hazards boldly quote;
Judicious Rymer oft review,
Wise Dennis, and profound Bossu;
Read all the prefaces of Dryden—
For these our critics much confide in,
(Though merely writ at first for filling,
To raise the volume's price a shilling.)

A forward critic often dupes us
With sham quotations *Peri Hupsous.*
And if we have not read Longinus,
Will magisterially outshine us.

Then, lest with Greek he overrun ye,
Procure the book for love or money,
Translated from Boileau's translation,
And quote quotation on quotation.
  At Will's you hear a poem read,
Where Battus from the table-head,
Reclining on his elbow-chair,
Gives judgment with decisive air;
To whom the tribes of circling wits
As to an oracle submits.
He gives directions to the town,
To cry it up, or run it down;
Like courtiers, when they send a note,
Instructing members how to vote.
He sets the stamp of bad and good,
Though not a word he understood.
Your lesson learned, you 'll be secure
To get the name of connoisseur:
And, when your merits once are known,
Procure disciples of your own.
For poets, (you can never want 'em,)
Spread through Augusta Trinobantum,
Computing by their pecks of coals,
Amount to just nine thousand souls.
These o'er their proper districts govern,
Of wit and humour judges sovereign.
In every street a city-bard
Rules, like an alderman, his ward;
His undisputed rights extend
Through all the lane, from end to end;
The neighbours round admire his shrewdness
For songs of loyalty and lewdness;
Outdone by none in rhyming well,
Although he never learned to spell.
Two bordering wits contend for glory;

And one is Whig, and one is Tory:
And this for epics claims the bays,
And that for elegiac lays:
Some famed for numbers soft and smooth,
By lovers spoke in Punch's booth;
And some as justly Fame extols
For lofty lines in Smithfield drolls.
Bavius in Wapping gains renown,
And Mavius reigns o'er Kentish-town;
Tigellius, placed in Phœbus' car,
From Ludgate shines to Temple-bar:
Harmonious Cibber entertains
The court with annual birth-day strains;
Whence Gay was banished in disgrace;
Where Pope will never show his face;
Where Young must torture his invention
To flatter knaves, or lose his pension.

But these are not a thousandth part
Of jobbers in the poet's art;
Attending each his proper station,
And all in due subordination,
Through every alley to be found,
In garrets high, or under ground;
And when they join their pericranies,
Out skips a book of miscellanies.
Hobbes clearly proves that every creature
Lives in a state of war by nature;
The greater for the smallest watch,
But meddle seldom with their match.
A whale of moderate size will draw
A shoal of herrings down his maw;
A fox with geese his belly crams;
A wolf destroys a thousand lambs:
But search among the rhyming race,
The brave are worried by the base.

If on Parnassus' top you sit,
You rarely bite, are always bit.
Each poet of inferior size
On you shall rail and criticise,
And strive to tear you limb from limb;
While others do as much for him.
　　The vermin only tease and pinch
Their foes superior by an inch:
So, naturalists observe, a flea
Hath smaller fleas that on him prey;
And these have smaller still to bite 'em,
And so proceed *ad infinitum*.
Thus every poet in his kind
Is bit by him that comes behind:
Who, though too little to be seen,
Can tease, and gall, and give the spleen;
Call dunces fools and sons of whores,
Lay Grub Street at each other's doors;
Extol the Greek and Roman masters,
And curse our modern poetasters;
Complain, as many an ancient bard did,
How genius is no more rewarded;
How wrong a taste prevails among us;
How much our ancestors out-sung us;
Can personate an awkward scorn
For those who are not poets born;
And all their brother-dunces lash,
Who crowd the press with hourly trash.
　　O Grub Street! how do I bemoan thee,
Whose graceless children scorn to own thee!
Their filial piety forgot,
Deny their country like a Scot;
Though by their idiom and grimace,
They soon betray their native place.
Yet thou hast greater cause to be

Ashamed of them, than they of thee,
Degenerate from their ancient brood
Since first the court allowed them food.
   Remains a difficulty still,
To purchase fame by writing ill.
From Flecknoe down to Howard's time,
How few have reached the low sublime!
For when our high-born Howard died,
Blackmore alone his place supplied;
And lest a chasm should intervene,
When death had finished Blackmore's reign,
The leaden crown devolved to thee,
Great poet of the Hollow Tree.
But ah! how unsecure thy throne!
A thousand bards thy right disown;
They plot to turn, in factious zeal,
Duncenia to a commonweal;
And with rebellious arms pretend
An equal privilege to defend.
   In bulk there are not more degrees
From elephants to mites in cheese,
Than what a curious eye may trace
In creatures of the rhyming race.
From bad to worse, and worse, they fall;
But who can reach the worst of all?
For though in nature, depth and height
Are equally held infinite;
In poetry, the height we know;
'Tis only infinite below.
For instance, when you rashly think
No rhymer can like Welsted sink,
His merits balanced, you shall find
The laureate leaves him far behind;
Concannen, more aspiring bard,
Soars downwards deeper by a yard;

Smart Jemmy Moor with vigour drops;
The rest pursue as thick as hops.
With heads to point, the gulf they enter,
Linked perpendicular to the centre;
And, as their heels elated rise,
Their heads attempt the nether skies.
　Oh, what indignity and shame,
To prostitute the Muse's name,
By flattering kings, whom Heaven designed
The plagues and scourges of mankind;
Bred up in ignorance and sloth,
And every vice that nurses both.
　Fair Britain, in thy monarch blest,
Whose virtues bear the strictest test;
Whom never faction could bespatter,
Nor minister nor poet flatter;
What justice in rewarding merit!
What magnanimity of spirit!
What lineaments divine we trace
Through all his figure, mien, and face!
Though peace with olive bind his hands,
Confessed the conquering hero stands.
Hydaspes, Indus, and the Ganges,
Dread from his hand impending changes;
From him the Tartar and the Chinese,
Short by the knees, entreat for peace.
The comfort of his throne and bed,
A perfect goddess born and bred;
Appointed sovereign judge to sit
On learning, eloquence and wit.
Our eldest hope, divine Iülus,
(Late, very late, oh, may he rule us!)
What early manhood has he shown,
Before his downy beard was grown!
Then think what wonders will be done,

By going on as he begun,
An heir for Britain to secure
As long as sun and moon endure.
   The remnant of the royal blood
Comes pouring on me like a flood:
Bright goddesses, in number five;
Duke William, sweetest prince alive!
   Now sings the minister of state,
Who shines alone without a mate.
Observe with what majestic port
This Atlas stands to prop the court,
Intent the public debts to pay,
Like prudent Fabius, by delay.
Thou great vicegerent of the king,
Thy praises every Muse shall sing!
In all affairs thou sole director,
Of wit and learning chief protector;
Though small the time thou hast to spare,
The church is thy peculiar care.
Of pious prelates what a stock
You choose, to rule the sable flock!
You raise the honour of your peerage,
Proud to attend you at the steerage;
You dignify the noble race,
Content yourself with humbler place.
Now learning, valour, virtue, sense,
To titles give the sole pretence.
St George beheld thee with delight
Vouchsafe to be an azure knight,
When on thy breasts and sides herculean
He fixed the star and string cerulean.
   Say, poet, in what other nation,
Shone ever such a constellation!
Attend, ye Popes, and Youngs, and Gays,
And tune your harps, and strew your bays:

Your panegyrics here provide;
You cannot err on flattery's side.
Above the stars exalt your style,
You still are low ten thousand mile.
On Louis all his bards bestowed
Of incense many a thousand load;
But Europe mortified his pride,
And swore the fawning rascals lied.
Yet what the world refused to Louis,
Applied to George, exactly true is.
Exactly true! invidious poet!
'Tis fifty thousand times below it.

   Translate me now some lines, if you can,
From Virgil, Martial, Ovid, Lucan.
They could all power in heaven divide,
And do no wrong on either side;
They, teach you how to split a hair,
Give George and Jove an equal share.
Yet why should we be laced so strait?
I 'll give my monarch butter weight;
And reason good, for many a year
Jove never intermeddled here:
Nor, though his priests be duly paid,
Did ever we desire his aid:
We now can better do without him,
Since Woolston gave us arms to rout him.

ON THE DEATH OF DR SWIFT.

Occasioned by reading the following maxim in Rochefoucault, 'Dans l'adversité
de nos meilleurs amis, nous trouvons toujours quelque chose qui ne nous
déplaît pas;'—'In the adversity of our best friends, we always find something that doth not displease us.'

   As Rochefoucault his maxims drew
   From nature, I believe them true:

They argue no corrupted mind
In him; the fault is in mankind.
　This maxim more than all the rest
Is thought too base for human breast:
'In all distresses of our friends,
We first consult our private ends;
While nature, kindly bent to ease us,
Points out some circumstance to please us.'
　If this perhaps your patience move,
Let reason and experience prove.
　We all behold with envious eyes
Our equals raised above our size.
Who would not at a crowded show
Stand high himself, keep others low?
I love my friend as well as you:
But why should he obstruct my view?
Then let me have the higher post;
Suppose it but an inch at most.
If in a battle you should find
One, whom you love of all mankind,
Had some heroic action done,
A champion killed, or trophy won;
Rather than thus be over-topped,
Would you not wish his laurels cropped?
Dear honest Ned is in the gout,
Lies racked with pain, and you without:
How patiently you hear him groan!
How glad the case is not your own!
　What poet would not grieve to see
His brother write as well as he?
But, rather than they should excel,
Would wish his rivals all in hell?
　Her end when emulation misses,
She turns to envy, stings, and hisses:

The strongest friendship yields to pride,
Unless the odds be on our side.
Vain human-kind! fantastic race!
Thy various follies who can trace?
Self-love, ambition, envy, pride,
Their empire in our hearts divide.
Give others riches, power, and station,
'Tis all on me an usurpation.
I have no title to aspire;
Yet, when you sink, I seem the higher.
In Pope I cannot read a line,
But, with a sigh, I wish it mine:
When he can in one couplet fix
More sense than I can do in six,
It gives me such a jealous fit,
I cry, 'Pox take him and his wit!'
I grieve to be outdone by Gay
In my own humorous, biting way.
Arbuthnot is no more my friend,
Who dares to irony pretend,
Which I was born to introduce,
Refined at first, and showed its use.
St John, as well as Pultney, knows
That I had some repute for prose;
And, till they drove me out of date,
Could maul a minister of state.
If they have mortified my pride,
And made me throw my pen aside;
If with such talents Heaven hath blest 'em,
Have I not reason to detest 'em?
　To all my foes, dear Fortune, send
Thy gifts; but never to my friend:
I tamely can endure the first;
But this with envy makes me burst.

Thus much may serve by way of proem;
Proceed we therefore to our poem.
  The time is not remote when I
Must by the course of nature die;
When, I foresee, my special friends
Will try to find their private ends:
And, though 'tis hardly understood
Which way my death can do them good,
Yet thus, methinks, I hear them speak:
'See how the Dean begins to break!
Poor gentleman, he droops apace!
You plainly find it in his face.
That old vertigo in his head
Will never leave him, till he's dead.
Besides, his memory decays:
He recollects not what he says;
He cannot call his friends to mind;
Forgets the place where last he dined;
Plies you with stories o'er and o'er;
He told them fifty times before.
How does he fancy we can sit
To hear his out-of-fashion wit?
But he takes up with younger folks,
Who for his wine will bear his jokes.
Faith! he must make his stories shorter,
Or change his comrades once a quarter:
In half the time he talks them round,
There must another set be found.
  'For poetry, he's past his prime:
He takes an hour to find a rhyme;
His fire is out, his wit decayed,
His fancy sunk, his Muse a jade.
I'd have him throw away his pen;—
But there's no talking to some men!'

70

And then their tenderness appears
By adding largely to my years:
'He 's older than he would be reckoned,
And well remembers Charles the Second.
He hardly drinks a pint of wine;
And that, I doubt, is no good sign.
His stomach too begins to fail:
Last year we thought him strong and hale;
But now he 's quite another thing:
I wish he may hold out till spring!'
They hug themselves, and reason thus:
'It is not yet so bad with us!'
　　In such a case, they talk in tropes,
And by their fears express their hopes.
Some great misfortune to portend,
No enemy can match a friend.
With all the kindness they profess,
The merit of a lucky guess
(When daily how-d'ye's come of course,
And servants answer, 'Worse and worse!')
Would please them better, than to tell,
That, 'God be praised, the Dean is well.'
Then he who prophesied the best,
Approves his foresight to the rest:
'You know, I always feared the worst,
And often told you so at first.'
He 'd rather choose that I should die,
Than his predictions prove a lie.
Not one foretells I shall recover;
But all agree to give me over.
　　Yet, should some neighbour feel a pain
Just in the parts where I complain;
How many a message would he send!
What hearty prayers that I should mend!

71

Inquire what regimen I kept;
What gave me ease, and how I slept;
And more lament when I was dead,
Than all the snivellers round my bed.

   My good companions, never fear;
For, though you may mistake a year,
Though your prognostics run too fast,
They must be verified at last.

   Behold the fatal day arrive!
'How is the Dean?'—'He's just alive.'
Now the departing prayer is read;
He hardly breathes—The Dean is dead.

   Before the passing-bell begun,
The news through half the town is run.
'Oh! may we all for death prepare!
What has he left? and who's his heir?'
'I know no more than what the news is;
'Tis all bequeathed to public uses.'
'To public uses! there's a whim!
What had the public done for him?
Mere envy, avarice, and pride:
He gave it all—but first he died.
And had the Dean, in all the nation,
No worthy friend, no poor relation?
So ready to do strangers good,
Forgetting his own flesh and blood!'

   Now Grub-Street wits are all employed;
With elegies the town is cloyed:
Some paragraph in every paper,
To curse the Dean, or bless the Drapier.

   The doctors, tender of their fame,
Wisely on me lay all the blame.
'We must confess, his case was nice;
But he would never take advice.

Had he been ruled, for aught appears,
He might have lived these twenty years:
For, when we opened him, we found
That all his vital parts were sound.'
  From Dublin soon to London spread,
'Tis told at court, ' The Dean is dead.'
And Lady Suffolk, in the spleen,
Runs laughing up to tell the queen.
The queen, so gracious, mild, and good,
Cries, ' Is he gone! 'tis time he should.
He 's dead, you say; then let him rot.
I 'm glad the medals were forgot.
I promised him, I own; but when?
I only was the princess then;
But now, as consort of the king,
You know, 'tis quite another thing.'
  Now Chartres, at Sir Robert's levee,
Tells with a sneer the tidings heavy:
' Why, if he died without his shoes,'
Cries Bob, ' I 'm sorry for the news:
Oh, were the wretch but living still,
And in his place my good friend Will!
Or had a mitre on his head,
Provided Bolingbroke were dead!'
  Now Curll his shop from rubbish drains:
Three genuine tomes of Swift's remains!
And then, to make them pass the glibber,
Revised by Tibbalds, Moore, and Cibber.
He 'll treat me as he does my betters,
Publish my will, my life, my letters;
Revive the libels born to die:
Which Pope must bear, as well as I.
  Here shift the scene, to represent
How those I love my death lament.

Poor Pope will grieve a month, and Gay
A week, and Arbuthnot a day.
    St John himself will scarce forbear
To bite his pen, and drop a tear.
The rest will give a shrug, and cry,
'I 'm sorry—but we all must die!'
    Indifference, clad in Wisdom's guise,
All fortitude of mind supplies:
For how can stony bowels melt
In those who never pity felt!
When we are lashed, they kiss the rod,
Resigning to the will of God.
    The fools, my juniors by a year,
Are tortured with suspense and fear;
Who wisely thought my age a screen,
When death approached, to stand between:
The screen removed, their hearts are trembling;
They mourn for me without dissembling.
    My female friends, whose tender hearts
Have better learned to act their parts,
Receive the news in doleful dumps:
'The Dean is dead: (Pray, what is trumps?)
Then, Lord have mercy on his soul!
(Ladies, I 'll venture for the vole.)
Six Deans, they say, must bear the pall:
(I wish I knew what king to call.)
Madam, your husband will attend
The funeral of so good a friend.'
'No, madam, 'tis a shocking sight;
And he 's engaged to-morrow night:
My Lady Club will take it ill,
If he should fail her at quadrille.
He loved the Dean—(I lead a heart)—
But dearest friends, they say, must part.

His time was come; he ran his race;
We hope he 's in a better place.'
    Why do we grieve that friends should die?
No loss more easy to supply.
One year is past; a different scene!
No further mention of the Dean,
Who now, alas! no more is missed,
Than if he never did exist.
Where 's now the favourite of Apollo?
Departed:—and his works must follow;
Must undergo the common fate;
His kind of wit is out of date.
    Some country squire to Lintot goes,
Inquires for Swift in verse and prose.
Says Lintot, ' I have heard the name;
He died a year ago.'—'The same.'
He searches all the shop in vain.
' Sir, you may find them in Duck Lane:
I sent them, with a load of books,
Last Monday, to the pastry-cook's.
To fancy they could live a year!
I find you 're but a stranger here.
The Dean was famous in his time,
And had a kind of knack at rhyme.
His way of writing now is past:
The town has got a better taste.
I keep no antiquated stuff;
But spick and span I have enough.
Pray, do but give me leave to show 'em:
Here 's Colley Cibber's birthday poem.
This ode you never yet have seen,
By Stephen Duck, upon the queen.
Then here 's a letter finely penned
Against the Craftsman and his friend:

It clearly shows that all reflection
On ministers is disaffection.
Next, here 's Sir Robert's vindication,
And Mr Henley's last oration.
The hawkers have not got them yet;
Your honour please to buy a set?
  ' Here 's Wolston's tracts, the twelfth edition;
'Tis read by every politician:
The country-members, when in town,
To all their boroughs send them down:
You never met a thing so smart;
The courtiers have them all by heart:
Those maids of honour who can read,
Are taught to use them for their creed.
The reverend author's good intention
Hath been rewarded with a pension:
He doth an honour to his gown,
By bravely running priestcraft down:
He shows, as sure as God 's in Gloucester,
That Moses was a grand impostor;
That all his miracles were cheats,
Performed as jugglers do their feats:
The church had never such a writer;
A shame he hath not got a mitre!'
  Suppose me dead; and then suppose
A club assembled at the Rose;
Where, from discourse of this and that,
I grow the subject of their chat.
And while they toss my name about,
With favour some, and some without;
One, quite indifferent in the cause,
My character impartial draws:
  'The Dean, if we believe report,
Was never ill received at court,

Although, ironically grave,
He shamed the fool, and lashed the knave;
To steal a hint was never known,
But what he writ was all his own.'
  'Sir, I have heard another story;
He was a most confounded Tory,
And grew, or he is much belied,
Extremely dull, before he died.'
  'Can we the Drapier then forget?
Is not our nation in his debt?
'Twas he that writ the Drapier's letters!'—
  'He should have left them for his betters;
We had a hundred abler men,
Nor need depend upon his pen.—
Say what you will about his reading,
You never can defend his breeding;
Who, in his satires running riot,
Could never leave the world in quiet;
Attacking, when he took the whim,
Court, city, camp,—all one to him.—
But why would he, except he slobbered,
Offend our patriot, great Sir Robert,
Whose counsels aid the sovereign power
To save the nation every hour!
What scenes of evil he unravels
In satires, libels, lying travels,
Not sparing his own clergy cloth,
But eats into it, like a moth!'
  'Perhaps I may allow the Dean
Had too much satire in his vein,
And seemed determined not to starve it,
Because no age could more deserve it.
Yet malice never was his aim;
He lashed the vice, but spared the name.

No individual could resent,
Where thousands equally were meant:
His satire points at no defect,
But what all mortals may correct;
For he abhorred the senseless tribe
Who call it humour when they gibe:
He spared a hump or crooked nose,
Whose owners set not up for beaux.
True genuine dulness moved his pity,
Unless it offered to be witty.
Those who their ignorance confessed
He ne'er offended with a jest;
But laughed to hear an idiot quote
A verse from Horace learned by rote.
Vice, if it e'er can be abashed,
Must be or ridiculed, or lashed.
If you resent it, who's to blame?
He neither knows you, nor your name.
Should vice expect to 'scape rebuke,
Because its owner is a duke?
His friendships, still to few confined,
Were always of the middling kind;
No fools of rank, or mongrel breed,
Who fain would pass for lords indeed:
Where titles give no right or power,
And peerage is a withered flower;
He would have deemed it_a disgrace,
If such a wretch had known his face.
On rural squires, that kingdom's bane,
He vented oft his wrath in vain:
* * * * * * squires to market brought,
Who sell their souls and * * * * for nought.
The * * * * * * * go joyful back,
To rob the church, their tenants rack;

Go snacks with * * * * * justices,
And keep the peace to pick up fees;
In every job to have a share,
A gaol or turnpike to repair;
And turn * * * * * * to public roads
Commodious to their own abodes.
    'He never thought an honour done him,
Because a peer was proud to own him;
Would rather slip aside, and choose
To talk with wits in dirty shoes;
And scorn the tools with stars and garters,
So often seen caressing Chartres.
He never courted men in station,
Nor persons held in admiration;
Of no man's greatness was afraid,
Because he sought for no man's aid.
Though trusted long in great affairs,
He gave himself no haughty airs:
Without regarding private ends,
Spent all his credit for his friends;
And only chose the wise and good;
No flatterers; no allies in blood:
But succoured virtue in distress,
And seldom failed of good success;
As numbers in their hearts must own,
Who, but for him, had been unknown.
    'He kept with princes due decorum;
Yet never stood in awe before 'em.
He followed David's lesson just,
In princes never put his trust:
And, would you make him truly sour,
Provoke him with a slave in power.
The Irish senate if you named,
With what impatience he declaimed!

Fair LIBERTY was all his cry;
For her he stood prepared to die;
For her he boldly stood alone;
For her he oft exposed his own.
Two kingdoms, just as faction led,
Had set a price upon his head;
But not a traitor could be found,
To sell him for six hundred pound.

   'Had he but spared his tongue and pen,
He might have rose like other men:
But power was never in his thought,
And wealth he valued not a groat:
Ingratitude he often found,
And pitied those who meant to wound;
But kept the tenor of his mind,
To merit well of human-kind;
Nor made a sacrifice of those
Who still were true, to please his foes.
He laboured many a fruitless hour,
To reconcile his friends in power;
Saw mischief by a faction brewing,
While they pursued each other's ruin.
But, finding vain was all his care,
He left the court in mere despair.

   'And, oh! how short are human schemes!
Here ended all our golden dreams.
What St John's skill in state affairs,
What Ormond's valour, Oxford's cares,
To save their sinking country lent,
Was all destroyed by one event.
Too soon that precious life was ended,
On which alone our weal depended.
When up a dangerous faction starts,
With wrath and vengeance in their hearts;

By solemn league and covenant bound,
To ruin, slaughter, and confound;
To turn religion to a fable,
And make the government a Babel;
Pervert the laws, disgrace the gown,
Corrupt the senate, rob the crown;
To sacrifice old England's glory,
And make her infamous in story:
When such a tempest shook the land,
How could unguarded virtue stand!
  'With horror, grief, despair, the Dean
Beheld the dire destructive scene:
His friends in exile, or the Tower,
Himself within the frown of power;
Pursued by base envenomed pens,
Far to the land of S—— and fens;
A servile race in folly nursed,
Who truckle most, when treated worst.
  'By innocence and resolution,
He bore continual persecution;
While numbers to preferment rose,
Whose merit was to be his foes;
When even his own familiar friends,
Intent upon their private ends,
Like renegadoes now he feels,
Against him lifting up their heels.
  'The Dean did, by his pen, defeat
An infamous destructive cheat;
Taught fools their interest how to know,
And gave them arms to ward the blow.
Envy hath owned it was his doing,
To save that hapless land from ruin;
While they who at the steerage stood,
And reaped the profit, sought his blood.

'To save them from their evil fate,
In him was held a crime of state.
A wicked monster on the bench,
Whose fury blood could never quench;
As vile and profligate a villain,
As modern Scroggs, or old Tressilian;
Who long all justice had discarded,
Nor feared he God, nor man regarded;
Vowed on the Dean his rage to vent,
And make him of his zeal repent:
But Heaven his innocence defends,
The grateful people stand his friends;
Not strains of law, nor judges' frown,
Nor topics brought to please the crown,
Nor witness hired, nor jury picked,
Prevail to bring him in convict.
  'In exile, with a steady heart,
He spent his life's declining part;
Where folly, pride, and faction sway,
Remote from St John, Pope, and Gay.'
  'Alas, poor Dean! his only scope
Was to be held a misanthrope.
This into general odium drew him,
Which if he liked, much good may 't do him.
His zeal was not to lash our crimes,
But discontent against the times:
For, had we made him timely offers
To raise his post, or fill his coffers,
Perhaps he might have truckled down,
Like other brethren of his gown;
For party he would scarce have bled:—
I say no more—because he 's dead.—
What writings has he left behind?'-
  'I hear they' re of a different kind:

A few in verse; but most in prose——'
  'Some high-flown pamphlets, I suppose:—
All scribbled in the worst of times,
To palliate his friend Oxford's crimes;
To praise Queen Anne, nay more, defend her,
As never favouring the Pretender:
Or libels yet concealed from sight,
Against the court to show his spite:
Perhaps his travels, part the third;
A lie at every second word—
Offensive to a loyal ear:—
But—not one sermon, you may swear.'
  'He knew an hundred pleasing stories,
With all the turns of Whigs and Tories:
Was cheerful to his dying-day;
And friends would let him have his way.
  'As for his works in verse or prose,
I own myself no judge of those.
Nor can I tell what critics thought them;
But this I know, all people bought them,
As with a moral view designed,
To please and to reform mankind:
And, if he often missed his aim,
The world must own it to their shame,
The praise is his, and theirs the blame.
He gave the little wealth he had
To build a house for fools and mad;
To show, by one satiric touch,
No nation wanted it so much.
That kingdom he hath left his debtor,
I wish it soon may have a better.
And, since you dread no further lashes,
Methinks you may forgive his ashes.'

A CHARACTER, PANEGYRIC, AND DESCRIPTION OF THE
LEGION-CLUB.   1736.

As I stroll the city, oft I
See a building large and lofty,
Not a bow-shot from the college;
Half the globe from sense and knowledge:
By the prudent architect,
Placed against the church direct,
Making good thy grandame's jest,
' Near the church'—you know the rest.
　　Tell us what the pile contains?
Many a head that holds no brains.
These demoniacs let me dub
With the name of Legion-Club.
Such assemblies, you might swear,
Meet when butchers bait a bear;
Such a noise, and such haranguing,
When a brother thief is hanging:
Such a rout and such a rabble
Run to hear Jack-pudden gabble;
Such a crowd their ordure throws
On a far less villain's nose.
　　Could I from the building's top
Hear the rattling thunder drop,
While the devil upon the roof
(If the devil be thunder-proof)
Should with poker fiery red
Crack the stones, and melt the lead;
Drive them down on every skull,
While the den of thieves is full;
Quite destroy the harpies' nest;
How might then our isle be blest!
For divines allow that God

Sometimes makes the devil his rod;
And the gospel will inform us,
He can punish sins enormous.
    Yet should Swift endow the schools,
For his lunatics and fools,
With a rood or two of land,
I allow the pile may stand.
You perhaps will ask me, Why so?
But it is with this proviso:
Since the house is like to last,
Let the royal grant be passed,
That the club have right to dwell
Each within his proper cell,
With a passage left to creep in,
And a hole above for peeping.
Let them when they once get in,
Sell the nation for a pin;
While they sit a-picking straws,
Let them rave at making laws;
While they never hold their tongue,
Let them dabble in their dung;
Let them form a grand committee,
How to plague and starve the city;
Let them stare, and storm, and frown,
When they see a clergy gown;
Let them, ere they crack a louse,
Call for the orders of the house;
Let them, with their gosling quills,
Scribble senseless heads of bills.
We may, while they strain their throats,
Wipe our a——s with their votes.
    Let Sir Tom,[1] that rampant ass,
Stuff his guts with flax and grass;

---

[1] 'Sir Tom:' Sir Thomas Prendergrast, a privy councillor.

But, before the priest he fleeces,
Tear the Bible all to pieces :
At the parsons, Tom, halloo, boy,
Worthy offspring of a shoe-boy,
Footman, traitor, vile seducer,
Perjured rebel, bribed accuser,
Lay thy privilege aside,
Sprung from Papist regicide ;
Fall a-working like a mole,
Raise the dirt about your hole.

    Come, assist me, muse obedient!
Let us try some new expedient ;
Shift the scene for half an hour,
Time and place are in thy power.
Thither, gentle muse, conduct me ;
I shall ask, and you instruct me.

    See the muse unbars the gate!
Hark, the monkeys, how they prate !

    All ye gods who rule the soul !
Styx, through hell whose waters roll !
Let me be allowed to tell
What I heard in yonder cell.

    Near the door an entrance gapes,
Crowded round with antic shapes,
Poverty, and Grief, and Care,
Causeless Joy, and true Despair ;
Discord periwigged with snakes,
See the dreadful strides she takes !

    By this odious crew beset,
I began to rage and fret,
And resolved to break their pates,
Ere we entered at the gates ;
Had not Clio in the nick
Whispered me, ' Lay down your stick.'

What, said I, is this the mad-house?
These, she answered, are but shadows,
Phantoms bodiless and vain,
Empty visions of the brain.'
In the porch Briareus stands,
Shows a bribe in all his hands;
Briareus, the secretary,
But we mortals call him Carey.
When the rogues their country fleece,
They may hope for pence a-piece.
Clio, who had been so wise
To put on a fool's disguise,
To bespeak some approbation,
And be thought a near relation,
When she saw three hundred brutes
All involved in wild disputes,
Roaring till their lungs were spent,
'Privilege of Parliament.'
Now a new misfortune feels,
Dreading to be laid by the heels.
Never durst the muse before
Enter that infernal door;
Clio, stifled with the smell,
Into spleen and vapours fell,
By the Stygian steams that flew
From the dire infectious crew.
Not the stench of Lake Avernus
Could have more offended her nose;
Had she flown but o'er the top,
She had felt her pinions drop,
And by exhalations dire,
Though a goddess, must expire.
In a fright she crept away;
Bravely I resolved to stay.

When I saw the keeper frown,
Tipping him with half-a-crown,
Now, said I, we are alone,
Name your heroes one by one.
Who is that hell-featured brawler?
Is it Satan?   No, 'tis Waller.
In what figure can a bard dress
Jack the grandson of Sir Hardress?
Honest keeper, drive him fûrther,
In his looks are hell and murther;
See the scowling visage drop,
Just as when he murdered T——p.
Keeper, show me where to fix
On the puppy pair of Dicks;
By their lantern jaws and leathern,
You might swear they both are brethren:
Dick Fitzbaker, Dick the player,
Old acquaintance, are you there?
Dear companions, hug and kiss,
Toast Old Glorious in your piss:
Tie them, keeper, in a tether,
Let them starve and stink together;
Both are apt to be unruly,
Lash them daily, lash them duly;
Though 'tis hopeless to reclaim them,
Scorpion rods perhaps may tame them.
Keeper, yon old dotard smoke,
Sweetly snoring in his cloak;
Who is he?   'Tis humdrum Wynne,
Half encompassed by his kin:
There observe the tribe of Bingham,
For he never fails to bring 'em;
While he sleeps the whole debate,
They submissive round him wait;

88

Yet would gladly see the hunks
In his grave, and search his trunks.
See, they gently twitch his coat,
Just to yawn and give his vote,
Always firm in his vocation,
For the court, against the nation.

   Those are A—s Jack and Bob,
First in every wicked job,
Son and brother to a queer
Brain-sick brute, they call a peer.
We must give them better quarter,
For their ancestor trod mortar,
And at H—th, to boast his fame,
On a chimney cut his name.

   There sit Clements, D—ks, and Harrison,
How they swagger from their garrison!
Such a triplet could you tell
Where to find on this side hell?
Harrison, D—ks, and Clements,
Keeper, see they have their payments;
Every mischief's in their hearts;
If they fail, 'tis want of parts.

   Bless us, Morgan! art thou there, man!
Bless mine eyes! art thou the chairman!
Chairman to yon damned committee!
Yet I look on thee with pity.
Dreadful sight! what! learned Morgan
Metamorphosed to a Gorgon?
For thy horrid looks I own,
Half convert me to a stone,
Hast thou been so long at school,
Now to turn a factious tool?
Alma Mater was thy mother,
Every young divine thy brother.

Thou a disobedient varlet,
Treat thy mother like a harlot!
Thou ungrateful to thy teachers,
Who are all grown reverend preachers!
Morgan, would it not surprise one!
Turn thy nourishment to poison!
When you walk among your books,
They reproach you with your looks.
Bind them fast, or from their shelves
They will come and right themselves;
Homer, Plutarch, Virgil, Flaccus,
All in arms prepare to back us.
Soon repent, or put to slaughter
Every Greek and Roman author.
Will you, in your faction's phrase,
Send the clergy all to graze,
And, to make your project pass,
Leave them not a blade of grass?

     How I want thee, humorous Hogarth!
Thou, I hear, a pleasing rogue art,
Were but you and I acquainted,
Every monster should be painted:
You should try your graving-tools
On this odious group of fools:
Draw the beasts as I describe them
From their features, while I gibe them;
Draw them like; for I assure you,
You will need no *car'catura;*
Draw them so, that we may trace
All the soul in every face.

     Keeper, I must now retire,
You have done what I desire:
But I feel my spirits spent
With the noise, the sight, the scent.

'Pray be patient; you shall find
Half the best are still behind:
You have hardly seen a score;
I can show two hundred more.'
Keeper, I have seen enough.—
Taking then a pinch of snuff,
I concluded, looking round them,
'May their god, the devil, confound them.
Take them, Satan, as your due,
All except the Fifty-two.'

ISAAC WATTS.

WE feel relieved, and so doubtless do our readers, in passing
from the dark tragic story of Swift, and his dubious and unhappy
character, to contemplate the useful career of a much smaller, but
a much better man, Isaac Watts. This admirable person was
born at Southampton on the 17th of July 1674. His father, of
the same name, kept a boarding-school for young gentlemen, and
was a man of intelligence and piety. Isaac was the eldest of
nine children, and began early to display precocity of genius.
At four he commenced to study Latin at home, and afterwards,
under one Pinhorn, a clergyman, who kept the free-school at
Southampton, he learned Latin, Hebrew, and Greek. A subscription was proposed for sending him to one of the great uni-
versities, but he preferred casting in his lot with the Dissenters.
He repaired accordingly, in 1690, to an academy kept by the
Rev. Thomas Rowe, whose son, we believe, became the husband
of the celebrated Elizabeth Rowe, the once popular author of
'Letters from the Dead to the Living.' The Rowes belonged to
the Independent body. At this academy Watts began to write
poetry, chiefly in the Latin language, and in the then popular
Pindaric measure. At the age of twenty, he returned to his
father's house, and spent two quiet years in devotion, meditation,

and study. He became next a tutor in the family of Sir John Hartopp for five years. He was afterwards chosen assistant to Dr Chauncey, and, after the Doctor's death, became his successor. His health, however, failed, and, after getting an assistant for a while, he was compelled to resign. In 1712, Sir Thomas Abney, a benevolent gentleman of the neighbourhood, received Watts into his house, where he continued during the rest of his life—all his wants attended to, and his feeble frame so tenderly cared for that he lived to the age of seventy-five. Sir Thomas died eight years after Dr Watts entered his establishment, but the widow and daughters continued unwearied in their attentions. Abney House was a mansion surrounded by fine gardens and pleasure-grounds, where the Doctor became thoroughly at home, and was wont to refresh his body and mind in the intervals of study. He preached regularly to a congregation, and in the pulpit, although his stature was low, not exceeding five feet, the excellence of his matter, the easy flow of his language, and the propriety of his pronunciation, rendered him very popular. In private he was exceedingly kind to the poor and to children, giving to the former a third part of his small income of £100 a-year, and writing for the other his inimitable hymns. Besides these, he published a well-known treatise on Logic, another on ' The Improvement of the Mind,' besides various theological productions, amongst which his ' World to Come ' has been pre-eminently popular. In 1728, he received from Edinburgh and Aberdeen an unsolicited diploma of Doctor of Divinity. As age advanced, he found himself unable to discharge his ministerial duties, and offered to remit his salary, but his congregation refused to accept his demission. On the 25th November 1748, quite worn out, but without suffering, this able and worthy man expired.

If to be eminently useful 'is to fulfil the highest purpose of humanity, it was certainly fulfilled by Isaac Watts. His logical and other treatises have served to brace the intellects, methodise the studies, and concentrate the activities of thousands—we had nearly said of millions of minds. This has given him an enviable distinction, but he shone still more in that other province he so felicitously chose and so successfully occupied—that of the hearts

of the young. One of his detractors called him 'Mother Watts.'
He might have taken up this epithet, and bound it as a crown
unto him. We have heard of a pious foreigner, possessed of im-
perfect English, who, in an agony of supplication to God for some
sick friend, said, 'O Fader, hear me! O Mudder, hear me!' It
struck us as one of the finest of stories, and containing one of the
most beautiful tributes to the Deity we ever heard, recognising in
Him a pity which not even a father, which only a mother can
feel. Like a tender mother does good Watts bend over the little
children, and secure that their first words of song shall be those
of simple, heartfelt trust in God, and of faith in their Elder Brother. To create a little heaven in the nursery by hymns, and
these not mawkish or twaddling, but beautifully natural and exquisitely simple breathings of piety and praise, was the high task
to which Watts consecrated, and by which he has immortalised,
his genius.

FEW HAPPY MATCHES.

1 Stay, mighty Love, and teach my song,
  To whom thy sweetest joys belong,
    And who the happy pairs,
  Whose yielding hearts, and joining hands,
  Find blessings twisted with their bands,
    To soften all their cares.

2 Not the wild herds of nymphs and swains
  That thoughtless fly into thy chains,
    As custom leads the way:
  If there be bliss without design,
  Ivies and oaks may grow and twine,
    And be as blest as they.

3 Not sordid souls of earthly mould
  Who, drawn by kindred charms of gold,
    To dull embraces move:

So two rich mountains of Peru
May rush to wealthy marriage too,
   And make a world of love.

4 Not the mad tribe that hell inspires
With wanton flames; those raging fires
   The purer bliss destroy:
On Ætna's top let furies wed,
And sheets of lightning dress the bed,
   To improve the burning joy.

5 Nor the dull pairs whose marble forms
None of the melting passions warms
   Can mingle hearts and hands:
Logs of green wood that quench the coals
Are married just like stoic souls,
   With osiers for their bands.

6 Not minds of melancholy strain,
Still silent, or that still complain,
   Can the dear bondage bless:
As well may heavenly concerts spring
Fróm two old lutes with ne'er a string,
   Or none besides the bass.

7 Nor can the soft enchantments hold
Two jarring souls of angry mould,
   The rugged and the keen:
Samson's young foxes might as well
In bonds of cheerful wedlock dwell,
   With firebrands tied between.

8 Nor let the cruel fetters bind
A gentle to a savage mind,
   For love abhors the sight:

94

    Loose the fierce tiger from the deer,
    For native rage and native fear
      Rise and forbid delight.

9 Two kindest souls alone must meet;
  'Tis friendship makes the bondage sweet,
    And feeds their mutual loves:
  Bright Venus on her rolling throne
  Is drawn by gentlest birds alone,
    And Cupids yoke the doves.

THE SLUGGARD.

1 'Tis the voice of the sluggard; I heard him complain,
'You have waked me too soon, I must slumber again.'
As the door on its hinges, so he on his bed,
Turns his sides, and his shoulders, and his heavy head.

2 'A little more sleep, and a little more slumber;'
Thus he wastes half his days, and his hours without
    number;
And when he gets up, he sits folding his hands,
Or walks about sauntering, or trifling he stands.

3 I passed by his garden, and saw the wild brier,
The thorn and thistle grew broader and higher;
The clothes that hang on him are turning to rags,
And his money still wastes till he starves or he begs.

4 I made him a visit, still hoping to find
He had took better care for improving his mind;
He told me his dreams, talked of eating and drinking,
But he scarce reads his Bible, and never loves thinking.

5 Said I then to my heart, 'Here's a lesson for me:
That man's but a picture of what I might be;
But thanks to my friends for their care in my breeding,
Who taught me betimes to love working and reading.'

THE ROSE.

1 How fair is the rose! what a beautiful flower!
    The glory of April and May!
But the leaves are beginning to fade in an hour,
    And they wither and die in a day.

2 Yet the rose has one powerful virtue to boast,
    Above all the flowers of the field:
When its leaves are all dead, and fine colours are lost,
    Still how sweet a perfume it will yield!

3 So frail is the youth and the beauty of men,
    Though they bloom and look gay like the rose:
But all our fond care to preserve them is vain;
    Time kills them as fast as he goes.

4 Then I 'll not be proud of my youth or my beauty,
    Since both of them wither and fade:
But gain a good name by well doing my duty;
    This will scent, like a rose, when I 'm dead.

A CRADLE HYMN.

1 Hush! my dear, lie still and slumber,
    Holy angels guard thy bed!
Heavenly blessings without number
    Gently falling on thy head.

2 Sleep, my babe; thy food and raiment,
    House and home, thy friends provide;
All without thy care or payment,
    All thy wants are well supplied.

3 How much better thou 'rt attended
    Than the Son of God could be,
When from heaven he descended,
    And became a child like thee!

96

4 Soft and easy in thy cradle:
    Coarse and hard thy Saviour lay,
When his birthplace was a stable,
    And his softest bed was hay.

5 Blessed babe! what glorious features,
    Spotless fair, divinely bright!
Must he dwell with brutal creatures?
    How could angels bear the sight?

6 Was there nothing but a manger
    Cursed sinners could afford,
To receive the heavenly Stranger!
    Did they thus affront their Lord?

7 Soft, my child, I did not chide thee,
    Though my song might sound too hard;
'Tis thy { mother[1] / nurse that } sits beside thee,
    And her arms shall be thy guard.

8 Yet to read the shameful story,
    How the Jews abused their King,
How they served the Lord of glory,
    Makes me angry while I sing.

9 See the kinder shepherds round him,
    Telling wonders from the sky!
Where they sought him, where they found him,
    With his virgin mother by.

10 See the lovely babe a-dressing;
    Lovely infant, how he smiled!
When he wept, the mother's blessing
    Soothed and hushed the holy child.

[1] Here you may use the words, brother, sister, neighbour, friend.

11 Lo! he slumbers in his manger,
        Where the horned oxen fed:
    Peace, my darling, here's no danger,
        Here's no ox a-near thy bed.

12 'Twas to save thee, child, from dying,
        Save my dear from burning flame,
    Bitter groans, and endless crying,
        That thy blest Redeemer came.

13 Mayst thou live to know and fear him,
        Trust and love him, all thy days;
    Then go dwell for ever near him,
        See his face, and sing his praise!

14 I could give thee thousand kisses,
        Hoping what I most desire;
    Not a mother's fondest wishes
        Can to greater joys aspire.

BREATHING TOWARD THE HEAVENLY COUNTRY.

The beauty of my native land
    Immortal love inspires;
I burn, I burn with strong desires,
And sigh and wait the high command.
There glides the moon her shining way,
And shoots my heart through with a silver ray,
    Upward my heart aspires:
A thousand lamps of golden light,
Hung high in vaulted azure, charm my sight,
And wink and beckon with their amorous fires.
O ye fair glories of my heavenly home,
Bright sentinels who guard my Father's court,
    Where all the happy minds resort!
    When will my Father's chariot come?

Must ye for ever walk the ethereal round,
  For ever see the mourner lie
    An exile of the sky,
    A prisoner of the ground?
Descend, some shining servants from on high,
  Build me a hasty tomb;
  A grassy turf will raise my head;
  The neighbouring lilies dress my bed,
    And shed a sweet perfume.
Here I put off the chains of death,
  My soul too long has worn:
  Friends, I forbid one groaning breath,
    Or tear to wet my urn.
Raphael, behold me all undressed;
Here gently lay this flesh to rest,
Then mount and lead the path unknown.
Swift I pursue thee, flaming guide, on pinions of my own.

TO THE REV. MR JOHN HOWE.

Great man, permit the muse to climb,
  And seat her at thy feet;
Bid her attempt a thought sublime,
  And consecrate her wit.
I feel, I feel the attractive force
  Of thy superior soul:
My chariot flies her upward course,
  The wheels divinely roll.
Now let me chide the mean affairs
  And mighty toil of men:
How they grow gray in trifling cares,
Or waste the motion of the spheres
  Upon delights as vain!
A puff of honour fills the mind,
And yellow dust is solid good;

Thus, like the ass of savage kind,
We snuff the breezes of the wind,
　　Or steal the serpent's food.
　　　　Could all the choirs
　　　　That charm the poles
　　But strike one doleful sound,
'Twould be employed to mourn our souls,
Souls that were framed of sprightly fires,
　　In floods of folly drowned.
Souls made for glory seek a brutal joy;
How they disclaim their heavenly birth,
Melt their bright substance down to drossy earth,
And hate to be refined from that impure alloy.

Oft has thy genius roused us hence
　　With elevated song,
Bid us renounce this world of sense,
Bid us divide the immortal prize
　　With the seraphic throng:
'Knowledge and love make spirits blest,
Knowledge their food, and love their rest;'
But flesh, the unmanageable beast,
Resists the pity of thine eyes,
　　And music of thy tongue.
Then let the worms of grovelling mind
Round the short joys of earthly kind
　　In restless windings roam;
Howe hath an ample orb of soul,
Where shining worlds of knowledge roll,
Where love, the centre and the pole,
　　Completes the heaven at home.

———————

AMBROSE PHILIPS.

THIS gentleman—remembered now chiefly as Pope's temporary rival—was born in 1671, in Leicestershire; studied at Cambridge; and, being a great Whig, was appointed by the government of George I. to be Commissioner of the Collieries, and afterwards to some lucrative appointments in Ireland. He was also made one of the Commissioners of the Lottery. He was elected member for Armagh in the Irish House of Commons. He returned home in 1748, and died the next year in his lodgings at Vauxhall.

His works are 'The Distressed Mother,' a tragedy translated from Racine, and greatly praised in the *Spectator;* two deservedly forgotten plays, 'The Briton,' and 'Humphrey, Duke of Gloucester;' some miscellaneous pieces, of which an epistle to the Earl of Dorset, dated Copenhagen, has some very vivid lines; his Pastorals, which were commended by Tickell at the expense of those of Pope, who took his revenge by damning them, not with 'faint' but with fulsome and ironical praise, in the *Guardian;* and the subjoined fragment from Sappho, which is, particularly in the first stanza, melody itself. Some conjecture that it was touched up by Addison.

A FRAGMENT OF SAPPHO.

1 Blessed as the immortal gods is he,
  The youth who fondly sits by thee,
  And hears and sees thee all the while
  Softly speak, and sweetly smile.

2 'Twas this deprived my soul of rest,
  And raised such tumults in my breast;
  For while I gazed, in transport tossed,
  My breath was gone, my voice was lost.

3 My bosom glowed: the subtle flame
  Ran quickly through my vital frame;

O'er my dim eyes a darkness hung,
My ears with hollow murmurs rung.

4 In dewy damps my limbs were chilled,
My blood with gentle horrors thrilled;
My feeble pulse forgot to play,
I fainted, sunk, and died away.

WILLIAM HAMILTON.

WILLIAM HAMILTON, of Bangour, was born in Ayrshire in 1704. He was of an ancient family, and mingled from the first in the most fashionable circles. Ere he was twenty he wrote verses in Ramsay's 'Tea-Table Miscellany.' In 1745, to the surprise of many, he joined the standard of Prince Charles, and wrote a poem on the battle of Gladsmuir, or Prestonpans. When the reverse of his party came, after many wanderings and hair's-breadth escapes in the Highlands, he found refuge in France. As he was a general favourite, and as much allowance was made for his poetical temperament, a pardon was soon procured for him by his friends, and he returned to his native country. His health, however, originally delicate, had suffered by his Highland privations, and he was compelled to seek the milder clime of Lyons, where he died in 1754.

Hamilton was what is called a ladies'-man, but his attachments were not deep, and he rather flirted than loved. A Scotch lady, who was annoyed at his addresses, asked John Home how she could get rid of them. He, knowing Hamilton well, advised her to appear to favour him. She acted on the advice, and he immediately withdrew his suit. And yet his best poem is a tale of love, and a tale, too, told with great simplicity and pathos. We refer to his 'Braes of Yarrow,' the beauty of which we never felt fully till we saw some time ago that lovely region, with its 'dowie dens,'—its clear living stream,—Newark Castle, with its woods and memories,—and the green wildernesses of

102

silent hills which stretch on all sides around ; saw it, too, in that aspect of which Wordsworth sung in the words—

> 'The grace of forest charms decayed
> And pastoral melancholy.'

It is the highest praise we can bestow upon Hamilton's ballad that it ranks in merit near Wordsworth's fine trinity of poems, 'Yarrow Unvisited,' 'Yarrow Visited,' and 'Yarrow Revisited.'

THE BRAES OF YARROW.

1 *A.* Busk ye, busk ye, my bonny bonny bride,
    Busk ye, busk ye, my winsome marrow!
Busk ye, busk ye, my bonny bonny bride,
    And think nae mair on the Braes of Yarrow.

2 *B.* Where gat ye that bonny bonny bride?
    Where gat ye that winsome marrow?
A. I gat her where I darena weil be seen,
    Pouing the birks on the Braes of Yarrow.

3 Weep not, weep not, my bonny bonny bride,
    Weep not, weep not, my winsome marrow!
Nor let thy heart lament to leave
    Pouing the birks on the Braes of Yarrow.

4 *B.* Why does she weep, thy bonny bonny bride?
    Why does she weep, thy winsome marrow?
And why dare ye nae mair weil be seen,
    Pouing the birks on the Braes of Yarrow?

5 *A.* Lang maun she weep, lang maun she, maun she
      weep,
    Lang maun she weep with dule and sorrow,
And lang maun I nae mair weil be seen
    Pouing the birks on the Braes of Yarrow.

6 For she has tint her lover lover dear,
    Her lover dear, the cause of sorrow,
  And I hae slain the comeliest swain
    That e'er poued birks on the Braes of Yarrow.

7 Why runs thy stream, O Yarrow, Yarrow, red?
    Why on thy braes heard the voice of sorrow?
  And why yon melancholious weeds
    Hung on the bonny birks of Yarrow?

8 What's yonder floats on the rueful rueful flude?
    What's yonder floats?   O dule and sorrow!
  'Tis he, the comely swain I slew
    Upon the duleful Braes of Yarrow.

9 Wash, oh wash his wounds his wounds in tears,
    His wounds in tears with dule and sorrow,
  And wrap his limbs in mourning weeds,
    And lay him on the Braes of Yarrow.

10 Then build, then build, ye sisters sisters sad,
    Ye sisters sad, his tomb with sorrow,
  And weep around in waeful wise,
    His helpless fate on the Braes of Yarrow.

11 Curse ye, curse ye, his useless useless shield,
    My arm that wrought the deed of sorrow,
  The fatal spear that pierced his breast,
    His comely breast, on the Braes of Yarrow.

12 Did I not warn thee not to lue,
    And warn from fight, but to my sorrow;
  O'er rashly bauld a stronger arm
    Thou met'st, and fell on the Braes of Yarrow.

13 Sweet smells the birk, green grows, green grows the
        grass,
      Yellow on Yarrow bank the gowan,
    Fair hangs the apple frae the rock,
      Sweet the wave of Yarrow flowan.

14 Flows Yarrow sweet? as sweet, as sweet flows Tweed,
      As green its grass, its gowan as yellow,
    As sweet smells on its braes the birk,
      The apple frae the rock as mellow.

15 Fair was thy love, fair fair indeed thy love
      In flowery bands thou him didst fetter;
    Though he was fair and weil beloved again,
      Than me he never lued thee better.

16 Busk ye then, busk, my bonny bonny bride,
      Busk ye, busk ye, my winsome marrow,
    Busk ye, and lue me on the banks of Tweed,
      And think nae mair on the Braes of Yarrow.

17 C. How can I busk a bonny bonny bride,
      How can I busk a winsome marrow,
    How lue him on the banks of Tweed,
      That slew my love on the Braes of Yarrow?

18 O Yarrow fields! may never never rain
      Nor dew thy tender blossoms cover,
    For there was basely slain my love,
      My love, as he had not been a lover.

19 The boy put on his robes, his robes of green,
      His purple vest, 'twas my ain sewin',
    Ah! wretched me! I little little kenned
      He was in these to meet his ruin.

20 The boy took out his milk-white milk-white steed,
        Unheedful of my dule and sorrow,
     But e'er the to-fall of tho night
        He lay a corpse on the Braes of Yarrow.

21 Much I rejoiced that waeful waeful day;
        I sang, my voice the woods returning,
     But lang ere night the spear was flown
        That slew my love, and left me mourning.

22 What can my barbarous barbarous father do,
        But with his cruel rage pursue me?
     My lover's blood is on thy spear,
        How canst thou, barbarous man, then woo me?

23 My happy sisters may be may be proud;
        With cruel and ungentle scoffin',
     May bid me seek on Yarrow Braes
        My lover nailed in his coffin.

24 My brother Douglas may upbraid, upbraid,
        And strive with threatening words to move me;
     My lover's blood is on thy spear,
        How canst thou ever bid me love thee?

25 Yes, yes, prepare the bed, the bed of love,
        With bridal sheets my body cover,
     Unbar, ye bridal maids, the door,
        Let in the expected husband lover.

26 But who the expected husband husband is?
        His hands, methinks, are bathed in slaughter.
     Ah mo! what ghastly spectre 's yon,
        Comes, in his pale shroud, bleeding after?
     106

27 Pale as he is, here lay him lay him down,
    Oh, lay his cold head on my pillow!
  Take aff take aff these bridal weeds,
    And crown my careful head with willow. ˎ

28 Pale though thou art, yet best yet best beloved;
    Oh, could my warmth to life restore thee,
  Ye'd lie all night between my breasts!
    No youth lay ever there before thee.

29 Pale pale, indeed, O lovely lovely youth;
    Forgive, forgive so foul a slaughter,
  And lie all night between my breasts;
    No youth shall ever lie there after.

30 *A.* Return, return, O mournful mournful bride,
    Return-and dry thy useless sorrow:
  Thy lover heeds nought of thy sighs,
    He lies a corpse on the Braes of Yarrow.

ALLAN RAMSAY.

CRAWFORD MUIR, in Lanarkshire, was the birthplace of this
true poet.   His father was manager of the Earl of Hope-
toun's lead-mines.   Allan was born in 1686.   His mother was
Alice Bower, the daughter of an Englishman who had emigrated
from Derbyshire.   His father died while his son was yet in
infancy; his mother married again in the same district; and
young Allan was educated at the parish school of Leadhills.
At the age of fifteen, he was sent to Edinburgh, and bound
apprentice to a wig-maker there.   This trade, however, he left
after finishing his term.   He displayed rather early a passion
for literature, and made a little reputation by some pieces of
verse,—such as 'An Address to the Easy Club,' a convivial society

with which he was connected,—and a considerable time after by
a capital continuation of King James' 'Christis Kirk on the
Green.' In 1712, he married a writer's daughter, Christiana
Ross, who was his affectionate companion for thirty years. Soon
after, he set up a bookseller's shop opposite Niddry's Wynd, and
in this capacity edited and published two collections,—the one
of songs, some of them his own, entitled 'The Tea-Table Miscellany,' and the other of early Scottish poems, entitled 'The
Evergreen.' In 1725, he published 'The Gentle Shepherd.' It
was the expansion of one or two pastoral scenes which he had
shewn to his delighted friends. The poem became instantly
popular, and was republished in London and Dublin, and widely
circulated in the Colonies. Pope admired it. Gay, then in
Scotland with his patrons the Queensberry family, used to
lounge into Ramsay's shop to get explanations of its Scotch
phrases to transmit to Twickenham, and to watch from the window the notable characters whom Allan pointed out to him in
the Edinburgh Exchange. He now removed to a better shop,
and set up for his sign the heads of Ben Jonson and Drummond,
who agreed better in figure than they had done in reality at
Hawthornden. He established the first circulating library in
Scotland. His shop became a centre of intelligence, and Ramsay
sat a Triton among the minnows of that rather mediocre day—
giving his little senate laws, and inditing verses, songs, and
fables. At forty-five—an age when Sir Walter Scott had scarcely
commenced his Waverley novels, and Dryden had by far his
greatest works to produce—honest Allan imagined his vein exhausted, and ceased to write, although he lived and enjoyed life
for nearly thirty years more. At last, after having lost money
and gained obloquy, in a vain attempt to found the first theatre
in Edinburgh, and after building for himself a curious octagon-
shaped house on the north side of the Castle Hill, which, while
he called it Ramsay Lodge, his enemies nicknamed 'The Goose-
pie,' and which, though altered, still, we believe, stands, under
the name of Ramsay Garden, the author of 'The Gentle Shepherd' breathed his last on the 7th of January 1758. He died of
a scurvy in the gums. His son became a distinguished painter,
intimate with Johnson, Burke, and the rest of that splendid set,

although now chiefly remembered from his connexion with them
and with his father.

Allan Ramsay was a poet with very few of the usual poetical
faults. He had an eye for nature, but he had also an eye for
the main chance. He 'kept his shop, and his shop kept him.'
He might sing of intrigues, and revels, and houses of indifferent
reputation; but he was himself a quiet, *canny*, domestic man,
seen regularly at kirk and market. He had a great reverence
for the gentry, with whom he fancied himself, and perhaps was,
through the Dalhousie family, connected. He had a vast opinion
of himself; and between pride of blood, pride of genius, and
plenty of means, he was tolerably happy. How different from
poor maudlin Fergusson, or from that dark-browed, dark-eyed,
impetuous being who was, within a year of Ramsay's death, to
appear upon the banks of Doon, coming into the world to sing
divinely, to act insanely, and prematurely to die!

A bard, in the highest use of the word, in which it approaches
the meaning of prophet, Ramsay was not, else he would not
have ceased so soon to sing. Whatever lyrical impulse was in
him speedily wore itself out, and left him to his milder mission
as a broad reflector of Scottish life—in its humbler, gentler, and
better aspects. His 'Gentle Shepherd' is a chapter of Scottish
still-life; and, since the pastoral is essentially the poetry of peace,
the 'Gentle Shepherd' is the finest pastoral in the world. No
thunders roll among these solitary crags; no lightnings affright
these lasses among their *claes* at Habbie's Howe; the air is still
and soft; the plaintive bleating of the sheep upon the hills, the
echoes of the city are distant and faintly heard, so that the very
sounds seem in unison and in league with silence. One thinks
of Shelley's isle 'mid the Ægean deep:—

> 'It is an isle under Ionian skies,
>   Beautiful as the wreck of Paradise;
>   And for the harbours are not safe and good,
>   The land would have remained a solitude,
>   But for some pastoral people, native there,
>   Who from the Elysian clear and sunny air
>   Draw the last spirit of the age of gold,
>   Simple and generous, innocent and bold.

*   *   *   *   *

109

> The winged storms, chanting their thunder psalm
> To other lands, leave azure chasms of calm
> Over this isle, or weep themselves in dew,
> From whence the fields and woods ever renew
> Their green and golden immortality.'

Yet in the little circle of calm carved out by the magician of 'The Gentle Shepherd' there is no insipidity. Lust is sternly excluded, but love of the purest and warmest kind there breathes. The parade of learning is not there; but strong common sense thinks, and robust and manly eloquence declaims. Humour too is there, and many have laughed at Mause and Baldy, whom all the frigid wit of 'Love for Love' and the 'School for Scandal' could only move to contempt or pity. A *dénouement* of great skill is not wanting to stir the calm surface of the story by the wind of surprise; the curtain falls over a group of innocent, guileless, and happy hearts, and as we gaze at them we breathe the prayer, that Scotland's peerage and Scotland's peasantry may always thus be blended into one bond of mutual esteem, endearment, and excellence. Well might Campbell say—'Like the poetry of Tasso and Ariosto, that of the "Gentle Shepherd" is engraven on the memory of its native country. Its verses have passed into proverbs, and it continues to be the delight and solace of the peasantry whom it describes.'

Ramsay has very slightly touched on the religion of his countrymen. This is to be regretted; but if he had no sympathy with that, he, at least, disdained to counterfeit it, and its poetical aspects have since been adequately sung by other minstrels.

LOCHABER NO MORE.

1 Farewell to Lochaber, and farewell, my Jean,
  Where heartsome with thee I've mony day been;
  For Lochaber no more, Lochaber no more,
  We'll maybe return to Lochaber no more.
  These tears that I shed they are a' for my dear,
  And no for the dangers attending on weir;
  Though borne on rough seas to a far bloody shore,
  Maybe to return to Lochaber no more.

2 Though hurricanes rise, and rise every wind,
They 'll ne'er make a tempest like that in my mind;
Though loudest of thunder on louder waves roar,
That 's naething like leaving my love on the shore.
To leave thee behind me my heart is sair pained;
By ease that 's inglorious no fame can be gained;
And beauty and love 's the reward of the brave,
And I must deserve it before I can crave.

3 Then glory, my Jeany, maun plead my excuse;
Since honour commands me, how can 1 refuse?
Without it I ne'er can have merit for thee,
And without thy favour I 'd better not be.
I gae then, my lass, to win honour and fame,
And if I should luck to come gloriously hame,
I 'll bring a heart to thee with love running o'er,
And then I 'll leave thee and Lochaber no more!

THE LAST TIME I CAME O'ER THE MOOR.

1 The last time I came o'er the moor,
    I left my love behind me;
  Ye powers! what pain do I endure,
    When soft ideas mind me!
  Soon as the ruddy morn displayed
    The beaming day ensuing,
  I met betimes my lovely maid,
    In fit retreats for wooing.

2 Beneath the cooling shade we lay,
    Gazing and chastely sporting;
  We kissed and promised time away,
    Till night spread her black curtain.

111

I pitied all beneath the skies,
  E'en kings, when she was nigh me;
In raptures I beheld her eyes,
  Which could but ill deny me.

3 Should I be called where cannons roar,
  Where mortal steel may wound me;
Or cast upon some foreign shore,
  Where dangers may surround me;
Yet hopes again to see my love,
  To feast on glowing kisses,
Shall make my cares at distance move,
  In prospect of such blisses.

4 In all my soul there's not one place
  To let a rival enter;
Since she excels in every grace,
  In her my love shall centre.
Sooner the seas shall cease to flow,
  Their waves the Alps shall cover,
On Greenland ice shall roses grow,
  Before I cease to love her.

5 The next time I go o'er the moor,
  She shall a lover find me;
And that my faith is firm and pure,
  Though I left her behind me:
Then Hymen's sacred bonds shall chain
  My heart to her fair bosom;
There, while my being does remain,
  My love more fresh shall blossom.

FROM 'THE GENTLE SHEPHERD.'

ACT I.—SCENE II.

PROLOGUE.

A flowrie howm[1] between twa verdant braes,
Where lasses used to wash and spread their claes,[2]
A trotting burnie wimpling through the ground,
Its channel peebles shining smooth and round:
Here view twa barefoot beauties clean and clear;
First please your eye, then gratify your ear;
While Jenny what she wishes discommends,
And Meg with better sense true love defends.

PEGGY AND JENNY.

Jenny. Come, Meg, let's fa' to wark upon this green,
This shining day will bleach our linen clean;
The water's clear, the lift[3] unclouded blue,
Will mak them like a lily wet with dew.
Peggy. Gae farrer up the burn to Habbie's How,
Where a' that's sweet in spring and simmer grow:
Between twa birks, out o'er a little linn,[4]
The water fa's, and maks a singin' din:
A pool breast-deep, beneath as clear as glass,
Kisses with easy whirls the bordering grass.
We'll end our washing while the morning's cool,
And when the day grows het we'll to the pool,
There wash oursells; 'tis healthfu' now in May,
And sweetly caller on sae warm a day.
Jenny. Daft lassie, when we're naked, what'll ye
      say,
Giff our twa herds come brattling down the brae,
And see us sae?—that jeering fellow, Pate,
Wad taunting say, 'Haith, lasses, ye're no blate.'[5]
Peggy. We're far frae ony road, and out of sight;

---

[1] 'Howm:' holm.—[2] 'Claes:' clothes.—[3] 'Lift:' sky.—[4] 'Linn:' a waterfall.
—[5] 'Blate:' bashful.

The lads they 're feeding far beyont the height;
But tell me now, dear Jenny, we 're our lane,
What gars ye plague your wooer with disdain?
The neighbours a' tent this as well as I;
That Roger lo'es ye, yet ye carena by.
What ails ye at him? Troth, between us twa,
He 's wordy you the best day e'er ye saw.
  Jenny. I dinna like him, Peggy, there 's an end;
A herd mair sheepish yet I never kenn'd.
He kames his hair, indeed, and gaes right snug,
With ribbon-knots at his blue bonnet lug;
Whilk pensylie[1] he wears a thought a-jee,[2]
And spreads his garters diced beneath his knee.
He falds his owrelay[3] down his breast with care,
And few gangs trigger to the kirk or fair;
For a' that, he can neither sing nor say,
Except, 'How d'ye?'—or, 'There 's a bonny day.'
  Peggy. Ye dash the lad with constant slighting pride,
Hatred for love is unco sair to bide:
But ye 'll repent ye, if his love grow cauld;—
What like 's a dorty[4] maiden when she 's auld?
Like dawted wean[5] that tarrows at its meat,[6]
That for some feckless[7] whim will orp[8] and greet:
The lave laugh at it till the dinner 's past,
And syne the fool thing is obliged to fast,
Or scart anither's leavings at the last.
Fy, Jenny! think, and dinna sit your time.
  Jenny. I never thought a single life a crime.
  Peggy. Nor I: but love in whispers lets us ken
That men were made for us, and we for men.
  Jenny. If Roger is my jo, he kens himsell,

---

[1] 'Pensylie:' sprucely.—[2] 'A-jee:' to one side.—[3] 'Owrelay:' cravat.—[4] 'Dorty:'
pettish.—[5] 'Dawted wean:' spoiled child.—[6] 'Tarrows at its meat:' refuses its
food.—[7] 'Feckless:' silly.—[8] 'Orp:' fret.

114

For sic a tale I never heard him tell.
He glowers[1] and sighs, and I can guess the cause:
But wha's obliged to spell his hums and haws?
Whene'er he likes to tell his mind mair plain,
I'se tell him frankly ne'er to do't again.
They're fools that slavery like, and may be free;
The chiels may a' knit up themselves for me.

　　Peggy. Be doing your ways: for me, I have a mind
To be as yielding as my Patie's kind.

　　Jenny. Heh! lass, how can ye lo'e that rattleskull?
A very deil, that aye maun have his will!
We soon will hear what a poor fechtin' life
You twa will lead, sae soon's ye're man and wife.

　　Peggy. I'll rin the risk; nor have I ony fear,
But rather think ilk langsome day a year,
Till I with pleasure mount my bridal-bed,
Where on my Patie's breast I'll lay my head.
There he may kiss as lang as kissing's good,
And what we do there's nane dare call it rude. .
He's get his will; why no? 'tis good my part
To give him that, and he'll give me his heart.

　　Jenny. He may indeed for ten or fifteen days
Mak meikle o' ye, with an unco fraise,
And daut ye baith afore fowk and your lane: ·
But soon as your newfangleness is gane,
He'll look upon you as his tether-stake,
And think he's tint his freedom for your sake.
Instead then of lang days of sweet delight,
Ae day be dumb, and a' the neist he'll flyte:
And maybe, in his barlichood's,[2] ne'er stick
To lend his loving wife a loundering lick.

　　Peggy. Sic coarse-spun thoughts as that want pith to
　　　　move

____

[1] 'Glowers:' stares.—[2] 'Barlichoods:' cross-moods.

My settled mind; I'm o'er far gane in love.
Patie to me is dearer than my breath,
But want of him, I dread nae other skaith.[1]
There's nane of a' the herds that tread the green
Has sic a smile, or sic twa glancing een.
And then he speaks with sic a taking art,
His words they thirl like music through my heart.
How blithely can he sport, and gently rave,
And jest at little fears that fright the lave.
Ilk day that he's alane upon the hill,
He reads feil[2] books that teach him meikle skill;
He is—but what need I say that or this,
I'd spend a month to tell you what he is!
In a' he says or does there's sic a gate,
The rest seem coofs compared with my dear Pate;
His better sense will lang his love secure :
Ill-nature hefts in sauls are weak and poor.
  Jenny. Hey, ' bonny lass of Branksome!' or 't be lang,
Your witty Pate will put you in a sang.
Oh, 'tis a pleasant thing to be a bride!
Syne whinging gets about your ingle-side,
Yelping for this or that with fasheous[3] din :
To mak them brats then ye maun toil and spin.
Ae wean fa's sick, and scads itself wi' brue,[4]
Ane breaks his shin, anither times his shoe :
The ' Deil gaes o'er John Wabster:'[5] hame grows hell,
When Pate misca's ye waur than tongue can tell.
  Peggy. Yes, it's a heartsome thing to be a wife,
When round the ingle-edge young sprouts are rife.
Gif I'm sae happy, I shall have delight
To hear their little plaints, and keep them right.

---

[1] 'Skaith :' harm.—[2] 'Feil:' many.—[3] 'Fasheous :' troublesome.—[4] 'Scads itself wi' brue:' scalds itself with broth.—[5] 'Deil gaes o'er John Wabster:' all goes
wrong.

Wow, Jenny! can there greater pleasure be,
Than see sic wee tots toolying at your knee;
When a' they ettle at, their greatest wish,
Is to be made of, and obtain a kiss?
Can there be toil in tenting day and night
The like of them, when loves makes care delight?

 Jenny. But poortith, Peggy, is the warst of a',
Gif o'er your heads ill chance should beggary draw:
There little love or canty cheer can come
Frae duddy doublets, and a pantry toom.[1]
Your nowt may die; the speat[2] may bear away
Frae aff the howms your dainty rucks of hay;
The thick-blawn wreaths of snaw, or blashy thows,
May smoor your wethers, and may rot your ewes;
A dyvour[3] buys your butter, woo', and cheese,
But, or the day of payment, breaks and flees;
With gloomin' brow the laird seeks in his rent,
'Tis no to gie, your merchant's to the bent;
His honour maunna want, he poinds your gear;
Syne driven frae house and hald, where will ye steer?—
Dear Meg, be wise, and lead a single life;
Troth, it's nae mows[4] to be a married wife.

 Peggy. May sic ill luck befa' that silly she,
Wha has sic fears, for that was never me.
Let fowk bode weel, and strive to do their best;
Nae mair's required—let Heaven make out the rest.
I've heard my honest uncle aften say,
That lads should a' for wives that's vertuous pray;
For the maist thrifty man could never get
A well-stored room, unless his wife wad let:
Wherefore nocht shall be wanting on my part
To gather wealth to raise my shepherd's heart.
Whate'er he wins, I'll guide with canny care,

---

[1] 'Toom:' empty.—[2] 'Speat:' land-flood.—[3] 'A dyvour:' bankrupt.—[4] 'Mows:' jest.

And win the vogue at market, tron, or fair,
For healsome, clean, cheap, and sufficient ware.
A flock of lambs, cheese, butter, and some woo',
Shall first be sald to pay the laird his due;
Syne a' behind 's our ain.—Thus without fear,
With love and rowth[1] we through the warld will steer;
And when my Pate in bairns and gear grows rife,
He 'll bless the day he gat me for his wife.

 Jenny. But what if some young giglet on the green,
With dimpled cheeks, and twa bewitching een,
Should gar your Patie think his half-worn Meg,
And her kenn'd kisses, hardly worth a feg?

 Peggy. Nae mair of that:—dear Jenny, to be free,
There 's some men constanter in love than we:
Nor is the ferly great, when Nature kind
Has blest them with solidity of mind;
They 'll reason calmly, and with kindness smile,
When our short passions wad our peace beguile:
Sae, whensoe'er they slight their maiks[2] at hame,
'Tis ten to ane their wives are maist to blame.
Then I 'll employ with pleasure a' my art
To keep him cheerfu', and secure his heart.
At even, when he comes weary frae the hill,
I 'll have a' things made ready to his will:
In winter, when he toils through wind and rain,
A bleezing ingle, and a clean hearth-stane:
And soon as he flings by his plaid and staff,
The seething-pot 's be ready to take aff;
Clean hag-abag[3] I 'll spread upon his board,
And serve him with the best we can afford:
Good-humour and white bigonets[4] shall be
Guards to my face, to keep his love for me.

---

[1] 'Rowth:' plenty.—[2] 'Maiks:' mates.—[3] 'Hag-abag:' huckaback.—[4] 'White
bigonets:' linen caps or coifs.

118

Jenny. A dish of married love right soon grows cauld,
And dozins[1] down to nane, as fowk grow auld.

Peggy. But we 'll grow auld together, and ne'er find
The loss of youth, when love grows on the mind.
Bairns and their bairns make sure a firmer tie,
Than aught in love the like of us can spy.
See yon twa elms that grow up side by side,
Suppose them some years syne bridegroom and bride;
Nearer and nearer ilka year they 've pressed,
Till wide their spreading branches are increased,
And in their mixture now are fully blessed:
This shields the other frae the eastlin' blast;
That in return defends it frae the wast.
Sic as stand single, (a state sae liked by you,)
Beneath ilk storm frae every airt[2] maun bow.

Jenny. I 've done,—I yield, dear lassie; I maun yield,
Your better sense has fairly won the field.
With the assistance of a little fae
Lies dern'd within my breast this mony a day.

Peggy. Alake, poor pris'ner!—Jenny, that 's no fair,
That ye 'll no let the wee thing take the air:
Haste, let him out; we 'll tent as well 's we can,
Gif he be Bauldy's, or poor Roger's man.

Jenny. Anither time 's as good; for see the sun
Is right far up, and we 're not yet begun
To freath the graith: if canker'd Madge, our aunt,
Come up the burn, she 'll gie 's a wicked rant;
But when we 've done, I 'll tell you a' my mind;
For this seems true—nae lass can be unkind.

[Exeunt.

---

[1] 'Dozins:' dwindles.—[2] 'Airt:' quarter.

119

WE come now to another cluster of minor poets,—such as Robert Dodsley, who rose, partly through Pope's influence, from a footman to be a respectable bookseller, and who, by the verses entitled ' The Parting Kiss,'—

> 'One fond kiss before we part,
> Drop a tear and bid adieu ;
> Though we sever, my fond heart,
> Till we meet, shall pant for you,' &c.—

seems to have suggested to Burns his ' Ae fond kiss, and then we sever;'—John Brown, author of certain tragedies and other works, including the once famous ' Estimate of the Manners and Principles of Modern Times,' of which Cowper says—

> ' The inestimable Estimate of Brown
> Rose like a paper kite and charmed the town ;
> But measures planned and executed well
> Shifted the wind that raised it, and it fell :'

and who went mad and died by his own hands ;—John Gilbert Cooper, author of a fine song to his wife, one stanza of which has often been quoted :—

> ' And when with envy Time transported
> Shall think to rob us of our joys ;
> You 'll in your girls again be courted,
> And I 'll go wooing in my boys ;'—

Cuthbert Shaw, an unfortunate author of the Savage type, who wrote an affecting monody on the death of his wife ;—Thomas Scott, author of ' Lyric Poems, Devotional and Moral : London, 1773 ;'—Edward Thompson, a native of Hull, and author of some tolerable sea-songs ;—Henry Headley, a young man of uncommon talents, a pupil of Dr Parr in Norwich, who, when only twenty-one, published ' Select Beauties of the Ancient English Poets,' accompanied by critical remarks discovering rare ripeness of mind for his years, who wrote poetry too, but was seized with consumption, and died at twenty-two ;—Nathaniel Cotton, the physician, under whose care, at St Alban's, Cowper for a time was ;—William Hayward Roberts, author of ' Judah Restored,' a poem of much ambition and considerable merit ;—

120

John Bampfylde, who went mad, and died in that state, after having published, when young, some sweet sonnets, of which the following is one:—

> 'Cold is the senseless heart that never strove
> With the mild tumult of a real flame;
> Rugged the breast that music cannot tame,
> Nor youth's enlivening graces teach to love
> The pathless vale, the long-forsaken grove,
> The rocky cave that bears the fair one's name,
> With ivy mantled o'er. For empty fame
> Let him amidst the rabble toil, or rove
> In search of plunder far to western clime.
> Give me to waste the hours in amorous play
> With Delia, beauteous maid, and build the rhyme,
> Praising her flowing hair, her snowy arms,
> And all that prodigality of charms,
> Formed to enslave my heart, and grace my lay;'—

Lord Chesterfield, who wrote some lines on 'Beau Nash's Picture at full length, between the Busts of Newton and Pope at Bath,' of which this is the last stanza—

> 'The picture placed the busts between,
>   Adds to the thought much strength;
> Wisdom and Wit are little seen,
>   But Folly's at full length;'—

Thomas Penrose, who is more memorable as a warrior than as a poet, having fought against Buenos Ayres, as well as having written some elegant war-verses;—Edward Moore, a contributor to the *World;*—Sir John Henry Moore, a youth of promise, who died in his twenty-fifth year, leaving behind him such songs as the following:—

> 'Cease to blame my melancholy,
>   Though with sighs and folded arms
>   I muse with silence on her charms;
> Censure not—I know 'tis folly;
> Yet these mournful thoughts possessing,
>   Such delights I find in grief
>   That, could heaven afford relief,
> My fond heart would scorn the blessing;'—

the Rev. Richard Jago, a friend of Shenstone's, and author of a pleasing fable entitled 'Labour and Genius;'—Henry Brooke,

121

better known for a novel, once much in vogue, called 'The Fool of Quality,' than for his elaborate poem entitled 'Universal Beauty,' which formed a prototype of Darwin's 'Botanic Garden,' but did not enjoy that poem's fame;—George Alexander Stevens, a comic actor, lecturer on 'heads,' and writer of some poems, novels, and Bacchanalian songs;—and, in fine, Mrs Greville, whose 'Prayer for Indifference' displays considerable genius.   We quote some stanzas :—

> 'I ask no kind return in love,
>   No tempting charm to please ;
>   Far from the heart such gifts remove
>   That sighs for peace and ease.
>
> 'Nor ease, nor peace, that heart can know
>   That, like the needle true,
>   Turns at the touch of joy and woe,
>   But, turning, trembles too.
>
> 'Far as distress the soul can wound,
>   'Tis pain in each degree ;
>   'Tis bliss but to a certain bound—
>   Beyond, is agony.
>
> 'Then take this treacherous sense of mine,
>   Which dooms me still to smart,
>   Which pleasure can to pain refine,
>   To pain new pangs impart.
>
> 'Oh, haste to shed the sovereign balm,
>   My shattered nerves new string,
>   And for my guest, serenely calm,
>   The nymph Indifference bring.'

ISAAC HAWKINS BROWNE.

THIS writer was born at Burton-on-Trent, in 1705. He was educated at Westminster and Cambridge, and studied law at Lincoln's Inn. He was a man of fortune, and sat in two parliaments for Wenlock, in Shropshire. He died in 1760. His imitations of authors are clever and amusing, and seem to have got their hint from 'The Splendid Shilling,' and to have given it to the 'Rejected Addresses.'

IMITATION OF THOMSON.

——Prorumpit ad æthera nubem
Turbine, fumantem piceo.   VIRG.

O thou, matured by glad Hesperian suns,
Tobacco, fountain pure of limpid truth,
That looks the very soul; whence pouring thought
Swarms all the mind; absorpt is yellow care,
And at each puff imagination burns:
Flash on thy bard, and with exalting fires
Touch the mysterious lip that chants thy praise
In strains to mortal sons of earth unknown.
Behold an engine, wrought from tawny mines
Of ductile clay, with plastic virtue formed,
And glazed magnific o'er, I grasp, I fill.
From Pætotheke with pungent powers perfumed,
Itself one tortoise all, where shines imbibed
Each parent ray; then rudely rammed, illume
With the red touch of zeal-enkindling sheet,
Marked with Gibsonian lore; forth issue clouds
Thought-thrilling, thirst-inciting clouds around,
And many-mining fires; I all the while,
Lolling at ease, inhale the breezy balm.
But chief, when Bacchus wont with thee to join,
In genial strife and orthodoxal ale,
Stream life and joy into the Muse's bowl.
Oh, be thou still my great inspirer, thou
My Muse; oh, fan me with thy zephyrs boon,
While I, in clouded tabernacle shrined,
Burst forth all oracle and mystic song.

IMITATION OF POPE.

——Solis ad ortus
Vanescit fumus.   LUCAN.

Blest leaf! whose aromatic gales dispense
To Templars modesty, to parsons sense:
So raptured priests, at famed Dodona's shrine,
Drank inspiration from the steam divine.
Poison that cures, a vapour that affords
Content, more solid than the smile of lords:
Rest to the weary, to the hungry food,
The last kind refuge of the wise and good.
Inspired by thee, dull cits adjust the scale
Of Europe's peace, when other statesmen fail.
By thee protected, and thy sister, beer,
Poets rejoice, nor think the bailiff near.
Nor less the critic owns thy genial aid,
While supperless he plies the piddling trade.
What though to love and soft delights a foe,
By ladies hated, hated by the beau,
Yet social freedom, long to courts unknown,
Fair health, fair truth, and virtue are thy own.
Come to thy poet, come with healing wings,
And let me taste thee unexcised by kings.

IMITATION OF SWIFT.

Ex fumo dare lucem.—HOR.

Boy! bring an ounce of Freeman's best,
And bid the vicar be my guest:
Let all be placed in manner due,
A pot wherein to spit or spew,
And London Journal, and Free-Briton,
Of use to light a pipe or   *   *
          *   *   *   *

124

This village, unmolested yet
By troopers, shall be my retreat:
Who cannot flatter, bribe, betray;
Who cannot write or vote for * * *
Far from the vermin of the town,
Here let me rather live, my own,
Doze o'er a pipe, whose vapour bland
In sweet oblivion lulls the land;
Of all which at Vienna passes,
As ignorant as * * Brass is:
And scorning rascals to caress,
Extol the days of good Queen Bess,
When first tobacco blessed our isle,
Then think of other queens—and smile.

Come, jovial pipe, and bring along
Midnight revelry and song;
The merry catch, the madrigal,
That echoes sweet in City Hall;
The parson's pun, the smutty tale
Of country justice o'er his ale.
I ask not what the French are doing,
Or Spain, to compass Britain's ruin:
Britons, if undone, can go
Where tobacco loves to grow.

WILLIAM OLDYS.

OLDYS was born in 1696, and died in 1761. He was a very
diligent collector of antiquarian materials, and the author of a
Life of Raleigh. He was intimate with Captain Grose, Burns'
friend, who used to rally him on his inordinate thirst for ale,
although, if we believe Burns, it was paralleled by Grose's liking
for port. The following Anacreontic is characteristic:—

SONG, OCCASIONED BY A FLY DRINKING OUT OF A CUP OF ALE.

Busy, curious, thirsty fly,
Drink with me, and drink as I;
Freely welcome to my cup,
Couldst thou sip and sip it up.
Make the most of life you may—
Life is short, and wears away.

Both alike are, mine and thine,
Hastening quick to their decline:
Thine's a summer, mine no more,
Though repeated to threescore;
Threescore summers, when they're gone,
Will appear as short as one.

ROBERT LLOYD.

ROBERT LLOYD was born in London in 1733. He was the son
of one of the under-masters of Westminster School. He went
to Cambridge, where he became distinguished for his talents
and notorious for his dissipation. He became an usher under
his father, but soon tired of the drudgery, and commenced professional author. He published a poem called 'The Actor,'
which attracted attention, and was the precursor of 'The
Rosciad.' He wrote for periodicals, produced some theatrical
pieces of no great merit, and edited the *St James' Magazine*.
This failed, and Lloyd, involved in pecuniary distresses, was
cast into the Fleet. Here he was deserted by all his boon companions except Churchill, to whose sister he was attached, and
who allowed him a guinea a-week and a servant, besides pro-
moting a subscription for his benefit. When the news of
Churchill's death arrived, Lloyd was seated at dinner; he became instantly sick, cried out 'Poor Charles! I shall follow him
soon,' and died in a few weeks. Churchill's sister, a woman

126

of excellent abilities, waited on Lloyd during his illness, and died soon after him of a broken heart. This was in 1764.

Lloyd was a minor Churchill. He had not his brawny force, but he had more than his liveliness of wit, and was a much better-conditioned man, and more temperate in his satire. Cowper knew, loved, admired, and in some of his verses imitated, Robert Lloyd.

THE MISERIES OF A POET'S LIFE.

The harlot Muse, so passing gay,
Bewitches only to betray.
Though for a while with easy air
She smooths the rugged brow of care,
And laps the mind in flowery dreams,
With Fancy's transitory gleams;
Fond of the nothings she bestows,
We wake at last to real woes.
Through every age, in every place,
Consider well the poet's case;
By turns protected and caressed,
Defamed, dependent, and distressed.
The joke of wits, the bane of slaves,
The curse of fools, the butt of knaves;
Too proud to stoop for servile ends,
To lacquey rogues or flatter friends;
With prodigality to give,
Too careless of the means to live;
The bubble fame intent to gain,
And yet too lazy to maintain;
He quits the world he never prized,
Pitied by few, by more despised,
And, lost to friends, oppressed by foes,
Sinks to the nothing whence he rose.
　　O glorious trade! for wit's a trade,

Where men are ruined more than made!
Let crazy Lee, neglected Gay,
The shabby Otway, Dryden gray,
Those tuneful servants of the Nine,
(Not that I blend their names with mine,)
Repeat their lives, their works, their fame.
And teach the world some useful shame.

HENRY CAREY.

OF Carey, the author of the popular song, ' Sally in our Alley,'
we know only that he was a professional musician, composing
the air as well as the words of ' Sally,' and that in 1763 he died
by his own hands.

SALLY IN OUR ALLEY.

1 Of all the girls that are so smart,
    There's none like pretty Sally;
She is the darling of my heart,
    And she lives in our alley.
There is no lady in the land
    Is half so sweet as Sally:
She is the darling of my heart,
    And she lives in our alley.

2 Her father he makes cabbage-nets,
    And through the streets does cry 'em;
Her mother she sells laces long,
    To such as please to buy 'em:
But sure such folks could ne'er beget
    So sweet a girl as Sally!
She is the darling of my heart,
    And she lives in our alley.

3 When she is by, I leave my work,
 (I love her so sincerely,)
My master comes like any Turk,
 And bangs me most severely:
But, let him bang his belly full,
 I'll bear it all for Sally;
She is the darling of my heart,
 And she lives in our alley.

4 Of all the days that's in the week,
 I dearly love but one day;
And that's the day that comes betwixt
 A Saturday and Monday;
For then I'm dressed all in my best,
 To walk abroad with Sally;
She is the darling of my heart,
 And she lives in our alley.

5 My master carries me to church,
 And often am I blamed,
Because I leave him in the lurch,
 As soon as text is named:
I leave the church in sermon time,
 And slink away to Sally;
She is the darling of my heart,
 And she lives in our alley.

6 When Christmas comes about again,
 O then I shall have money;
I'll hoard it up, and box it all,
 I'll give it to my honey:
I would it were ten thousand pounds,
 I'd give it all to Sally;
She is the darling of my heart,
 And she lives in our alley.

> 7 My master, and the neighbours all,
>   Make game of me and Sally;
>   And, but for her, I 'd better be
>   A slave, and row a galley:
>   But when my seven long years are out,
>   O then I 'll marry Sally,
>   O then we 'll wed, and then we 'll bed,
>   But not in our alley.

DAVID MALLETT.

DAVID MALLETT was the son of a small innkeeper in Crieff, Perthshire, where he was born in the year 1700. Crieff, as many of our readers know, is situated on the western side of a hill, and commands a most varied and beautiful prospect, including Drummond Castle, with its solemn shadowy woods, and the Ochils, on the south,—Ochtertyre, one of the loveliest spots in Scotland, and the gorge of Glenturrett, on the north,—and the bold dark hills which surround the romantic village of Comrie, on the west. Crieff is now a place of considerable note, and forms a centre of summer attraction to multitudes; but at the commencement of the eighteenth century it must have been a miserable hamlet. *Malloch* was originally the name of the poet, and the name is still common in that part of Perthshire. David attended the college of Aberdeen, and became, afterwards, an unsalaried tutor in the family of Mr Home of Dreghorn, near Edinburgh. We find him next in the Duke of Montrose's family, with a salary of £30 per annum. In 1723, he accompanied his pupils to London, and changed his name to Mallett, as more euphonious. Next year, he produced his pretty ballad of 'William and Margaret,' and published it in Aaron Hill's 'Plain Dealer.' This served as an introduction to the literary society of the metropolis, including such names as Young and Pope. In 1733, he disgraced himself by a satire on the greatest man then living, the venerable Richard Bentley. Mallett was one of those mean creatures who always worship a rising, and turn their backs on a setting sun. By his very considerable talents, his management, and his address, he soon rose in the world. He was appointed under-secretary to the Prince of Wales, with a salary of £200 a-year. In conjunction with Thomson, to whom he was really kind, he wrote in 1740, 'The Masque of Alfred,' in honour of the birthday of the Princess Augusta. His first wife, of whom nothing is recorded, having died, he married the daughter of Lord Carlisle's steward, who brought him a fortune of £10,000. Both she and Mallett himself gave themselves out as Deists. This was partly owing to his intimacy with Bolingbroke, to gratify whom, he heaped abuse upon Pope in a preface to 'The Patriot-King,' and was rewarded by Bolingbroke leaving him the whole of his works and MSS. These he afterwards published, and exposed himself to the vengeful sarcasm of Johnson, who said that Bolingbroke was a scoundrel and a coward;—a scoundrel, to charge a blunderbuss against Christianity; and a coward, because he durst not fire it himself, but left a shilling to a beggarly Scotsman to draw the trigger after his death. Mallett ranked himself among the calumniators and, as it proved, murderers of Admiral Byng. He wrote a Life of Lord Bacon, in which, it was said, he forgot that Bacon was a philosopher, and would probably, when he came to write the Life of Marlborough, forget that he was a general. This Life of Bacon is now utterly forgotten. We happened to read it in our early days, and thought it a very contemptible performance. The Duchess of Marlborough left £1000 in her will between Glover and Mallett to write a Life of her husband. Glover threw up his share of the work, and Mallett engaged to perform the whole, to which, besides, he was stimulated by a pension from the second Duke of Marlborough. He got the money, but when he died it was found that he had not written a line of the work. In his latter days he held the lucrative office of Keeper of the Book of Entries for the port of London. He died on the 21st April 1765.

Mallett is, on the whole, no credit to Scotland. He was a bad, mean, insincere, and unprincipled man, whose success was procured by despicable and dastardly arts. He had doubtless some genius, and his 'Birks of Invermay,' and 'William and

131

Margaret,' shall preserve his name after his clumsy imitation of Thomson, called 'The Excursion,' and his long, rambling 'Amyntor and Theodora,' have been forgotten.

WILLIAM AND MARGARET.

1 'Twas at the silent, solemn hour
    When night and morning meet;
In glided Margaret's grimly ghost,
    And stood at William's feet.

2 Her face was like an April-morn,
    Clad in a wintry cloud;
And clay-cold was her lily hand,
    That held her sable shroud.

3 So shall the fairest face appear,
    When youth and years are flown:
Such is the robe that kings must wear,
    When death has reft their crown.

4 Her bloom was like the springing flower,
    That sips the silver dew;
The rose was budded in her cheek,
    Just opening to the view.

5 But love had, like the canker-worm,
    Consumed her early prime:
The rose grew pale, and left her cheek;
    She died before her time.

6 'Awake!' she cried, 'thy true love calls,
    Come from her midnight-grave;
Now let thy pity hear the maid,
    Thy love refused to save.

7 ‘ This is the dumb and dreary hour,
      When injured ghosts complain;
  When yawning graves give up their dead,
      To haunt the faithless swain.

8 ‘ Bethink thee, William, of thy fault,
      Thy pledge and broken oath!
  And give me back my maiden-vow,
      And give me back my troth.

9 ‘ Why did you promise love to me,
      And not that promise keep?
  Why did you swear my eyes were bright,
      Yet leave those eyes to weep?

10 ‘ How could you say my face was fair,
      And yet that face forsake?
  How could you win my virgin-heart,
      Yet leave that heart to break?

11 ‘ Why did you say my lip was sweet,
      And made the scarlet pale?
  And why did I, young witless maid!
      Believe the flattering tale?

12 ‘ That face, alas! no more is fair,
      Those lips no longer red:
  Dark are my eyes, now closed in death,
      And every charm is fled.

13 ‘ The hungry worm my sister is;
      This winding-sheet I wear:
  And cold and weary lasts our night,
      Till that last morn appear.

14 'But, hark! the cock has warned me hence;
    A long and late adieu!
Come, see, false man, how low she lies,
    Who died for love of you.'

15 The lark sung loud; the morning smiled,
    With beams of rosy red:
Pale William quaked in every limb,
    And raving left his bed.

16 He hied him to the fatal place
    Where Margaret's body lay;
And stretched him on the green-grass turf,
    That wrapped her breathless clay.

17 And thrice he called on Margaret's name,
    And thrice he wept full sore;
Then laid his cheek to her cold grave,
    And word spake never more!

THE BIRKS OF INVERMAY.

The smiling morn, the breathing spring,
Invite the tunefu' birds to sing;
And, while they warble from the spray,
Love melts the universal lay.
Let us, Amanda, timely wise,
Like them, improve the hour that flies;
And in soft raptures waste the day,
Among the birks of Invermay.

For soon the winter of the year,
And age, life's winter, will appear;
At this thy living bloom will fade,
As that will strip the verdant shade.

Our taste of pleasure then is o'er,
The feathered songsters are no more;
And when they drop and we decay,
Adieu the birks of Invermay!

JAMES MERRICK.

MERRICK was a clergyman, as well as a writer of verse. He
was born in 1720, and became a Fellow of Trinity College,
Oxford, where Lord North was one of his pupils. He took
orders, but owing to incessant pains in the head, could not perform duty. He died in 1769. His works are a translation of
Tryphiodorus, done at twenty, a version of the Psalms, a collec-
tion of Hymns, and a few miscellaneous pieces, one good speci-
men of which we subjoin.

THE CHAMELEON.

Oft has it been my lot to mark
A proud, conceited, talking spark,
With eyes that hardly served at most
To guard their master 'gainst a post;
Yet round the world the blade has been,
To see whatever could be seen.
Returning from his finished tour,
Grown ten times perter than before;
Whatever word you chance to drop,
The travelled fool your mouth will stop:
'Sir, if my judgment you 'll allow—
I 've seen—and sure I ought to know.'—
So begs you 'd pay a due submission,
And acquiesce in his decision.

Two travellers of such a cast,
As o'er Arabia's wilds they passed,

And on their way, in friendly chat,
Now talked of this, and then of that;
Discoursed a while, 'mongst other matter,
Of the chameleon's form and nature.
' A stranger animal,' cries one,
'Sure never lived beneath the sun:
A lizard's body lean and long,
A fish's head, a serpent's tongue,
Its foot with triple claw disjoined;
And what a length of tail behind!
How slow its pace! and then its hue—
Who ever saw so fine a blue?'
  ' Hold there,' the other quick replies,
' 'Tis green, I saw it with these eyes,
As late with open mouth it lay,
And warmed it in the sunny ray;
Stretched at its ease the beast I viewed,
And saw it eat the air for food.'
  ' I 've seen it, sir, as well as you,
And must again affirm it blue;
At leisure I the beast surveyed
Extended in the cooling shade.'
  ' 'Tis green, 'tis green, sir, I assure ye.'
' Green!' cries the other in a fury:
' Why, sir, d' ye think I 've lost my eyes?'
' 'Twere no great loss,' the friend replies;
' For if they always serve you thus,
You 'll find them but of little use.'
  So high at last the contest rose,
From words they almost came to blows:
When luckily came by a third;
To him the question they referred:
And begged he 'd tell them, if he knew,
Whether the thing was green or blue.

136

'Sirs,' cries the umpire, 'cease your pother;
The creature's neither one nor t'other.
I caught the animal last night,
And viewed it o'er by candle-light:
I marked it well, 'twas black as jet—
You stare—but sirs, I've got it yet,
And can produce it.'—'Pray, sir, do;
I'll lay my life the thing is blue.'
'And I'll be sworn, that when you've seen
The reptile, you'll pronounce him green.'

'Well, then, at once to ease the doubt,'
Replies the man, 'I'll turn him out:
And when before your eyes I've set him,
If you don't find him black, I'll eat him.'
He said; and full before their sight
Produced the beast, and lo!—'twas white.
Both stared, the man looked wondrous wise—
'My children,' the chameleon cries,
(Then first the creature found a tongue,)
'You all are right, and all are wrong:
When next you talk of what you view,
Think others see as well as you:
Nor wonder if you find that none
Prefers your eyesight to his own.'

DR JAMES GRAINGER.

THIS writer possessed some true imagination, although his claim
to immortality lies in the narrow compass of one poem—his
'Ode to Solitude.' Little is known of his personal history. He
was born in 1721—belonging to a gentleman's family in Cumberland. He studied medicine, and was for some time a surgeon
connected with the army. When the peace came, he established
himself in London as a medical practitioner. In 1755, he pub-

lished his 'Solitude,' which found many admirers, including Dr Johnson, who pronounced its opening lines 'very noble.' He afterwards indited several other pieces, wrote a translation of Tibullus, and became one of the critical staff of the *Monthly Review.* He was unable, however, through all these labours to secure a competence, and, in 1759, he sought the West Indies. In St Christopher's he commenced practising as a physician, and married the Governor's daughter, who brought him a fortune. He wrote a poem entitled 'The Sugar-cane.' This was sent over to London in MS., and was read at Sir Joshua Reynold's table to a literary coterie, who, according to Boswell, all burst out into a laugh when, after much blank-verse pomp, the poet began a new paragraph thus—

'Now, Muse, let's sing of rats.'

And what increased the ridicule was, that one of the company, slily overlooking the reader, found that the word had been originally 'mice,' but had been changed to rats as more dignified.

Boswell goes on to record Johnson's opinion of Grainger. He said, 'He was an agreeable man, a man that would do any good that was in his power.' His translation of Tibullus was very well done, but 'The Sugar-cane, a Poem,' did not please him. 'What could he make of a Sugar-cane? one might as well write "The Parsley-bed, a Poem," or "The Cabbage Garden, a Poem."' Boswell—'You must then *pickle* your cabbage with the *sal Atticum.*' Johnson—'One could say a great deal about cabbage. The poem might begin with the advantages of civilised society over a rude state, exemplified by the Scotch, who had no cabbages till Oliver Cromwell's soldiers introduced them, and one might thus shew how arts are propagated by conquest, as they were by the Roman arms.' Cabbage, by the way, in a metaphorical sense, might furnish a very good subject for a literary *satire.*

Grainger died of the fever of the country in 1767. Bishop Percy corroborates Johnson's character of him as a man. He says, 'He was not only a man of genius and learning, but had many excellent virtues, being one of the most generous, friendly, benevolent men I ever knew.'

Grainger in some points reminds us of Dyer. Dyer staked his reputation on 'The Fleece;' but it is his lesser poem, 'Grongar Hill,' which preserves his name; that fine effusion has survived the laboured work. And so Grainger's 'Solitude' has supplanted the stately 'Sugar-cane.' The scenery of the West Indies had to wait till its real poet appeared in the author of 'Paul and Virginia.' Grainger was hardly able to cope with the strange and gorgeous contrasts it presents of cliffs and crags, like those of Iceland, with vegetation rich as that of the fairest parts of India, and of splendid sunshine, with tempests of such tremendous fury that, but for their brief continuance, no property could be secure, and no life could be safe.

The commencement of the 'Ode to Solitude' is fine, but the closing part becomes tedious. In the middle of the poem there is a tumult of personifications, some of them felicitous and others forced.

> 'Sage Reflection, bent with years,'

may pass, but

> 'Conscious Virtue, void of fears,'

is poor.

> 'Halcyon Peace on moss reclined,'

is a picture;

> 'Retrospect that scans the mind,'

is nothing;

> 'Health that snuffs the morning air,'

is a living image; but what sense is there in

> 'Full-eyed Truth, with bosom bare?'

and how poor his

> 'Laughter in loud peals that breaks,'

to Milton's

> 'Laughter, holding both his sides!'

The paragraph, however, commencing

> 'With you roses brighter bloom,'

and closing with

> 'The bournless macrocosm's thine,'

is very spirited, and, along with the opening lines, proves Grainger a poet.

ODE TO SOLITUDE.

O solitude, romantic maid!
Whether by nodding towers you tread,
Or haunt the desert's trackless gloom,
Or hover o'er the yawning tomb,
Or climb the Andes' clifted side,
Or by the Nile's coy source abide,
Or starting from your half-year's sleep
From Hecla view the thawing deep,
Or, at the purple dawn of day,
Tadmor's marble wastes survey,
You, recluse, again I woo,
And again your steps pursue.

Plumed Conceit himself surveying,
Folly with her shadow playing,
Purse-proud, elbowing Insolence,
Bloated empiric, puffed Pretence,
Noise that through a trumpet speaks,
Laughter in loud peals that breaks,
Intrusion with a fopling's face,
Ignorant of time and place,
Sparks of fire Dissension blowing,
Ductile, court-bred Flattery, bowing,
Restraint's stiff neck, Grimace's leer,
Squint-eyed Censure's artful sneer,
Ambition's buskins, steeped in blood,
Fly thy presence, Solitude.

Sage Reflection, bent with years,
Conscious Virtue, void of fears,
Muffled Silence, wood-nymph shy,
Meditation's piercing eye,

Halcyon Peace on moss reclined,
Retrospect that scans the mind,
Rapt, earth-gazing Reverie,
Blushing, artless Modesty,
Health that snuffs the morning air,
Full-eyed Truth, with bosom bare,
Inspiration, Nature's child,
Seek the solitary wild.

You, with the tragic muse retired,
The wise Euripides inspired,
You taught the sadly-pleasing air
That Athens saved from ruins bare.
You gave the Cean's tears to flow,
And unlocked the springs of woe;
You penned what exiled Naso thought,
And poured the melancholy note.
With Petrarch o'er Vaucluse you strayed,
When death snatched his long-loved maid;
You taught the rocks her loss to mourn,
Ye strewed with flowers her virgin urn.
And late in Hagley you were seen,
With bloodshot eyes, and sombre mien,
Hymen his yellow vestment tore,
And Dirge a wreath of cypress wore.
But chief your own the solemn lay
That wept Narcissa young and gay,
Darkness clapped her sable wing,
While you touched the mournful string,
Anguish left the pathless wild,
Grim-faced Melancholy smiled,
Drowsy Midnight ceased to yawn,
The starry host put back the dawn,
Aside their harps even seraphs flung

To hear thy sweet Complaint, O Young!
When all nature's hushed asleep,
Nor Love nor Guilt their vigils keep,
Soft you leave your caverned den,
And wander o'er the works of men;
But when Phosphor brings the dawn
By her dappled coursers drawn,
Again you to the wild retreat
And the early huntsman meet,
Where as you pensive pace along,
You catch the distant shepherd's song,
Or brush from herbs the pearly dew,
Or the rising primrose view.
Devotion lends her heaven-plumed wings,
You mount, and nature with you sings.
But when mid-day fervours glow,
To upland airy shades you go,
Where never sunburnt woodman came,
Nor sportsman chased the timid game;
And there beneath an oak reclined,
With drowsy waterfalls behind,
You sink to rest.
Till the tuneful bird of night
From the neighbouring poplar's height
Wake you with her solemn strain,
And teach pleased Echo to complain.

With you roses brighter bloom,
Sweeter every sweet perfume,
Purer every fountain flows,
Stronger every wilding grows.
Let those toil for gold who please,
Or for fame renounce their ease.
What is fame? an empty bubble.

Gold ? a transient shining trouble.
Let them for their country bleed,
What was Sidney's, Raleigh's meed ?
Man's not worth a moment's pain,
Base, ungrateful, fickle, vain.
Then let me, sequestered fair,
To your sibyl grot repair;
On yon hanging cliff it stands,
Scooped by nature's salvage hands,
Bosomed in the gloomy shade
Of cypress not with age decayed.
Where the owl still-hooting sits,
Where the bat incessant flits,
There in loftier strains I'll sing
Whence the changing seasons spring,
Tell how storms deform the skies,
Whence the waves subside and rise,
Trace the comet's blazing tail,
Weigh the planets in a scale;
Bend, great God, before thy shrine,
The bournless macrocosm's thine.

*   *   *   *

MICHAEL BRUCE.

WE refer our readers to Dr Mackelvie's well-known and very
able Life of poor Bruce, for his full story, and for the evidence on
which his claim to the 'Cuckoo' is rested. Apart from external
evidence, we think that poem more characteristic of Bruce's
genius than of Logan's, and have therefore ranked it under
Bruce's name.

Bruce was born on the 27th of March 1746, at Kinnesswood,
parish of Portmoak, county of Kinross. His father was a
weaver, and Michael was the fifth of a family of eight children.

Poor as his parents were, they were intelligent, religious, and most conscientious in the discharge of their duties to their children. In the summer months Michael was sent out to herd cattle; and one loves to imagine the young poet wrapt in his plaid, under a whin-bush, while the storm was blowing,—or gazing at the rainbow from the summit of a fence,—or admiring at Lochleven and its old ruined castle,—or weaving around the form of some little maiden, herding in a neighbouring field—some 'Jeanie Morrison'—one of those webs of romantic early love which are beautiful and evanescent as the gossamer, but how exquisitely relished while they last! Say not, with one of his biographers, that his 'education was retarded by this employment;' he was receiving in these solitary fields a kind of education which no school and no college could furnish; nay, who knows but, as he saw the cuckoo winging her way from one deep woodland recess to another, or heard her dull, divine monotone coming from the heart of the forest, the germ of that exquisite strain, 'least in the kingdom' of the heaven of poetry in size, but immortal in its smallness, was sown in his mind? In winter he went to school, and profited there so much, that at fifteen (not a very early period, after all, for a Scotch student beginning his curriculum—in our day twelve was not an uncommon age) he was judged fit for going to college. And just in time a windfall came across the path of our poet, the mention of which may make many of our readers smile. This was a legacy which was left his father by a relative, amounting to 200 merks, or £11, 2s. 6d. With this munificent sum in his pocket, Bruce was sent to study at Edinburgh College. Here he became distinguished by his attainments, and particularly his taste and poetic powers; and here, too, he became acquainted with John Logan, afterwards his biographer. After spending three sessions at college, supported by his parents and other friends, he returned to the country, and taught a school at Gairney Bridge (a place famous for the first meeting of the first presbytery of the Seceders) for £11 of salary. Thence he removed to Foresthill, near Alloa, where a damp school-room, poverty, and hard labour in teaching, united to injure his health and depress his spirits. At Foresthill he wrote his poem 'Lochleven,' which discovers

144

no small descriptive power. Consumption began now to make
its appearance, and he returned to the cottage of his parents,
where he wrote his 'Elegy on Spring,' in which he refers with
dignified pathos to his approaching dissolution. On the 5th of
July 1767, this remarkable youth died, aged twenty-one years
and three months. His Bible was found on his pillow, marked
at the words, Jer. xxii. 10, ' Weep ye not for the dead, neither
bemoan him : but weep sore for him that goeth away : for he
shall return no more, nor see his native country.'

Lord Craig wrote some time afterwards an affecting paper in
the *Mirror*, recording the fate, and commending the genius of
Bruce. John Logan, in 1770, published his poems. In the
year 1807, the kind-hearted Principal Baird published an edition
of the poems for the behoof of Bruce's mother, then an aged
widow. And in 1837, Dr William Mackelvie, Balgedie, Kin-
ross-shire, published what may be considered the standard Life of
this poet, along with a complete edition of his Works.

It is impossible from so small a segment of a circle as Bruce's
life describes, to infer with any certainty the whole. So far as we
can judge from the fragments left, his power was rather in the
beautiful, than in the sublime or in the strong. The lines on
Spring, from the words ' Now spring returns ' to the close, form a
continuous stream of pensive loveliness. How sweetly he sings
in the shadow of death ! Nor let us too severely blame his allu-
sion to the old Pagan mythology, in the words—

' I hear the helpless wail, the shriek of woe,
I see the muddy wave, the dreary shore ;'

remembering that he was still a mere student, and not recovered from that fine intoxication in which classical literature
drenches a young imaginative soul, and that at last we find him
' resting in the hopes of an eternal day.' ' Lochleven' is the spent
echo of the ' Seasons,' although, as we said before, its descriptions possess considerable merit. His ' Last Day' is more ambi-
tious than successful. If we grant the ' Cuckoo ' to be his, as we
are inclined decidedly to do, it is a sure title to fame, being one
of the sweetest little poems in any language. Shakspeare would
have been proud of the verse—

> 'Sweet bird! thy bower is ever green,
> Thy sky is ever clear;
> Thou hast no sorrow in thy song,
> No winter in thy year.'

Bruce has not, however, it has always appeared to us, caught so well as Wordsworth the *differentia* of the cuckoo,—its invisible, shadowy, shifting, supernatural character—heard, but seldom seen—its note so limited and almost unearthly :—

> 'O Cuckoo, shall I call thee bird,
> Or but a *wandering voice?*'

How fine this conception of a separated voice—'The viewless spirit of a *lonely* sound,' plaining in the woods as if seeking for some incarnation it cannot find, and saddening the spring groves by a note so contradictory to the genius of the season. In reference to the note of the cuckoo we find the following remarks among the fragments from the commonplace-book of Dr Thomas Brown, printed by Dr Welsh :—'The name of the cuckoo has generally been considered as a very pure instance of imitative harmony. But in giving that name, we have most unjustly defrauded the poor bird of a portion of its very small variety of sound. The second syllable is not a mere echo of the first; it is the sound reversed, like the reading of a sotadic line; and to preserve the strictness of the imitation we should give it the name of Ook-koo.' *This* is the prose of the cuckoo after its poetry.

TO THE CUCKOO.

1 Hail, beauteous stranger of the grove!
 The messenger of spring!
Now Heaven repairs thy rural seat,
 And woods thy welcome sing.

2 Soon as the daisy decks the green,
 Thy certain voice we hear;
Hast thou a star to guide thy path,
 Or mark the rolling year?

3 Delightful visitant! with thee
      I hail the time of flowers,
  And hear the sound of music sweet,
      From birds among the bowers.

4 The school-boy, wandering through the wood
      To pull the primrose gay,
  Starts thy curious voice to hear,
      And imitates the lay.

5 What time the pea puts on the bloom,
      Thou fli'st thy vocal vale,
  An annual guest in other lands,
      Another spring to hail.

6 Sweet bird! thy bower is ever green,
      Thy sky is ever clear;
  Thou hast no sorrow in thy song,
      No winter in thy year.

7 Oh, could I fly, I 'd fly with thee!
      We 'd make with joyful wing
  Our annual visit o'er the globe,
      Attendants on the spring.

ELEGY, WRITTEN IN SPRING.

1 'Tis past: the North has spent his rage;
      Stern Winter now resigns the lengthening day;
  The stormy howlings of the winds assuage,
      And warm o'er ether western breezes play.

2 Of genial heat and cheerful light the source,
      From southern climes, beneath another sky,
  The sun, returning, wheels his golden course:
      Before his beams all noxious vapours fly.

3 Far to the North grim Winter draws his train,
    To his own clime, to Zembla's frozen shore;
 Where, throned on ice, he holds eternal reign,
    Where whirlwinds madden, and where tempests roar.

4 Loosed from the bonds of frost, the verdant ground
    Again puts on her robe of cheerful green,
 Again puts forth her flowers, and all around,
    Smiling, the cheerful face of Spring is seen.

5 Behold! the trees new-deck their withered boughs;
    Their ample leaves, the hospitable plane,
 The taper elm, and lofty ash disclose;
    The blooming hawthorn variegates the scene.

6 The lily of the vale, of flowers the queen,
    Puts on the robe she neither sewed nor spun:
 The birds on ground, or on the branches green,
    Hop to and fro, and glitter in the sun.

7 Soon as o'er eastern hills the morning peers,
    From her low nest the tufted lark upsprings;
 And cheerful singing, up the air she steers;
    Still high she mounts, still loud and sweet she sings.

8 On the green furze, clothed o'er with golden blooms
    That fill the air with fragrance all around,
 The linnet sits, and tricks his glossy plumes,
    While o'er the wild his broken notes resound.

9 While the sun journeys down the western sky,
    Along the green sward, marked with Roman mound,
 Beneath the blithesome shepherd's watchful eye,
    The cheerful lambkins dance and frisk around.

148

10 Now is the time for those who wisdom love,
  Who love to walk in Virtue's flowery road,
Along the lovely paths of Spring to rove,
  And follow Nature up to Nature's God.

11 Thus Zoroaster studied Nature's laws;
  Thus Socrates, the wisest of mankind;
Thus heaven-taught Plato traced the Almighty cause,
  And left the wondering multitude behind.

12 Thus Ashley gathered academic bays;
  Thus gentle Thomson, as the seasons roll,
Taught them to sing the great Creator's praise,
  And bear their poet's name from pole to pole.

13 Thus have I walked along the dewy lawn;
  My frequent foot the blooming wild hath worn:
Before the lark I 've sung the beauteous dawn,
  And gathered health from all the gales of morn.

14 And even when Winter chilled the aged year,
  I wandered lonely o'er the hoary plain:
Though frosty Boreas warned me to forbear,
  'Boreas, with all his tempests, warned in vain.

15 Then sleep my nights, and quiet blessed my days;
  I feared no loss, my mind was all my store;
No anxious wishes e'er disturbed my ease;
  Heaven gave content and health—I asked no
    more.

16 Now Spring returns: but not to me returns
  The vernal joy my better years have known;
Dim in my breast life's dying taper burns,
  And all the joys of life with health are flown.

17 Starting and shivering in the inconstant wind,
    Meagre and pale, the ghost of what I was,
  Beneath some blasted tree I lie reclined,
    And count the silent moments as they pass:

18 The winged moments, whose unstaying speed
    No art can stop, or in their course arrest;
  Whose flight shall shortly count me with the dead,
    And lay me down at peace with them at rest.

19 Oft morning-dreams presage approaching fate;
    And morning-dreams, as poets tell, are true.
  Led by pale ghosts, I enter Death's dark gate,
    And bid the realms of light and life adieu.

20 I hear the helpless wail, the shriek of woe;
    I see the muddy wave, the dreary shore,
  The sluggish streams that slowly creep below,
    Which mortals visit, and return no more.

21 Farewell, ye blooming fields! ye cheerful plains!
    Enough for me the churchyard's lonely mound,
  Where Melancholy with still Silence reigns,
    And the rank grass waves o'er the cheerless
      ground.

22 There let me wander at the shut of eve,
    When sleep sits dewy on the labourer's eyes:
  The world and all its busy follies leave,
    And talk of wisdom where my Daphnis lies.

23 There let me sleep forgotten in the clay,
    When death shall shut these weary, aching eyes;
  Rest in the hopes of an eternal day,
    Till the long night is gone, and the last morn
      arise.

150

CHRISTOPHER SMART.

WE hear of 'Single-speech Hamilton.' We have now to say something of 'Single-poem Smart,' the author of one of the grandest bursts of devotional and poetical feeling in the English language—the 'Song to David.' This poor unfortunate was born at Shipbourne, Kent, in 1722. His father was steward to Lord Barnard, who, after his death, continued his patronage to the son, who was then eleven years of age. The Duchess of Cleveland, through Lord Barnard's influence, bestowed on Christopher an allowance of £40 a-year. With this he went to Pembroke Hall, Cambridge, in 1739; was in 1745 elected a Fellow of Pembroke, and in 1747 took his degree of M.A. At college, Smart began to display that reckless dissipation which led afterwards to such melancholy consequences. He studied hard, however, at intervals; wrote poetry both in Latin and English; produced a comedy called a 'Trip to Cambridge; or, The Grateful Fair,' which was acted in the hall of Pembroke College; and, in spite of his vices and follies, was popular on account of his agreeable manners and amiable dispositions. Having become acquainted with Newberry, the benevolent, red-nosed bookseller commemorated in 'The Vicar of Wakefield,'—for whom he wrote some trifles,—he married his step-daughter, Miss Carnan, in the year 1753. He now removed to London, and became an author to trade. He wrote a clever satire, entitled 'The Hilliad,' against Sir John Hill, who had attacked him in an underhand manner. He translated the fables of Phædrus into verse,—Horace into prose ('Smart's Horace' used to be a great favourite, under the rose, with schoolboys); made an indifferent version of the Psalms and Paraphrases, and a good one, at a former period, of Pope's 'Ode on St Cecilia's Day,' with which that poet professed himself highly pleased. He was employed on a monthly publication called *The Universal Visitor.* We find Johnson giving the following account of this matter in Boswell's Life:—'Old Gardner, the bookseller, employed Rolt and Smart to write a monthly miscellany called *The Universal Visitor.*' There was a formal written contract. They were bound to write nothing else,—they were to have, I think, a third of the profits of the sixpenny pamphlet, and the contract was for ninety-nine years. I wrote for some months in *The Universal Visitor* for poor Smart, while he was mad, not then knowing the terms on which he was engaged to write, and thinking I was doing him good. I hoped his wits would soon return to him. Mine returned to me, and I wrote in *The Universal Visitor* no longer.'

Smart at last was called to pay the penalty of his blended labour and dissipation. In 1763 he was shut up in a madhouse. His derangement had exhibited itself in a religious way: he insisted upon people kneeling down along with him in the street and praying. During his confinement, writing materials were denied him, and he used to write his poetical pieces with a key on the wainscot. Thus, 'scrabbling,' like his own hero, on the wall, he produced his immortal ' Song to David.'. He became by and by sane; but, returning to his old habits, got into debt, and died in the King's Bench prison, after a short illness, in 1770.

The ' Song to David ' has been well called one of the greatest curiosities of literature. It ranks in this point with the tragedies written by Lee, and the sermons and prayers uttered by Hall in a similar melancholy state of mind. In these cases, as well as in Smart's, the thin partition between genius and madness was broken down in thunder,—the thunder of a higher poetry than perhaps they were capable of even conceiving in their saner moments. Lee produced in that state—which was, indeed, nearly his normal one—some glorious extravagancies. Hall's sermons, monologised and overheard in the madhouse, are said to have transcended all that he preached in his healthier moods. And, assuredly, the other poems by Smart scarcely furnish a point of comparison with the towering and sustained loftiness of some parts of the ' Song to David.' Nor is it loftiness alone, —although the last three stanzas are absolute inspiration, and you see the waters of Castalia tossed by a heavenly wind to the very summit of Parnassus, — but there are innumerable exquisite beauties and subtleties, dropt as if by the hand of rich haste, in every corner of the poem. Witness his description of David's muse, as a

'Blest light, still gaining on the gloom,
The more *than Michal of his bloom*,
The *Abishag of his age.'* ‑

The account of David's object—

'To further knowledge, silence vice,
And plant perpetual paradise,
When *God had calmed the world.'*

Of David's Sabbath—

''Twas then his thoughts self-conquest pruned,
And heavenly melancholy tuned,
To bless and bear the rest.'

One of David's themes—

'The multitudinous abyss,
Where secrecy remains in bliss,
And wisdom hides her skill.'

And, not to multiply instances to repletion, this stanza about gems—

'Of gems—their virtue and their price,
Which, hid in earth from man's device,
Their *darts of lustre sheath ;*
The jasper of the master's stamp,
The topaz blazing like a lamp,
Among the mines beneath.'

Incoherence and extravagance we find here and there; but it is not the flutter of weakness, it is the fury of power: from the very stumble of the rushing steed, sparks are kindled. And, even as Baretti, when he read the *Rambler*, in Italy, thought within himself, If such are the lighter productions of the English mind, what must be the grander and sterner efforts of its genius? and formed, consequently, a strong desire to visit that country; so might he have reasoned, If such poems as 'David' issue from England's very madhouses, what must be the writings of its saner and nobler poetic souls? and thus might he, from the parallax of a Smart, have been able to rise toward the ideal altitudes of a Shakspeare or a Milton. Indeed, there are portions of the 'Song to David,' which a Milton or a Shakspeare has never surpassed. The blaze of the meteor often eclipses the light of

'The loftiest star of unascended heaven,
Pinnacled dim in the intense inane.'

153

SONG TO DAVID.

1 O thou, that sitt'st upon a throne,
  With harp of high, majestic tone,
    To praise the King of kings:
  'And voice of heaven, ascending, swell,
  Which, while its deeper notes excel,
    Clear as a clarion rings:

2 To bless each valley, grove, and coast,
  And charm the cherubs to the post
    Of gratitude in throngs;
  To keep the days on Zion's Mount,
  And send the year to his account,
    With dances and with songs:

3 O servant of God's holiest charge,
  The minister of praise at large,
    Which thou mayst now receive;
  From thy blest mansion hail and hear,
  From topmost eminence appear
    To this the wreath I weave.

4 Great, valiant, pious, good, and clean,
  Sublime, contemplative, serene,
    Strong, constant, pleasant, wise!
  Bright effluence of exceeding grace;
  Best man! the swiftness and the race,
    The peril and the prize!

5 Great—from the lustre of his crown,
  From Samuel's horn, and God's renown,
    Which is the people's voice;
  For all the host, from rear to van,
  Applauded and embraced the man—
    The man of God's own choice.

6 Valiant—the word, and up he rose;
  The fight—he triumphed o'er the foes
      Whom God's just laws abhor;
  And, armed in gallant faith, he took
  Against the boaster, from the brook,
      The weapons of the war.

7 Pious—magnificent and grand,
  'Twas he the famous temple planned,
      (The seraph in his soul :)
  Foremost to give the Lord his dues,
  Foremost to bless the welcome news,
      And foremost to condole.

8 Good—from Jehudah's genuine vein,
  From God's best nature, good in grain,
      His aspect and his heart:
  To pity, to forgive, to save,
  Witness En-gedi's conscious cave,
      And Shimei's blunted dart.

9 Clean—if perpetual prayer be pure,
  And love, which could itself inure
      To fasting and to fear—
  Clean in his gestures, hands, and feet,
  To smite the lyre, the dance complete,
      To play the sword and spear.

10 Sublime—invention ever young,
   Of vast conception, towering tongue,
       To God the eternal theme;
   Notes from yon exaltations caught,
   Unrivalled royalty of thought,
       O'er meaner strains supreme.

11 Contemplative—on God to fix
      His musings, and above the six
         The Sabbath-day he blessed;
   'Twas then his thoughts self-conquest pruned,
   And heavenly melancholy tuned,
         To bless and bear the rest.

12 Serene—to sow the seeds of peace,
      Remembering when he watched the fleece,
         How sweetly Kidron purled—
   To further knowledge, silence vice,
   And plant perpetual paradise,
         When God had calmed the world.

13 Strong—in the Lord, who could defy
      Satan, and all his powers that lie
         In sempiternal night;
   And hell, and horror, and despair
   Were as the lion and the bear
         To his undaunted might.

14 Constant—in love to God, the Truth,
      Age, manhood, infancy, and youth;
         To Jonathan his friend
   Constant, beyond the verge of death;
   And Ziba, and Mephibosheth,
         His endless fame attend.

15 Pleasant—and various as the year;
      Man, soul, and angel without peer,
         Priest, champion, sage, and boy;
   In armour or in ephod clad,
   His pomp, his piety was glad;
         Majestic was his joy.

16 Wise—in recovery from his fall,
Whence rose his eminence o'er all,
　Of all the most reviled;
The light of Israel in his ways,
Wise are his precepts, prayer, and praise,
　And counsel to his child.

17 His muse, bright angel of his verse,
Gives balm for all the thorns that pierce,
　For all the pangs that rage;
Blest light, still gaining on the gloom,
The more than Michal of his bloom,
　The Abishag of his age.

18 He sang of God—the mighty source
Of all things—the stupendous force
　On which all strength depends;
From whose right arm, beneath whose eyes,
All period, power, and enterprise
　Commences, reigns, and ends.

19 Angels—their ministry and meed,
Which to and fro with blessings speed,
　Or with their citterns wait;
Where Michael, with his millions, bows,
Where dwells the seraph and his spouse,
　The cherub and her mate.

20 Of man—the semblance and effect
Of God and love—the saint elect
　For infinite applause—
To rule the land, and briny broad,
To be laborious in his laud,
　And heroes in his cause.

21 The world—the clustering spheres he made,
    The glorious light, the soothing shade,
        Dale, champaign, grove, and hill;
    The multitudinous abyss,
    Where secrecy remains in bliss,
        And wisdom hides her skill.

22 Trees, plants, and flowers—of virtuous root;
    Gem yielding blossom, yielding fruit,
        Choice gums and precious balm;
    Bless ye the nosegay in the vale,
    And with the sweetness of the gale
        Enrich the thankful psalm.

23 Of fowl—even every beak and wing
    Which cheer the winter, hail the spring,
        That live in peace, or prey;
    They that make music, or that mock,
    The quail, the brave domestic cock,
        The raven, swan, and jay.

24 Of fishes—every size and shape,
    Which nature frames of light escape,
        Devouring man to shun:
    The shells are in the wealthy deep,
    The shoals upon the surface leap,
        And love the glancing sun.

25 Of beasts—the beaver plods his task;
    While the sleek tigers roll and bask,
        Nor yet the shades arouse;
    Her cave the mining coney scoops;
    Where o'er the mead the mountain stoops,
        The kids exult and browse.

26 Of gems—their virtue and their price,
   Which, hid in earth from man's device,
     Their darts of lustre sheath;
   The jasper of the master's stamp,
   The topaz blazing like a lamp,
     Among the mines beneath.

27 Blest was the tenderness he felt,
   When to his graceful harp he knelt,
     And did for audience call;
   When Satan with his hand he quelled,
   And in serene suspense he held
     The frantic throes of Saul.

28 His furious foes no more maligned
   As he such melody divined,
     And sense and soul detained;
   Now striking strong, now soothing soft,
   He sent the godly sounds aloft,
     Or in delight refrained.

29 When up to heaven his thoughts he piled,
   From fervent lips fair Michal smiled,
     As blush to blush she stood;
   And chose herself the queen, and gave
   Her utmost from her heart—'so brave,
     And plays his hymns so good.'

30 The pillars of the Lord are seven,
   Which stand from earth to topmost heaven;
     His wisdom drew the plan;
   His Word accomplished the design,
   From brightest gem to deepest mine,
     From Christ enthroned to man.

31   Alpha, the cause of causes, first
       In station, fountain, whence the burst
           Of light and blaze of day;
       Whence bold attempt, and brave advance,
       Have motion, life, and ordinance,
           And heaven itself its stay.

32   Gamma supports the glorious arch
       On which angelic legions march,
           And is with sapphires paved;
       Thence the fleet clouds are sent adrift,
       And thence the painted folds that lift
           The crimson veil, are waved.

33   Eta with living sculpture breathes,
       With verdant carvings, flowery wreathes
           Of never-wasting bloom;
       In strong relief his goodly base
       All instruments of labour grace,
           The trowel, spade, and loom.

34   Next Theta stands to the supreme—
       Who formed in number, sign, and scheme,
           The illustrious lights that are;
       And one addressed his saffron robe,
       And one, clad in a silver globe,
           Held rule with every star.

35   Iota's tuned to choral hymns
       Of those that fly, while he that swims
           In thankful safety lurks;
       And foot, and chapiter, and niche,
       The various histories enrich
           Of God's recorded works.

160

36 Sigma presents the social droves
      With him that solitary roves,
          And man of all the chief;
      Fair on whose face, and stately frame,
      Did God impress his hallowed name,
          For ocular belief.

37 Omega! greatest and the best,
      Stands sacred to the day of rest,
          For gratitude and thought;
      Which blessed the world upon his pole,
      And gave the universe his goal,
          And closed the infernal draught.

38 O David, scholar of the Lord!
      Such is thy science, whence reward,
          And infinite degree;
      O strength, O sweetness, lasting ripe!
      God's harp thy symbol, and thy type
          The lion and the bee!

39 There is but One who ne'er rebelled,
      But One by passion unimpelled,
          By pleasures unenticed;
      He from himself his semblance sent,
      Grand object of his own content,
          And saw the God in Christ.

40 Tell them, I Am, Jehovah said
      To Moses; while earth heard in dread,
          And, smitten to the heart,
      At once above, beneath, around,
      All nature, without voice or sound,
          Replied, O Lord, Thou Art.

41 Thou art—to give and to confirm,
　For each his talent and his term;
　　All flesh thy bounties share:
　Thou shalt not call thy brother fool;
　The porches of the Christian school
　　Are meekness, peace, and prayer.

42 Open and naked of offence,
　Man's made of mercy, soul, and sense:
　　God armed the snail and wilk;
　Be good to him that pulls thy plough;
　Due food and care, due rest allow
　　For her that yields thee milk.

43 Rise up before the hoary head,
　And God's benign commandment dread,
　　Which says thou shalt not die:
　'Not as I will, but as thou wilt,'
　Prayed He, whose conscience knew no guilt;
　　With whose blessed pattern vie.

44 Use all thy passions!—love is thine,
　And joy and jealousy divine;
　　Thine hope's eternal fort,
　And care thy leisure to disturb,
　With fear concupiscence to curb,
　　And rapture to transport.

45 Act simply, as occasion asks;
　Put mellow wine in seasoned casks;
　　Till not with ass and bull:
　Remember thy baptismal bond;
　Keep from commixtures foul and fond,
　　Nor work thy flax with wool.

162

46 Distribute; pay the Lord his tithe,
   And make the widow's heart-strings blithe;
       Resort with those that weep:
   As you from all and each expect,
   For all and each thy love direct,
       And render as you reap.

47 The slander and its bearer spurn,
   And propagating praise sojourn
       To make thy welcome last;
   Turn from old Adam to the New:
   By hope futurity pursue:
       Look upwards to the past.

48 Control thine eye, salute success,
   Honour the wiser, happier bless,
       And for thy neighbour feel;
   Grutch not of mammon and his leaven,
   Work emulation up to heaven
       By knowledge and by zeal.

49 O David, highest in the list
   Of worthies, on God's ways insist,
       The genuine word repeat!
   Vain are the documents of men,
   And vain the flourish of the pen
       That keeps the fool's conceit.

50 Praise above all—for praise prevails;
   Heap up the measure, load the scales,
       And good to goodness add:
   The generous soul her Saviour aids,
   But peevish obloquy degrades;
       The Lord is great and glad.

51 For Adoration all the ranks
   Of angels yield eternal thanks,
      And David in the midst;
   With God's good poor, which, last and least
   In man's esteem, thou to thy feast,
      O blessed bridegroom, bidst.

52 For Adoration seasons change,
   And order, truth, and beauty range,
      Adjust, attract, and fill:
   The grass the polyanthus checks;
   And polished porphyry reflects,
      By the descending rill.

53 Rich almonds colour to the prime
   For Adoration; tendrils climb,
      And fruit-trees pledge their gems;
   And Ivis, with her gorgeous vest,
   Builds for her eggs her cunning nest,
      And bell-flowers bow their stems.

54 With vinous syrup cedars spout;
   From rocks pure honey gushing out,
      For Adoration springs:
   All scenes of painting crowd the map
   Of nature; to the mermaid's pap
      The scaled infant clings.

55 The spotted ounce and playsome cubs
   Run rustling 'mongst the flowering shrubs,
      And lizards feed the moss;
   For Adoration beasts embark,
   While waves upholding halcyon's ark
      No longer roar and toss.

164

56 While Israel sits beneath his fig,
   With coral root and amber sprig
     The weaned adventurer sports;
   Where to the palm the jasmine cleaves,
   For Adoration 'mong the leaves
     The gale his peace reports.

57 Increasing days their reign exalt,
   Nor in the pink and mottled vault
     The opposing spirits tilt;
   And by the coasting reader spied,
   The silverlings and crusions glide
     For Adoration gilt.

58 For Adoration ripening canes,
   And cocóa's purest milk detains
     The western pilgrim's staff;
   Where rain in clasping boughs enclosed,
   And vines with oranges disposed,
     Embower the social laugh.

59 Now labour his reward receives,
   For Adoration counts his sheaves
     To peace, her bounteous prince;
   The nect'rine his strong tint imbibes,
   And apples of ten thousand tribes,
     And quick peculiar quince.

60 The wealthy crops of whitening rice
   'Mongst thyine woods and groves of spice,
     For Adoration grow;
   And, marshalled in the fenced land,
   The peaches and pomegranates stand,
     Where wild carnations blow.

61　The laurels with the winter strive;
　　The crocus burnishes alive
　　　　Upon the snow-clad earth:
　　For Adoration myrtles stay
　　To keep the garden from dismay,
　　　　And bless the sight from dearth.

62　The pheasant shows his pompous neck;
　　And ermine, jealous of a speck,
　　　　With fear eludes offence:
　　The sable, with his glossy pride,
　　For Adoration is descried,
　　　　Where frosts the waves condense.

63　The cheerful holly, pensive yew,
　　And holy thorn, their trim renew;
　　　　The squirrel hoards his nuts:
　　All creatures batten o'er their stores,
　　And careful nature all her doors
　　　　For Adoration shuts.

64　For Adoration, David's Psalms
　　Lift up the heart to deeds of alms;
　　　　And he, who kneels and chants,
　　Prevails his passions to control,
　　Finds meat and medicine to the soul,
　　　　Which for translation pants.

65　For Adoration, beyond match,
　　The scholar bullfinch aims to catch
　　　　The soft flute's ivory touch;
　　And, careless, on the hazel spray
　　The daring redbreast keeps at bay
　　　　The damsel's greedy clutch.

166

66 For Adoration, in the skies,
The Lord's philosopher espies
    The dog, the ram, and rose;
The planets' ring, Orion's sword;
Nor is his greatness less adored
    In the vile worm that glows.

67 For Adoration, on the strings
The western breezes work their wings,
    The captive ear to soothe—
Hark! 'tis a voice—how still, and small—
That makes the cataracts to fall,
    Or bids the sea be smooth!

68 For Adoration, incense comes
From bezoar, and Arabian gums,
    And from the civet's fur:
But as for prayer, or e'er it faints,
Far better is the breath of saints
    Than galbanum or myrrh.

69 For Adoration, from the down
Of damsons to the anana's crown,
    God sends to tempt the taste;
And while the luscious zest invites
The sense, that in the scene delights,
    Commands desire be chaste.

70 For Adoration, all the paths
Of grace are open, all the baths
    Of purity refresh;
And all the rays of glory beam
To deck the man of God's esteem,
    Who triumphs o'er the flesh.

71 For Adoration, in the dome
     Of Christ, the sparrows find a home;
        And on his olives perch:
     The swallow also dwells with thee,
     O man of God's humility,
        Within his Saviour's church.

72 Sweet is the dew that falls betimes,
     And drops upon the leafy limes;
        Sweet Hermon's fragrant air:
     Sweet is the lily's silver bell,
     And sweet the wakeful tapers' smell
        That watch for early prayer.

73 Sweet the young nurse, with love intense,
     Which smiles o'er sleeping innocence;
        Sweet when the lost arrive:
     Sweet the musician's ardour beats,
     While his vague mind's in quest of sweets,
        The choicest flowers to hive.

74 Sweeter, in all the strains of love,
     The language of thy turtle-dove,
        Paired to thy swelling chord;
     Sweeter, with every grace endued,
     The glory of thy gratitude,
        Respired unto the Lord.

75 Strong is the horse upon his speed;
     Strong in pursuit the rapid glede,
        Which makes at once his game:
     Strong the tall ostrich on the ground;
     Strong through the turbulent profound
        Shoots xiphias to his aim.

76 Strong is the lion—like a coal
   His eyeball—like a bastion's mole
      His chest against the foes:
   Strong the gier-eagle on his sail,
   Strong against tide the enormous whale
      Emerges as he goes.

77 But stronger still in earth and air,
   And in the sea the man of prayer,
      And far beneath the tide:
   And in the seat to faith assigned,
   Where ask is have, where seek is find,
      Where knock is open wide.

78 Beauteous the fleet before the gale;
   Beauteous the multitudes in mail,
      Ranked arms, and crested heads;
   Beauteous the garden's umbrage mild,
   Walk, water, meditated wild,
      And all the bloomy beds.

79 Beauteous the moon full on the lawn;
   And beauteous when the veil's withdrawn,
      The virgin to her spouse:
   Beauteous the temple, decked and filled,
   When to the heaven of heavens they build
      Their heart-directed vows.

80 Beauteous, yea beauteous more than these,
   The Shepherd King upon his knees,
      For his momentous trust;
   With wish of infinite conceit,
   For man, beast, mute, the small and great,
      And prostrate dust to dust.

81　Precious the bounteous widow's mite;
　　And precious, for extreme delight,
　　　　The largess from the churl:
　　Precious the ruby's blushing blaze,
　　And alba's blest imperial rays,
　　　　And pure cerulean pearl.

82　Precious the penitential tear;
　　And precious is the sigh sincere;
　　　　Acceptable to God:
　　And precious are the winning flowers,
　　In gladsome Israel's feast of bowers,
　　　　Bound on the hallowed sod.

83　More precious that diviner part
　　Of David, even the Lord's own heart,
　　　　Great, beautiful, and new:
　　In all things where it was intent,
　　In all extremes, in each event,
　　　　Proof—answering true to true.

84　Glorious the sun in mid career;
　　Glorious the assembled fires appear;
　　　　Glorious the comet's train:
　　Glorious the trumpet and alarm;
　　Glorious the Almighty's stretched-out arm;
　　　　Glorious the enraptured main:

85　Glorious the northern lights astream;
　　Glorious the song, when God's the theme;
　　　　Glorious the thunder's roar:
　　Glorious hosannah from the den;
　　Glorious the catholic amen;
　　　　Glorious the martyr's gore:

170

86 Glorious—more glorious is the crown
Of Him that brought salvation dówn,
By meekness called thy Son;
Thou that stupendous truth believed,
And now the matchless deed's achieved,
Determined, Dared, and Done.

THOMAS CHATTERTON.

THE history of this 'marvellous boy' is familiar to all the readers of English poetry, and requires only a cursory treatment here. Thomas Chatterton was born in Bristol, November 20, 1752. His father, a teacher in the free-school there, had died before his birth, and he was sent to be educated at a charity-school. He first learned to read from a black-letter Bible. At the age of fourteen, he was put apprentice to an attorney; a situation which, however uncongenial, left him ample leisure for pursuing his private studies. In an unlucky hour, some evil genius seemed to have whispered to this extraordinary youth,—'Do not find or force, but forge thy way to renown; the other paths to the summit of the hill are worn and common-place; try a new and dangerous course, the rather as I forewarn thee that thy time is short.' When, accordingly, the new bridge at Bristol was finished in October 1768, Chatterton sent to a newspaper a fictitious account of the opening of the old bridge, alleging in a note that he had found the principal part of the description in an ancient MS. And having thus fairly begun to work the mint of forgery, it was amazing what a number of false coins he threw off, and with what perfect ease and mastery! Ancient poems, pretending to have been written four hundred and fifty years before; fragments of sermons on the Holy Spirit, dated from the fifteenth century; accounts of all the churches of Bristol as they had appeared three hundred years before; with drawings and descriptions of the castle—most of them professing to be drawn from the writings of 'ane gode prieste, Thomas Rowley'—issued in thick succession from this wonderful, and, to use the Shaks-pearean word in a twofold sense, ' forgetive' brain. He next ventured to send to Horace Walpole, who was employed on a History of British Painters, an account of eminent ' Carvellers and Peynctcrs,' who, according to him, once flourished in Bristol. These labours he plied in secret, and with the utmost enthu-siasm. He used to write by the light of the moon, deeming that there was a special inspiration in the rays of that planet, and reminding one of poor Nat Lee inditing his insane tragedies in his asylum under the same weird lustre. On Sabbaths he was wont to stroll away into the country around Bristol, which is very beautiful, and to draw sketches of those objects which impressed his imagination. He often lay down on the meadows near St Mary's Redcliffe Church, admiring the ancient edifice; and some years ago we saw a chamber near the summit of that edifice where he used to sit and write, his ' eye in a fine frenzy rolling,' and where we could imagine him, when. a moonless night fell, composing his wild Runic lays by the light of a candle burning in a human skull. It was actually in one of the rooms of this church that some ancient chests had been deposited, in-cluding one called the ' Coffre of Mr Canynge,' an eminent mer-chant in Bristol, who had rebuilt the church in the reign of Edward IV. This coffer had been broken up by public autho-rity in 1727, and some valuable deeds had been taken out. Besides these, they contained various MSS., some of which Chatterton's father, whose uncle was sexton of the church, had carried off and used as covers to the copy-books of his scholars. This furnished a hint to Chatterton's inventive genius. He gave out that among these parchments he had found many productions of Mr Canynge's, and of the aforesaid Thomas Rowley's, a priest of the fifteenth century, and a friend of Canynge's. Chatterton had become a contributor to a pe-riodical of the day called *The Town and Country Magazine*, and to it from time to time he sent these poems. A keen con-troversy arose as to their genuineness. Horace Walpole shewed some of them, which Chatterton had sent him, to Gray and Mason, who were deemed, justly, first-rate authorities on anti-quarian matters, and who at once pronounced them forgeries.

172

It is deeply to be regretted that these men, perceiving, as they must have done, the great merit of these productions, had not made more particular inquiries about them, and tried to help and save the poet. Walpole, to say the least of it, treated him coldly, telling him, when he had discovered the forgery, to attend to his own business, and keeping some of his MSS. iu his hands, till an indignant letter from the author compelled him to restore them.

Chatterton now determined to go to London. His three years' apprenticeship had expired, and there was in Bristol no further field for his aspiring genius. He found instant employment among the booksellers, and procured an introduction to Beckford, the patriot mayor, who tried to get him engaged upon the Opposition side in politics. Our capricious and unprincipled poet, however, declared that he was a poor author that could not write on both sides; and although his leanings were to the popular party, yet on the death of Beckford he addressed a letter to Lord North in support of his administration. He had projected some large works, such as a History of England and a History of London, and wrote flaming letters to his mother and sisters about his prospects, enclosing them at the same time small remittances of money. But his bright hopes were soon overcast. Instead of a prominent political character, he found himself a mere bookseller's hack. To this his poverty no more than his will would consent, for though that was great it was equalled by his pride. His life in the country had been regular, although his religious principles were loose ; but in town, misery drove him to intemperance, and intemperance, in its reaction, to remorse and a desperate tampering with the thought,

' There is one remedy for all.'

At last, after a vain attempt to obtain an appointment as a surgeon's mate to Africa, he made up his mind to suicide. A guinea had been sent him by a gentleman, which he declined. Mrs Angel, his landlady, knowing him to be in want, the day before his death offered him his dinner, but this also he spurned; and, on the 25th of August 1770, having first destroyed all his papers, he swallowed arsenic, and was found dead in his bed.

173

He was buried in a shell in the burial-place of Shoe-Lane Workhouse. He was aged seventeen years nine months and a few days. Alas for

‘The sleepless soul that perished in his pride !’

Chatterton, had he lived, would, perhaps, have become a powerful poet, or a powerful character of some kind. But we must now view him chiefly as a prodigy. Some have treated his power as unnatural—resembling a huge hydrocephalic head, the magnitude of which implies disease, ultimate weakness, and early death. Others maintain that, apart from the extraordinary elements that undoubtedly characterised Chatterton, and constituted him a premature and prodigious birth intellectually, there was also in parts of his poems evidence of a healthy vigour which only needed favourable circumstances to develop into transcendent excellence. Hazlitt, holding with the one of these opinions, cries, ‘If Chatterton had had a great work to do by living, he would have lived!’ Others retort on the critic, ‘On the same principle, why did Keats, whom you rate so high, perish so early?’ The question altogether is nugatory, seeing it can never be settled. Suffice it that these songs and rhymes of Chatterton have great beauties, apart from the age and position of their author. There may at times be madness, but there is method in it. The flight of the rhapsody is ever upheld by the strength of the wing, and while the reading discovered is enormous for a boy, the depth of feeling exhibited is equally extraordinary; and the clear, firm judgment which did not characterise his conduct, forms the root and the trunk of much of his poetry. It was said of his eyes that it seemed as if fire rolled under them ; and it rolls still, and shall ever roll, below many of his verses.

BRISTOWE TRAGEDY.

1 The feathered songster, chanticleer,
   Hath wound his bugle-horn,
  And told the early villager
   The coming of the morn.

2 King Edward saw the ruddy streaks
   Of light eclipse the gray,
And heard the raven's croaking throat
   Proclaim the fated day.

3 'Thou 'rt right,' quoth he, 'for by the God
   That sits enthroned on high!
Charles Bawdin and his fellows twain
   To-day shall surely die.'

4 Then with a jug of nappy ale
   His knights did on him wait;
'Go tell the traitor that to-day
   He leaves this mortal state.'

5 Sir Canterlone then bended low,
   With heart brimful of woe;
He journeyed to the castle-gate,
   And to Sir Charles did go.

6 But when he came, his children twain,
   And eke his loving wife,
With briny tears did wet the floor,
   For good Sir Charles' life.

7 'O good Sir Charles!' said Canterlone,
   'Bad tidings I do bring.'
'Speak boldly, man,' said brave Sir Charles;
   'What says the traitor king?'

8 'I grieve to tell; before that sun
   Doth from the heaven fly,
He hath upon his honour sworn,
   That thou shalt surely die.'

9 'We all must die,' quoth brave Sir Charles;
      'Of that I 'm not afeard;
    What boots to live a little space?
      Thank Jesus, I 'm prepared:

10 'But tell thy king, for mine he 's not,
      I 'd sooner die to-day
    Than live his slave, as many are,
      Though I should live for aye.'

11 Then Canterlone he did go out,
      To tell the mayor straight
    To get all things in readiness
      For good Sir Charles' fate.

12 Then Master Canynge sought the king,
      And fell down on his knee;
    'I 'm come,' quoth he, 'unto your Grace
      To move your clemency.'

13 'Then,' quoth the king, 'your tale speak out;
      You have been much our friend;
    Whatever your request may be,
      We will to it attend.'

14 'My noble liege! all my request
      Is for a noble knight,
    Who, though perhaps he has done wrong,
      He thought it still was right:

15 'He has a spouse and children twain—
      All ruined are for aye,
    If that you are resolved to let
      Charles Bawdin die to-day.'

176

16 'Speak not of such a traitor vile,'
        The king in fury said;
    ' Before the evening star doth shine,
        Bawdin shall lose his head:

17 ' Justice does loudly for him call,
        And he shall have his meed;
    Speak, Master Canynge! what thing else
        At present do you need?'

18 ' My noble liege!' good Canynge said,
        ' Leave justice to our God,
    And lay the iron rule aside;—
        Be thine the olive rod.

19 ' Was God to search our hearts and reins,
        The best were sinners great;
    Christ's vicar only knows no sin,
        In all this mortal state.

20 ' Let mercy rule thine infant reign;
        'Twill fix thy crown full sure;
    From race to race thy family
        All sovereigns shall endure:

21 ' But if with blood and slaughter thou
        Begin thy infant reign,
    Thy crown upon thy children's brow
        Will never long remain.'

22 'Canynge, away! this traitor vile
        Has scorned my power and me;
    How canst thou then for such a man
        Entreat my clemency?'

23 'My noble liege! the truly brave
    Will valorous actions prize;
Respect a brave and noble mind,
    Although in enemies.'

24 'Canynge, away! By God in heaven,
    That did me being give,
I will not taste a bit of bread
    While this Sir Charles doth live.

25 'By Mary, and all saints in heaven,
    This sun shall be his last.'—
Then Canynge dropped a briny tear,
    And from the presence passed.

26 With heart brimful of gnawing grief,
    He to Sir Charles did go,
And sat him down upon a stool,
    And tears began to flow.

27 'We all must die,' quoth brave Sir Charles;
    'What boots it how or when?
Death is the sure, the certain fate
    Of all us mortal men.

28 'Say why, my friend, thy honest soul
    Runs over at thine eye?
Is it for my most welcome doom
    That thou dost child-like cry?'

29 Quoth godly Canynge, 'I do weep,
    That thou so soon must die,
And leave thy sons and helpless wife;
    'Tis this that wets mine eye.'

30 'Then dry the tears that out thine eye
    From godly fountains spring;
Death I despise, and all the power
    Of Edward, traitor king.

31 'When through the tyrant's welcome means
    I shall resign my life,
The God I serve will soon provide
    For both my sons and wife.

32 'Before I saw the lightsome sun,
    This was appointed me;—
Shall mortal man repine or grudge
    What God ordains to be?

33 'How oft in battle have I stood,
    When thousands died around;
When smoking streams of crimson blood
    Imbrued the fattened ground?

34 'How did I know that every dart,
    That cut the airy way,
Might not find passage to my heart,
    And close mine eyes for aye?

35 'And shall I now from fear of death
    Look wan and be dismayed?
No! from my heart fly childish fear,
    Be all the man displayed.

36 'Ah, godlike Henry! God forefend
    And guard thee and thy son,
If 'tis his will; but if 'tis not,
    Why, then his will be done.

37 'My honest friend, my fault has been
    To serve God and my prince;
  And that I no timeserver am,
    My death will soon convince.

38 'In London city was I born,
    Of parents of great note;
  My father did a noble arms
    Emblazon on his coat:

39 'I make no doubt that he is gone
    Where soon I hope to go;
  Where we for ever shall be blest,
    From out the reach of woe.

40 'He taught me justice and the laws
    With pity to unite;
  And likewise taught me how to know
    The wrong cause from the right:

41 'He taught me with a prudent hand
    To feed the hungry poor;
  Nor let my servants drive away
    The hungry from my door:

42 'And none can say but all my life
    I have his counsel kept,
  And summed the actions of each day
    Each night before I slept.

43 'I have a spouse; go ask of her
    If I defiled her bed;
  I have a king, and none can lay
    Black treason on my head.

44 ' In Lent, and on the holy eve,
        From flesh I did refrain;
    Why should I then appear dismayed
        To leave this world of pain?

45 ' No, hapless Henry! I rejoice
        I shall not see thy death;
    Most willingly in thy just cause
        Do I resign my breath.

46 ' O fickle people, ruined land!
        Thou wilt know peace no moe;
    While Richard's sons exalt themselves,
        Thy brooks with blood will flow.

47 ' Say, were ye tired of godly peace,
        And godly Henry's reign,
    That you did change your easy days
        For those of blood and pain?

48 ' What though I on a sledge be drawn,
        And mangled by a hind?
    I do defy the traitor's power,—
        He cannot harm my mind!

49 ' What though uphoisted on a pole,
        My limbs shall rot in air,
    And no rich monument of brass
        Charles Bawdin's name shall bear?

50 ' Yet in the holy book above,
        Which time can't eat away,
    There, with the servants of the Lord,
        My name shall live for aye.

51 'Then welcome death! for life eterne
        I leave this mortal life:
    Farewell, vain world! and all that's dear,
        My sons and loving wife!

52 'Now death as welcome to me comes
        As e'er the month of May;
    Nor would I even wish to live,
        With my dear wife to stay.'

53 Quoth Canynge, ''Tis a goodly thing
        To be prepared to die;
    And from this world of pain and grief
        To God in heaven to fly.'

54 And now the bell began to toll,
        And clarions to sound;
    Sir Charles he heard the horses' feet
        A-prancing on the ground:

55 And just before the officers
        His loving wife came in,
    Weeping unfeigned tears of woe,
        With loud and dismal din.

56 'Sweet Florence! now, I pray, forbear;
        In quiet let me die;
    Pray God that every Christian soul
        May look on death as I.

57 'Sweet Florence! why those briny tears?
        They wash my soul away,
    And almost make me wish for life,
        With thee, sweet dame, to stay.

58   ' 'Tis but a journey I shall go
     Unto the land of bliss;
  Now, as a proof of husband's love,
     Receive this holy kiss.'

59   Then Florence, faltering in her say,
     Trembling these words she spoke,—
  'Ah, cruel Edward! bloody king!
     My heart is well-nigh broke.

60   ' Ah, sweet Sir Charles! why wilt thou go
     Without thy loving wife?
  The cruel axe that cuts thy neck
     Shall also end my life.'

61   And now the officers came in
     To bring Sir Charles away,
  Who turned to his loving wife,
     And thus to her did say:

62   'I go to life, and not to death;
     Trust thou in God above,
  And teach thy sons to fear the Lord,
     And in their hearts him love:

63   ' Teach them to run the noble race
     That I their father run;
  Florence! should death thee take—adieu!—
     Ye officers, lead on.'

64   Then Florence raved as any mad,
     And did her tresses tear;—
  ' Oh, stay, my husband, lord, and life!'—
     Sir Charles then dropped a tear;—

65 Till tired out with raving loud,
    She fell upon the floor:
    Sir Charles exerted all his might,
    And marched from out the door.

66 Upon a sledge he mounted then,
    With looks full brave and sweet;
    Looks that did show no more concern
    Than any in the street.

67 Before him went the council-men,
    In scarlet robes and gold,
    And tassels spangling in the sun,
    Much glorious to behold:

68 The friars of St Augustine next
    Appeared to the sight,
    All clad in homely russet woods
    Of godly monkish plight:

69 In different parts a godly psalm
    Most sweetly they did chaunt;
    Behind their backs six minstrels came,
    Who tuned the strong bataunt.

70 Then five-and-twenty archers came;
    Each one the bow did bend,
    From rescue of King Henry's friends
    Sir Charles for to defend.

71 Bold as a lion came Sir Charles,
    Drawn on a cloth-laid sled
    By two black steeds, in trappings white,
    With plumes upon their head.

72 Behind him five-and-twenty more
  Of archers strong and stout,
 With bended bow each one in hand,
  Marched in goodly rout:

73 Saint James's friars marched next,
  Each one his part did chaunt;
 Behind their backs six minstrels came
  Who tuned the strong bataunt:

74 Then came the mayor and aldermen,
  In cloth of scarlet decked;
 And their attending men, each one
  Like eastern princes tricked:

75 And after them a multitude
  Of citizens did throng;
 The windows were all full of heads,
  As he did pass along.

76 And when he came to the high cross,
  Sir Charles did turn and say,—
 'O Thou that savest man from sin,
  Wash my soul clean this day!'

77 At the great minster window sat
  The king in mickle state,
 To see Charles Bawdin go along
  To his most welcome fate.

78 Soon as the sledge drew nigh enough
  That Edward he might hear,
 The brave Sir Charles he did stand up,
  And thus his words declare:

185

79 'Thou seest me, Edward! traitor vile!
      Exposed to infamy;
    But be assured, disloyal man!
      I 'm greater now than thee.

80 'By foul proceedings, murder, blood,
      Thou wearest now a crown;
    And hast appointed me to die,
      By power not thine own.

81 'Thou thinkest I shall die to-day;
      I have been dead till now,
    And soon shall live to wear a crown
      For ever on my brow:

82 'Whilst thou, perhaps, for some few years
      Shall rule this fickle land,
    To let them know how wide the rule
      'Twixt king and tyrant hand:

83 'Thy power unjust, thou traitor slave!
      Shall fall on thy own head'——
    From out of hearing of the king
      Departed then the sled.

84 King Edward's soul rushed to his face,
      He turned his head away,
    And to his brother Gloucester
      He thus did speak and say:

85 'To him that so much dreaded death
      No ghastly terrors bring,
    Behold the man! he spake the truth,
      He 's greater than a king!'

186

86 'So let him die!' Duke Richard said;
    'And may each of our foes
Bend down their necks to bloody axe,
    And feed the carrion crows!'

87 And now the horses gently drew
    Sir Charles up the high hill;
The axe did glisten in the sun,
    His precious blood to spill.

88 Sir Charles did up the scaffold go,
    As up a gilded car
Of victory, by valorous chiefs,
    Gained in the bloody war:

89 And to the people he did say,—
    'Behold, you see me die,
For serving loyally my king,
    My king most rightfully.

90 'As long as Edward rules this land,
    No quiet you will know;
Your sons and husbands shall be slain,
    And brooks with blood shall flow.

91 'You leave your good and lawful king
    When in adversity;
Like me unto the true cause stick,
    And for the true cause die.'

92 Then he with priests, upon his knees,
    A prayer to God did make,
Beseeching him unto himself
    His parting soul to take.

93 Then, kneeling down, he laid his head
  Most seemly on the block;
  Which from his body fair at once
  The able headsman stroke :

94 And out the blood began to flow,
  And round the scaffold twine;
  And tears, enough to wash 't away,
  Did flow from each man's eyne.

95 The bloody axe his body fair
  Into four quarters cut;
  And every part, likewise his head,
  Upon a pole was put.

96 One part did rot on Kinwulph-hill,
  One on the minster-tower,
  And one from off the castle-gate
  The crowen did devour:

97 The other on Saint Paul's good gate,
  A dreary spectacle;
  His head was placed on the high cross,
  In high street most nobile.

98 Thus was the end of Bawdin's fate;—
  God prosper long our king,
  And grant he may, with Bawdin's soul,
  In heaven God's mercy sing!

MINSTREL'S SONG.

1 O! sing unto my roundelay,
  O! drop the briny tear with me;
  Dance no more at holy-day,
  Like a running river be:

My love is dead,
Gone to his death-bed,
All under the willow-tree.

2 Black his cryne[1] as the winter night,
White his rode[2] as the summer snow,
Red his face as the morning light,
Cold he lies in the grave below:
My love is dead,
Gone to his death-bed,
All under the willow-tree.

3 Sweet his tongue as the throstle's note,
Quick in dance as thought can be,
Deft his tabour, cudgel stout;
O! he lies by the willow-tree:
My love is dead,
Gone to his death-bed,
All under the willow-tree.

4 Hark! the raven flaps his wing,
In the briared dell below;
Hark! the death-owl loud doth sing
To the night-mares as they go:
My love is dead,
Gone to his death-bed,
All under the willow-tree.

5 See! the white moon shines on high;
Whiter is my true love's shroud,
Whiter than the morning sky,
Whiter than the evening cloud:
My love is dead,
Gone to his death-bed,
All under the willow-tree.

[1] 'Cryne:' hair.—[2] 'Rode:' complexion.

189

6 Here upon my true love's grave,
   Shall the barren flowers be laid,
Not one holy saint to save
   All the celness of a maid:
     My love is dead,
     Gone to his death-bed,
     All under the willow-tree.

7 With my hands I 'll dent[1] the briars
   Round his holy corse to gree;[2]
Ouphant[3] fairy, light your fires—
   Here my body still shall be:
     My love is dead,
     Gone to his death-bed,
     All under the willow-tree.

8 Come, with acorn-cup and thorn,
   Drain my hearté's-blood away;
Life and all its goods I scorn,
   Dance by night, or feast by day:
     My love is dead,
     Gone to his death-bed,
     All under the willow-tree.

9 Water-witches, crowned with reytes,[4]
   Bear me to your lethal tide.
'I die! I come! my true love waits!'
   Thus the damsel spake, and died.

THE STORY OF WILLIAM CANYNGE.

1 Anent a brooklet as I lay reclined,
   Listening to hear the water glide along,
Minding how thorough the green meads it twined,
   Whilst the cavés responsed its muttering song,

---

[1] 'Dent:' fix.—[2] 'Gree:' grow.—[3] 'Ouphant:' elfish.—[4] 'Reytes:' water-flags.

190

At distant rising Avon to he sped,
Amenged[1] with rising hills did show its head;

2 Engarlanded with crowns of osier-weeds
   And wraytes[2] of alders of a bercie scent,
And sticking out with cloud-agested reeds,
   The hoary Avon showed dire semblament,
Whilst blatant Severn, from Sabrina cleped,
Roars flemie o'er the sandës that she heaped.

3 These eyne-gears swithin[3] bringeth to my thought
   Of hardy champions knowen to the flood,
How on the banks thereof brave Ælle fought,
   Ælle descended from Merce kingly blood,
Warder of Bristol town and castle stede,
Who ever and anon made Danes to bleed.

4 Methought such doughty men must have a sprite
   Dight in the armour brace that Michael bore,
When he with Satan, king of Hell, did fight,
   And earth was drenched in a sea of gore;
Or, soon as they did see the worldë's light,
Fate had wrote down, 'This man is born to fight.'

5 Ælle, I said, or else my mind did say,
   Why is thy actions left so spare in story?
Were I to dispone, there should liven aye,
   In earth and heaven's rolls thy tale of glory;
Thy acts so doughty should for aye abide,
And by their test all after acts be tried.

6 Next holy Wareburghus filled my mind,
   As fair a saint as any town can boast,

[1] 'Amenged:' mixed.—[2] 'Wraytes:' flags.—[3] 'Swithin:' quickly.

Or be the earth with light or mirk ywrynde,[1]
  I see his image walking through the coast:
Fitz-Hardynge, Bithrickus, and twenty moe,
In vision 'fore my fantasy did go.

7 Thus all my wandering faitour[2] thinking strayed,
  And each digne[3] builder dequaced on my mind,
When from the distant stream arose a maid,
  Whose gentle tresses moved not to the wind;
Like to the silver moon in frosty night,
The damoiselle did come so blithe and sweet.

8 No broidered mantle of a scarlet hue,
  No shoe-pikes plaited o'er with riband gear,
No costly robes of woaden blue,
  Nought of a dress, but beauty did she wear;
Naked she was, and looked sweet of youth,
All did bewrayen that her name was Truth.

9 The easy ringlets of her nut-brown hair
  What ne a man should see did sweetly hide,
Which on her milk-white bodykin so fair
  Did show like brown streams fouling the white
    tide,
Or veins of brown hue in a marble cuarr,[4]
Which by the traveller is kenned from far.

10 Astounded mickle there I silent lay,
  Still scauncing wondrous at the walking sight;
My senses forgard,[5] nor could run away,
  But was not forstraught[6] when she did alight
Anigh to me, dressed up in naked view,
Which might in some lascivious thoughts abrew.

[1] 'Ywrynde:' covered.—[2] 'Faitour:' vagrant.—[3] 'Digne:' worthy.—[4] 'Cuarr:'
quarry.—[5] 'Forgard:' lose.—[6] 'Forstraught:' distracted.

11 But I did not once think of wanton thought;
      For well I minded what by vow I hete,
   And in my pocket had a crochee[1] brought;
      Which in the blossom would such sins aneto;
   I looked with eyes as pure as angels do,
   And did the every thought of foul eschew.

12 With sweet semblatë, and an angel's grace,
      She 'gan to lecture from her gentle breast;
   For Truth's own wordës is her mindë's face,
      False oratories she did aye detest:
   Sweetness was in each word she did ywreene,
   Though she strove not to make that sweetness seen.

13 She said, 'My manner of appearing here
      My name and slighted myndruch may thee tell;
   I'm Truth, that did descend from heaven-were,
      Goulers and courtiers do not know me well;
   Thy inmost thoughts, thy labouring brain I saw,
   And from thy gentle dream will thee adawe.[2]

14 Full many champions, and men of lore,
      Painters and carvellers[3] have gained good name,
   But there's a Canynge to increase the store,
      A Canynge who shall buy up all their fame.
   Take thou my power, and see in child and man
   What true nobility in Canynge ran.'

15 As when a bordelier[4] on easy bed,
      Tired with the labours maynt[5] of sultry day,
   In sleepë's bosom lays his weary head,
      So, senses sunk to rest, my body lay;

---

[1] 'A crochee:' a cross.—[2] 'Adawe:' awake.—[3] 'Carvellers:' sculptors.—[4] 'A bordelier:' a cottager.—[5] 'Maynt:' many.

Eftsoons my sprite, from earthly bands untied,
Emerged in flanched air with Truth aside.

16 Straight was I carried back to times of yore,
      Whilst Canynge swathed yet in fleshly bed,
    And saw all actions which had been before,
      And all the scroll of fate unravelled;
    And when the fate-marked babe had come to sight,
    I saw him eager gasping after light.

17 In all his shepen gambols and child's play,
      In every merry-making, fair, or wake,
    I knew a purple light of wisdom's ray;
      He eat down learning with a wastle cake.
    As wise as any of the aldermen,
    He'd wit enough to make a mayor at ten.

18 As the dulce[1] downy barbe began to gre,
      So was the well thighte texture of his lore
    Each day enheedynge mockler[2] for to be,
      Great in his counsel for the days he bore.
    All tongues, all carols did unto him sing,
    Wond'ring at one so wise, and yet so ying.[3]

19 Increasing in the years of mortal life,
      And hasting to his journey unto heaven,
    He thought it proper for to choose a wife,
      And use the sexes for the purpose given.
    He then was youth of comely semelikede,
    And he had made a maiden's heart to bleed.

20 He had a father (Jesus rest his soul!)
      Who loved money, as his cherished joy;

    [1] 'Dulce:' sweet.—[2] 'Mockler:' more.—[3] 'Ying:' young.

He had a brother (happy man be 's dole !)
  In mind and body his own father's boy:
What then could Canynge wishen as a part
To give to her who had made exchange of heart ?

21 But lands and castle tenures, gold and bighes,[1]
  And hoards of silver rusted in the ent,[2]
Canynge and his fair sweet did that despise,
  To change of truly love was their content;
They lived together in a house adigne,[3]
Of good sendaument commily and fine.

22 But soon his brother and his sire did die,
  And left to William states and renting-rolls,
And at his will his brother John supply.
  He gave a chauntry to redeem their souls;
And put his brother into such a trade,
That he Lord Mayor of London town was made.

23 Eftsoons his morning turned to gloomy night;
  His dame, his second self, gave up her breath,
Seeking for eterne life and endless light,
  And slew good Canynge; sad mistake of Death !
So have I seen a flower in summer-time
Trod down and broke and wither in its prime.

24 Near Redcliff Church (oh, work of hand of Heaven!
  Where Canynge showeth as an instrument)
Was to my bismarde eyesight newly given;
  'Tis past to blazon it to good content.
You that would fain the festive building see
Repair to Redcliff, and contented be.

---

[1] 'Bighes:' jewels.—[2] 'Ent:' bag.—[3] 'Adigne:' worthy.

25 I saw the myndbruch of his notte soul
   When Edward menaced a second wife;
  I saw what Pheryons in his mind did roll:
   Now fixed from second dames, a priest for life,
  This is the man of men, the vision spoke;
  Then bell for even-song my senses woke.

KENRICK.

TRANSLATED FROM THE SAXON.

When winter yelled through the leafless grove; when the black waves rode over the roaring winds, and the dark-brown clouds hid the face of the sun; when the silver brook stood still, and snow environed the top of the lofty mountain; when the flowers appeared not in the blasted fields, and the boughs of the leafless trees bent with the loads of ice; when the howling of the wolf affrighted the darkly glimmering light of the western sky; Kenrick, terrible as the tempest, young as the snake of the valley, strong as the mountain of the slain; his armour shining like the stars in the dark night, when the moon is veiled in sable, and the blasting winds howl over the wide plain; his shield like the black rock, prepared himself for war.

Ceolwolf of the high mountain, who viewed the first rays of the morning star, swift as the flying deer, strong as the young oak, fierce as an evening wolf, drew his sword; glittering like the blue vapours in the valley of Horso; terrible as the red lightning, bursting from the dark-brown clouds; his swift bark rode over the foaming waves, like the wind in the tempest; the arches fell at his blow, and he wrapped the towers in flames: he followed Kenrick, like a wolf roaming for prey.

Centwin of the vale arose, he seized the massy spear; terrible was his voice, great was his strength; he hurled the rocks into the sea, and broke the strong oaks of the

196

forest. Slow in the race as the minutes of impatience. His spear, like the fury of a thunderbolt, swept down whole armies; his enemies melted before him, like the stones of hail at the approach of the sun.

Awake, O Eldulph! thou that sleepest on the white mountain, with the fairest of women. No more pursue the dark-brown wolf: arise from the mossy bank of the falling waters; let thy garments be stained in blood, and the streams of life discolour thy girdle; let thy flowing hair be hid in a helmet, and thy beauteous countenance be writhed into terror.

Egward, keeper of the barks, arise like the roaring waves of the sea: pursue the black companies of the enemy.

Ye Saxons, who live in the air and glide over the stars, act like yourselves.

Like the murmuring voice of the Severn, swelled with rain, the Saxons moved along; like a blazing star the sword of Kenrick shone among the Britons; Tenyan bled at his feet; like the red lightning of heaven he burnt up the ranks of his enemy.

Centwin raged like a wild boar. Tatward sported in blood; armies melted at his stroke. Eldulph was a flaming vapour; destruction sat upon his sword. Ceolwolf was drenched in gore, but fell like a rock before the sword of Mervin.

Egward pursued the slayer of his friend; the blood of Mervin smoked on his hand.

Like the rage of a tempest was the noise of the battle; like the roaring of the torrent, gushing from the brow of the lofty mountain.

The Britons fled, like a black cloud dropping hail, flying before the howling winds.

Ye virgins! arise and welcome back the pursuers; deck their brows with chaplets of jewels; spread the branches of the oak beneath their feet.   Kenrick is returned from the war, the clotted gore hangs terrible upon his crooked sword, like the noxious vapours on the black rock; his knees are red with the gore of the foe.

Ye sons of the song, sound the instruments of music; ye virgins, dance around him.

Costan of the lake, arise, take thy harp from the willow, sing the praise of Kenrick, to the sweet sound of the white waves sinking to the foundation of the black rock.

Rejoice, O ye Saxons! Kenrick is victorious.

FEBRUARY, AN ELEGY.

1 Begin, my muse, the imitative lay,
    Æonian doxies, sound the thrumming string;
  Attempt no number of the plaintive Gray;
    Let me like midnight cats, or Collins, sing.

2 If in the trammels of the doleful line,
    The bounding hail or drilling rain descend;
  Come, brooding Melancholy, power divine,
    And every unformed mass of words amend.

3 Now the rough Goat withdraws his curling horns,
    And the cold Waterer twirls his circling mop:
  Swift sudden anguish darts through altering corns,
    And the spruce mercer trembles in his shop.

4 Now infant authors, maddening for renown,
    Extend the plume, and hum about the stage,
  Procure a benefit, amuse the town,
    And proudly glitter in a title-page.

5 Now, wrapped in ninefold fur, his squeamish Grace
    Defies the fury of the howling storm;
  And whilst the tempest whistles round his face,
    Exults to find his mantled carcase warm.

6 Now rumbling coaches furious drive along,
    Full of the majesty of city dames,
  Whose jewels, sparkling in the gaudy throng,
    Raise strange emotions and invidious flames.

7 Now Merit, happy in the calm of place,
    To mortals as a Highlander appears,
  And conscious of the excellence of lace,
    With spreading frogs and gleaming spangles glares:

8 Whilst Envy, on a tripod seated nigh,
    In form a shoe-boy, daubs the valued fruit,
  And darting lightnings from his vengeful eye,
    Raves about Wilkes, and politics, and Bute.

9 Now Barry, taller than a grenadier,
    Dwindles into a stripling of eighteen;
  Or sabled in Othello breaks the ear,
    Exerts his voice, and totters to the scene.

10 Now Foote, a looking-glass for all mankind,
    Applies his wax to personal defects;
  But leaves untouched the image of the mind;—
    His art no mental quality reflects.

11 Now Drury's potent king extorts applause,
    And pit, box, gallery, echo, 'How divine!'
  Whilst, versed in all the drama's mystic laws,
    His graceful action saves the wooden line.

12 Now—but what further can the muses sing?
    Now dropping particles of water fall;
Now vapours riding on the north wind's wing,
    With transitory darkness shadows all.

13 Alas! how joyless the descriptive theme,
    When sorrow on the writer's quiet preys;
And like a mouse in Cheshire cheese supreme,
    Devours the substance of the lessening bays.

14 Come, February, lend thy darkest sky,
    There teach the wintered muse with clouds to soar:
Come, February, lift the number high;
    Let the sharp strain like wind through alleys roar.

15 Ye channels, wandering through the spacious street,
    In hollow murmurs roll the dirt along,
With inundations wet the sabled feet,
    Whilst gouts, responsive, join the elegiac song.

16 Ye damsels fair, whose silver voices shrill
    Sound through meandering folds of Echo's horn;
Let the sweet cry of liberty be still,
    No more let smoking cakes awake the morn.

17 O Winter! put away thy snowy pride;
    O Spring! neglect the cowslip and the bell;
O Summer! throw thy pears and plums aside;
    O Autumn! bid the grape with poison swell.

18 The pensioned muse of Johnson is no more!
    Drowned in a butt of wine his genius lies.
Earth! Ocean! Heaven! the wondrous loss deplore,
    The dregs of nature with her glory dies.

19 What iron Stoic can suppress the tear!
   What sour reviewer read with vacant eye!
   What bard but decks his literary bier !—
   Alas! I cannot sing—I howl—I cry!

LORD LYTTELTON.

DR JOHNSON said once of Chesterfield, 'I thought him a lord among wits, but I find him to be only a wit among lords.' And so we may say of Lord Lyttelton, 'He is a poet among lords, if not a lord among poets.' He was the son of Sir Thomas Lyttelton, of Hagley in Worcestershire, and was born in 1709. He went to Eton and Oxford, where he distinguished himself. Having gone the usual grand tour, he entered Parliament, and became an opponent of Sir Robert Walpole. He was made secretary to the Prince of Wales, and was in this capacity useful to Mallett and Thomson. In 1741, he married Lucy Fortescue, of Devonshire, who died five years afterwards. Lyttelton grieved sincerely for her, and wrote his affecting ' Monody ' on the subject. When his party triumphed, he was created a Lord of the Treasury, and afterwards Chancellor of the Exchequer, with a peerage. He employed much of his leisure in literary composition, writing a good little book on the Conversion of St Paul, a laboured History of Henry II., and some verses, including the stanza in the 'Castle of Indolence' describing Thomson—

    ' A bard there dwelt, more fat than bard beseems,' &c.—

and a very spirited prologue to Thomson's ' Coriolanus,' which was written after that author's death, and says of him,

    ——' His chaste muse employed her heaven-taught lyre
    None but the noblest passions to inspire:
    Not one immoral, one corrupted thought,
    One line which dying he could wish to blot.'

Lyttelton himself died August 22, 1773, aged sixty-four. His History is now little read. It took him, it is said, thirty years to write it, and he employed another man to point it—a fact recalling what is told of Macaulay, that he sent the first

volume of his ' History of England ' to Lord Jeffrey, who over-
looked the punctuation and criticised the style.   Of a series of
Dialogues issued by this writer, Dr Johnson remarked, with his
usual pointed severity, ' Here is a man telling the world what
the world had all his life been telling him.'   His ' Monody '
expresses real grief in an artificial style, but has some stanzas as
natural in the expression as they are pathetic in the feeling.

FROM THE ' MONODY.'

At length escaped from every human eye,
   From every duty, every care,
That in my mournful thoughts might claim a share,
Or force my tears their flowing stream to dry;
Beneath the gloom of this embowering shade,
This lone retreat, for tender sorrow made,
I now may give my burdened heart relief,
   And pour forth all my stores of grief;
Of grief surpassing every other woe,
Far as the purest bliss, the happiest love
   Can on the ennobled mind bestow,
   Exceeds the vulgar joys that move
Our gross desires, inelegant and low.

  *   *   *   *   *

   In vain I look around
   O'er all the well-known ground,
My Lucy's wonted footsteps to descry;
   Where oft we used to walk,
   Where oft in tender talk
We saw the summer sun go down the sky;
   Nor by yon fountain's side,
   Nor where its waters glide
Along the valley, can she now be found:
In all the wide-stretched prospect's ample bound

202

No more my mournful eye
Can aught of her espy,
But the sad sacred earth where her dear relics lie.

*   *   *   *

Sweet babes, who, like the little playful fawns,
Were wont to trip along these verdant lawns
By your delighted mother's side:
Who now your infant steps shall guide?
Ah! where is now the hand whose tender care
To every virtue would have formed your youth,
And strewed with flowers the thorny ways of truth?
O loss beyond repair!
O wretched father! left alone,
To weep their dire misfortune and thy own:
How shall thy weakened mind, oppressed with woe,
And drooping o'er thy Lucy's grave,
Perform the duties that you doubly owe!
Now she, alas! is gone,
From folly and from vice their helpless age to save?

*   *   *   *

O best of wives! O dearer far to me
Than when thy virgin charms
Were yielded to my arms:
How can my soul endure the loss of thee?
How in the world, to me a desert grown,
Abandoned and alone,
Without my sweet companion can I live?
Without thy lovely smile,
The dear reward of every virtuous toil,
What pleasures now can palled ambition give?
Even the delightful sense of well-earned praise,
Unshared by thee, no more my lifeless thoughts could
raise.

For my distracted mind
What succour can I find?
On whom for consolation shall I call?
Support me, every friend;
Your kind assistance lend,
To bear the weight of this oppressive woe.
Alas! each friend of mine,
My dear departed love, so much was thine,
That none has any comfort to bestow.
My books, the best relief
In every other grief,
Are now with your idea saddened all:
Each favourite author we together read
My tortured memory wounds, and speaks of Lucy dead.

We were the happiest pair of human kind;
The rolling year its varying course performed,
And back returned again;
Another and another smiling came,
And saw our happiness unchanged remain:
Still in her golden chain
Harmonious concord did our wishes bind:
Our studies, pleasures, taste, the same.
O fatal, fatal stroke,
That all this pleasing fabric love had raised
Of rare felicity,
On which even wanton vice with envy gazed,
And every scheme of bliss our hearts had formed,
With soothing hope, for many a future day,
In one sad moment broke!—
Yet, O my soul, thy rising murmurs stay;
Nor dare the all-wise Disposer to arraign,
Or against his supreme decree
With impious grief complain;

That all thy full-blown joys at once should fade,
Was his most righteous will—and be that will obeyed.

JOHN CUNNINGHAM.

WE know very little of the history of this pleasing poet. He
was born in 1729, the son of a wine-cooper in Dublin. At the
age of seventeen he wrote a farce, entitled 'Love in a Mist,' and
shortly after came to Britain as an actor. He was for a long
time a performer in Digges' company in Edinburgh, and subsequently resided in Newcastle-upon-Tyne. Here he seems to
have fallen into distressed circumstances, and was supported by
a benevolent printer, at whose house he died in 1773. His
poetry is distinguished by a charming simplicity. This characterises 'Kate of Aberdeen,' given below, and also his 'Content : a Pastoral,' in which he says allegorically—

> 'Her air was so modest, her aspect so meek,
>   So simple yet sweet were her charms !
> I kissed the ripe roses that glowed on her cheek,
>   And locked the dear maid in my arms.

> 'Now jocund together we tend a few sheep,
>   And if, by yon prattler, the stream,
> Reclined on her bosom, I sink into sleep,
>   Her image still softens my dream.'

MAY-EVE; OR, KATE OF ABERDEEN.

1 The silver moon's enamoured beam
    Steals softly through the night,
  To wanton with the winding stream,
    And kiss reflected light.
  To beds of state go, balmy sleep,
    ('Tis where you 've seldom been,)
  May's vigil whilst the shepherds keep
    With Kate of Aberdeen.

2 Upon the green the virgins wait,
  In rosy chaplets gay,
Till Morn unbar her golden gate,
  And give the promised May.
Methinks I hear the maids declare,
  The promised May, when seen,
Not half so fragrant, half so fair,
  As Kate of Aberdeen.

3 Strike up the tabor's boldest notes,
  We 'll rouse the nodding grove;
The nested birds shall raise their throats,
  And hail the maid I love:
And see—the matin lark mistakes,
  He quits the tufted green:
Fond bird! 'tis not the morning breaks,
  'Tis Kate of Aberdeen.

4 Now lightsome o'er the level mead,
  Where midnight fairies rove,
Like them the jocund dance we 'll lead,
  Or tune the reed to love:
For see the rosy May draws nigh;
  She claims a virgin queen!
And hark, the happy shepherds cry,
  'Tis Kate of Aberdeen.

ROBERT FERGUSSON.

This unfortunate Scottish bard was born in Edinburgh on the 17th (some say the 5th) of October 1751. His father, who had been an accountant to the British Linen Company's Bank, died early, leaving a widow and four children. Robert spent six

years at the grammar schools of Edinburgh and Dundee, went
for a short period to Edinburgh College, and then, having
obtained a bursary, to St Andrews, where he continued till his
seventeenth year. He was at first designed for the ministry of
the Scottish Church. He distinguished himself at college for
his mathematical knowledge, and became a favourite of Dr
Wilkie, Professor of Natural Philosophy, on whose death he
wrote an elegy. He early discovered a passion for poetry, and
collected materials for a tragedy on the subject of Sir William
Wallace, which he never finished. He once thought of studying
medicine, but had neither patience nor funds for the needful
preliminary studies. He went away to reside with a rich uncle,
named John Forbes, in the north, near Aberdeen. This person,
however, and poor Fergusson unfortunately quarrelled; and,
after residing some months in his house, he left it in disgust,
and with a few shillings in his pocket proceeded southwards.
He travelled on foot, and such was the effect of his vexation and
fatigue, that when he reached his mother's house he fell into a
severe fit of illness.

He became, on his recovery, a copying-clerk in a solicitor's,
and afterwards in a sheriff-clerk's office, and began to contribute
to *Ruddiman's Weekly Magazine*. We remember in boyhood
reading some odd volumes of this production, the general matter
in which was inconceivably poor, relieved only by Fergusson's
racy little Scottish poems. His evenings were spent chiefly in
the tavern, amidst the gay and dissipated youth of the metropolis, to whom he was the ' wit, songster, and mimic.' That his
convivial powers were extraordinary, is proved by the fact of
one of his contemporaries, who survived to be a correspondent of
Burns, doubting if even he equalled the fascination of Fergusson's converse. Dissipation gradually stole in upon him, in
spite of resolutions dictated by remorse. In 1773, he collected
his poems into a volume, which was warmly received, but
brought him, it is believed, little pecuniary benefit. At last,
under the pressure of poverty, toil, and intemperance, his reason
gave way, and he was by a stratagem removed to an asylum.
Here, when he found himself and became aware of his situation,
he uttered a dismal shriek, and cast a wild and startled look

around his cell. The history of his confinement was very similar to that of Nat Lee and Christopher Smart. For instance, a
story is told of him which is an exact duplicate of one recorded
of Lee. He was writing by the light of the moon, when a thin
cloud crossed its disk. 'Jupiter, snuff the moon,' roared the
impatient poet. The cloud thickened, and entirely darkened
the light. 'Thou stupid god,' he exclaimed, 'thou hast snuffed
it out.' By and by he became calmer, and had some affecting
interviews with his mother and sister. A removal to his
mother's house was even contemplated, but his constitution was
exhausted, and on the 16th of October 1774, poor Fergusson
breathed his last. It is interesting to know that the New Tes-
tament was his favourite companion in his cell. A little after
his death arrived a letter from an old friend, a Mr Burnet, who
had made a fortune in the East Indies, wishing him to come
out to India, and enclosing a remittance of £100 to defray the
expenses of the journey.

Thus in his twenty-fourth year perished Robert Fergusson.
He was buried in the Canongate churchyard, where Burns
afterwards erected a monument to his memory, with an inscrip-
tion which is familiar to most of our readers.

Burns in one of his poems attributes to Fergusson 'glorious
pairts.' He was certainly a youth of remarkable powers, although
'pairts' rather than high genius seems to express his calibre.
He can hardly be said to sing, and he never soars. His best
poems, such as 'The Farmer's Ingle,' are just lively daguerreo-
types of the life he saw around him—there is nothing ideal or
lofty in any of them. His 'ingle-bleeze' burns low compared
to that which in 'The Cottar's Saturday Night' springs up aloft
to heaven, like the tongue of an altar-fire. He stuffs his poems,
too, with Scotch to a degree which renders them too 'rich for
even a Scotchman's taste, and as repulsive as a haggis to that
of an Englishman. On the whole, Fergusson's best claim to
fame arises from the influence he exerted on the far higher
genius of Burns, who seems, strangely enough, to have preferred
him to Allan Ramsay.

THE FARMER'S INGLE.

Et multo imprimis hilarans convivia Baccho,
Ante focum, si frigus erit.—VIRG.

1 Whan gloamin gray out owre the welkin keeks;[1]
    Whan Batie ca's his owsen[2] to the byre;
Whan Thrasher John, sair dung,[3] his barn-door
        steeks,[4]
    An' lusty lasses at the dightin'[5] tire;
What bangs fu' leal[6] the e'enin's coming cauld,
    An' gars[7] snaw-tappit Winter freeze in vain;
Gars dowie mortals look baith blithe an' bauld,
    Nor fley'd[8] wi' a' the poortith o' the plain;
    Begin, my Muse! and chant in hamely strain.

2 Frae the big stack, weel winnow't on the hill,
    Wi' divots theekit[9] frae the weet an' drift,
Sods, peats, and heathery turfs the chimley[10] fill,
    An' gar their thickening smeek[11] salute the lift.
The gudeman, new come hame, is blithe to find,
    Whan he out owre the hallan[12] flings his een,
That ilka turn is handled to his mind;
    That a' his housie looks sae cosh[13] an' clean;
    For cleanly house lo'es he, though e'er sae mean.

3 Weel kens the gudewife, that the pleughs require
    A heartsome meltith,[14] an' refreshin' synd[15]
O' nappy liquor, owre a bleezin' fire:
    Sair wark an' poortith downa[16] weel be joined.

---

[1] 'Keeks:' peeps.—[2] 'Owsen:' oxen.—[3] 'Sair dung:' fatigued.—[4] 'Steeks:'
shuts.—[5] 'Dightin':' winnowing.—[6] 'What bangs fu' leal:' what shuts out most
comfortably.—[7] 'Gars:' makes.—[8] 'Fley'd:' frightened.—[9] 'Wi' divots theekit:'
thatched with turf.—[10] 'Chimley:' chimney.—[11] 'Smeek:' smoke.—[12] 'Hallan:'
the inner wall of a cottage.—[13] 'Cosh:' comfortable.—[14] 'Meltith:' meal.—
[15] 'Synd:' drink.—[16] 'Downa:' should not.

Wi' butter'd bannocks now the girdle[1] reeks;
 I' the far nook the bowie[2] briskly reams;
The readied kail[3] stands by the chimley cheeks,
 An' haud the riggin' het wi' welcome streams,
 Whilk than the daintiest kitchen[4] nicer seems.

4 Frae this, lat gentler gabs[5] a lesson lear:
 Wad they to labouring lend an eident[6] hand,
They'd rax fell strang upo' the simplest fare,
 Nor find their stamacks ever at a stand.
Fu' hale an' healthy wad they pass the day;
 At night, in calmest slumbers dose fu' sound;
Nor doctor need their weary life to spae,[7]
 Nor drogs their noddle and their sense confound,
 Till death slip sleely on, an' gie the hindmost
  wound.

5 On siccan food has mony a doughty deed
 By Caledonia's ancestors been done;
By this did mony a wight fu' weirlike bleed
 In brulzies[8] frae the dawn to set o' sun.
'Twas this that braced their gardies[9] stiff an' strang;
 That bent the deadly yew in ancient days;
Laid Denmark's daring sons on yird[10] alang;
 Garr'd Scottish thristles bang the Roman bays;
 For near our crest their heads they dought na raise.

6 The couthy cracks[11] begin whan supper's owre;
 The cheering bicker[12] gars them glibly gash[13]
O' Simmer's showery blinks, an Winter's sour,
 Whase floods did erst their mailins' produce hash.[14]

[1] 'Girdle:' a flat iron for toasting cakes.—[2] 'Bowie:' beer-barrel.—[3] 'Kail:' broth with greens.—[4] 'Kitchen:' anything eaten with bread.—[5] 'Gabs:' palates. —[6] 'Eident:' assiduous.—[7] 'Spae:' foretell.—[8] 'Brulzies:' contests.—[9] 'Gardies:' arms.—[10] 'Yird:' earth.—[11] 'Cracks:' pleasant talk.—[12] 'Bicker:' the cup.— [13] 'Gash:' chat.—[14] 'Their mailins' produce hash:' destroy the produce of their farms.

'Bout kirk an' market eke their tales gae on;
　　How Jock woo'd Jenny here to be his bride;
An' there, how Marion, for a bastard son,
　　Upo' the cutty-stool was forced to ride;
　　The waefu' scauld o' our Mess John to bide.

7 The fient a cheep[1] 's amang the bairnies now;
　　For a' their anger 's wi' their hunger gane:
Aye maun the childer, wi' a fastin' mou,
　　Grumble an' greet, an' mak an unco maen.[2]
In rangles[3] round, before the ingle's low,
　　Frae gudame's[4] mouth auld-warld tales they hear,
O' warlocks loupin round the wirrikow:[5]
　　O' ghaists, that win[6] in glen an kirkyard drear,
　　Whilk touzles a' their tap, an' gars them shake
　　　　wi' fear!

8 For weel she trows that fiends an' fairies be
　　Sent frae the deil to fleetch[7] us to our ill;
That kye hae tint[8] their milk wi' evil ee;
　　An' corn been scowder'd[9] on the glowin' kiln.
O mock nae this, my friends! but rather mourn,
　　Ye in life's brawest spring wi' reason clear;
Wi' eild[10] our idle fancies a' return,
　　And dim our dolefu' days wi' bairnly[11] fear;
　　The mind 's aye cradled whan the grave is near.

9 Yet Thrift, industrious, bides her latest days,
　　Though Age her sair-dow'd front wi' runcles
　　　　wave;
　　Yet frae the russet lap the spindle plays;
　　Her e'enin stent[12] reels she as weel 's the lave.[13]

---

[1] 'The fient a cheep:' not a whimper.—[2] 'Maen:' moan.—[3] 'Rangles:' circles.
—[4] 'Gudame's:' grandame.—[5] 'Wirrikow:' scare-crow.—[6] 'Win:' abide.—
[7] 'Fleetch:' entice.—[8] 'Tint:' lost.—[9] 'Scowder'd:' scorched.—[10] 'Eild:' age.—
[11] 'Bairnly:' childish.—[12] 'Stent:' task.—[13] 'Lave:' the rest.

On some feast-day, tho wee things buskit braw,
  Shall heese her heart up wi' a silent joy,
Fu' cadgie that her head was up an' saw
  Her ain spun cleedin' on a darlin' oy;[1]
Careless though death should mak the feast
    her foy.[2]

10 In its auld lerroch[3] yet the deas[4] remains,
  Where the gudeman aft streeks[5] him at his
    case;
A warm and canny lean for weary banes
  O'. labourers doylt upo' the wintry leas.
Round him will baudrins[6] an' the collie come,
  To wag their tail, and cast a thankfu' ee,
To him wha kindly flings them mony a crumb
  O' kebbuck[7] whang'd, an' dainty fadge[8] to prie;[9]
  This a' the boon they crave, an' a' the fee.

11 Frae him the lads their mornin' counsel tak:
  What stacks he wants to thrash; what rigs to
    till;
How big a birn[10] maun lie on bassie's[11] back,
  For meal an' mu'ter[12] to the thirlin' mill.
Neist, the gudewife her hirelin' damsels bids
  Glower through the byre, an' see the hawkies[13]
    bound;
Tak tent, case Crummy tak her wonted tids,[14]
  An' ca' the laiglen's[15] treasure on the ground;
  Whilk spills a kebbuck nice, or yellow pound.

[1] 'Oy:' grandchild.—[2] 'Her foy:' her farewell entertainment.—[3] 'Lerroch:' corner.—[4] 'Deas:' bench.—[5] 'Streeks:' stretches.—[6] 'Baudrins:' the cat.—[7] 'Kebbuck:' cheese.—[8] 'Fadge:' loaf.—[9] 'To prie:' to taste.—[10] 'Birn:' burden.—[11] 'Bassie:' the horse.—[12] 'Mu'ter:' the miller's perquisite.—[13] 'Hawkies:' cows.—[14] 'Tids:' fits.—[15] 'The laiglen:' the milk-pail.

12 Then a' the house for sleep begin to green,[1]
      Their joints to slack frae industry a while;
   The leaden god fa's heavy on their een,
      An hafflins stecks them frae their daily toil:
   The cruizy,[2] too, can only blink and bleer;
      The reistit ingle's done the maist it dow;
   Tacksman an' cottar eke to bed maun steer,
      Upo' the cod[3] to clear their drumly pow,[4]
      Till waukened by the dawnin's ruddy glow.

13 Peace to the husbandman, an' a' his tribe,
      Whase care fells a' our wants frae year to year!
   Lang may his sock[5] and cou'ter turn the gleyb,[6]
      An' banks o' corn bend down wi' laded ear!
   May Scotia's simmers aye look gay an' green;
      Her yellow ha'rsts frae scowry blasts decreed!
   May a' her tenants sit fu' snug an' bien,[7]
      Frae the hard grip o' ails, and poortith freed;
      An' a lang lasting train o' peacefu' hours succeed!

DR WALTER HARTE.

CAMPBELL, in his 'Specimens,' devotes a large portion of space
to Dr Walter Harte, and has quoted profusely from a poem of
his entitled 'Eulogius.' We may give some of the best lines
here :—

      'This spot for dwelling fit Eulogius chose,
        And in a month a decent homestall rose,
        Something between a cottage and a cell ;
        Yet virtue here could sleep, and peace could dwell.

      'The site was neither granted him nor given ;
        'Twas Nature's, and the ground-rent due to Heaven.

[1] 'To green:' to long.—[2] 'The cruizy:' the lamp.—[3] 'Cod:' pillow.—[4] 'Drumly
pow:' thick heads.—[5] 'Sock:' ploughshare.—[6] 'Gleyb:' soil.—[7] 'Bien:' comfortable.

> Wife he had none, nor had he love to spare,—
> An aged mother wanted all his care.
> They thanked their Maker for a pittance sent,
> Supped on a turnip, slept upon content.'

Again, of a neighbouring matron, who died leaving Eulogius
money—

> 'This matron, whitened with good works and age,
> Approached the Sabbath of her pilgrimage ;
> Her spirit to himself the Almighty drew,
> *Breathed on the alembic, and exhaled the dew.'*

And once more—

> 'Who but Eulogius now exults for joy ?
> New thoughts, new hopes, new views his mind employ ;
> Pride pushed forth buds at every branching shoot,
> And virtue shrank almost beneath the root.
> High raised on fortune's hill, new Alps he spies,
> O'ershoots the valley which beneath him lies,
> Forgets the depths between, and travels with his eyes.'

EDWARD LOVIBOND.

HAMPTON in Middlesex was the birthplace of our next poet,
Edward Lovibond.   He was a gentleman of fortune, who chiefly
employed his time in rural occupations.   He became a director
of the East India Company.   He helped his friend Moore in
conducting the periodical called *The World*, to which he contributed several papers, including the very pleasing poem entitled 'The Tears of Old May-Day.'   He died in 1775.

THE TEARS OF OLD MAY-DAY.

WRITTEN ON THE REFORMATION OF THE CALENDAR IN 1754.

1 Led by the jocund train of vernal hours
    And vernal airs, uprose the gentle May;
  Blushing she rose, and blushing rose the flowers
    That sprung spontaneous in her genial ray.

214

2 Her locks with heaven's ambrosial dews were bright,
    And amorous zephyrs fluttered on her breast:
With every shifting gleam of morning light,
    The colours shifted of her rainbow vest.

3 Imperial ensigns graced her smiling form,
    A golden key and golden wand she bore;
This charms to peace each sullen eastern storm,
    And that unlocks the summer's copious store.

4 Onward in conscious majesty she came,
    The grateful honours of mankind to taste:
To gather fairest wreaths of future fame,
    And blend fresh triumphs with her glories past.

5 Vain hope! no more in choral bands unite
    Her virgin votaries, and at early dawn,
Sacred to May and love's mysterious rite,
    Brush the light dew-drops from the spangled
        lawn.

6 To her no more Augusta's wealthy pride
    Pours the full tribute from Potosi's mine:
Nor fresh-blown garlands village maids provide,
    A purer offering at her rustic shrine.

7 No more the Maypole's verdant height around
    To valour's games the ambitious youth advance;
No merry bells and tabor's sprightlier sound
    Wake the loud carol, and the sportive dance.

8 Sudden in pensive sadness drooped her head,
    Faint on her cheeks the blushing crimson died—
'O chaste victorious triumphs! whither fled?
    My maiden honours, whither gone?' she cried.

9 Ah! once to fame and bright dominion born,
    The earth and smiling ocean saw me rise,
  With time coeval and the star of morn,
    The first, the fairest daughter of the skies.

10 Then, when at Heaven's prolific mandate sprung
    The radiant beam of new-created day,
  Celestial harps, to airs of triumph strung,
    Hailed the glad dawn, and angels called me May.

11 Space in her empty regions heard the sound,
    And hills, and dales, and rocks, and valleys rung;
  The sun exulted in his glorious round,
    And shouting planets in their courses sung.

12 For ever then I led the constant year;
    Saw youth, and joy, and love's enchanting wiles;
  Saw the mild graces in my train appear,
    And infant beauty brighten in my smiles.

13 No winter frowned.   In sweet embrace allied,
    Three sister seasons danced the eternal green;
  And Spring's retiring softness gently vied
    With Autumn's blush, and Summer's lofty mien.

14 Too soon, when man profaned the blessings given,
    And vengeance armed to blot a guilty age,
  With bright Astrea to my native heaven
    I fled, and flying saw the deluge rage;

15 Saw bursting clouds eclipse the noontide beams,
    While sounding billows from the mountains rolled,
  With bitter waves polluting all my streams,
    My nectared streams, that flowed on sands of gold.
  216

16 Then vanished many a sea-girt isle and grove,
    Their forests floating on the watery plain:
  Then, famed for arts and laws derived from Jove,
    My Atalantis sunk beneath the main.

17 No longer bloomed primeval Eden's bowers,
    Nor guardian dragons watched the Hesperian
        steep:
  With all their fountains, fragrant fruits and flowers,
    Torn from the continent to glut the deep.

18 No more to dwell in sylvan scenes I deigned,
    Yet oft descending to the languid earth,
  With quickening powers the fainting mass sustained,
    And waked her slumbering atoms into birth.

19 And every echo taught my raptured name,
    And every virgin breathed her amorous vows,
  And precious wreaths of rich immortal fame,
    Showered by the Muses, crowned my lofty brows.

20 But chief in Europe, and in Europe's pride,
    My Albion's favoured realms, I rose adored;
  And poured my wealth, to other climes denied;
    From Amalthea's horn with plenty stored.

21 Ah me! for now a younger rival claims
    My ravished honours, and to her belong
  My choral dances, and victorious games,
    To her my garlands and triumphal song.

22 O say what yet untasted beauties flow,
    What purer joys await her gentler reign?
  Do lilies fairer, violets sweeter blow?
    And warbles Philomel a softer strain?

217

23 Do morning suns in ruddier glory rise?
        Does evening fan her with serener gales?
    Do clouds drop fatness from the wealthier skies,
        Or wantons plenty in her happier vales?

24 Ah! no: the blunted beams of dawning light
        Skirt the pale orient with uncertain day;
    And Cynthia, riding on the car of night,
        Through clouds embattled faintly wings her way.

25 Pale, immature, the blighted verdure springs,
        Nor mounting juices feed the swelling flower;
    Mute all the groves, nor Philomela sings
        When silence listens at the midnight hour.

26 Nor wonder, man, that Nature's bashful face,
        And opening charms, her rude embraces fear:
    Is she not sprung from April's wayward race,
        The sickly daughter of the unripened year?

27 With showers and sunshine in her fickle eyes,
        With hollow smiles proclaiming treacherous peace,
    With blushes, harbouring, in their thin disguise,
        The blasts that riot on the Spring's increase?

28 Is this the fair invested with my spoil
        By Europe's laws, and senates' stern command?
    Ungenerous Europe! let me fly thy soil,
        And waft my treasures to a grateful land;

29 Again revive, on Asia's drooping shore,
        My Daphne's groves, or Lycia's ancient plain;
    Again to Afric's sultry sands restore
        Embowering shades, and Lybian Ammon's fane:
    218

30 Or haste to northern Zembla's savage coast,
      There hush to silence elemental strife;
   Brood o'er the regions of eternal frost,
      And swell her barren womb with heat and life.

31 Then Britain—Here she ceased.   Indignant grief,
      And parting pangs, her faltering tongue suppressed:
   Veiled in an amber cloud she sought relief,
      And tears and silent anguish told the rest.

FRANCIS FAWKES.

THIS 'learned and jovial parson,' as Campbell calls him, was
born in 1721, in Yorkshire.   He studied at Cambridge, and
became curate at Croydon, in Surrey.   Here he obtained the
friendship of Archbishop Herring, and was by him appointed
vicar of Orpington in Kent, a situation which he ultimately
exchanged for the rectory of Hayes, in the same county.   He
translated various minor Greek poets, including Anacreon, Sappho,
Bion and Moschus, Theocritus, &c.   He died in 1777.   His
'Brown Jug' breathes some of the spirit of the first of these
writers, and two or three lines of it were once quoted triumph-
antly in Parliament by Sheil, while charging Peel, we think it
was, with appropriating arguments from Bishop Philpotts—
'Harry of Exeter.'

> 'Dear Tom, this brown jug that now foams with mild ale,
>   Was once Toby Philpotts,' &c.

THE BROWN JUG.

1 Dear Tom, this brown jug that now foams with
      mild ale,
   (In which I will drink to sweet Nan of the Vale,)
   Was once Toby Fillpot, a thirsty old soul
   As e'er drank a bottle, or fathomed a bowl;

219

In boosing about 'twas his praise to excel,
And among jolly topers he bore off the bell.

2 It chanced as in dog-days he sat at his ease
In his flower-woven arbour as gay as you please,
With a friend and a pipe puffing sorrows away,
And with honest old stingo was soaking his clay,
His breath-doors of life on a sudden were shut,
And he died full as big as a Dorchester butt.

3 His body, when long in the ground it had lain,
And time into clay had resolved it again,
A potter found out in its covert so snug,
And with part of fat Toby he formed this brown
    jug,
Now sacred to friendship, and mirth, and mild ale;
So here's to my lovely sweet Nan of the Vale.

JOHN LANGHORNE.

THIS poetical divine was born in 1735, at Kirkby Steven, in Westmoreland. Left fatherless at four years old, his mother fulfilled her double charge of duty with great tenderness and assiduity. He was educated at Appleby, and subsequently became assistant at the free-school of Wakefield, took deacon's orders, and gave promise, although very young, of becoming a popular preacher. After various vicissitudes of life and fortune, and publishing a number of works in prose and verse, Langhorne repaired to London, and obtained, in 1764, the curacy and lectureship of St John's, Clerkenwell. He soon afterwards became assistant-preacher in Lincoln's Inn Chapel, where he had a very intellectual audience to address, and bore a somewhat trying ordeal with complete success. He continued for a number of years in London, maintaining his reputation both as a preacher and writer. His most popular works were the 'Letters

of Theodosius and Constantia,' and a translation of Plutarch's
Lives, which Wrangham afterwards corrected and improved, and
which is still standard.   He was twice married, and survived
both his wives.   He obtained the living of Blagden in Somer-
setshire, and in addition to it, in 1777, a prebend in the Cathedral
of Wells.   He died in 1779, aged only forty-four; his death, it
is supposed, being accelerated by intemperance, although it does
not seem to have been of a gross or aggravated description.

Langhorne, an amiable man, and highly popular as well as
warmly beloved in his day, survives now in memory chiefly
through his Plutarch's Lives, and through a few lines in his
'Country Justice,' which are immortalised by the well-known
story of Scott's interview with Burns.   Campbell puts in a plea
besides for his 'Owen of Carron,' but the plea, being founded on
early reading, is partial, and has not been responded to by the
public.

FROM 'THE COUNTRY JUSTICE.'

The social laws from insult to protect,
To cherish peace, to cultivate respect;
The rich from wanton cruelty restrain,
To smooth the bed of penury and pain;
The hapless vagrant to his rest restore,
The maze of fraud, the haunts of theft explore;
The thoughtless maiden, when subdued by art,
To aid, and bring her rover to her heart;
Wild riot's voice with dignity to quell,
Forbid unpeaceful passions to rebel,
Wrest from revenge the meditated harm,
For this fair Justice raised her sacred arm;
For this the rural magistrate, of yore,
Thy honours, Edward, to his mansion bore.
    Oft, where old Air in conscious glory sails,
On silver waves that flow through smiling vales;
In Harewood's groves, where long my youth was laid,
Unseen beneath their ancient world of shade;

With many a group of antique columns crowned,
In Gothic guise such mansion have I found.
   Nor lightly deem, ye apes of modern race,
Ye cits that sore bedizen nature's face,
Of the more manly structures here ye view;
They rose for greatness that ye never knew!
Ye reptile cits, that oft have moved my spleen
With Venus and the Graces on your green!
Let Plutus, growling o'er his ill-got wealth,
Let Mercury, the thriving god of stealth,
The shopman, Janus, with his double looks,
Rise on your mounts, and perch upon your books!
But spare my Venus, spare each sister Grace,
Ye cits, that sore bedizen nature's face!
   Ye royal architects, whose antic taste
Would lay the realms of sense and nature waste;
Forgot, whenever from her steps ye stray,
That folly only points each other way;
Here, though your eye no courtly creature sees,
Snakes on the ground, or monkeys in the trees;
Yet let not too severe a censure fall
On the plain precincts of the ancient hall.
   For though no sight your childish fancy meets,
Of Thibet's dogs, or China's paroquets;
Though apes, asps, lizards, things without a tail,
And all the tribes of foreign monsters fail;
Here shall ye sigh to see, with rust o'ergrown,
The iron griffin and the sphinx of stone;
And mourn, neglected in their waste abodes,
Fire-breathing drakes, and water-spouting gods.
   Long have these mighty monsters known disgrace,
Yet still some trophies hold their ancient place;
Where, round the hall, the oak's high surbase rears
The field-day triumphs of two hundred years.
   222

The enormous antlers here recall the day
That saw the forest monarch forced away;
Who, many a flood, and many a mountain passed,
Not finding those, nor deeming these the last,
O'er floods, o'er mountains yet prepared to fly,
Long ere the death-drop filled his failing eye!
Here famed for cunning, and in crimes grown old,
Hangs his gray brush, the felon of the fold.
Oft as the rent-feast swells the midnight cheer,
The maudlin farmer kens him o'er his beer,
And tells his old, traditionary tale,
Though known to every tenant of the vale.
Here, where of old the festal ox has fed,
Marked with his weight, the mighty horns are spread:
Some ox, O Marshall, for a board like thine,
Where the vast master with the vast sirloin
Vied in round magnitude—Respect I bear
To thee, though oft the ruin of the chair.
These, and such antique tokens that record
The manly spirit, and the bounteous board,
Me more delight than all the gewgaw train,
The whims and zigzags of a modern brain,
More than all Asia's marmosets to view,
Grin, frisk, and water in the walks of Kew.
Through these fair valleys, stranger, hast thou
        strayed,
By any chance, to visit Harewood's shade,
And seen with honest, antiquated air,
In the plain hall the magistratial chair?
There Herbert sat—The love of human kind,
Pure light of truth, and temperance of mind,
In the free eye the featured soul displayed,
Honour's strong beam, and Mercy's melting shade:
Justice that, in the rigid paths of law,

Would still some drops from Pity's fountain draw,
Bend o'er her urn with many a generous fear,
Ere his firm seal should force one orphan's tear;
Fair equity, and reason scorning art,
And all the sober virtues of the heart—
These sat with Herbert, these shall best avail
Where statutes order, or where statutes fail.

Be this, ye rural magistrates, your plan:
Firm be your justice, but be friends to man.

He whom the mighty master of this ball
We fondly deem, or farcically call,
To own the patriarch's truth, however loth,
Holds but a mansion crushed before the moth.

Frail in his genius, in his heart too frail,
Born but to err, and erring to bewail,
Shalt thou his faults with eye severe explore,
And give to life one human weakness more?

Still mark if vice or nature prompts the deed;
Still mark the strong temptation and the need:
On pressing want, on famine's powerful call,
At least more lenient let thy justice fall.

For him who, lost to every hope of life,
Has long with fortune held unequal strife,
Known to no human love, no human care,
The friendless, homeless object of despair;
For the poor vagrant feel, while he complains,
Nor from sad freedom send to sadder chains.
Alike, if folly or misfortune brought
Those last of woes his evil days have wrought;
Believe with social mercy and with me,
Folly 's misfortune in the first degree.

Perhaps on some inhospitable shore
The houseless wretch a widowed parent bore;
Who then, no more by golden prospects led,

224

Of the poor Indian begged a leafy bed.
Cold on Canadian hills, or Minden's plain,
Perhaps that parent mourned her soldier slain;
Bent o'er her babe, her eye dissolved in dew,
The big drops mingling with the milk he drew,
Gave the sad presage of his future years,
The child of misery, baptized in tears!

GIPSIES.

FROM THE SAME.

The gipsy-race my pity rarely move;
Yet their strong thirst of liberty I love:
Not Wilkes, our Freedom's holy martyr, more;
Nor his firm phalanx of the common shore.
  For this in Norwood's patrimonial groves
The tawny father with his offspring roves;
When summer suns lead slow the sultry day,
In mossy caves, where welling waters play,
Fanned by each gale that cools the fervid sky,
With this in ragged luxury they lie.
Oft at the sun the dusky elfins strain
The sable eye, then snugging, sleep again;
Oft as the dews of cooler evening fall,
For their prophetic mother's mantle call.
  Far other cares that wandering mother wait,
The mouth, and oft the minister of fate!
From her to hear, in evening's friendly shade,
Of future fortune, flies the village-maid,
Draws her long-hoarded copper from its hold,
And rusty halfpence purchase hopes of gold.
  But, ah! ye maids, beware the gipsy's lures!
She opens not the womb of time, but yours.
Oft has her hands the hapless Marian wrung,
Marian, whom Gay in sweetest strains has sung!

The parson's maid—sore cause had she to rue
The gipsy's tongue; the parson's daughter too.
Long had that anxious daughter sighed to know
What Vellum's sprucy clerk, the valley's beau,
Meant by those glances which at church he stole,
Her father nodding to the psalm's slow drawl;
Long had she sighed; at length a prophet came,
By many a sure prediction known to fame,
To Marian known, and all she told, for true:
She knew the future, for the past she knew.

A CASE WHERE MERCY SHOULD HAVE MITIGATED JUSTICE.

FROM THE SAME.

Unnumbered objects ask thy honest care,
Beside the orphan's tear, the widow's prayer:
Far as thy power can save, thy bounty bless,
Unnumbered evils call for thy redress.
    Seest thou afar yon solitary thorn,
Whose aged limbs the heath's wild winds have torn?
While yet to cheer the homeward shepherd's eye,
A few seem straggling in the evening sky!
Not many suns have hastened down the day,
Or blushing moons immersed in clouds their way,
Since there, a scene that stained their sacred light,
With horror stopped a felon in his flight;
A babe just born that signs of life expressed,
Lay naked o'er the mother's lifeless breast.
The pitying robber, conscious that, pursued,
He had no time to waste, yet stood and viewed;
To the next cot the trembling infant bore,
And gave a part of what he stole before;
Nor known to him the wretches were, nor dear,
He felt as man, and dropped a human tear.
    226

Far other treatment she who breathless lay,
Found from a viler animal of prey.
　Worn with long toil on many a painful road,
That toil increased by nature's growing load,
When evening brought the friendly hour of rest,
And all the mother thronged about her breast,
The ruffian officer opposed her stay,
And, cruel, bore her in her pangs away,
So far beyond the town's last limits drove,
That to return were hopeless, had she strove;
Abandoned there, with famine, pain, and cold,
And anguish, she expired,—The rest I've told.
　'Now let me swear.　For by my soul's last sigh,
That thief shall live, that overseer shall die.'
　Too late!—his life the generous robber paid,
Lost by that pity which his steps delayed!
No soul-discerning Mansfield sat to hear,
No Hertford bore his prayer to mercy's ear;
No liberal justice first assigned the gaol,
Or urged, as Camplin would have urged, his tale.

SIR WILLIAM BLACKSTONE.

THIS is not the place for writing the life of the great lawyer
whose awful wig has been singed by the sarcasm of Junius.
He was born in London in 1723, and died in 1780. He had
early coquetted with poetry, but on entering the Middle Temple
he bade a 'Farewell to his Muse' in the verses subjoined. So
far as lucre was concerned, he chose the better part, and rose
gradually on the ladder of law to be a knight and a judge in
the Court of Common Pleas. It has been conjectured, from
some notes on Shakspeare published by Stevens, that Sir William continued till the end of his days to hold occasional flirta-
tions with his old flame.

THE LAWYER'S FAREWELL TO HIS MUSE.

As, by some tyrant's stern command,
A wretch forsakes his native land,
In foreign climes condemned to roam
An endless exile from his home;
Pensive he treads the destined way,
And dreads to go, nor dares to stay;
Till on some neighbouring mountain's brow
He stops, and turns his eyes below;
There, melting at the well-known view,
Drops a last tear, and bids adieu:
So I, thus doomed from thee to part,
Gay queen of Fancy, and of Art,
Reluctant move, with doubtful mind
Oft stop, and often look behind.

Companion of my tender age,
Serenely gay, and sweetly sage,
How blithesome were we wont to rove
By verdant hill, or shady grove,
Where fervent bees, with humming voice,
Around the honeyed oak rejoice,
And aged elms with awful bend
In long cathedral walks extend!
Lulled by the lapse of gliding floods,
Cheered by the warbling of the woods,
How blessed my days, my thoughts how free,
In sweet society with thee!
Then all was joyous, all was young,
And years unheeded rolled along:
But now the pleasing dream is o'er,
These scenes must charm me now no more.
Lost to the fields, and torn from you,—
Farewell!—a long, a last adieu.

228

Mo wrangling courts, and stubborn law,
To smoke, and crowds, and cities draw:
There selfish faction rules the day,
And pride and avarice throng the way;
Diseases taint the murky air,
And midnight conflagrations glare;
Loose Revelry and Riot bold
In frighted streets their orgies hold;
Or, where in silence all is drowned,
Fell Murder walks his lonely round;
No room for peace, no room for you,
Adieu, celestial nymph, adieu!

Shakspeare no more, thy sylvan son,
Nor all the art of Addison,
Pope's heaven-strung lyre, nor Waller's ease,
Nor Milton's mighty self, must please:
Instead of these a formal band,
In furs and coifs, around me stand;
With sounds uncouth and accents dry,
That grate the soul of harmony,
Each pedant sage unlocks his store
Of mystic, dark, discordant lore;
And points with tottering hand the ways
That lead me to the thorny maze.

There, in a winding close retreat,
Is Justice doomed to fix her seat;
There, fenced by bulwarks of the law,
She keeps the wondering world in awe;
And there, from vulgar sight retired,
Like eastern queens, is more admired.

Oh, let me pierce the sacred shade
Where dwells the venerable maid!
There humbly mark, with reverent awe,
The guardian of Britannia's law;

Unfold with joy her sacred page,
The united boast of many an age;
Where mixed, yet uniform, appears
The wisdom of a thousand years.
In that pure spring the bottom view,
Clear, deep, and regularly true;
And other doctrines thence imbibe
Than lurk within the sordid scribe;
Observe how parts with parts unite
In one harmonious rule of right;
See countless wheels distinctly tend
By various laws to one great end:
While mighty Alfred's piercing soul
Pervades, and regulates the whole.
   Then welcome business, welcome strife,
Welcome the cares, the thorns of life,
The visage wan, the poreblind sight,
The toil by day, the lamp at night,
The tedious forms, the solemn prate,
The pert dispute, the dull debate,
The drowsy bench, the babbling Hall,
For thee, fair Justice, welcome all!
Thus though my noon of life be passed,
Yet let my setting sun, at last,
Find out the still, the rural cell,
Where sage Retirement loves to dwell!
There let me taste the homefelt bliss
Of innocence and inward peace;
Untainted by the guilty bribe;
Uncursed amid the harpy tribe;
No orphan's cry to wound my ear;
My honour and my conscience clear;
Thus may I calmly meet my end,
Thus to the grave in peace descend.

JOHN SCOTT.

THIS poet is generally known as 'Scott of Amwell.' This ar'
from the fact that his father, a draper in Southwark, where Joh.
was born in 1730, retired ten years afterwards to Amwell. He
had never been inoculated with the small-pox, and such was his
dread of the disease, and that of his family, that for twenty
years, although within twenty miles of London, he never visited
it. His parents, who belonged to the amiable sect of Quakers,
sent him to a day-school at Ware, but that too he left upon the
first alarm of infection. At seventeen, although his education
was much neglected, he began to relish reading, and was mate-
rially assisted in his studies by a neighbour of the name of
Frogley, a master bricklayer, who, though somewhat illiterate,
admired poetry. Scott sent his first essays to the *Gentleman's
Magazine*, and in his thirtieth year published four elegies, which
met with a kind reception, although Dr Johnson said only of
them, 'They are very well, but such as twenty people might
write.' He produced afterwards 'The Garden,' 'Amwell,' and
other poems, besides some rather narrow 'Critical Essays on
the English Poets.' When thirty-six years of age, he sub-
mitted to inoculation, and henceforward visited London fre-
quently, and became acquainted with Dr Johnson, Sir William
Jones, Mrs Montague, and other eminent characters. He was a
very active promoter of local improvements, and diligent in cul-
tivating his grounds and garden. He was twice married, his
first wife being a daughter of his friend Frogley. He died in
1783, not of that disease which he so 'greatly feared,' but of a
putrid fever, at Radcliff. One note of his, entitled 'Ode on
Hearing the Drum,' still reverberates on the ear of poetic readers.
Wordsworth has imitated it in his 'Andrew Jones.' Sir Walter
makes Rachel Geddes say, in 'Redgauntlet,' alluding to books
of verse, 'Some of our people do indeed hold that every writer
who is not with us is against us, but brother Joshua is mitigated
in his opinions, and correspondeth with our friend John Scott
of Amwell, who hath himself constructed verses well approved
of even in the world.'

ODE ON HEARING THE DRUM.

1 I hate that drum's discordant sound,
 Parading round, and round, and round:
 To thoughtless youth it pleasure yields,
 And lures from cities and from fields,
 To sell their liberty for charms
 Of tawdry lace, and glittering arms;
 And when ambition's voice commands,
To march, and fight, and fall, in foreign lands.

2 I hate that drum's discordant sound,
 Parading round, and round, and round:
 To me it talks of ravaged plains,
 And burning towns, and ruined swains,
 And mangled limbs, and dying groans, `
 And widows' tears, and orphans' moans;
 And all that misery's hand bestows,
To fill the catalogue of human woes.

THE TEMPESTUOUS EVENING.

AN ODE.

1 There's grandeur in this sounding storm,
 That drives the hurrying clouds along,
 That on each other seem to throng,
 And mix in many a varied form;
 While, bursting now and then between,
 The moon's dim misty orb is seen,
 And casts faint glimpses on the green.

2 Beneath the blast the forests bend,
 And thick the branchy ruin lies,
 And wide the shower of foliage flies;
 The lake's black waves in tumult blend,

Revolving o'er and o'er and o'er,
And foaming on the rocky shore,
Whose caverns echo to their roar.

3 The sight sublime enrapts my thought,
  And swift along the past it strays,
  And much of strange event surveys,
  What history's faithful tongue has taught,
  Or fancy formed, whose plastic skill
  The page with fabled change can fill
  Of ill to good, or good to ill.

4 But can my soul the scene enjoy,
  That rends another's breast with pain?
  O hapless he, who, near the main,
  Now sees its billowy rage destroy!
  Beholds the foundering bark descend,
  Nor knows but what its fate may end
  The moments of his dearest friend!

ALEXANDER ROSS.

OF this fine old Scottish poet we regret that we can tell our
readers so little. He was born in 1698, became parish schoolmaster at Lochlee in Angusshire, and published, by the advice
of Dr Beattie, in 1768, a volume entitled 'Helenore; or, The
Fortunate Shepherdess: a Pastoral Tale in the Scottish Dialect;
along with a few Songs.' Some of these latter, such as 'Woo'd,
and Married, and a',' became very popular. Beattie loved the
'good-humoured, social, happy old man,' who was 'passing rich'
on twenty pounds a-year, and wrote in the *Aberdeen Journal* a
poetical letter in the Scotch language to promote the sale of his
poem. Ross died in 1784, about eighty-six years old, and is
buried in a churchyard at the east end of the loch.

Lochlee is a very solitary and romantic spot. The road to it from the low country, or Howe of the Mearns, conducts us through a winding, unequal, but very interesting glen, which, after bearing at its foot many patches of corn, yellowing amidst thick green copsewood and birch trees, fades and darkens gradually into a stern, woodless, and rocky defile, which emerges on a solitary loch, lying 'dern and dreary' amidst silent hills. It is one of those lakes which divide the distance between the loch and the tarn, being two miles in length and one in breadth. The hills, which are stony and savage, sink directly down upon its brink. A house or two are all the dwellings in view. The celebrated Thomas Guthrie dearly loves this lake, lives beside it for months at a time, and is often seen rowing his lonely boat in the midst of it, by sunlight and by moonlight too. On the west, one bold, sword-like summit, Craig Macskeldie by name, cuts the air, and relieves the monotony of the other mountains. Fit rest has Ross found in that calm, rural burying-place, beside 'the rude forefathers of the hamlet,' with short, sweet, flower-sprinkled grass covering his dust, the low voice of the lake sounding a few yards from his cold ear, and a plain grave-stone uniting with his native mountains to form his memorial. 'Fortunate Shepherd,' (shall we call him?) to have obtained a grave so intensely characteristic of a Scottish poet!

WOO'D, AND MARRIED, AND A'.

1 The bride cam' out o' the byre,
    And, O, as she dighted her cheeks!
'Sirs, I'm to be married the night,
    And have neither blankets nor sheets;
Have neither blankets nor sheets,
    Nor scarce a coverlet too;
The bride that has a' thing to borrow,
    Has e'en right muckle ado.'
        Woo'd, and married, and a',
           Married, and woo'd, and a'!
        And was she nae very weel off,
           That was woo'd, and married, and a'?

2 Out spake the bride's father,
    As he cam' in frae the pleugh:
'O, haud your tongue my dochter,
    And ye'se get gear enough;
The stirk stands i' the tether,
    And our braw bawsint yade,
Will carry ye hame your corn—
    What wad ye be at, ye jade?'

3 Out spake the bride's mither:
    'What deil needs a' this pride?
I had nae a plack in my pouch
    That night I was a bride;
My gown was linsey-woolsey,
    And ne'er a sark ava;
And ye hae ribbons and buskins,
    Mae than ane or twa.'
      *   *   *   *

4 Out spake the bride's brither,
    As he cam' in wi' the kye:
'Poor Willie wad ne'er hae ta'en ye,
    Had he kent ye as weel as I;
For ye're baith proud and saucy,
    And no for a poor man's wife;
Gin I canna get a better,
    I'se ne'er tak ane i' my life.'
      *   *   *   *

THE ROCK AN' THE WEE PICKLE TOW.

1 There was an auld wife had a wee pickle tow,
    And she wad gae try the spinnin' o't;
But lootin' her doun, her rock took a-lowe,
    And that was an ill beginnin' o't.

She spat on 't, she flat on 't, and tramped on its pate,
But a' she could do it wad ha'e its ain gate;
At last she sat down on 't and bitterly grat,
    For e'er ha'in' tried the spinnin' o't.

2 Foul fa' them that ever advised me to spin,
    It minds me o' the beginnin' o't;
I weel might ha'e ended as I had begun,
    And never ha'e tried the spinnin' o't.
But she's a wise wife wha kens her ain weird,
I thought ance a day it wad never be spier'd,
How let ye the lowe tak' the rock by the beard,
    When ye gaed to try the spinnin' o't?

3 The spinnin', the spinnin', it gars my heart sab
    To think on the ill beginnin' o't;
I took 't in my head to mak' me a wab,
    And that was the first beginnin' o't.
But had I nine daughters, as I ha'e but three,
The safest and soundest advice I wad gi'e,
That they wad frae spinnin' aye keep their heads free,
    For fear o' an ill beginnin' o't.

4 But if they, in spite o' my counsel, wad run
    The dreary, sad task o' the spinnin' o't;
Let them find a lown seat by the light o' the sun,
    And syne venture on the beginnin' o't.
For wha's done as I 've done, alake and awowe!
To busk up a rock at the cheek o' a lowe;
They 'll say that I had little wit in my pow—
    O the muckle black deil tak' the spinnin' o't.

RICHARD GLOVER.

GLOVER was a man so remarkable as to be thought capable of having written the letters of Junius, although no one now almost names his name or reads his poetry. He was the son of a Hamburgh merchant in London, and born (1712) in St Martin's Lane, Cannon Street. He was educated at a private school in Surrey, but being designed for trade, was never sent to a university, yet by his own exertions he became an excellent classical scholar. At sixteen he wrote a poem to the memory of Sir Isaac Newton, and at twenty-five produced nine books of his 'Leonidas.' Partly through its own merits, partly through its liberal political sentiments, and partly through the influence of Lord Cobham, to whom it was inscribed, and the praise of Fielding and Chatham, it became very popular. In 1739, he produced a poem entitled 'London; or, The Progress of Commerce,' and a spirited ballad entitled 'Admiral Hosier's Ghost,' which we have given, both designed to rouse the national spirit against the Spaniards.

Glover was a merchant, and very highly esteemed among his commercial brethren, although at one time unfortunate in business. When forced by his failure to seek retirement, he produced a tragedy on the subject of Boadicea, which ran the usual nine nights, although it has long since ceased to be acted or read. In his later years his affairs improved; he returned again to public life, was elected to Parliament, and approved himself a painstaking and popular M.P. In 1770, he enlarged his 'Leonidas' from nine books to twelve, and afterwards wrote a sequel to it, entitled 'The Athenais.' Glover spent his closing years in opulent retirement, enjoying the intimacy and respect of the most eminent men of the day, and died in 1785.

'Leonidas' may be called the epic of the eighteenth century, and betrays the artificial genius of its age. The poet rises to his flight like a heavy heron—not a hawk or eagle. Passages in it are good, but the effect of the whole is dulness. It reminds you of Cowper's 'Homer,' in which all is accurate, but all is cold, and where even the sound of battle lulls to slumber—or of Edwin

Atherstone's 'Fall of Nineveh,' where you are fatigued with
uniform pomp, and the story struggles and staggers under a load
of words. Thomson exclaimed when he heard of the work of
Glover, 'He write an epic, who never saw a mountain!' And
there was justice in the remark. The success of 'Leonidas'
was probably one cause of the swarm of epics which appeared
in the close of the eighteenth and the beginning of the nineteenth
century.—Cottle himself being, according to De Quincey, 'the
author of four epic poems, *and* a new kind of blacking.' Their
day seems now for ever at an end.

FROM BOOK XII

Song of the Priestess of the Muses to the chosen band after their return from
the inroad into the Persian camp, on the night before the Battle of Ther-
mopylæ.

Back to the pass in gentle march he leads
The embattled warriors.   They, behind the shrubs,
Where Medon sent such numbers to the shades,
In ambush lie.   The tempest is o'erblown.
Soft breezes only from the Malian wave
O'er each grim face, besmeared with smoke and gore,
Their cool refreshment breathe.   The healing gale,
A crystal rill near Œta's verdant feet,
Dispel the languor from their harassed nerves,
Fresh braced by strength returning.   O'er their heads
Lo! in full blaze of majesty appears
Melissa, bearing in her hand divine
The eternal guardian of illustrious deeds,
The sweet Phœbean lyre.   Her graceful train
Of white-robed virgins, seated on a range
Half down the cliff, o'ershadowing the Greeks,
All with concordant strings, and accents clear,
A torrent pour of melody, and swell
A high, triumphal, solemn dirge of praise,
Anticipating fame.   Of endless joys

In blessed Elysium was the song.   Go, meet
Lycurgus, Solon, and Zaleucus sage,
Let them salute the children of their laws.
Meet Homer, Orpheus, and the Ascræan bard,
Who with a spirit, by ambrosial food
Refined, and more exalted, shall contend
Your splendid fate to warble through the bowers
Of amaranth and myrtle ever young,
Like your renown.   Your ashes we will cull.
In yonder fane deposited, your urns,
Dear to the Muses, shall our lays inspire.
Whatever offerings, genius, science, art
Can dedicate to virtue, shall be yours,
The gifts of all the Muses, to transmit
You on the enlivened canvas, marble, brass,
In wisdom's volume, in the poet's song,
In every tongue, through every age and clime,
You of this earth the brightest flowers, not cropt,
Transplanted only to immortal bloom
Of praise with men, of happiness with gods.

ADMIRAL HOSIER'S GHOST.

ON THE TAKING OF PORTO-BELLO FROM THE SPANIARDS BY ADMIRAL VERNON—
Nov. 22, 1739.

1 As near Porto-Bello lying
      On the gently swelling flood,
   At midnight with streamers flying,
      Our triumphant navy rode:
   There while Vernon sat all-glorious
      From the Spaniards' late defeat;
   And his crews, with shouts victorious,
      Drank success to England's fleet:

2 On a sudden shrilly sounding,
　　Hideous yells and shrieks were heard;
　Then each heart with fear confounding,
　　A sad troop of ghosts appeared,
　All in dreary hammocks shrouded,
　　Which for winding-sheets they wore,
　And with looks by sorrow clouded,
　　Frowning on that hostile shore.

3 On them gleamed the moon's wan lustre,
　　When the shade of Hosier brave
　His pale bands was seen to muster,
　　Rising from their watery grave:
　O'er the glimmering wave he hied him,
　　Where the Burford[1] reared her sail,
　With three thousand ghosts beside him,
　　And in groans did Vernon hail:

4 'Heed, O heed, our fatal story,
　　I am Hosier's injured ghost,
　You, who now have purchased glory
　　At this place where I was lost;
　Though in Porto-Bello's ruin
　　You now triumph free from fears,
　When you think on our undoing,
　　You will mix your joy with tears.

5 'See these mournful spectres, sweeping
　　Ghastly o'er this hated wave,
　Whose wan cheeks are stained with weeping;
　　These were English captains brave:
　Mark those numbers pale and horrid,
　　Those were once my sailors bold,
　Lo! each hangs his drooping forehead,
　　While his dismal tale is told.

[1] 'The Burford:' Admiral Vernon's ship.

6 'I, by twenty sail attended,
    Did·this Spanish town affright:
Nothing then its wealth defended
    But my orders not to fight:
Oh! that in this rolling ocean
    I had cast them with disdain,
And obeyed my heart's warm motion,
    To have quelled the pride of Spain.

7 'For resistance I could fear none,
    But with twenty ships had done
What thou, brave and happy Vernon,
    Hast achieved with six alone.
Then the Bastimentos never
    Had our foul dishonour seen,
Nor the sea the sad receiver
    Of this gallant train had been.

8 'Thus, like thee, proud Spain dismaying,
    And her galleons leading home,
Though condemned for disobeying,
    I had met a traitor's doom;
To have fallen, my country crying,
    He has played an English part,
Had been better far than dying
    Of a grieved and broken heart.

9 'Unrepining at thy glory,
    Thy successful arms we hail;
But remember our sad story,
    And let Hosier's wrongs prevail.
Sent in this foul clime to languish,
    Think what thousands fell in vain,
Wasted with disease and anguish,
    Not in glorious battle slain.

10 'Hence, with all my train attending
      From their oozy tombs below,
   Through the hoary foam ascending,
      Here I feed my constant woe:
   Here the Bastimentos viewing,
      We recall our shameful doom,
   And our plaintive cries renewing,
      Wander through the midnight gloom.

11 'O'er these waves for ever mourning
      Shall we roam deprived of rest,
   If to Britain's shores returning,
      You neglect my just request.
   After this proud foe subduing,
      When your patriot friends you see,
   Think on vengeance for my ruin,
      And for England shamed in me.'

WILLIAM WHITEHEAD.

THERE was also a Paul Whitehead, who wrote a satire entitled
'Manners,' which is highly praised by Boswell, and mentioned
contemptuously by Campbell, and who lives in the couplet of
Churchill—

> 'May I (can worse disgrace on manhood fall?)
> Be born a Whitehead, and baptized a Paul.'

William Whitehead was the son of a baker in Cambridge,
was born in 1715, and studied first at Winchester, and then in
Clare Hall, in his own city. He became tutor to the son of the
Earl of Jersey, wrote one or two poor plays, and in 1757, on
the death of Colley Cibber, was appointed Poet-Laureate—the
office having previously been refused by Gray. This roused
against him a large class of those 'beings capable of envying
even a poet-laureate,' to use Gray's expression, and especially

242

the wrath of Churchill, then the man-mountain of satiric literature, who, in his 'Ghost,' says—

> 'But he who in the laureate chair,
> By grace, not merit, planted there,
> In awkward pomp is seen to sit,
> And by his patent proves his wit,' &c.

To these attacks Whitehead, who was a good-natured and
modest man, made no reply. In his latter years the Laureate
resided in the family of Lord Jersey, and died in 1785. His
poem called 'Variety' is light and pleasant, and deserves a
niche in our 'Specimens.'

VARIETY.

A TALE FOR MARRIED PEOPLE.

A gentle maid, of rural breeding,
By Nature first, and then by reading,
Was filled with all those soft sensations
Which we restrain in near relations,
Lest future husbands should be jealous,
And think their wives too fond of fellows.
  The morning sun beheld her rove
A nymph, or goddess of the grove!
At eve she paced the dewy lawn,
And called each clown she saw, a faun!
Then, scudding homeward, locked her door,
And turned some copious volume o'er.
For much she read; and chiefly those
Great authors, who in verse, or prose,
Or something betwixt both, unwind
The secret springs which move the mind.
These much she read; and thought she knew
The human heart's minutest clue;
Yet shrewd observers still declare,
(To show how shrewd observers are,)
Though plays, which breathed heroic flame,

And novels, in profusion, came,
Imported fresh-and-fresh from France,
She only read the heart's romance.
    The world, no doubt, was well enough
To smooth the manners of the rough;
Might please the giddy and the vain,
Those tinselled slaves of folly's train:
But, for her part, the truest taste
She found was in retirement placed,
Where, as in verse it sweetly flows,
'On every thorn instruction grows.'
    Not that she wished to 'be alone,'
As some affected prudes have done;
She knew it was decreed on high
We should 'increase and multiply;'
And therefore, if kind Fate would grant
Her fondest wish, her only want,
A cottage with the man she loved
Was what her gentle heart approved;
In some delightful solitude
Where step profane might ne'er intrude;
But Hymen guard the sacred ground,
And virtuous Cupids hover round.
Not such as flutter on a fan
Round Crete's vile bull, or Leda's swan,
(Who scatter myrtles, scatter roses,
And hold their fingers to their noses,)
But simpering, mild, and innocent,
As angels on a monument.
    Fate heard her prayer: a lover came,
Who felt, like her, the innoxious flame;
One who had trod, as well as she,
The flowery paths of poesy;
Had warmed himself with Milton's heat,

244

Could every line of Pope repeat,
Or chant in Shenstone's tender strains,
'The lover's hopes,' 'the lover's pains.'
    Attentive to the charmer's tongue,
With him she thought no evening long;
With him she sauntered half the day;
And sometimes, in a laughing way,
Ran o'er the catalogue by rote
Of who might marry, and who not;
'Consider, sir, we're near relations—'
'I hope so in our inclinations.'—
In short, she looked, she blushed consent;
He grasped her hand, to church they went;
And every matron that was there,
    With tongue so voluble and supple,
Said for her part, she must declare,
    She never saw a finer couple.
O halcyon days! 'Twas Nature's reign,
'Twas Tempe's vale, and Enna's plain,
The fields assumed unusual bloom,
And every zephyr breathed perfume,
The laughing sun with genial beams
Danced lightly on the exulting streams;
And the pale regent of the night
In dewy softness shed delight.
'Twas transport not to be expressed;
'Twas Paradise!—But mark the rest.
    Two smiling springs had waked the flowers
That paint the meads, or fringe the bowers,
(Ye lovers, lend your wondering ears,
Who count by months, and not by years,)
Two smiling springs had chaplets wove
To crown their solitude, and love:
When lo, they find, they can't tell how,

Their walks are not so pleasant now.
The seasons sure were changed; the place
Had, somehow, got a different face.
Some blast had struck the cheerful scene;
The lawns, the woods, were not so green.
The purling rill, which murmured by,
And once was liquid harmony,
Became a sluggish, reedy pool:
The days grew hot, the evenings cool.
The moon, with all the starry reign,
Were melancholy's silent train.
And then the tedious winter night—
They could not read by candle-light.

    Full oft, unknowing why they did,
They called in adventitious aid.
A faithful, favourite dog ('twas thus
With Tobit and Telemachus)
Amused their steps; and for a while
They viewed his gambols with a smile.
The kitten too was comical,
She played so oddly with her tail,
Or in the glass was pleased to find
Another cat, and peeped behind.

    A courteous neighbour at the door
Was deemed intrusive noise no more.
For rural visits, now and then,
Are right, as men must live with men.
Then cousin Jenny, fresh from town,
    A new recruit, a dear delight!
Made many a heavy hour go down,
At morn, at noon, at eve, at night:
Sure they could hear her jokes for ever,
She was so sprightly, and so clever!

    Yet neighbours were not quite the thing;

What joy, alas! could converse bring
With awkward creatures bred at home?—
The dog grew dull, or troublesome.
The cat had spoiled the kitten's merit,
And, with her youth, had lost her spirit.
And jokes repeated o'er and o'er,
Had quite exhausted Jenny's store.
—'And then, my dear, I can't abide
This always sauntering side by side.'
'Enough!' he cries, 'the reason 's plain:
For causes never rack your brain.
Our neighbours are like other folks,
Skip's playful tricks, and Jenny's jokes,
Are still delightful, still would please;
Were we, my dear, ourselves at ease.
Look round, with an impartial eye,
On yonder fields, on yonder sky;
The azure cope, the flowers below,
With all their wonted colours glow.
The rill still murmurs; and the moon
Shines, as she did, a softer sun.
No change has made the seasons fail,
No comet brushed us with his tail.
The scene 's the same, the same the weather—
We live, my dear, too much together.'
    Agreed.   A rich old uncle dies,
And added wealth the means supplies.
With eager haste to town they flew,
Where all must please, for all was new.
    But here, by strict poetic laws,
Description claims its proper pause.
    The rosy morn had raised her head
From old Tithonus' saffron bed;
And embryo sunbeams from the east,

247

Half-choked, were struggling through the mist,
When forth advanced the gilded chaise;
The village crowded round to gaze.
The pert postilion, now promoted
From driving plough, and neatly booted,
His jacket, cap, and baldric on,
(As greater folks than he have done,)
Looked round; and, with a coxcomb air,
Smacked loud his lash.   The happy pair
Bowed graceful, from a separate door,
And Jenny, from the stool before.
    Roll swift, ye wheels! to willing eyes
New objects every moment rise.
Each carriage passing on the road,
From the broad waggon's ponderous load
To the light car, where mounted high
The giddy driver seems to fly,
Were themes for harmless satire fit,
And gave fresh force to Jenny's wit.
Whate'er occurred, 'twas all delightful,
No noise was harsh, no danger frightful.
The dash and splash through thick and thin,
The hairbreadth 'scapes, the bustling inn,
(Where well-bred landlords were so ready
To welcome in the 'squire and lady,)
Dirt, dust, and sun, they bore with ease,
Determined to be pleased, and please.
    Now nearer town, and all agog,
They know dear London by its fog.
Bridges they cross, through lanes they wind,
Leave Hounslow's dangerous heath behind,
Through Brentford win a passage free
By roaring, 'Wilkes and Liberty!'
At Knightsbridge bless the shortening way,
248

Where Bays's troops in ambush lay,
O'er Piccadilly's pavement glide,
With palaces to grace its side,
Till Bond Street with its lamps a-blaze
Concludes the journey of three days.
    Why should we paint, in tedious song,
How every day, and all day long,
They drove at first with curious haste
Through Lud's vast town; or, as they passed
'Midst risings, fallings, and repairs
Of streets on streets, and squares on squares,
Describe how strong their wonder grew
At buildings—and at builders too?
    Scarce less astonishment arose
At architects more fair than those—
Who built as high, as widely spread
The enormous loads that clothed their head.
For British dames new follies love,
And, if they can't invent, improve.
Some with erect pagodas vie,
Some nod, like Pisa's tower, awry,
Medusa's snakes, with Pallas' crest,
Convolved, contorted, and compressed;
With intermingling trees, and flowers,
And corn, and grass, and shepherd's bowers,
Stage above stage the turrets run,
Like pendent groves of Babylon,-
Till nodding from the topmost wall
Otranto's plumes envelop all!
Whilst the black ewes, who owned the hair,
Feed harmless on, in pastures fair,
Unconscious that their tails perfume,
In scented curls, the drawing-room.
    When Night her murky pinions spread,

And sober folks retire to bed,
To every public place they flow,
Where Jenny told them who was who.
Money was always at command,
And tripped with pleasure hand in hand.
Money was equipage, was show,
Gallini's, Almack's, and Soho;
The *passe-partout* through every vein
Of dissipation's hydra reign.

O London, thou prolific source,
Parent of vice, and folly's nurse!
Fruitful as Nile, thy copious springs
Spawn hourly births—and all with stings:
But happiest far the he, or she,
I know not which, that livelier dunce
Who first contrived the coterie,
To crush domestic bliss at once.
Then grinned, no doubt, amidst the dames,
As Nero fiddled to the flames.

Of thee, Pantheon, let me speak
With reverence, though in numbers weak;
Thy beauties satire's frown beguile,
We spare the follies for the pile.
Flounced, furbelowed, and tricked for show,
With lamps above, and lamps below,
Thy charms even modern taste defied,
They could not spoil thee, though they tried.

Ah, pity that Time's hasty wings
Must sweep thee off with vulgar things!
Let architects of humbler name
On frail materials build their fame,
Their noblest works the world might want,
Wyatt should build in adamant.

But what are these to scenes which lie

Secreted from the vulgar eye,
And baffle all the powers of song?—
A brazen throat, an iron tongue,
(Which poets wish for, when at length
Their subject soars above their strength,)
Would shun the task.   Our humbler Muse,
Who only reads the public news
And idly utters what she gleans
From chronicles and magazines,
Recoiling feels her feeble fires,
And blushing to her shades retires,
Alas! she knows not how to treat
The finer follies of the great,
Where even, Democritus, thy sneer
Were vain as Heraclitus' tear.
    Suffice it that by just degrees
They reached all heights, and rose with ease;
(For beauty wins its way, uncalled,
And ready dupes are ne'er black-balled.)
Each gambling dame she knew, and he
Knew every shark of quality;
From the grave cautious few who live
On thoughtless youth, and living thrive,
To the light train who mimic France,
And the soft sons of *nonchalance*.
While Jenny, now no more of use,
Excuse succeeding to excuse,
Grew piqued, and prudently withdrew
To shilling whist, and chicken loo.
    Advanced to fashion's wavering head,
They now, where once they followed, led.
Devised new systems of delight,
A-bed all day, and up all night,
In different circles reigned supreme.

Wives copied her, and husbands him;
Till so divinely life ran on,
So separate, so quite *bon-ton*,
That meeting in a public place,
They scarcely knew each other's face.
　　At last they met, by his desire,
A *tête-à-tête* across the fire;
Looked in each other's face awhile,
With half a tear, and half a smile.
The ruddy health, which wont to grace
With manly glow his rural face,
Now scarce retained its faintest streak;
So sallow was his leathern cheek.
She lank, and pale, and hollow-eyed,
With rouge had striven in vain to hide
What once was beauty, and repair
The rapine of the midnight air.
　　Silence is eloquence, 'tis said.
Both wished to speak, both hung the head.
At length it burst.——' 'Tis time,' he cries,
' When tired of folly, to be wise.
Are you too tired ? '—then checked a groan.
She wept consent, and he went on:
　' How delicate the married life !
You love your husband, I my wife !
Not even satiety could tame,
Nor dissipation quench the flame.
　' True to the bias of our kind,
'Tis happiness we wish to find.
In rural scenes retired we sought
In vain the dear, delicious draught,
Though blest with love's indulgent store,
We found we wanted something more.
'Twas company, 'twas friends to share

252

The bliss we languished to declare.
'Twas social converse, change of scene,
To soothe the sullen hour of spleen;
Short absences to wake desire,
And sweet regrets to fan the fire.
  ' We left the lonesome place; and found,
In dissipation's giddy round,
A thousand novelties to wake
The springs of life and not to break.
As, from the nest not wandering far,
In light excursions through the air,
The feathered tenants of the grove
Around in mazy circles move,
Sip the cool springs that murmuring flow,
Or taste the blossom on the bough.
We sported freely with the rest;
And still, returning to the nest,
In easy mirth we chatted o'er
The trifles of the day before.
  ' Behold us now, dissolving quite
In the full ocean of delight;
In pleasures every hour employ,
Immersed in all the world calls joy;
Our affluence easing the expense
Of splendour and magnificence;
Our company, the exalted set
Of all that's gay, and all that's great:
Nor happy yet!—and where's the wonder!—
We live, my dear, too much asunder.'
  The moral of my tale is this,
Variety's the soul of bless;
But such variety alone
As makes our home the more our own.
As from the heart's impelling power

The life-blood pours its genial store;
Though taking each a various way,
The active streams meandering play
Through every artery, every vein,
All to the heart return again;
From thence resume their new career,
But still return and centre there:
So real happiness below
Must from the heart sincerely flow;
Nor, listening to the syren's song,
Must stray too far, or rest too long.
All human pleasures thither tend;
Must there begin, and there must end;
Must there recruit their languid force,
And gain fresh vigour from their source.

WILLIAM JULIUS MICKLE.

THIS poet was born in Langholm, Dumfriesshire, in 1734.
His father was minister of the parish, but removed to Edinburgh,
where William, after attending the High School, became clerk
to a brewery, and ultimately a partner in the concern. In this
he failed, however; and in 1764 he repaired to London to prosecute literature. Lord Lyttelton became his patron, although
he did him so little service in a secular point of view, that
Mickle was fain to accept the situation of corrector to the Cla-
rendon Press at Oxford. Here he published his ' Pollio,' his
' Concubine,'—a poem in the manner of Spenser, very sweetly
and musically written, which became popular,—and in 1771 the
first canto of a translation of the 'Lusiad' of Camoens. This
translation, which he completed in 1775, was published by subscription, and at once increased his fortune and established his
fame. He had resigned his office of corrector of the press, and
was residing with Mr Tomkins, a farmer at Foresthill, near

254

Oxford.   In 1779, he went out to Portugal as secretary to Commodore Johnstone, and, as the translator of Camoens, was received with much distinction.   On his return with a little money, he married Mr Tomkins' daughter, who had a little more, and took up his permanent residence at Foresthill, where he died of a short illness in 1788.

His translation of the 'Lusiad' is understood to be too free and flowery, and the translator stands in the relation to Camoens which Pope does to Homer. 'Cumnor Hall' has suggested to Scott his brilliant romance of 'Kenilworth,' and is a garland worthy of being bound up in the beautiful locks of Amy Robsart for evermore. 'Are ye sure the news is true?' is a song true to the very soul of Scottish and of general nature, and worthy, as Burns says, of 'the first poet.'

CUMNOR HALL.

1 The dews of summer night did fall,
    The moon, sweet regent of the sky,
Silvered the walls of Cumnor Hall,
    And many an oak that grew thereby.

2 Now nought was heard beneath the skies,
    The sounds of busy life were still,
Save an unhappy lady's sighs,
    That issued from that lonely pile.

3 'Leicester,' she cried, 'is this thy love
    That thou so oft hast sworn to me,
To leave me in this lonely grove,
    Immured in shameful privity?

4 'No more thou com'st, with lover's speed,
    Thy once beloved bride to see ;
But be she alive, or be she dead,
    I fear, stern Earl, 's the same to thee.

5 'Not so the usage I received
      When happy in my father's hall;
  No faithless husband then me grieved,
      No chilling fears did me appal.

6 'I rose up with the cheerful morn,
      No lark so blithe, no flower more gay;
  And, like the bird that haunts the thorn,
      So merrily sung the livelong day.

7 'If that my beauty is but small,
      Among court ladies all despised,
  Why didst thou rend it from that hall,
      Where, scornful Earl, it well was prized?

8 'And when you first to me made suit,
      How fair I was, you oft would say!
  And, proud of conquest, plucked the fruit,
      Then left the blossom to decay.

9 'Yes! now neglected and despised,
      The rose is pale, the lily's dead;
  But he that once their charms so prized,
      Is sure the cause those charms are fled.

10 'For know, when sickening grief doth prey,
      And tender love's repaid with scorn,
  The sweetest beauty will decay:
      What floweret can endure the storm?

11 'At court, I'm told, is beauty's throne,
      Where every lady's passing rare,
  That eastern flowers, that shame the sun,
      Are not so glowing, not so fair.

12 'Then, Earl, why didst thou leave the beds
    Where roses and where lilies vie,
To seek a primrose, whose pale shades
    Must sicken when those gauds are by?

13 ''Mong rural beauties I was one;
    Among the fields wild-flowers are fair;
Some country swain might me have won,
    And thought my passing beauty rare.

14 'But, Leicester, or I much am wrong,
    It is not beauty lures thy vows;
Rather ambition's gilded crown
    Makes thee forget thy humble spouse.

15 'Then, Leicester, why, again I plead,
    The injured surely may repine,
Why didst thou wed a country maid,
    When some fair princess might be thine?

16 'Why didst thou praise my humble charms,
    And, oh! then leave them to decay?
Why didst thou win me to thy arms,
    Then leave me to mourn the livelong day?.

17 'The village maidens of the plain
    Salute me lowly as they go:
Envious they mark my silken train,
    Nor think a countess can have woe.

18 'The simple nymphs! they little know
    How far more happy's their estate;
To smile for joy, than sigh for woe;
    To be content, than to be great.

19 'How far less blessed am I than them,
       Daily to pine and waste with care!
    Like the poor plant, that, from its stem
       Divided, feels the chilling air.

20 'Nor, cruel Earl! can I enjoy
       The humble charms of solitude;
    Your minions proud my peace destroy,
       By sullen frowns, or pratings rude.

21 'Last night, as sad I chanced to stray,
       The village death-bell smote my ear;
    They winked aside, and seemed to say,
       "Countess, prepare—thy end is near."

22 'And now, while happy peasants sleep,
       Here I sit lonely and forlorn;
    No one to soothe me as I weep,
       Save Philomel on yonder thorn.

23 'My spirits flag, my hopes decay;
       Still that dread death-bell smites my ear;
    And many a body seems to say,
       "Countess, prepare—thy end is near."'

24 Thus sore and sad that lady grieved
       In Cumnor Hall, so lone and drear;
    And many a heartfelt sigh she heaved,
       And let fall many a bitter tear.

25 And ere the dawn of day appeared,
       In Cumnor Hall, so lone and drear,
    Full many a piercing scream was heard,
       And many a cry of mortal fear.

258

26 The death-bell thrice was heard to ring,
    An aërial voice was heard to call,
And thrice the raven flapped his wing
    Around the towers of Cumnor Hall.

27 The mastiff howled at village door,
    The oaks were shattered on the green;
Woe was the hour, for never more
    That hapless Countess e'er was seen.

28 And in that manor, now no more
    Is cheerful feast or sprightly ball;
For ever since that dreary hour
    Have spirits haunted Cumnor Hall.

29 The village maids, with fearful glance,
    Avoid the ancient moss-grown wall;
Nor never lead the merry dance
    Among the groves of Cumnor Hall.

30 Full many a traveller has sighed,
    And pensive wept the Countess' fall,
As wandering onwards they 've espied
    The haunted towers of Cumnor Hall.

THE MARINER'S WIFE.

1 But are yo sure the news is true?
    And are ye sure he 's weel?
Is this a time to think o' wark?
    Ye jauds, fling by your wheel.
      For there 's nae luck about the house,
        There 's nae luck at a',
      There 's nae luck about the house,
      When our gudeman 's awa.

2 Is this a time to think o' wark,
    When Colin's at the door?
  Rax down my cloak—I'll to the quay,
    And see him come ashore.

3 Rise up and mak a clean fireside,
    Put on the mickle pat;
  Gie little Kate her cotton goun,
    And Jock his Sunday's coat.

4 And mak their shoon as black as slaes,
    Their stockins white as snaw;
  It's a' to pleasure our gudeman—
    He likes to see them braw.

5 There are twa hens into the crib,
    Hae fed this month and mair;
  Mak haste and thraw their necks about,
    That Colin weel may fare.

6 My Turkey slippers I'll put on,
    My stockins pearl blue—
  It's a' to pleasure our gudeman,
    For he's baith leal and true.

7 Sae sweet his voice, sae smooth his tongue;
    His breath's like caller air;
  His very fit has music in 't,
    As he comes up the stair.

8 And will I see his face again?
    And will I hear him speak?
  I'm downright dizzy wi' the thought:
    In troth I'm like to greet.

LORD NUGENT.

ROBERT CRAGGS, afterwards created Lord Nugent, was an Irishman, a younger son of Michael Nugent, by the daughter of Robert, Lord Trimlestown, and born in 1709. He was in 1741 elected M.P. for St Mawes, in Cornwall, and became in 1747 comptroller to the Prince of Wales' household. He afterwards made peace with the Court, and received various promotions and marks of favour besides the peerage. In 1739, he published anonymously a volume of poems possessing considerable merit. He was converted from Popery, and wrote some vigorous verses on the occasion. Unfortunately, however, he relapsed, and again celebrated the event in a very weak poem, entitled 'Faith.' He died in 1788. Although a man of decided talent, as his 'Ode to Mankind' proves, Nugent does not stand very high either in the catalogue of Irish patriots or of 'royal and noble authors.'

ODE TO MANKIND.

1 Is there, or do the schoolmen dream?
   Is there on earth a power supreme,
     The delegate of Heaven,
   To whom an uncontrolled command,
   In every realm o'er sea and land,
     By special grace is given?

2 Then say, what signs this god proclaim?
   Dwells he amidst the diamond's flame,
     A throne his hallowed shrine?
   The borrowed pomp, the armed array,
   Want, fear, and impotence, betray
     Strange proofs of power divine!

3 If service due from human kind,
   To men in slothful ease reclined,
     Can form a sovereign's claim:

Hail, monarchs! ye, whom Heaven ordains,
Our toils unshared, to share our gains,
   Ye idiots, blind and lame!

4 Superior virtue, wisdom, might,
Create and mark the ruler's right,
   So reason must conclude:
Then thine it is, to whom belong
The wise, the virtuous, and the strong,
   Thrice sacred multitude!

5 In thee, vast All! are these contained,
For thee are those, thy parts ordained,
   So nature's systems roll:
The sceptre 's thine, if such there be;
If none there is, then thou art free,
   Great monarch! mighty whole!

6 Let the proud tyrant rest his cause
On faith, prescription, force, or laws,
   An host's or senate's voice!
His voice affirms thy stronger due,
Who for the many made the few,
   And gave the species choice.

7 Unsanctified by thy command,
Unowned by thee, the sceptred hand
   The trembling slave may bind;
But loose from nature's moral ties,
The oath by force imposed belies
   The unassenting mind.

8 Thy will 's thy rule, thy good its end;
You punish only to defend
   What parent nature gave:

And he who dares her gifts invade,
By nature's oldest law is made
　　Thy victim or thy slave.

9　Thus reason founds the just degree
On universal liberty,
　　Not private rights resigned:
Through various nature's wide extent,
No private beings e'er were meant
　　To hurt the general kind.

10　Thee justice guides, thee right maintains,
The oppressor's wrongs, the pilferer's gains,
　　Thy injured weal impair.
Thy warmest passions soon subside,
Nor partial envy, hate, nor pride,
　　Thy tempered counsels share.

11　Each instance of thy vengeful rage,
Collected from each clime and age,
　　Though malice swell the sum,
Would seem a spotless scanty scroll,
Compared with Marius' bloody roll,
　　Or Sylla's hippodrome.

12　But thine has been imputed blame,
The unworthy few assume thy name,
　　The rabble weak and loud;
Or those who on thy ruins feast,
The lord, the lawyer, and the priest;
　　A more ignoble crowd.

13　Avails it thee, if one devours,
Or lesser spoilers share his powers,
　　While both thy claim oppose?

Monsters who wore thy sullied crown,
Tyrants who pulled those monsters down,
    Alike to thee were foes.

14 Far other shone fair Freedom's band,
Far other was the immortal stand,
    When Hampden fought for thee:
They snatched from rapine's gripe thy spoils,
The fruits and prize of glorious toils,
    Of arts and industry.

15 On thee yet foams the preacher's rage,
On thee fierce frowns the historian's page,
    A false apostate train:
Tears stream adown the martyr's tomb;
Unpitied in their harder doom,
    Thy thousands strow the plain.

16 These had no charms to please the sense,
No graceful port, no eloquence,
    To win the Muse's throng:
Unknown, unsung, unmarked they lie;
But Cæsar's fate o'ercasts the sky,
    And Nature mourns his wrong.

17 Thy foes, a frontless band, invade;
Thy friends afford a timid aid,
    And yield up half the right.
Even Locke beams forth a mingled ray,
Afraid to pour the flood of day
    On man's too feeble sight.

18 Hence are the motley systems framed,
Of right transferred, of power reclaimed;
    Distinctions weak and vain.

Wise nature mocks the wrangling herd;
For unreclaimed, and untransferred,
  Her powers and rights remain.

19 While law the royal agent moves,
The instrument thy choice approves,
  We bow through him to you.
But change, or cease the inspiring choice,
The sovereign sinks a private voice,
  Alike in one, or few!

20 Shall then the wretch, whose dastard heart
Shrinks at a tyrant's nobler part,
  And only dares betray;
With reptile wiles, alas! prevail,
Where force, and rage, and priestcraft fail,
  To pilfer power away?

21 Oh! shall the bought, and buying tribe,
The slaves who take, and deal the bribe,
  A people's claims enjoy!
So Indian murderers hope to gain
The powers and virtues of the slain,
  Of wretches they destroy.

22 'Avert it, Heaven! you love the brave,
You hate the treacherous, willing slave,
  The self-devoted head;
Nor shall an hireling's voice convey
That sacred prize to lawless sway,
  For which a nation bled.'

23 Vain prayer, the coward's weak resource!
Directing reason, active force,
  Propitious Heaven bestows.

> But ne'er shall flame the thundering sky,
> To aid the trembling herd that fly
>   Before their weaker foes.

24 In names there dwell no magic charms,
    The British virtues, British arms
        Unloosed our fathers' band:
    Say, Greece and Rome! if these should fail,
    What names, what ancestors avail,
        To save a sinking land?

25 Far, far from us such ills shall be,
    Mankind shall boast one nation free,
        One monarch truly great:
    Whose title speaks a people's choice,
    Whose sovereign will a people's voice,
        Whose strength a prosperous state.

JOHN LOGAN.

JOHN LOGAN was born in the year 1748.   He was the son of a
farmer at Soutra, in the parish of Fala, Mid-Lothian.   He was
educated for the church at Edinburgh, where he became intimate with Robertson, afterwards the historian.   So, at least,
Campbell asserts; but he strangely calls him a student of the
same standing, whereas, in fact, Robertson saw light in 1721,
and had been a settled minister five years before Logan was
born.   After finishing his studies, he became tutor in the family
of Mr Sinclair of Ulbster, and the late well-known Sir John
Sinclair was one of his pupils.   When licensed to preach, Logan
became popular, and was in his twenty-fifth year appointed one
of the ministers of South Leith.   In 1781, he read in Edinburgh
a course of lectures on the Philosophy of History, and in 1782,
he printed one of them, on the Government of Asia.   In the same
year he published a volume of poems, which were well received.

266

In 1783, he wrote a tragedy called 'Runnymede,' which was, owing to some imagined incendiary matter, prohibited from being acted on the London boards, but which was produced on the Edinburgh stage, and afterwards published. This, along with some alleged irregularities of conduct on the part of Logan, tended to alienate his flock, and he was induced to retire on a small annuity. He betook himself to London, where, in conjunction with the Rev. Mr Thomson,—who had left the parish of Monzievaird, in Perthshire, owing to a scandal,—he wrote for the *English Review*, and was employed to defend Warren Hastings. This he did in an able manner, although a well-known story describes him as listening to Sheridan, on the Oude case, with intense interest, and exclaiming, after the first hour, 'This is mere declamation without proof'—after the next two, 'This is a man of extraordinary powers '—and ere the close of the matchless oration, 'Of all the monsters in history, Warren Hastings is the vilest.' Logan died in the year 1788, in his lodgings, Marlborough Street. His sermons were published shortly after his death, and if parts of them are, as is alleged, pilfered from a Swiss divine, (George Joachim Zollikofer,) they have not remained exclusively with the thief, since no sermons have been so often reproduced in Scottish pulpits as the elegant orations issued under the name of Logan.

We have already declined to enter on the controversy about 'The Cuckoo,' intimating, however, our belief, founded partly upon Logan's unscrupulous character and partly on internal evidence, that it was originally written by Bruce, but probably polished to its present perfection by Logan, whose other writings give us rather the impression of a man of varied accomplishments and excellent taste, than of deep feeling or original genius. If Logan were not the author of 'The Cuckoo,' there was a special baseness connected with the fact, that when Burke sought him out in Edinburgh, solely from his admiration of that poem, he owned the soft and false impeachment, and rolled as a sweet morsel praise from the greatest man of the age, which he knew was the rightful due of another.

THE LOVERS.

1   *Har.* 'Tis midnight dark: 'tis silence deep,
My father's house is hushed in sleep;
In dreams the lover meets his bride,
She sees her lover at her side;
The mourner's voice is now suppressed,
A while the weary are at rest:
'Tis midnight dark; 'tis silence deep;
I only wake, and wake to weep.

2 The window's drawn, the ladder waits,
I spy no watchman at the gates;
No tread re-echoes through the hall,
No shadow moves along the wall.
I am alone. 'Tis dreary night,
Oh, come, thou partner of my flight!
Shield me from darkness, from alarms;
Oh, take me trembling to thine arms!

3 The dog howls dismal in the heath,
The raven croaks the dirge of death;
Ah me! disaster's in the sound!
The terrors of the night are round;
A sad mischance my fears forebode,
The demon of the dark's abroad,
And lures, with apparition dire,
The night-struck man through flood and fire.

4 The owlet screams ill-boding sounds,
The spirit walks unholy rounds;
The wizard's hour eclipsing rolls;
The shades of hell usurp the poles;
The moon retires; the heaven departs.
From opening earth a spectre starts:

My spirit dies—Away, my fears!
My love, my life, my lord, appears!

5   *Hen.* I come, I come, my love! my life!
And, nature's dearest name, my wife!
Long have I loved thee; long have sought:
And dangers braved, and battles fought;
In this embrace our evils end;
From this our better days ascend;
The year of suffering now is o'er,
At last we meet to part no more!

6 My lovely bride! my consort, come!
The rapid chariot rolls thee home.
   Har. I fear to go——I dare not stay.
Look back.——I dare not look that way.
   Hen. No evil ever shall betide
My love, while I am at her side.
Lo! thy protector and thy friend,
The arms that fold thee will defend.

7   *Har.* Still beats my bosom with alarms:
I tremble while I'm in thy arms!
What will impassioned lovers do?
What have I done—to follow you?
I leave a father torn with fears;
I leave a mother bathed in tears;
A brother, girding on his sword,
Against my life, against my lord.

8 Now, without father, mother, friend,
On thee my future days depend;
Wilt thou, for ever true to love,
A father, mother, brother, prove?

O Henry!——to thy arms I fall,
My friend! my husband! and my all!
Alas! what hazards may I run?
Shouldst thou forsake me—I 'm undone.

9   *Hen.* My Harriet, dissipate thy fears,
And let a husband wipe thy tears;
For ever joined our fates combine,
And I am yours, and you are mine.
The fires the firmament that rend,
On this devoted head descend,
If e'er in thought from thee I rove,
Or love thee less than now I love!

10 Although our fathers have been foes,
From hatred stronger love arose;
From adverse briars that threatening stood,
And threw a horror o'er the wood,
Two lovely roses met on high,
Transplanted to a better sky;
And, grafted in one stock, they grow,
In union spring, in beauty blow.

11   *Har.* My heart believes my love; but still
My boding mind presages ill:
For luckless ever was our love,
Dark as the sky that hung above.
While we embraced, we shook with fears,
And with our kisses mingled tears;
We met with murmurs and with sighs,
And parted still with watery eyes.

12 An unforeseen and fatal hand
Crossed all the measures love had planned;
270

Intrusion marred the tender hour,
A demon started in the bower;
If, like the past, the future run,
And my dark day is but begun,
What clouds may hang above my head?
What tears may I have yet to shed?

13   *Hen.* Oh, do not wound that gentle breast,
Nor sink, with fancied ills oppressed;
For softness, sweetness, all, thou art,
And love is virtue in thy heart.
That bosom ne'er shall heave again
But to the poet's tender strain;
And never more these eyes o'erflow
But for a hapless lover's woe.

14 Long on the ocean tempest-tossed,
At last we gain the happy coast;
And safe recount upon the shore
Our sufferings past, and dangers o'er:
Past scenes, the woes we wept erewhile,
Will make our future minutes smile:
When sudden joy from sorrow springs,
How the heart thrills through all its strings!

15   *Har.* My father's castle springs to sight;
Ye towers that gave me to the light!
O hills! O vales! where I have played;
Ye woods, that wrap me in your shade!
O scenes I've often wandered o'er!
O scenes I shall behold no more!
I take a long, last, lingering view:
Adieu! my native land, adieu!

16 O father, mother, brother dear!
    O names still uttered with a tear!
    Upon whose knees I 've sat and smiled,
    Whose griefs my blandishments beguiled;
    Whom I forsake in sorrows old,
    Whom I shall never more behold!
    Farewell, my friends, a long farewell,
    Till time shall toll the funeral knoll.

17   *Hen.* Thy friends, thy father's house resign;
    My friends, my house, my all is thine:
    Awake, arise, my wedded wife,
    To higher thoughts, and happier life!
    For thee the marriage feast is spread,
    For thee the virgins deck the bed;
    The star of Venus shines above,
    And all thy future life is love.

18 They rise, the dear domestic hours!
    The May of love unfolds her flowers;
    Youth, beauty, pleasure spread the feast,
    And friendship sits a constant guest;
    In cheerful peace the morn ascends,
    In wine and love the evening ends;
    At distance grandeur sheds a ray,
    To gild the evening of our day.

19 Connubial love has dearer names,
    And finer ties, and sweeter claims,
    Than e'er unwedded hearts can feel,
    Than wedded hearts can e'er reveal;
    Pure as the charities above,
    Rise the sweet sympathies of love;
    And closer cords than those of life
    Unite the husband to the wife.

20 Like cherubs now come from the skies,
   Henries and Harriets round us rise;
   And playing wanton in the hall,
   With accent sweet their parents call;
   To your fair images I run,
   You clasp the husband in the son;
   Oh, how the mother's heart will bound!
   Oh, how the father's joy be crowned!

WRITTEN IN A VISIT TO THE COUNTRY IN AUTUMN.

1 'Tis past! no more the Summer blooms!
     Ascending in the rear,
   Behold congenial Autumn comes,
     The Sabbath of the year!
   What time thy holy whispers breathe,
   The pensive evening shade beneath,
     And twilight consecrates the floods;
   While nature strips her garment gay,
   And wears the vesture of decay,
   Oh, let me wander through the sounding woods!

2 Ah! well-known streams!—ah! wonted groves,
     Still pictured in my mind!
   Oh! sacred scene of youthful loves,
     Whose image lives behind!
   While sad I ponder on the past,
   The joys that must no longer last;
     The wild-flower strown on Summer's bier
   The dying music of the grove,
   And the last elegies of love,
   Dissolve the soul, and draw the tender tear!

3 Alas! the hospitable hall,
     Where youth and friendship played,

Wide to the winds a ruined wall
  Projects a death-like shade !
The charm is vanished from the vales;
No voice with virgin-whisper hails
  A stranger to his native bowers :
No more Arcadian mountains bloom,
Nor Enna valleys breathe perfume;
The fancied Eden fades with all its flowers !

4 Companions of the youthful scene,
    Endeared from earliest days !
  With whom I sported on the green,
    Or roved the woodland maze !
  Long exiled from your native clime,
  Or by the thunder-stroke of time
    Snatched to the shadows of despair;
  I hear your voices in the wind,
  Your forms in every walk I find;
  I stretch my arms: ye vanish into air !

5 My steps, when innocent and young,
    These fairy paths pursued;
  And wandering o'er the wild, I sung
    My fancies to the wood.
  I mourned the linnet-lover's fate,
  Or turtle from her murdered mate,
    Condemned the widowed hours to wail :
  Or while the mournful vision rose,
  I sought to weep for imaged woes,
  Nor real life believed a tragic tale !

6 Alas ! misfortune's cloud unkind
    May summer soon o'ercast !
  And cruel fate's untimely wind
    All human beauty blast !

The wrath of nature smites our bowers,
And promised fruits and cherished flowers,
  The hopes of life in embryo sweeps;
Pale o'er the ruins of his prime,
And desolate before his time,
In silence sad the mourner walks and weeps!

7 Relentless power! whose fated stroke
    O'er wretched man prevails!
Ha! love's eternal chain is broke,
    And friendship's covenant fails!
Upbraiding forms! a moment's ease—
O memory! how shall I appease
    The bleeding shade, the unlaid ghost?
What charm can bind the gushing eye,
What voice console the incessant sigh,
And everlasting longings for the lost?

8 Yet not unwelcome waves the wood
    That hides me in its gloom,
While lost in melancholy mood
    I muse upon the tomb.
Their chequered leaves the branches shed;
Whirling in eddies o'er my head,
    They sadly sigh that Winter's near:
The warning voice I hear behind,
That shakes the wood without a wind,
And solemn sounds the death-bell of the year.

9 Nor will I court Lethean streams,
    The sorrowing sense to steep;
Nor drink oblivion of the themes
    On which I love to weep.
Belated oft by fabled rill,

While nightly o'er the hallowed hill
  Aërial music seems to mourn;
I 'll listen Autumn's closing strain;
Then woo the walks of youth again,
And pour my sorrows o'er the untimely urn !

COMPLAINT OF NATURE.

1 Few are thy days and full of woe,
    O man of woman born !
  Thy doom is written, dust thou art,
    And shalt to dust return.

2 Determined are the days that fly
    Successive o'er thy head;
  The numbered hour is on the wing
    That lays thee with the dead.

3 Alas ! the little day of life
    Is shorter than a span;
  Yet black with thousand hidden ills
    To miserable man.

4 Gay is thy morning, flattering hope
    Thy sprightly step attends;
  But soon the tempest howls behind,
    And the dark night descends.

5 Before its splendid hour the cloud
    Comes o'er the beam of light;
  A pilgrim in a weary land,
    Man tarries but a night.

6 Behold, sad emblem of thy state !
    The flowers that paint the field;
  Or trees that crown the mountain's brow,
    And boughs and blossoms yield.

7 When chill the blast of Winter blows,
      Away the Summer flies,
   The flowers resign their sunny robes,
      And all their beauty dies.

8 Nipt by the year the forest fades;
      And shaking to the wind,
   The leaves toss to and fro, and streak
      The wilderness behind.

9 The Winter past, reviving flowers
      Anew shall paint the plain,
   The woods shall hear the voice of Spring,
      And flourish green again.

10 But man departs this earthly scene,
      Ah! never to return!
   No second Spring shall e'er revive
      The ashes of the urn.

11 The inexorable doors of death
      What hand can e'er unfold?
   Who from the cerements of the tomb
      Can raise the human mould?

12 The mighty flood that rolls along
      Its torrents to the main,
   The waters lost can ne'er recall
      From that abyss again.

13 The days, the years, the ages, dark
      Descending down to night,
   Can never, never be redeemed
      Back to the gates of light.

14 So man departs the living scene,
     To night's perpetual gloom;
   The voice of morning ne'er shall break
     The slumbers of the tomb.

15 Where are our fathers? Whither gone
     The mighty men of old?
   The patriarchs, prophets, princes, kings,
     In sacred books enrolled?

16 Gone to the resting-place of man,
     The everlasting home,
   Where ages past have gone before,
     Where future ages come.

17 Thus nature poured the wail of woe,
     And urged her earnest cry;
   Her voice, in agony extreme,
     Ascended to the sky.

18 The Almighty heard: then from his throne
     In majesty he rose;
   And from the heaven, that opened wide,
     His voice in mercy flows:

19 'When mortal man resigns his breath,
     And falls a clod of clay,
   The soul immortal wings its flight
     To never-setting day.

20 'Prepared of old for wicked men
     The bed of torment lies;
   The just shall enter into bliss
     Immortal in the skies.'

THOMAS BLACKLOCK.

THE amiable Dr Blacklock deserves praise for his character and for his conduct under very peculiar circumstances, much more than for his poetry. He was born at Annan, where his father was a bricklayer, in 1721. When about six months old, he lost his eyesight by small-pox. His father used to read to him, especially poetry, and through the kindness of friends he acquired some knowledge of the Latin tongue. His father having been accidentally killed when Thomas was nineteen, it might have fared hard with him, but Dr Stevenson, an eminent medical man in Edinburgh, who had seen some verses composed by the blind youth, took him to the capital, sent him to college to study divinity, and encouraged him to write and to publish poetry. His volume, to which was prefixed an account of the author, by Professor Spence of Oxford, attracted much attention. Blacklock was licensed to preach in 1759, and three years afterwards was married to a Miss Johnstone of Dumfries, an exemplary but plain-looking lady, whose beauty her husband was wont to praise so warmly that his friends were thankful that his infirmity was never removed, and thought how justly Cupid had been painted blind. He was even, through the influence of the Earl of Selkirk, appointed to the parish of Kirkcudbright, but the parishioners opposed his induction on the plea of his want of sight, and, in consideration of a small annuity, he withdrew his claims. He finally settled down in Edinburgh, where he supported himself chiefly by keeping young gentlemen as boarders in his house. His chief amusements were poetry and music. His conduct to (1786) and correspondence with Burns are too well known to require to be noticed at length here. He published a paper of no small merit in the 'Encyclopædia Britannica' on Blindness, and is the author of a work entitled 'Paraclesis; or, Consolations of Religion,'—which surely none require more than the blind. He died of a nervous fever on the 7th of July 1791, so far fortunate that he did not live to see the ruin of his immortal *protégé*.

Blacklock was a most amiable, genial, and benevolent being. He was sometimes subject to melancholy—*un*like many of the blind, and one especially, whom we name not, but who, still living, bears a striking resemblance to Blacklock in fineness of mind, warmth of heart, and high-toned piety, but who is cheerful as the day. As to his poetry, it is undoubtedly wonderful, considering the circumstances of its production, if not *per se*. Dr Johnson says to Boswell,—'As Blacklock had the misfortune to be blind, we may be absolutely sure that the passages in his poems descriptive of visible objects are combinations of what he remembered of the works of other writers who could see. That foolish fellow Spence has laboured to explain philosophically how Blacklock may have done, by his own faculties, what it is impossible he should do. The solution, as I have given it, is plain. Suppose I know a man to be so lame that he is absolutely incapable to move himself, and I find him in a different room from that in which I left him, shall I puzzle myself with idle conjectures that perhaps his nerves have, by some unknown change, all at once become effective? No, sir; it is clear how he got into a different room—he was CARRIED.'

Perhaps there is a fallacy in this somewhat dogmatic statement. Perhaps the blind are not so utterly dark but they may have certain dim *simulacra* of external objects before their eyes and minds. Apart from this, however, Blacklock's poetry endures only from its connexion with the author's misfortune, and from the fact that through the gloom he groped greatly to find and give the burning hand of the peasant poet the squeeze of a kindred spirit,—kindred, we mean, in feeling and heart, although very far removed in strength of intellect and genius.

THE AUTHOR'S PICTURE.

While in my matchless graces wrapt I stand,
And touch each feature with a trembling hand;
Deign, lovely self! with art and nature's pride,
To mix the colours, and the pencil guide.
    Self is the grand pursuit of half mankind;
How vast a crowd by self, like me, are blind!
By self the fop in magic colours shown,
Though scorned by every eye, delights his own:
280

When age and wrinkles seize the conquering maid,
Self, not the glass, reflects the flattering shade.
Then, wonder-working self! begin the lay;
Thy charms to others as to me display.
  Straight is my person, but of little size;
Lean are my cheeks, and hollow are my eyes;
My youthful down is, like my talents, rare;
Politely distant stands each single hair.
My voice too rough to charm a lady's ear;
So smooth, a child may listen without fear;
Not formed in cadence soft and warbling lays,
To soothe the fair through pleasure's wanton ways.
My form so fine, so regular, so new,
My port so manly, and so fresh my hue;
Oft, as I meet the crowd, they laughing say,
'See, see *Memento Mori* cross the way.'
The ravished Proserpine at last, we know,
Grew fondly jealous of her sable beau;
But, thanks to nature! none from me need fly;
One heart the devil could wound—so cannot I.
  Yet, though my person fearless may be seen,
There is some danger in my graceful mien:
For, as some vessel tossed by wind and tide,
Bounds o'er the waves and rocks from side to side;
In just vibration thus I always move:
This who can view and not be forced to love?
  Hail! charming self! by whose propitious aid
My form in all its glory stands displayed:
Be present still; with inspiration kind,
Let the same faithful colours paint the mind.
  Like all mankind, with vanity I'm blessed,
Conscious of wit I never yet possessed.
To strong desires my heart an easy prey,
Oft feels their force, but never owns their sway.

This hour, perhaps, as death I hate my foe;
The next, I wonder why I should do so.
Though poor, the rich I view with careless eye;
Scorn a vain oath, and hate a serious lie.
I ne'er for satire torture common sense;
Nor show my wit at God's nor man's expense.
Harmless I live, unknowing and unknown;
Wish well to all, and yet do good to none.
Unmerited contempt I hate to bear;
Yet on my faults, like others, am severe.
Dishonest flames my bosom never fire;
The bad I pity, and the good admire;
Fond of the Muse, to her devote my days,
And scribble—not for pudding, but for praise.
    These careless lines, if any virgin hears,
Perhaps, in pity to my joyless years, -
She may consent a generous flame to own,
And I no longer sigh the nights alone.
But should the fair, affected, vain, or nice,
Scream with the fears inspired by frogs or mice;
Cry, 'Save us, Heaven! a spectre, not a man!'
Her hartshorn snatch or interpose her fan:
If I my tender overture repeat;
Oh! may my vows her kind reception meet!
May she new graces on my form bestow,
And with tall honours dignify my brow!

ODE TO AURORA, ON MELISSA'S BIRTHDAY.

Of time and nature eldest born,
Emerge, thou rosy-fingered morn,
Emerge, in purest dress arrayed;
And chase from heaven night's envious shade,
That I once more may, pleased, survey,
And hail Melissa's natal day.
282

Of time and nature eldest born,
Emerge, thou rosy-fingered morn;
In order at the eastern gate
The hours to draw thy chariot wait;
Whilst zephyr, on his balmy wings
Mild nature's fragrant tribute brings,
With odours sweet to strew thy way,
And grace the bland revolving day.

But as thou leadst the radiant sphere,
That gilds its birth, and marks the year,
And as his stronger glories rise,
Diffused around the expanded skies,
Till clothed with beams serenely bright,
All heaven's vast concave flames with light;
So, when, through life's protracted day,
Melissa still pursues her way,
Her virtues with thy splendour vie,
Increasing to the mental eye:
Though less conspicuous, not less dear,
Long may they Bion's prospect cheer;
So shall his heart no more repine,
Blessed with her rays, though robbed of thine.

MISS ELLIOT AND MRS COCKBURN.

HERE we find two ladies amicably united in the composition
of one of Scotland's finest songs, the ' Flowers of the Forest.'
Miss Jane Elliot of Minto, sister of Sir Gilbert Elliot of Minto,
wrote the first and the finest of the two versions. Mrs Cockburn, the author of the second, was a remarkable person. Her
maiden name was Alicia Rutherford, and she was the daughter
of Mr Rutherford of Fernilee, in Selkirkshire. She married Mr
Patrick Cockburn, a younger son of Adam Cockburn of Ormis-
ton, Lord Justice-Clerk of Scotland. She became prominent

in the literary circles of Edinburgh, and an intimate friend of David Hume, with whom she carried on a long and serious correspondence on religious subjects, in which it is understood the philosopher opened up his whole heart, but which is unfortunately lost. Mrs Cockburn, who was born in 1714, lived to 1794, and saw and proclaimed the wonderful promise of Walter Scott. She wrote a great deal, but the 'Flowers of the Forest' is the only one of her effusions that has been published. A ludicrous story is told of her son, who was a dissipated youth, returning one night drunk, while a large party of *savans* was assembled in the house, and locking himself up in the room in which their coats and hats were deposited. Nothing would rouse him ; and the company had to depart in the best substitutes they could find for their ordinary habiliments,—Hume (characteristically) in a dreadnought, Monboddo in an old shabby hat, &c.—the echoes of the midnight Potterrow resounding to their laughter at their own odd figures. It is believed that Mrs Cockburn's song was really occasioned by the bankruptcy of a number of gentlemen in Selkirkshire, although she chose to throw the new matter of lamentation into the old mould of song.

THE FLOWERS OF THE FOREST.

BY MISS JANE ELLIOT.

1 I 've heard the lilting at our yowe-milking,
    Lasses a-lilting before the dawn of day;
  But now they are moaning on ilka green loaning—
    The Flowers of the Forest are a' wede away.

2 At buchts, in the morning, nae blithe lads are scorning,
    The lasses are lonely, and dowie, and wae;
  Nae daffin', nae gabbin', but sighing and sabbing,
    Ilk ane lifts her leglen and hies her away.

3 In hairst, at the shearing, nae youths now are jeering,
    The bandsters are lyart, and runkled, and gray;
  At fair, or at preaching, nae wooing, nae fleeching—
    The Flowers of the Forest are a' wede away.

284

4 At e'en, at the gloaming, nae swankies are roaming
    'Bout stacks wi' the lasses at bogle to play;
But ilk ane sits drearie, lamenting her dearie—
    The Flowers of the Forest are a' wede away.

5 Dule and wae for the order, sent our lads to the
        Border!
The English, for ance, by guile wan the day;
 ·The Flowers of the Forest, that foucht aye the foremost,
    The prime o' our land, are cauld in the clay.

6 We hear nae mair lilting at our yowe-milking,
    Women and bairns are heartless and wae;
Sighing and moaning on ilka green loaning—
    The Flowers of the Forest are a' wede away.

THE FLOWERS OF THE FOREST.

BY MRS COCKBURN.

1 I 've seen the smiling
    Of Fortune beguiling;
I 've felt all its favours, and found its decay:
    Sweet was its blessing,
    Kind its caressing;
But now 'tis fled—fled far away.

2 I 've seen the forest
    Adorned the foremost
With flowers of the fairest most pleasant and gay;
    Sae bonnie was their blooming!
    Their scent the air perfuming!
But now they are withered and weeded away.

3 I 've seen the morning
    With gold the hills adorning,
And loud tempest storming before the mid-day.

I've seen Tweed's silver streams,
Shining in the sunny beams,
Grow drumly and dark as he rowed on his way.

4 Oh, fickle Fortune,
Why this cruel sporting?
Oh, why still perplex us, poor sons of a day?
Nae mair your smiles can cheer me,
Nae mair your frowns can fear me;
For the Flowers of the Forest are a' wede away.

SIR WILLIAM JONES.

THIS extraordinary person, the 'Justinian of India,' the master
of twenty-eight languages, who into the short space of forty-eight
years (he was born in 1746, and died 27th of April 1794) compressed such a vast quantity of study and labour, is also the
author of two volumes of poetry, of unequal merit. We quote
the best thing in the book.

A PERSIAN SONG OF HAFIZ.

1 Sweet maid, if thou wouldst charm my sight,
And bid these arms thy neck enfold;
That rosy cheek, that lily hand,
Would give thy poet more delight
Than all Bokhara's vaunted gold,
Than all the gems of Samarcand.

2 Boy, let yon liquid ruby flow,
And bid thy pensive heart be glad,
Whate'er the frowning zealots say:
Tell them, their Eden cannot show
A stream so clear as Rocnabad,
A bower so sweet as Mosellay.

3 Oh! when these fair perfidious maids,
  Whose eyes our secret haunts infest,
  Their dear destructive charms display,
  Each glance my tender breast invades,
  And robs my wounded soul of rest,
  As Tartars seize their destined prey.

4 In vain with love our bosoms glow:
  Can all our tears, can all our sighs,
  New lustre to those charms impart?
  Can cheeks, where living roses blow,
  Where nature spreads her richest dyes,
  Require the borrowed gloss of art?

5 Speak not of fate: ah! change the theme,
  And talk of odours, talk of wine,
  Talk of the flowers that round us bloom:
  'Tis all a cloud, 'tis all a dream;
  To love and joy thy thoughts confine,
  Nor hope to pierce the sacred gloom.

6 Beauty has such resistless power,
  That even the chaste Egyptian dame
  Sighed for the blooming Hebrew boy:
  For her how fatal was the hour,
  When to the banks of Nilus came
  A youth so lovely and so coy!

7 But, ah! sweet maid, my counsel hear,
  (Youth should attend when those advise
  Whom long experience renders sage):
  While music charms the ravished ear,
  While sparkling cups delight our eyes,
  Be gay; and scorn the frowns of age.

8 What cruel answer have I heard?
   And yet, by Heaven, I love thee still:
   Can aught be cruel from thy lip?
   Yet say, how fell that bitter word
   From lips which streams of sweetness fill,
   Which nought but drops of honey sip?

9 Go boldly forth, my simple lay,
   Whose accents flow with artless ease,
   Like orient pearls at random strung:
   Thy notes are sweet, the damsels say;
   But, oh! far sweeter, if they please
   The nymph for whom these notes are sung.

SAMUEL BISHOP.

THIS gentleman was born in 1731, and died in 1795. He was
an English clergyman, master of Merchant Tailors' School,
London, and author of a volume of Latin pieces, entitled ' Feriæ
Poeticæ,' and of various other poetical pieces. We give some
verses to his wife, from which it appears that he remained an
ardent lover long after having become a husband.

TO MRS BISHOP,

WITH A PRESENT OF A KNIFE.

'A knife,' dear girl, 'cuts love,' they say!
Mere modish love, perhaps it may—
For any tool, of any kind,
Can separate—what was never joined.
   The knife, that cuts our love in two,
Will have much tougher work to do;
Must cut your softness, truth, and spirit,
Down to the vulgar size of merit;

To level yours, with modern taste,
Must cut a world of sense to waste;
And from your single beauty's store,
Clip what would dizen out a score.
　　That self-same blade from me must sever
Sensation, judgment, sight, for ever:
All memory of endearments past,
All hope of comforts long to last;
All that makes fourteen years with you,
A summer, and a short one too;
All that affection feels and fears,
When hours without you seem like years.
　　Till that be done, and I'd as soon
Believe this knife will chip the moon,
Accept my present, undeterred,
And leave their proverbs to the herd.
　　If in a kiss—delicious treat!—
Your lips acknowledge the receipt,
Love, fond of such substantial fare,
And proud to play the glutton there,
All thoughts of cutting will disdain,
Save only—'cut and come again.'

TO THE SAME,

ON THE ANNIVERSARY OF HER WEDDING-DAY, WHICH WAS ALSO HER BIRTH-DAY,
WITH A RING.

'Thee, Mary, with this ring I wed'—
So, fourteen years ago, I said.——
Behold another ring!—'For what?'
'To wed thee o'er again?'—Why not?
　　With that first ring I married youth,
Grace, beauty, innocence, and truth;
Taste long admired, sense long revered,
And all my Molly then appeared.

If she, by merit since disclosed,
Prove twice the woman I supposed,
I plead that double merit now,
To justify a double vow.
    Here then to-day, with faith as sure,
With ardour as intense, as pure,
As when, amidst the rites divine,
I took thy troth, and plighted mine,
To thee, sweet girl, my second ring
A token and a pledge I bring:
With this I wed, till death us part,
Thy riper virtues to my heart;
Those virtues which, before untried,
The wife has added to the bride:
Those virtues, whose progressive claim,
Endearing wedlock's very name,
My soul enjoys, my song approves,
For conscience' sake, as well as love's.
    And why?   They show me every hour,
Honour's high thought, Affection's power,
Discretion's deed, sound Judgment's sentence,
And teach me all things—but repentance.

SUSANNA BLAMIRE.

THIS lady was born at Cardew Hall, near Carlisle, and remained
there from the date of her birth (1747) till she was twenty years
of age, when she accompanied her sister—who had married
Colonel Graham of Duchray, Perthshire—to Scotland, and continued there some years. She became enamoured of Scottish
music and poetry, and thus qualified herself for writing such sweet
lyrics as 'The Nabob,' and 'What ails this heart o' mine?' On
her return to Cumberland she wrote several pieces illustrative of
Cumbrian manners. She died unmarried in 1794. Her poetical

pieces, some of which had been floating through the country in
the form of popular songs, were collected by Mr Patrick Max-
well, and published in 1842. The two we have quoted rank
with those of Lady Nairne in nature and pathos.

THE NABOB.

1 When silent time, wi' lightly foot,
    Had trod on thirty years,
I sought again my native land
    Wi' mony hopes and fears.
Wha kens gin the dear friends I left
    May still continue mine?
Or gin I e'er again shall taste
    The joys I left langsyne?

2 As I drew near my ancient pile,
    My heart beat a' the way;
Ilk place I passed seemed yet to speak
    O' some dear former day;
Those days that followed me afar,
    Those happy days o' mine,
Whilk made me think the present joys
    A' naething to langsyne!

3 The ivied tower now met my eye,
    Where minstrels used to blaw;
Nae friend stepped forth wi' open hand,
    Nae weel-kenned face I saw;
Till Donald tottered to the door,
    Wham I left in his prime,
And grat to see the lad return
    He bore about langsyne.

4 I ran to ilka dear friend's room,
    As if to find them there,

I knew where ilk ane used to sit,
　　And hang o'er mony a chair;
Till soft remembrance threw a veil
　　Across these een o' mine,
I closed the door, and sobbed aloud,
　　To think on auld langsyne!

5　Some pensy chiels, a new-sprung race,
　　Wad next their welcome pay,
Wha shuddered at my Gothic wa's,
　　And wished my groves away.
'Cut, cut,' they cried, 'those aged elms,
　　Lay low yon mournfu' pine.'
Na! na! our fathers' names grow there,
　　Memorials o' langsyne.

6　To wean me frae these waefu' thoughts,
　　·They took me to the town;
But sair on ilka weel-kenned face
　　I missed the youthfu' bloom.
At balls they pointed to a nymph
　　Wham a' declared divine;
But sure her mother's blushing cheeks
　　Were fairer far langsyne!

7　In vain I sought in music's sound
　　To find that magic art,
Which oft in Scotland's ancient lays
　　Has thrilled through a' my heart.
The sang had mony an artfu' turn;
　　My ear confessed 'twas fine;
But missed the simple melody
　　I listened to langsyne.

8　Ye sons to comrades o' my youth,
　　Forgie an auld man's spleen,

Wha 'midst your gayest scenes still mourns
    The days he ance has seen.
When time has passed and seasons fled,
    Your hearts will feel like mine;
And aye the sang will maist delight
    That minds ye o' langsyne!

WHAT AILS THIS HEART O' MINE?

1 What ails this heart o' mine?
    What ails this watery ee?
  What gars me a' turn pale as death
    When I tak leave o' thee?
  When thou art far awa',
    Thou 'lt dearer grow to me;
  But change o' place and change o' folk
    May gar thy fancy jee

2 When I gae out at e'en,
    Or walk at morning air,
  Ilk rustling bush will seem to say
    I used to meet thee there.
  Then I 'll sit down and cry,
    And live aneath the tree,
  And when a leaf fa's i' my lap,
    I 'll ca't a word frae thee.

3 I 'll hie me to the bower
    That thou wi' roses tied,
  And where wi' mony a blushing bud
    I strove myself to hide.
  I 'll doat on ilka spot
    Where I ha'e been wi' thee;
  And ca' to mind some kindly word
    By ilka burn and tree.

JAMES MACPHERSON.

Now we come to one who, with all his faults, was not only a real, but a great poet. The events of his life need not detain us long. He was born at Kingussie, Inverness-shire, in 1738, and educated at Aberdeen. At twenty he published a very juvenile production in verse, called 'The Highlandman: a Heroic Poem, in six cantos.' He taught for some time the school of Ruthven, near his native place, and became afterwards tutor in the family of Graham of Balgowan. While attending a scion of this family—afterwards Lord Lynedoch—at Moffat Wells, Macpherson became acquainted with Home, the author of 'Douglas,' and shewed to him some fragments of Gaelic poetry, translated by himself. Home was delighted with these specimens, and the consequence was, that our poet, under the patronage of Home, Blair, Adam Fergusson, and Dr Carlyle, (the once famous 'Jupiter Carlyle,' minister of Inveresk—called 'Jupiter' because he used to sit to sculptors for their statues of 'Father Jove,' and declared by Sir Walter Scott to have been the 'grandest demigod he ever saw,') published, in a small volume of sixty pages, his 'Fragments of Ancient Poetry, translated from the Gaelic or Erse language.' This *brochure* became popular, and Macpherson was provided with a purse to go to the Highlands to collect additional pieces. The result was, in 1762, 'Fingal: an Epic Poem;' and, in the next year, 'Temora,' another epic poem. Their sale was prodigious, and the effect not equalled till, twenty-four years later, the poems of Burns appeared. He realised £1200 by these productions. In 1764 he accompanied Governor Johnston to Pensacola as his secretary, but quarrelled with him, and returned to London. Here he became a professional pamphleteer, always taking the ministerial side, and diversifying these labours by publishing a translation of Homer, in the style of his Ossian, which, as Coleridge says of another production, was 'damned unanimously.' Our readers are familiar with his row with Dr Johnson, who, when threatened with personal chastisement for his obstinate and fierce incredulity in the matter of Ossian, thus wrote the author:—

'To Mr JAMES MACPHERSON.

'I received your foolish and impudent letter. Any violence offered me I shall do the best to repel, and what I cannot do for myself, the law shall do for me. I hope I shall not be deterred from detecting what I think a cheat by the menaces of a ruffian.

'What would you have me to retract? I thought your book an imposture. I think it an imposture still. For this opinion I have given my reasons to the public, which I dare you to refute. Your rage I defy. Your abilities, since your Homer, are not so formidable, and what I hear of your morals inclines me to pay regard, not to what you shall say, but to what you shall prove. You may print this if you will.

'SAM. JOHNSON.'

Nothing daunted by this, and a hundred other similar rebuffs, Macpherson, like Mallett before him, but with twenty times his abilities, pursued his peculiar course. He was appointed agent for the Nabob of Arcot, and became M.P. for Camelford. In this way he speedily accumulated a handsome fortune, and in 1789, while still a youngish man, he retired to his native parish, where he bought the estate of Raitts, and founded a splendid villa, called Belleville, where, in ease and affluence, he spent his remaining days. Surviving Johnson, his ablest opponent, by twelve years, he died on the 17th of February 1796, in the full view of Ossian's country. One of his daughters became his heir, and another was the first wife of Sir David Brewster. Macpherson in his will ordered that his body should be buried in Westminster Abbey, and left a sum of money to erect a monument to him near Belleville. He lies, accordingly, in Poets' Corner, and a marble obelisk to his memory may be seen near Kingussie, in the centre of some trees.

There is nothing new that is true, or true that is new, to be said about the questions connected with Ossian's Poems. That Macpherson is the sole author is a theory now as generally abandoned as the other, which held that he was simply a free translator of the old bard. To the real fragments of Ossian, which he found in the Highlands, he acted very much as he did to the ancient property of Raitts, in his own native parish. This he purchased in its crude state, and beautified into a mountain paradise. He changed, however, its name into Belleville, and it had been better if he had behaved in a similar way with the poems, and published them as, with some little groundwork from another,

295

the veritable writings of James Macpherson, Esq. The ablest opponent of his living reputation was, as we said, Johnson; and the ablest enemy of his posthumous fame has been Macaulay. We are at a loss to understand *his* animosity to the author of Ossian. Were the Macphersons and Macaulays ever at feud, and did the historian lose his great-great-grandmother in some onslaught made on the Hebrides by the progenitors of the pseudo-Ossian? Macpherson as a man we respect not, and we are persuaded that the greater part of Ossian's Poems can be traced no further than his teeming brain. Nor are we careful to defend his poetry from the common charges of monotony, affectation, and fustian. But we deem Macaulay grossly unjust in his treatment of Macpherson's genius and its results, and can fortify our judgment by that of Sir Walter Scott and Professor Wilson, two men as far superior to the historian in knowledge of the Highlands and of Highland song, and in genuine poetic taste, as they were confessedly in original imagination. The former says, ' Macpherson was certainly a man of high talents, and his poetic powers are honourable to his country.' Wilson, in an admirable paper in *Blackwood* for November 1839, while admitting many faults in Ossian, eloquently proclaims the presence in his strains of much of the purest, most pathetic, and most sublime poetry, instancing the ' Address to the Sun ' as equal to anything in Homer or Milton.   Both these great writers have paid Macpherson a higher compliment still,—they have imitated him, and the speeches of Allan Macaulay (a far greater genius than his namesake), Ranald MacEagh, and Elspeth MacTavish, in the ' Waverley Novels,' and such articles by Christopher North as ' Cottages,' ' Hints for the Holidays,' and a ' Glance at Selby's Ornithology,' are all coloured by familiarity and fellow-feeling with Ossian's style. Best of all, the Highlanders as a nation have accepted Ossian as their bard; he is as much the poet of Morven as Burns of Coila, and it is as hopeless to dislodge the one from the Highland as the other from the Lowland heart. The true way to learn to appreciate Ossian's poetry is not to hurry, as Macaulay seems to have done, in a steamer from Glasgow to Oban, and thence to Ballachulish, and thence through Glencoe, (mistaking a fine lake for a ' sullen pool ' on his way,

296

and ignoring altogether its peculiar features of grandeur,) and thence to Inverness or Edinburgh ; but it is to live for years—as Macpherson did while writing Ossian, and Wilson also did to some extent—under the shadow of the mountains,—to wander through lonely moors amidst drenching mists and rains,—to hold trysts with thunder-storms on the summit of savage hills,—to bathe after nightfall in dreary tarns,—to lie over the ledge and dip one's fingers in the spray of cataracts,—to plough a solitary path into the heart of forests, and to sleep and dream for hours amidst their sunless glades,—to meet on twilight hills the apparition of the winter moon rising over snowy wastes,—to descend by her ghastly light precipices where the eagles are sleeping,—and, returning home, to be haunted by night-visions of mightier mountains, wilder desolations, and giddier descents ;—experience somewhat like this is necessary to form a true 'Child of the Mist,' and to give the full capacity for sharing in or appreciating the shadowy, solitary, pensive, and magnificent spirit which tabernacles in Ossian's poetry.

Never, at least, can we forget how, in our boyhood, while feeling, but quite unable to express, the emotions which were suggested by the bold shapes of mountains resting against the stars, mirrored from below in lakes and wild torrents, and quaking sometimes in concert with the quaking couch of the half-slumbering earthquake, the poems of Ossian served to give our thoughts an expression which they could not otherwise have found—how they at once strengthened and consolidated enthusiasm, and are now regarded with feelings which, wreathed around earliest memories and the strongest fibres of the heart, no criticism can ever weaken or destroy.

OSSIAN'S ADDRESS TO THE SUN.

I feel the sun, O Malvina!—leave me to my rest. Perhaps they may come to my dreams; I think I hear a feeble voice! The beam of heaven delights to shine on the grave of Carthon: I feel it warm around.

O thou that rollest above, round as the shield of my

fathers! Whence are thy beams, O sun! thy everlasting light? Thou comest forth in thy awful beauty; the stars hide themselves in the sky; the moon, cold and pale, sinks in the western wave; but thou thyself movest alone. Who can be a companion of thy course? The oaks of the mountains fall; the mountains themselves decay with years; the ocean shrinks and grows again; the moon herself is lost in heaven, but thou art for ever the same, rejoicing in the brightness of thy course. When the world is dark with tempests, when thunder rolls and lightning flies, thou lookest in thy beauty from the clouds, and laughest at the storm. But to Ossian thou lookest in vain, for he beholds thy beams no more; whether thy yellow hair flows on the eastern clouds, or thou tremblest at the gates of the west. But thou art perhaps, like me, for a season; thy years will have an end. Thou shalt sleep in thy clouds careless of the voice of the morning. Exult then, O sun, in the strength of thy youth! Age is dark and unlovely; it is like the glimmering light of the moon when it shines through broken clouds, and the mist is on the hills: the blast of the north is on the plain; the traveller shrinks in the midst of his journey.

DESOLATION OF BALCLUTHA.

I have seen the walls of Balclutha, but they were desolate. The fire had resounded in the halls; and the voice of the people is heard no more. The stream of Clutha was removed from its place by the fall of the walls. The thistle shook there its lonely head; the moss whistled to the wind. The fox looked out from the windows; the rank grass of the wall waved round its head. Desolate is the dwelling of Moina; silence is in the house of her fathers. Raise the song of mourning, O bards!

over the land of strangers. They have but fallen before us: for one day we must fall. Why dost thou build the hall, son of the winged days? Thou lookest from thy towers to-day: yet a few years, and the blast of the desert comes; it howls in thy empty court, and whistles round thy half-worn shield. And let the blast of the desert come! we shall be renowned in our day! The mark of my arm shall be in battle; my name in the song of bards. Raise the song, send round the shell: let joy be heard in my hall. When thou, sun of heaven, shalt fail! if thou shalt fail, thou mighty light! if thy brightness is but for a season, like Fingal, our fame shall survive thy beams. Such was the song of Fingal in the day of his joy.

FINGAL AND THE SPIRIT OF LODA.

Night came down on the sea; Roma's bay received the ship. A rock bends along the coast with all its echoing wood. On the top is the circle of Loda, the mossy stone of power! A narrow plain spreads beneath, covered with grass and aged trees, which the midnight winds, in their wrath, had torn from the shaggy rock. The blue course of a stream is there! the lonely blast of ocean pursues the thistle's beard. The flame of three oaks arose: the feast is spread around: but the soul of the king is sad, for Carric-thura's chief distressed.

The wan, cold moon, rose in the east; sleep descended on the youths! Their blue helmets glitter to the beam; the fading fire decays. But sleep did not rest on the king: he rose in the midst of his arms, and slowly ascended the hill, to behold the flame of Sarno's tower.

The flame was dim and distant, the moon hid her red face in the east. A blast came from the mountain, on its wings was the spirit of Loda. He came to his place in his terrors, and shook his dusky spear. His eyes appear like flames in his dark face; his voice is like distant thunder. Fingal advanced his spear in night, and raised his voice on high.

Son of night, retire: call thy winds, and fly! Why dost thou come to my presence, with thy shadowy arms? Do I fear thy gloomy form, spirit of dismal Loda? Weak is thy shield of clouds: feeble is that meteor, thy sword! The blast rolls them together; and thou thyself art lost. Fly from my presence, son of night! Call thy winds, and fly!

Dost thou force me from my place? replied the hollow voice. The people bend before me. I turn the battle in the field of the brave. I look on the nations, and they vanish: my nostrils pour the blast of death. I come abroad on the winds: the tempests are before my face. But my dwelling is calm, above the clouds; the fields of my rest are pleasant.

Dwell in thy pleasant fields, said the king; let Comhal's son be forgot. Do my steps ascend, from my hills, into thy peaceful plains? Do I meet thee, with a spear, on thy cloud, spirit of dismal Loda? Why then dost thou frown on me? Why shake thine airy spear? Thou frownest in vain: I never fled from the mighty in war. And shall the sons of the wind frighten the king of Morven? No: he knows the weakness of their arms!

Fly to thy land, replied the form: receive the wind, and fly! The blasts are in the hollow of my hand: the course of the storm is mine. The king of Sora is my son, he bends at the storm of my power. His battle is around Carric-thura; and he will prevail! Fly to thy land, son of Comhal, or feel my flaming wrath!

He lifted high his shadowy spear! He bent forward his dreadful height. Fingal, advancing, drew his sword;
300

the blade of dark-brown Luno. The gleaming path of the steel winds through the gloomy ghost. The form fell shapeless into air, like a column of smoke, which the staff of the boy disturbs, as it rises from the half-extinguished furnace.

The spirit of Loda shrieked, as, rolled into himself, he rose on the wind. Inistore shook at the sound, the waves heard it on the deep. They stopped in their course with fear: the friends of Fingal started at once, and took their heavy spears. They missed the king; they rose in rage; all their arms resound!

ADDRESS TO THE MOON.

Daughter of heaven, fair art thou! the silence of thy face is pleasant! Thou comest forth in loveliness. The stars attend thy blue course in the east. The clouds rejoice in thy presence, O moon! they brighten their dark-brown sides. Who is like thee in heaven, light of the silent night? The stars are ashamed in thy presence. They turn away their sparkling eyes. Whither dost thou retire from thy course, when the darkness of thy countenance grows? hast thou thy hall, like Ossian? dwellest thou in the shadow of grief? have thy sisters fallen from heaven? are they who rejoiced with thee at night no more? Yes, they have fallen, fair light! and thou dost often retire to mourn. But thou thyself shalt fail one night, and leave thy blue path in heaven. The stars will then lift their heads: they, who were ashamed in thy presence, will rejoice. Thou art now clothed with thy brightness. Look from thy gates in the sky. Burst the cloud, O wind! that the daughter of night may look forth! that the shaggy mountains may brighten, and the ocean roll its white waves in light.

FINGAL'S SPIRIT-HOME.

His friends sit around the king, on mist! They hear the songs of Ullin: he strikes the half-viewless harp. He raises the feeble voice. The lesser heroes, with a thousand meteors, light the airy hall. Malvina rises in the midst; a blush is on her cheek. She beholds the unknown faces of her fathers. She turns aside her humid eyes. 'Art thou come so soon?' said Fingal, 'daughter of generous Toscar. Sadness dwells in the halls of Lutha. My aged son is sad! I hear the breeze of Cona, that was wont to lift thy heavy locks. It comes to the hall, but thou art not there. Its voice is mournful among the arms of thy fathers! Go, with thy rustling wing, O breeze! sigh on Malvina's tomb. It rises yonder beneath the rock, at the blue stream of Lutha. The maids are departed to their place. Thou alone, O breeze, mournest there!'

THE CAVE.

1 The wind is up, the field is bare,
    Some hermit lead me to his cell,
  Where Contemplation, lonely fair,
    With blessed content has chose to dwell.

2 Behold! it opens to my sight,
    Dark in the rock, beside the flood;
  Dry fern around obstructs the light;
    The winds above it move the wood.

3 Reflected in the lake, I see
    The downward mountains and the skies,
  The flying bird, the waving tree,
    The goats that on the hill arise.

4 The gray-cloaked herd[1] drives on the cow;
   The slow-paced fowler walks the heath;
A freckled pointer scours the brow;
   A musing shepherd stands beneath.

5 Curved o'er the ruin of an oak,
   The woodman lifts his axe on high;
The hills re-echo to the stroke;
   I see—I see the shivers fly!

6 Some rural maid, with apron full,
   Brings fuel to the homely flame;
I see the smoky columns roll,
   And, through the chinky hut, the beam.

7 Beside a stone o'ergrown with moss,
   Two well-met hunters talk at ease;
Three panting dogs beside repose;
   One bleeding deer is stretched on grass.

8 A lake at distance spreads to sight,
   Skirted with shady forests round;
In midst, an island's rocky height
   Sustains a ruin, once renowned.

9 One tree bends o'er the naked walls;
   Two broad-winged eagles hover nigh;
By intervals a fragment falls,
   As blows the blast along the sky.

10 The rough-spun hinds the pinnace guide
   With labouring oars along the flood;
An angler, bending o'er the tide,
   Hangs from the boat the insidious wood.

[1] 'Herd': neat-herd.

11 Beside the flood, beneath the rocks,
    On grassy bank, two lovers lean;
  Bend on each other amorous looks,
    And seem to laugh and kiss between.

12 The wind is rustling in the oak;
    They seem to hear the tread of feet;
  They start, they rise, look round the rock;
    Again they smile, again they meet.

13 But see! the gray mist from the lake
    Ascends upon the shady hills;
  Dark storms the murmuring forests shake,
    Rain beats around a hundred rills.

14 To Damon's homely hut I fly;
    I see it smoking on the plain;
  When storms are past and fair the sky,
    I'll often seek my cave again.

WILLIAM MASON.

THIS gentleman is now nearly forgotten, except as the friend, biographer, and literary executor of Gray. He was born in 1725, and died in 1797. His tragedies, ' Elfrida' and ' Caractacus,' are spirited declamations in dramatic form, not dramas. His odes have the turgidity without the grandeur of Gray's. His ' English Garden' is too long and too formal. His Life of Gray was an admirable innovation on the form of biography then prevalent, interspersing, as it does, journals and letters with mere narrative. Mason was a royal chaplain, held the living of Ashton, and was precentor of York Cathedral. We quote the best of his minor poems.

EPITAPH ON MRS MASON,

IN THE CATHEDRAL OF BRISTOL.

1 Take, holy earth! all that my soul holds dear:
    Take that best gift which Heaven so lately gave:
  To Bristol's fount I bore with trembling care
    Her faded form; she bowed to taste the wave,
  And died.   Does youth, does beauty, read the line?
    Does sympathetic fear their breasts alarm?
  Speak, dead Maria! breathe a strain divine:
    Even from the grave thou shalt have power to charm.

2 Bid them be chaste, be innocent, like thee;
    Bid them in duty's sphere as meekly move;
  And if so fair, from vanity as free;
    As firm in friendship, and as fond in love;
  Tell them, though 'tis an awful thing to die,
    ('Twas even to thee,) yet the dread path once trod,
  Heaven lifts its everlasting portals high,
    And bids 'the pure in heart behold their God.'

AN HEROIC EPISTLE TO SIR WILLIAM CHAMBERS, KNIGHT, COMPTROLLER-GENERAL OF HIS MAJESTY'S WORKS, ETC.

Knight of the Polar Star! by fortune placed
To shine the Cynosure of British taste;
Whose orb collects in one refulgent view
The scattered glories of Chinese virtù;
And spreads their lustre in so broad a blaze,
That kings themselves are dazzled while they gaze:
Oh, let the Muse attend thy march sublime,
And, with thy prose, caparison her rhyme;
Teach her, like thee, to gild her splendid song,
With scenes of Yven-Ming, and sayings of Li-Tsong;

Like thee to scorn dame Nature's simple fence;
Leap each ha-ha of truth and common sense;
And proudly rising in her bold career,
Demand attention from the gracious ear
Of him, whom we and all the world admit,
Patron supreme of science, taste, and wit.
Does envy doubt?   Witness, ye chosen train,
Who breathe the sweets of his Saturnian reign;
Witness, ye Hills, ye Johnsons, Scots, Shebbeares,
Hark to my call, for some of you have ears.
Let David Hume, from the remotest north,
In see-saw sceptic scruples hint his worth;
David, who there supinely deigns to lie
The fattest hog of Epicurus' sty;
Though drunk with Gallic wine, and Gallic praise,
David shall bless Old England's halcyon days;
The mighty Home, bemired in prose so long,
Again shall stalk upon the stilts of song:
While bold Mac-Ossian, wont in ghosts to deal,
Bids candid Smollett from his coffin steal;
Bids Mallock quit his sweet Elysian rest,
Sunk in his St John's philosophic breast,
And, like old Orpheus, make some strong effort
To come from Hell, and warble Truth at Court.
There was a time, 'in Esher's peaceful grove,
When Kent and Nature vied for Pelham's love,'
That Pope beheld them with auspicious smile,
And owned that beauty blest their mutual toil.
Mistaken bard! could such a pair design
Scenes fit to live in thy immortal line?
Hadst thou been born in this enlightened day,
Felt, as we feel, taste's oriental ray,
Thy satire sure had given them both a stab,
Called Kent a driveller, and the nymph a drab.
  306

For what is Nature? Ring her changes round,
Her three flat notes are water, plants, and ground;
Prolong the peal, yet, spite of all your clatter,
The tedious chime is still ground, plants, and water.
So, when some John his dull invention racks,
To rival Boodle's dinners, or Almack's;
Three uncouth legs of mutton shock our eyes,
Three roasted geese, three buttered apple-pies.
Come, then, prolific Art, and with thee bring
The charms that rise from thy exhaustless spring;
To Richmond come, for see, untutored Browne
Destroys those wonders which were once thy own.
Lo, from his melon-ground the peasant slave
Has rudely rushed, and levelled Merlin's cave;
Knocked down the waxen wizard, seized his wand,
Transformed to lawn what late was fairy-land;
And marred, with impious hand, each sweet design
Of Stephen Duck, and good Queen Caroline.
Haste, bid yon livelong terrace re-ascend,
Replace each vista, straighten every bend;
Shut out the Thames; shall that ignoble thing
Approach the presence of great Ocean's king?
No! let barbaric glories feast his eyes,
August pagodas round his palace rise,
And finished Richmond open to his view,
'A work to wonder at, perhaps a Kew.'
Nor rest we here, but, at our magic call,
Monkeys shall climb our trees, and lizards crawl;
Huge dogs of Tibet bark in yonder grove,
Here parrots prate, there cats make cruel love;
In some fair island will we turn to grass
(With the queen's leave) her elephant and ass.
Giants from Africa shall guard the glades,
Where hiss our snakes, where sport our Tartar maids;

Or, wanting these, from Charlotte Hayes we bring
Damsels, alike adroit to sport and sting.
Now to our lawns of dalliance and delight,
Join we the groves of horror and affright;
This to achieve no foreign aids we try,—
Thy gibbets, Bagshot! shall our wants supply;
Hounslow, whose heath sublimer terror fills,
Shall with her gibbets lend her powder-mills.
Here, too, O king of vengeance, in thy fane,
Tremendous Wilkes shall rattle his gold chain;
And round that fane, on many a Tyburn tree,
Hang fragments dire of Newgate-history;
On this shall Holland's dying speech be read,
Here Bute's confession, and his wooden head:
While all the minor plunderers of the age,
(Too numerous far for this contracted page,)
The Rigbys, Calcrafts, Dysons, Bradshaws there,
In straw-stuffed effigy, shall kick the air.
But say, ye powers, who come when fancy calls,
Where shall our mimic London rear her walls?
That eastern feature, Art must next produce,
Though not for present yet for future use,
Our sons some slave of greatness may behold,
Cast in the genuine Asiatic mould:
Who of three realms shall condescend to know
No more than he can spy from Windsor's brow;
For him, that blessing of a better time,
The Muse shall deal a while in brick and lime;
Surpass the bold *ΑΔΕΛΦΙ* in design,
And o'er the Thames fling one stupendous line
Of marble arches, in a bridge, that cuts
From Richmond Ferry slant to Brentford Butts.
Brentford with London's charms will we adorn;
Brentford, the bishopric of Parson Horne.

There, at one glance, the royal eye shall meet
Each varied beauty of St James's Street;
Stout Talbot there shall ply with hackney chair,
And patriot Betty fix her fruit-shop there.
Like distant thunder, now the coach of state
Rolls o'er the bridge, that groans beneath its weight.
The court hath crossed the stream; the sports begin;
Now Noel preaches of rebellion's sin:
And as the powers of his strong pathos rise,
Lo, brazen tears fall from Sir Fletcher's eyes.
While skulking round the pews, that babe of grace,
Who ne'er before at sermon showed his face,
See Jemmy Twitcher shambles; stop! stop thief!
He's stolen the Earl of Denbigh's handkerchief,
Let Barrington arrest him in mock fury,
And Mansfield hang the knave without a jury.
But hark, the voice of battle shouts from far,
The Jews and Maccaronis are at war:
The Jews prevail, and, thundering from the stocks,
They seize, they bind, they circumcise Charles Fox.
Fair Schwellenbergen smiles the sport to see,
And all the maids of honour cry 'Te! He!'
Be these the rural pastimes that attend
Great Brunswick's leisure: these shall best unbend
His royal mind, whene'er from state withdrawn,
He treads the velvet of his Richmond lawn;
These shall prolong his Asiatic dream,
Though Europe's balance trembles on its beam.
And thou, Sir William! while thy plastic hand
Creates each wonder which thy bard has planned,
While, as thy art commands, obsequious rise
Whate'er can please, or frighten, or surprise,
Oh, let that bard his knight's protection claim,
And share, like faithful Sancho, Quixote's fame.

JOHN LOWE.

THE author of 'Mary's Dream' was born in 1750, at Kenmore, Galloway, and was the son of a gardener.   He became a student of divinity, and acted as tutor in the family of a Mr M'Ghie of Airds.   A daughter of Mr M'Ghie was attached to a gentleman named Miller, a surgeon at sea, and on the occasion of his death Lowe wrote his beautiful 'Mary's Dream,' the exquisite simplicity and music of the first stanza of which has often been admired.   Lowe was betrothed to a sister of 'Mary,' but having emigrated to America, he married another, fell into dissipated habits, and died in a miserable plight at Fredericksburgh in 1798.   He wrote many other pieces, but none equal to 'Mary's Dream.'

MARY'S DREAM.

1 The moon had climbed the highest hill
   Which rises o'er the source of Dee,
And from the eastern summit shed
   Her silver light on tower and tree;
When Mary laid her down to sleep,
   Her thoughts on Sandy far at sea,
When, soft and low, a voice was heard,
   Saying, 'Mary, weep no more for me!'

2 She from her pillow gently raised
   Her head, to ask who there might be,
And saw young Sandy shivering stand,
   With visage pale, and hollow ee.
'O Mary dear, cold is my clay;
   It lies beneath a stormy sea.
Far, far from thee I sleep in death;
   So, Mary, weep no more for me!

3 'Three stormy nights and stormy days
   We tossed upon the raging main;

And long we strove our bark to save,
  But all our striving was in vain.
Even then, when horror chilled my blood,
  My heart was filled with love for thee:
The storm is past, and I at rest;
  So, Mary, weep no more for me!

4 'O maiden dear, thyself prepare;
  We soon shall meet upon that shore,
Where love is free from doubt and care,
  And thou and I shall part no more!'
Loud crowed the cock, the shadow fled,
  No more of Sandy could she see;
But soft the passing spirit said,
  'Sweet Mary, weep no more for me!'

JOSEPH WARTON.

THIS accomplished critic and poet was born in 1722.   He was
son to the Vicar of Basingstoke, and brother to Thomas Warton.
(See a former volume for his life.)   Joseph was educated at
Winchester College, and became intimate there with William
Collins.   He wrote when quite young some poetry in the *Gentleman's Magazine.*   He was in due time removed to Oriel College,
where he composed two poems, entitled 'The Enthusiast,' and
'The Dying Indian.'   In 1744, he took the degree of Bachelor
of Arts at Oxford, and was ordained to his father's curacy at
Basingstoke.   He went thence to Chelsea, but did not remain
there long, owing to some disagreement with his parishioners,
and returned to Basingstoke.   In 1746, he published a volume
of Odes, and in the preface expressed his hope that it might be
successful as an attempt to bring poetry back from the didactic
and satirical taste of the age, to the truer channels of fancy and
description.   The motive of this attempt was, however, more
praiseworthy than its success was conspicuous.

In 1748, Warton was presented by the Duke of Bolton to the rectory of Winslade, and he straightway married a Miss Daman, to whom he had for some time been attached. In the same year he began, and in 1753 he finished and printed, an edition of Virgil in English and Latin. Of this large, elaborate work, Warton himself supplied only the life of Virgil, with three essays on pastoral, didactic, and epic poetry, and a poetical version of the Eclogues and the Georgics, more correct but less spirited than Dryden's. He adopted Pitt's version of the Æneid, and his friends furnished some of the dissertations, notes, &c. Shortly after, he contributed twenty-four excellent papers, including some striking allegories, and some good criticisms on Shakspeare, to the *Adventurer*. In 1754, he was appointed to the living of Tunworth, and the next year was elected second master of Winchester School. Soon after this he published anonymously 'An Essay on the Writings and Genius of Pope,' which, whether because he failed in convincing the public that his estimate of Pope was the correct one, or because he stood in awe of Warburton, he did not complete or reprint for twenty-six years. It is a somewhat gossiping book, but full of information and interest.

In May 1766, he was made head-master of Winchester. In 1768, he lost his wife, and next year married a Miss Nicholas of Winchester. In 1782, he was promoted, through Bishop Lowth, to a prebend's post in St Paul's, and to the living of Thorley, which he exchanged for that of Wickham. Other livings dropped in upon him, and in 1793 he resigned the mastership of Winchester, and went to reside at Wickham. Here he employed himself in preparing an edition of Pope, which he published in 1797. In 1800 he died.

Warton, like his brother, did good service in resisting the literary despotism of Pope, and in directing the attention of the public to the forgotten treasures of old English poetry. He was a man of extensive learning, a very fair and candid, as well as acute critic, and his 'Ode to Fancy' proves him to have possessed no ordinary genius.

ODE TO FANCY.

O parent of each lovely Muse,
Thy spirit o'er my soul diffuse,
O'er all my artless songs preside,
My footsteps to thy temple guide,
To offer at thy turf-built shrine,
In golden cups no costly wine,
No murdered fatling of the flock,
But flowers and honey from the rock.
O nymph with loosely-flowing hair,
With buskined leg, and bosom bare,
Thy waist with myrtle-girdle bound,
Thy brows with Indian feathers crowned,
Waving in thy snowy hand
An all-commanding magic wand,
Of power to bid fresh gardens blow,
'Mid cheerless Lapland's barren snow,
Whose rapid wings thy flight convey
Through air, and over earth and sea,
While the vast various landscape lies
Conspicuous to thy piercing eyes.
O lover of the desert, hail!
Say, in what deep and pathless vale,
Or on what hoary mountain's side,
'Mid fall of waters, you reside,
'Mid broken rocks, a rugged scene,
With green and grassy dales between,
'Mid forests dark of aged oak,
Ne'er echoing with the woodman's stroke,
Where never human art appeared,
Nor even one straw-roofed cot was reared,
Where Nature seems to sit alone,
Majestic on a craggy throne;

Tell me the path, sweet wanderer, tell,
To thy unknown sequestered cell,
Where woodbines cluster round the door,
Where shells and moss o'erlay the floor,
And on whose top a hawthorn blows,
Amid whose thickly-woven boughs
Some nightingale still builds her nest,
Each evening warbling thee to rest:
Then lay me by the haunted stream,
Rapt in some wild, poetic dream,
In converse while methinks I rove
With Spenser through a fairy grove;
Till, suddenly awaked, I hear
Strange whispered music in my ear,
And my glad soul in bliss is drowned
By the sweetly-soothing sound!
Me, goddess, by the right hand lead
Sometimes through the yellow mead,
Where Joy and white-robed Peace resort,
And Venus keeps her festive court;
Where Mirth and Youth each evening meet,
And lightly trip with nimble feet,
Nodding their lily-crowned heads,
Where Laughter rose-lipped Hebe leads;
Where Echo walks steep hills among,
Listening to the shepherd's song:
Yet not these flowery fields of joy
Can long my pensive mind employ;
Haste, Fancy, from the scenes of folly,
To meet the matron Melancholy,
Goddess of the tearful eye,
That loves to fold her arms, and sigh;
Let us with silent footsteps go
To charnels and the house of woe,

To Gothic churches, vaults, and tombs,
Where each sad night some virgin comes,
With throbbing breast, and faded cheek,
Her promised bridegroom's urn to seek;
Or to some abbey's mouldering towers,
Where, to avoid cold wintry showers,
The naked beggar shivering lies,
While whistling tempests round her rise,
And trembles lest the tottering wall
Should on her sleeping infants fall.
Now let us louder strike the lyre,
For my heart glows with martial fire,—
I feel, I feel, with sudden heat,
My big tumultuous bosom beat;
The trumpet's clangours pierce my ear,
A thousand widows' shrieks I hear,
Give me another horse, I cry,
Lo! the base Gallic squadrons fly;
Whence is this rage?—what spirit, say,
To battle hurries me away?
'Tis Fancy, in her fiery car,
Transports me to the thickest war,
There whirls me o'er the hills of slain,
Where Tumult and Destruction reign;
Where, mad with pain, the wounded steed
Tramples the dying and the dead;
Where giant Terror stalks around,
With sullen joy surveys the ground,
And, pointing to the ensanguined field,
Shakes his dreadful gorgon shield!
Oh, guide me from this horrid scene,
To high-arched walks and alleys green,
Which lovely Laura seeks, to shun
The fervours of the mid-day sun;

The pangs of absence, oh, remove!
For thou canst place me near my love,
Canst fold in visionary bliss,
And let me think I steal a kiss,
While her ruby lips dispense
Luscious nectar's quintessence!
When young-eyed Spring profusely throws
From her green lap the pink and rose,
When the soft turtle of the dale
To Summer tells her tender tale;
When Autumn cooling caverns seeks,
And stains with wine his jolly cheeks;
When Winter, like poor pilgrim old,
Shakes his silver beard with cold;
At every season let my ear
Thy solemn whispers, Fancy, hear.
O warm, enthusiastic maid,
Without thy powerful, vital aid,
That breathes an energy divine,
That gives a soul to every line,
Ne'er may I strive with lips profane
To utter an unhallowed strain,
Nor dare to touch the sacred string,
Save when with smiles thou bidst me sing.
Oh, hear our prayer! oh, hither come
From thy lamented Shakspeare's tomb,
On which thou lovest to sit at eve,
Musing o'er thy darling's grave;
O queen of numbers, once again
Animate some chosen swain,
Who, filled with unexhausted fire,
May boldly smite the sounding lyre,
Who with some new unequalled song
May rise above the rhyming throng,

O'er all our listening passions reign,
O'erwhelm our souls with joy and pain,
With terror shake, and pity move,
Rouse with revenge, or melt with love;
Oh, deign to attend his evening walk,
With him in groves and grottoes talk;
Teach him to scorn with frigid art
Feebly to touch the enraptured heart;
Like lightning, let his mighty verse
The bosom's inmost foldings pierce;
With native beauties win applause
Beyond cold critics' studied laws;
Oh, let each Muse's fame increase!
Oh, bid Britannia rival Greece!

MISCELLANEOUS.

SONG.

FROM 'THE SHAMROCK, OR HIBERNIAN CROSSES.' DUBLIN, 1772.

1 Belinda's sparkling eyes and wit
    Do various passions raise;
And, like the lightning, yield a bright,
    But momentary blaze.

2 Eliza's milder, gentler sway,
    Her conquests fairly won,
Shall last till life and time decay,
    Eternal as the sun.

3 Thus the wild flood with deafening roar
    Bursts dreadful from on high;
But soon its empty rage is o'er,
    And leaves the channel dry:

4 While the pure stream, which still and slow
   Its gentler current brings,
Through every change of time shall flow
   With unexhausted springs.

VERSES,

COPIED FROM THE WINDOW OF AN OBSCURE LODGING-HOUSE, IN THE NEIGHBOURHOOD OF LONDON.

Stranger! whoe'er thou art, whose restless mind,
Like me within these walls is cribbed, confined;
Learn how each want that heaves our mutual sigh
A woman's soft solicitudes supply.
From her white breast retreat all rude alarms,
Or fly the magic circle of her arms;
While souls exchanged alternate grace acquire,
And passions catch from passion's glorious fire:
What though to deck this roof no arts combine,
Such forms as rival every fair but mine;
No nodding plumes, our humble couch above,
Proclaim each triumph of unbounded love;
No silver lamp with sculptured Cupids gay,
O'er yielding beauty pours its midnight ray;
Yet Fanny's charms could Time's slow flight beguile,
Soothe every care, and make each dungeon smile:
In her, what kings, what saints have wished, is given,
Her heart is empire, and her love is heaven.

THE OLD BACHELOR.

AFTER THE MANNER OF SPENSER.

1 In Phœbus' region while some bards there be
   That sing of battles, and the trumpet's roar;
Yet these, I ween, more powerful bards than me,
   Above my ken, on eagle pinions soar!

Haply a scene of meaner view to scan,
  Beneath their laurelled praise my verse may
      give,
To trace the features of unnoticed man;
  Deeds, else forgotten, in the verse may live!
Her lore, mayhap, instructive sense may teach,
From weeds of humbler growth within my lowly
      reach.

2 A wight there was, who single and alone
  Had crept from vigorous youth to waning age,
Nor e'er was worth, nor e'er was beauty known
  His heart to captive, or his thought engage:
Some feeble joyaunce, though his conscious mind
  Might female worth or beauty give to wear,
Yet to the nobler sex he held confined
  The genuine graces of the soul sincere,
And well could show with saw or proverb quaint
All semblance woman's soul, and all her beauty paint.

3 In plain attire this wight apparelled was,
  (For much he conned of frugal lore and knew,)
Nor, till some day of larger note might cause,
  From iron-bound chest his better garb he drew:
But when the Sabbath-day might challenge more,
  Or feast, or birthday, should it chance to be,
A glossy suit devoid of stain he wore,
  And gold his buttons glanced so fair to see,
Gold clasped his shoon, by maiden brushed so
      sheen,
And his rough beard he shaved, and donned his linen
      clean.

4 But in his common garb a coat he wore,
  A faithful coat that long its lord had known,

That once was black, but now was black no more,
  Attinged by various colours not its own.
All from his nostrils was the front embrowned,
  And down the back ran many a greasy line,
While, here and there, his social moments owned
  The generous signet of the purple wine.
Brown o'er the bent of eld his wig appeared,
Like fox's trailing tail by hunters sore affeared.

5 One only maid he had, like turtle true,
  But not like turtle gentle, soft, and kind;
For many a time her tongue bewrayed the shrew,
  And in meet words unpacked her peevish mind.
Ne formed was she to raise the soft desire
  That stirs the tingling blood in youthful vein,
Ne formed was she to light the tender fire,
  By many a bard is sung in many a strain:
Hooked was her nose, and countless wrinkles told
What no man durst to her, I ween, that she was old.

6 When the clock told the wonted hour was come
  When from his nightly cups the wight withdrew,
Right patient would she watch his wending home,
  His feet she heard, and soon the bolt she drew.
If long his time was past, and leaden sleep
  O'er her tired eyelids 'gan his reign to stretch,
Oft would she curse that men such hours should
    keep,
  And many a saw 'gainst drunkenness would
    preach;
Haply if potent gin had armed her tongue,
All on the reeling wight a thundering peal she rung.

7 For though the blooming queen of Cyprus' isle
  O'er her cold bosom long had ceased to reign,
320

On that cold bosom still could Bacchus smile,
  Such beverage to own if Bacchus deign:
For wine she prized not much, for stronger drink
  Its medicine, oft a cholic-pain will call,
And for the medicine's sake, might envy think,
  Oft would a cholic-pain her bowels enthral;
Yet much the proffer did she loathe, and say
No dram might maiden taste, and often answered nay.

8 So as in single animals he joyed,
  One cat, and eke one dog, his bounty fed;
The first the cate-devouring mice destroyed,
  Thieves heard the last, and from his threshold
    fled:
All in the sunbeams basked the lazy cat,
  Her mottled length in couchant posture laid;
On one accustomed chair while Pompey sat,
  And loud he barked should Puss his right invade.
The human pair oft marked them as they lay,
And haply sometimes thought like cat and dog were
    they.

9 A room he had that faced the southern ray,
  Where oft he walked to set his thoughts in tune,
Pensive he paced its length an hour or tway,
  All to the music of his creeking shoon.
And at the end a darkling closet stood,
  Where books he kept of old research and new,
In seemly order ranged on shelves of wood,
  And rusty nails and phials not a few:
Thilk place a wooden box beseemeth well,
And papers squared and trimmed for use unmeet to
    tell.

10 For still in form he placed his chief delight,
        Nor lightly broke his old accustomed rule,
    And much uncourteous would he hold the wight
        That e'er displaced a table, chair, or stool;
    And oft in meet array their ranks he placed,
        And oft with careful eye their ranks reviewed;
    For novel forms, though much those forms had
            graced,
        Himself and maiden-minister eschewed:
    One path he trod, nor ever would decline
  A hair's unmeasured breadth from off the even line.

11 A Club select there was, where various talk
        On various chapters passed the lingering hour,
    And thither oft he bent his evening walk,
        And warmed to mirth by wine's enlivening power.
    And oft on politics the preachments ran,
        If a pipe lent its thought-begetting fume:
    And oft important matters would they scan,
        And deep in council fix a nation's doom :
    And oft they chuckled loud at jest or jeer,
  Or bawdy tale the most, thilk much they loved to hear.

12 For men like him they were of like consort,
        Thilk much the honest muse must needs condemn,
    Who made of women's wiles their wanton sport,
        And blessed their stars that kept the curse from
            them!
    No honest love they knew, no melting smile
        That shoots the transports to the throbbing heart!
    Thilk knew they not but in a harlot's guile
        Lascivious smiling through the mask of art:
    And so of women deemed they as they knew,
  And from a Demon's traits an Angel's picture drew.
    322

13 But most abhorred they hymeneal rites,
　　And boasted oft the freedom of their fate:
　Nor 'vailed, as they opined, its best delights
　　Those ills to balance that on wedlock wait;
　And often would they tell of henpecked fool
　　Snubbed by the hard behest of sour-eyed dame.
　And vowed no tongue-armed woman's freakish rule
　　Their mirth should quail, or damp their generous
　　　　flame:
　Then pledged their hands, and tossed their bumpers
　　　　o'er,
　And Io! Bacchus! sung, and owned no other power.

14 If e'er a doubt of softer kind arose
　　Within some breast of less obdurate frame,
　Lo! where its hideous form a phantom shows
　　Full in his view, and Cuckold is its name.
　Him Scorn attended with a glance askew,
　　And Scorpion Shame for delicts not his own,
　Her painted bubbles while Suspicion blew,
　　And vexed the region round the Cupid's throne:
　'Far be from us,' they cried, 'the treacherous bane,
　Far be the dimply guile, and far the flowery chain!'

CARELESS CONTENT.

1 I am content, I do not care,
　　Wag as it will the world for me;
　When fuss and fret was all my fare,
　　It got no ground as I could see:
　So when away my caring went,
　I counted cost, and was content.

2 With more of thanks and less of thought,
　　I strive to make my matters meet;

To seek what ancient sages sought,
   Physic and food in sour and sweet:
To take what passes in good part,
And keep the hiccups from the heart.

3 With good and gentle-humoured hearts,
   I choose to chat where'er I come,
Whate'er the subject be that starts;
   But if I get among the glum,
I hold my tongue to tell the truth,
And keep my breath to cool my broth.

4 For chance or change of peace or pain,
   For Fortune's favour or her frown,
For lack or glut, for loss or gain,
   I never dodge, nor up nor down:
But swing what way the ship shall swim,
Or tack about with equal trim.

5 I suit not where I shall not speed,
   Nor trace the turn of every tide;
If simple sense will not succeed,
   I make no bustling, but abide:
For shining wealth, or scaring woe,
I force no friend, I fear no foe.

6 Of ups and downs, of ins and outs,
   Of they're i' the wrong, and we're i' the right,
I shun the rancours and the routs;
   And wishing well to every wight,
Whatever turn the matter takes,
   I deem it all but ducks and drakes.

7 With whom I feast I do not fawn,
    Nor if the folks should flout me, faint;
If wonted welcome be withdrawn,
    I cook no kind of a complaint:
With none disposed to disagree,
But like them best who best like me.

8 Not that I rate myself the rule
    How all my betters should behave
But fame shall find me no man's fool,
    Nor to a set of men a slave:
I love a friendship free and frank,
And hate to hang upon a hank.

9 Fond of a true and trusty tie,
    I never loose where'er I link;
Though if a business budges by,
    I talk thereon just as I think;
My word, my work, my heart, my hand,
Still on a side together stand.

10 If names or notions make a noise,
    Whatever hap the question hath,
The point impartially I poise,
    And read or write, but without wrath;
For should I burn, or break my brains,
Pray, who will pay me for my pains?

11 I love my neighbour as myself,
    Myself like him too, by his leave;
Nor to his pleasure, power, or pelf,
    Came I to crouch, as I conceive:
Dame Nature doubtless has designed
A man the monarch of his mind.

12 Now taste and try this temper, sirs,
    Mood it and brood it in your breast;
Or if ye ween, for worldly stirs,
    That man does right to mar his rest,
Let me be deft, and debonair,
I am content, I do not care.

A PASTORAL.

1 My time, O ye Muses, was happily spent,
When Phœbe went with me wherever I went;
Ten thousand sweet pleasures I felt in my breast:
Sure never fond shepherd like Colin was blest!
But now she is gone, and has left me behind,
What a marvellous change on a sudden I find!
When things were as fine as could possibly be,
I thought 'twas the Spring; but alas! it was she.

2 With such a companion to tend a few sheep,
To rise up and play, or to lie down and sleep:
I was so good-humoured, so cheerful and gay,
My heart was as light as a feather all day;
But now I so cross and so peevish am grown,
So strangely uneasy, as never was known.
My fair one is gone, and my joys are all drowned,
And my heart—I am sure it weighs more than a pound.

3 The fountain that wont to run sweetly along,
And dance to soft murmurs the pebbles among;
Thou know'st, little Cupid, if Phœbe was there,
'Twas pleasure to look at, 'twas music to hear:
But now she is absent, I walk by its side,
And still, as it murmurs, do nothing but chide;
Must you be so cheerful, while I go in pain?
Peace there with your bubbling, and hear me complain.

4 My lambkins around me would oftentimes play,
  And Phœbe and I were as joyful as they;
  How pleasant their sporting, how happy their time,
  When Spring, Love, and Beauty, were all in their
      prime!
  But now, in their frolics when by me they pass,
  I fling at their fleeces a handful of grass;
  Be still, then, I cry, for it makes me quite mad,
  To see you so merry while I am so sad.

5 My dog I was ever well pleased to see
  Come wagging his tail to my fair one and me;
  And Phœbe was pleased too, and to my dog said,
  'Come hither, poor fellow;' and patted his head.
  But now, when he's fawning, I with a sour look
  Cry 'Sirrah;' and give him a blow with my crook:
  And I'll give him another; for why should not Tray
  Be as dull as his master, when Phœbe's away?

6 When walking with Phœbe, what sights have I seen,
  How fair was the flower, how fresh was the green!
  What a lovely appearance the trees and the shade,
  The corn-fields and hedges, and everything made!
  But now she has left me, though all are still there,
  They none of them now so delightful appear:
  'Twas nought but the magic, I find, of her eyes,
  Made so many beautiful prospects arise.

7 Sweet music went with us both all the wood
      through,
  The lark, linnet, throstle, and nightingale too;
  Winds over us whispered, flocks by us did bleat,
  And chirp went the grasshopper under our feet.
  But now she is absent, though still they sing on,
  The woods are but lonely, the melody's gone:

Her voice in the concert, as now I have found,
Gave everything else its agreeable sound.

8 Rose, what is become of thy delicate hue?
   And where is the violet's beautiful blue?
   Does ought of its sweetness the blossom beguile?
   That meadow, those daisies, why do they not smile?
   Ah! rivals, I see what it was that you dressed,
   And made yourselves fine for—a place in her breast:
   You put on your colours to pleasure her eye,
   To be plucked by her hand, on her bosom to die.

9 How slowly Time creeps till my Phœbe return!
   While amidst the soft zephyr's cool breezes I burn:
   Methinks, if I knew whereabouts he would tread,
   I could breathe on his wings, and 'twould melt down
        the lead.
   Fly swifter, ye minutes, bring hither my dear,
   And rest so much longer for 't when she is here.
   Ah, Colin! old Time is full of delay,
   Nor will budge one foot faster for all thou canst say.

10 Will no pitying power, that hears me complain,
    Or cure my disquiet, or soften my pain?
    To be cured, thou must, Colin, thy passion remove;
    But what swain is so silly to live without love!
    No, deity, bid the dear nymph to return,
    For ne'er was poor shepherd so sadly forlorn.
    Ah! what shall I do?   I shall die with despair;
    Take heed, all ye swains, how ye part with your fair.

ODE TO A TOBACCO-PIPE.

Little tube of mighty power,
Charmer of an idle hour,
Object of my warm desire,
Lip of wax and eye of fire;
And thy snowy taper waist,
With my finger gently braced;
And thy pretty swelling crest,
With my little stopper pressed;
And the sweetest bliss of blisses,
Breathing from thy balmy kisses.
Happy thrice, and thrice again,
Happiest he of happy men;
Who when again the night returns,
When again the taper burns,
When again the cricket's gay,
(Little cricket full of play,)
Can afford his tube to feed
With the fragrant Indian weed:
Pleasure for a nose divine,
Incense of the god of wine.
Happy thrice, and thrice again,
Happiest he of happy men.

AWAY! LET NOUGHT TO LOVE DISPLEASING.

1 Away! let nought to love displeasing,
   My Winifreda, move your care;
Let nought delay the heavenly blessing,
   Nor squeamish pride, nor gloomy fear.

2 What though no grants of royal donors,
   With pompous titles grace our blood;
We 'll shine in more substantial honours,
   And, to be noble, we 'll be good.

3 Our name while virtue thus we tender,
    Will sweetly sound where'er 'tis spoke;
And all the great ones, they shall wonder
    How they respect such little folk.

4 What though, from fortune's lavish bounty,
    No mighty treasures we possess;
We'll find, within our pittance, plenty,
    And be content without excess.

5 Still shall each kind returning season
    Sufficient for our wishes give;
For we will live a life of reason,
    And that's the only life to live.

6 Through youth and age, in love excelling,
    We'll hand in hand together tread;
Sweet-smiling peace shall crown our dwelling,
    And babes, sweet-smiling babes, our bed.

7 How should I love the pretty creatures,
    While round my knees they fondly clung!
To see them look their mother's features,
    To hear them lisp their mother's tongue!

8 And when with envy Time transported,
    Shall think to rob us of our joys;
You'll in your girls again be courted,
    And I'll go wooing in my boys.

RICHARD BENTLEY'S SOLE POETICAL COMPOSITION.

1 Who strives to mount Parnassus' hill,
    And thence poetic laurels bring,
Must first acquire due force and skill,
    Must fly with swan's or eagle's wing.

2 Who Nature's treasures would explore,
    Her mysteries and arcana know,
Must high as lofty Newton soar,
    Must stoop as delving Woodward low.

3 Who studies ancient laws and rites,
    Tongues, arts, and arms, and history;
Must drudge, like Selden, days and nights,
    And in the endless labour die.

4 Who travels in religious jars,
    (Truth mixed with error, shades with rays,)
Like Whiston, wanting pyx or stars,
    In ocean wide or sinks or strays.

5 But grant our hero's hope, long toil
    And comprehensive genius crown,
All sciences, all arts his spoil,
    Yet what reward, or what renown?

6 Envy, innate in vulgar souls,
    Envy steps in and stops his rise;
Envy with poisoned tarnish fouls
    His lustre, and his worth decries.

7 He lives inglorious or in want,
    To college and old books confined:
Instead of learned, he's called pedant;
    Dunces advanced, he's left behind:
Yet left content, a genuine Stoic he,
Great without patron, rich without South Sea.

LINES ADDRESSED TO POPE.[1]

1 While malice, Pope, denies thy page
    Its own celestial fire;
  While critics and while bards in rage
    Admiring, won't admire:

2 While wayward pens thy worth assail,
    And envious tongues decry;
  These times, though many a friend bewail,
    These times bewail not I.

3 But when the world's loud praise is thine,
    And spleen no more shall blame;
  When with thy Homer thou shalt shine
    In one unclouded fame:

4 When none shall rail, and every lay
    Devote a wreath to thee;
  That day (for come it will) that day
    Shall I lament to see.

[1] Written by one Lewis, a schoolmaster, and highly commended by Johnson.—*See* Boswell.

THE END.

INDEX.

INDEX.

BALLANTYNE AND COMPANY, PRINTERS, EDINBURGH.

www.ingramcontent.com/pod-product-compliance
Lightning Source LLC
Chambersburg PA
CBHW021753110726
47902CB00006B/1503